Flora Speer
"Two Turtledoves"

"Ms. Speer crafts a touching romance, full of both sensual fire and tender love. Fans will be more than pleased."
—*Romantic Times* on *Lady Lure*

Stobie Piel
"A Partridge In A Pear Tree"

"Ms. Piel spices a rousing adventure with blistering sensual fire and adds a witty leavening of secondary characters whose sparkling interplay is well nigh irresistible."
—*Romantic Times* on *The White Sun*

Constance O'Banyon
"Eleven Pipers Piping"

"Constance O'Banyon is dynamic. Wonderful characters. One of the best writers of romantic adventure."
—*Romantic Times* on *Desert Song*

Lynsay Sands
"Three French Hens"

"Starting on page one, readers are swept up in a delicious, merry and often breath-catching roller coaster ride that will keep them on the edge of their seats and laughing out loud. A true delight!"
—*Romantic Times* on *The Deed*

Five Gold Rings

Constance O'Banyon,
Stobie Piel,
Lynsay Sands,
Flora Speer

LEISURE BOOKS NEW YORK CITY

A LEISURE BOOK®

October 1999

Published by

Dorchester Publishing Co., Inc.
276 Fifth Avenue
New York, NY 10001

ISBN 0-8439-4612-1

Two
Turtledoves

Flora Speer

Chapter One

Menton Castle was his for the taking. Easily accessed, easily assailed by a strong knight. Damien of Aquitaine envisioned the battle, and his pulse quickened like fire in his veins. The cold wind encircled him, a challenge to a brave heart. He stood alone outside Menton Castle, and he saw it fall to a well-planned assault.

He closed his eyes and saw himself, the most renowned knight in Aquitaine, leading the charge against the feeble English resistance, shouting orders his subordinates obeyed without hesitation, so great was their trust in his word. In his mind's eye, he rode a black charger, heavy-boned to withstand the weight of his glorious armor, caparisoned like a king's horse. Perhaps better. Certainly better than the steed of an English nobleman.

The haunting sounds of clashing armies echoed in

his ears. A faint sneer curved his lips, twisting into a smile as he imagined his victory. The subsequent cheers. The bedazzled gazes of wildly wealthy women who gazed up at him with adoration. Praise from a grateful liege . . .

No man ever led an army better. No man ever fought more bravely, with the fury of a lion. . . . His heart pounded at the thought. One English castle . . . His for the taking. Damien reached for the sword that hung at his side. He fingered the weapon and found its hilt.

He seized the weapon and drew it forth, then swung it in the air. Its blade sang as it was raised in the cold air. . . .

Twang.

Damien's arm froze in position, his weapon poised avenging at the sky. He opened one eye, then the other.

He held a mandolin upright, his thumb pressed against, not a sword's hilt, but a cursed string. The string that had twanged.

His thoughts of a glorious siege vanished, replaced by a fury darker still. He glared at the instrument as if his shame found voice in its music.

Sometimes, his imagination got the better of him. In a disgust that almost reached nausea, Damien returned the cursed instrument to his side. His broad shoulders slumped and he cast a dark, accusatory glance upward into the gray sky.

Festive sounds of music and laughter came from Menton Castle. His mouth curved in increasing disgust.

Reminding himself that a true knight does not yield until the battle is won, Damien headed through the castle gate.

*   *   *

Two Turtledoves

There was nothing so fair in all the world as a castle filled with music, bedecked in finery, and celebrating the magic of Yule. Pippa stood in the great hall of Menton Castle, her heart aching at its beauty. Here, all hearts would be lifted. From the most powerful nobleman to the lowest serf, the magic of Christmas was here for all.

Her gauze veil added an aura of mist to everything she saw. Mummers and minstrels flooded the hall. Nobles greeted their guests, and platters of food and drink were sent to tables. This was truly a place of wonder, and for the next twelve days, she would join the mummers and musicians here. She would sing ancient songs, and some that she had made up herself. As she sang, she would look out at her listeners, and see her words enter their hearts.

She would follow the path laid out before her, and she would do it with all her heart. Her mesmerizing voice was a gift she had been born with. She had learned to use it when still a young girl. Even when she'd lost everything else, the beauty of her voice had been the one thing that never deserted her.

The master of the castle, Lord Robert, entered the room. Pippa watched as he greeted his guests, but his expression seemed dark. The man's wife was small, and seemed tense. Pippa sensed an unhappiness between the couple, a chasm between them not recently bridged. Her own heart filled with strength. She would sing a song that would draw them back to each other. She had no doubt. There wasn't a heart made her voice couldn't reach.

The wide doors swung open again, and a cold wind blew in. She turned and her heart skipped a beat.

A young man entered the great hall. He greeted no one and despite the festivities, he looked miserable. He was clothed all in black, from high black boots, to snug black leggings, to a short black tunic. His sleeves were slashed to reveal more black beneath. Even his hair was black, she noticed as she studied the long soft black waves. The only color in his outfit was supplied by the golden brown mandolin hanging at his side.

He was the most beautiful man she had ever seen. Despite his frown, despite his immediately apparent irritation with his surroundings, despite the evidence of a deeply ingrained pride . . . his presence was so strong that she couldn't look away.

"There's a heart of stone." Angus of Perth spoke beside her, a note of regret in his voice. "Let it please God Almighty that we don't have to listen to *his* tongue again!"

Pippa glanced at Angus, then back at the man in black. He stopped in the center of the hall and looked around, his hands on his hips. He had beautiful hands, tender, capable of great artistry. He clenched one fist as if gripping a sword.

"Who is that man, Angus? Do you know him?"

Angus uttered a brief huff. "Aye, I know him. Damien of Aquitaine, ravager of music, tormentor of the ear."

Pippa exhaled a soft breath of wonder. "I cannot imagine that his voice would be anything less than . . . magic."

"A boar's death groan is sweeter, lass."

Pippa shifted her weight from foot to foot. She couldn't tear her gaze from the man in black. His face was sweet and young, but strong, as his body appeared to be.

She looked back at Angus. "Who did you say he was?"

"Damien of Aquitaine."

"Why is he here in England?"

Angus crossed his stout arms over his chest. "I don't know. I've heard that he offended Queen Eleanor herself."

"I cannot imagine him offending anyone, even Eleanor." She peered cautiously at the minstrel lest he notice her attention. "The French are gracious in the extreme."

"You've never been to France, have you, lass?"

"I have imagined it. I will sing there one day."

Angus eyed her doubtfully. "Don't know why you'd want to."

"Because it is beautiful . . . How did he offend the queen?"

She knew Angus liked gossip. He'd heard every tale in England, especially those involving the queen. Eleanor of Aquitaine had been the subject of many tales of chivalry and romance. "I don't know. Don't care," he said.

Pippa's heart moved as she contemplated the man in black's distress. "He looks so . . . vulnerable. I shall befriend him."

Angus stared at her for a moment, then shook his head. "*Vulnerable?* Stay away from him, lass. In fact, stay away from all men." Angus paused. "On second thought, I'm thinking you'd best stay away from all people."

She took his meaning and lifted her chin, offended. "I am not naive. I have simply learned to trust my own heart's voice."

Angus drew a long breath. "Don't you understand, lass? The heart's voice is the one thing most likely to betray you."

Within moments of his arrival, Damien knew the potential for both pleasure and an end to his infernal quest. A man had need for a woman to entertain him. The girl in white would fulfill that need. She was watching him even now, beneath a gauze veil. He spotted blond curls around her soft cheeks.

He fingered the gold ring hanging on a chain at his

11

neck. A shame that his quest had to be resolved in England, but not a grim enough circumstance to stop him. He would regain his knighthood in England, then spend his lifetime elsewhere. In Aquitaine.

A heavyset, red-haired man stood protectively beside the girl in white. The man patted the girl's shoulder. Yes, she had a fragility that would inspire such paternal attention. Not from himself, but from men with weaker hearts.

She, too, was clothed as a minstrel. He spotted a small harp hanging at her narrow hip. It was unusual for a woman to be a minstrel. The traveling, the performing, the profession was filled with perils to a lady's virtue and physical safety. Perhaps the stout man was her father. He looked big enough to protect her.

Damien let his gaze move on and he assessed the other performers. All wore ridiculous garb. One slender, overly frail man wore a checked cloth of magenta, light green, and a foul version of lavender. The toes of his shoes curled into two points, each with bells attached. Damien fought an urge to seize a guard's sword and do away with such a dubious specimen of manhood.

He sighed. He hadn't been so violence-minded when he'd been a knight. Skilled with a sword, dangerous, formidable, yes . . . but not bloodthirsty. But he hadn't been condemned to a life of utter humiliation then, either. Now, it wasn't a far stretch to imagine doing in the whole group of revelers.

Lord Robert's guests were depositing lavish gifts which threatened to overtake the central court. Damien eyed them—had he been a nobleman, he would have been expected to bestow a gift, too. As a minstrel, his only gift would be a song. Four men carried in a tree. A pear tree. Damien's brow quirked, for it seemed an odd gift. Some form of armor would have been better, he was sure.

His gaze caught on a cage where a fat partridge pecked relentlessly at the bars. Damien watched, fascinated. The foolish creature would never free itself that way. He started to look away, but as he watched the partridge stopped, then tried the cage door instead. It tried forcing it, again with no luck. Then, in a burst of inspiration, it tried the latch. No effort was required. The latch gave way, the door opened, and the partridge flew out.

A servant cursed and tried to catch the bird, but it flew to the top of the pear tree and sat there proudly, like a king. Damien took heart. Clearly, the bird's escape was portentous. He, too, would escape his confinement.

For every prison, there was a key, and he would find his. He would regain his status. He would become the knight on his fiery steed, the king on his throne. A partridge in a pear tree.

The Yule celebration at Menton Castle might prove to be just the situation he required. It had been a long journey north, but worth the effort if it should yield his redemption. He was a *warrior* and a warrior was to follow his chosen path with dedication and perseverance. Menton Castle might well harbor the goal of his quest.

Patience. All things in their time.

His attention was again captured by the lovely blond girl in white. Knowing she would, he waited until she glanced toward him. He didn't have to wait long. Her soft lips parted as if in awe. Damien smiled and offered a subdued bow.

Her little hands clenched over her heart in obvious appreciation of his attention. How was a man to resist being a seducer of beautiful women when it came so naturally to him? He approached her.

The red-haired man placed himself in front of the girl like a solid wall, but Damien moved around him as if he wasn't there. He seized her hand, gazed a moment into her eyes, then kissed the backs of her fingers.

"We entertain the nobles together, it seems, fair lady."

She opened her mouth to answer, but no words formed. Her lips remained parted, and he smiled. Such charming innocence!

"I am Damien of Aquitaine. And you are the most beautiful woman I have seen since I set foot on England's shore." She just stared up at him as if she beheld a thing of wonder. "What is your name?" he prompted.

"I am called Pippa." Her voice was soft, small, and lower than he'd expected.

"Pippa . . . A charming name, for an even more charming woman." He kissed her hand again and she looked at the spot as if she'd been touched by a god. "Is this your home, Pippa?"

"No." She seemed uncertain. Maybe she had no real home. "I am Welsh."

"The Welsh tend to be dark, do they not?"

"My mother is Welsh, but my father is English."

He sensed nervousness at this line of conversation, though he had no idea why. No matter. The girl's past was of no consequence, only her presence now. "What brings you to Menton Castle?"

"I travel with the Mummers of Cornwall."

"Ah. I, myself, travel alone."

She offered a shy smile. "But not unnoticed."

It was bold of her to flatter him, and unexpected. She looked so retiring and vulnerable. He studied her expression more closely and saw intelligence there, a wit crisp and quick. If he hadn't known that mummers

14

and minstrels were of the peasant classes, he would guess she had been educated.

The stout man wedged himself between them. "You, little rooster, I'd never thought to see again. After the last time you opened your mouth to squawk at a noble's guests, I'd have thought you'd be beheaded."

"Who are you?"

"Angus of Perth. I was in the vicinity when you bombarded Lord Gareth's spring festival with a . . . 'song.'"

Damien barely glanced Angus's way. "It seems I am afflicted with a persistent . . . hoarseness. Perhaps it is due to England's constant, relentless, never-ending mists and vapors."

"Ha! You're afflicted with nothing but arrogance and the worst singing voice I have ever heard!"

"Angus!" Pippa gasped in obvious embarrassment, but Damien squeezed her hand, which he still held in his own.

"If it were my true calling . . ." He stopped and sighed. "But I am not by nature a minstrel." He couldn't withhold an element of disgust at the term.

A wistful expression appeared on her small face. *"'What a man is, he then becomes.'"*

"What did you say?" *And what a horrid notion!*

She seemed nervous at having spoken this way. "It is a quote. It sounds better in Welsh."

Angus's brow puckered. "Lass, *nothing* sounds better in Welsh. It is the most peculiar language ever devised."

Damien ignored Angus. "From what comes this quote?"

Her cheeks turned a light and charming pink. "From a verse . . ."

Angus smiled and patted her shoulder. "One of your own?"

Pippa fixed her gaze on her feet and nodded.

Damien looked down at her bowed head. There was something unknowable about this woman. "What does it mean?" he asked.

She looked up and into his eyes. "It means that, over time, a man will most truly become that which he already carries within himself." She paused. "A woman, too."

"It is to be hoped so, my lady." Damien gripped his mandolin and elevated it without affection. "If your words are true, then this cursed instrument will soon be replaced by its rightful opponent. A sword."

The time he hated most had come. Noble men and ladies, servants and guards—every person in the banquet hall fell silent to listen to the one thing Damien loathed above all else. Singing. His singing.

All night, the revelers had prodded him for a song. Naturally, because he was handsome and dashing, he drew attention, and he'd been avoiding their pleas all night. But the time had come when he could avoid them no longer. He cursed Eleanor of Aquitaine with all his soul, then stood before his hosts. They were smiling, but not at each other.

At the head of the table sat Lady Elisa. She was rather plump, with light hair and dark eyes like Pippa. An attractive combination, he decided. Sensual. Next to her sat her husband, a dark man with an intelligent expression. Yes, he was the kind of man Damien could associate with—not the usual pale-haired, lackluster English toad.

Their daughter, Christina, sat nearby, radiant. She resembled her father more than her mother and she appeared bright, but distracted, as if she had something more interesting on her mind. She obviously hadn't heard of his situation yet, or her gaze would be on him, wondering at his tragedy, curious as to his quest for "love."

Two Turtledoves

It almost seemed too easy. He lifted the dreaded mandolin and fingered it idly, producing a sound he assumed was musical. It twanged, at any rate. The crowd hushed. Young women took notice of his good looks and leaned forward.

In his mind's eye, he saw himself facing a barbarian in battle. Perhaps a Viking. Or a Highlander. Or . . . an Englishman. The image was hardly enough to inspire song. Another image entered his mind. The memory of Eleanor of Aquitaine. *"You are banished. It is well deserved, Damien, for you scorn love. You seduce and dismiss women, never glancing back at the shattered hearts you leave behind."* He saw her lean toward him, eyes ablaze with both anger and power. *"Take this gold ring. Sing the praises of the love it honors far and wide. And when you find a woman on whose finger you can place this ring without dishonoring all it upholds, your banishment will end and your title be restored. Now, begone."*

Grudgingly, he began to sing. He sang the first Yule song that entered his head. Perhaps a combination of several. He sang as if he challenged a vile opponent. He did so before he actually considered his words, and as the mention of blood and battle replaced certain holy phrases, he realized what he did. His voice was garbled, though, so he assumed no one noticed. At least the war ballads he sang were good ones, he thought. Much more intriguing than the lifeless tones the crowd likely expected at Yuletide.

He added an extra verse that hinted at a grim death for meddling women, praised a young knight for his skill with a sword, and then added something dutiful about the Christmas celebration.

He finished, and the crowd remained silent. It was not an unusual reaction, though. Lady Elisa whispered something to her daughter, and seemed concerned.

Maybe he'd gone too far by adding the verse about the woman's death. He cleared his throat as if it were sore. It wasn't. He couldn't get himself banished from Lord Robert's domain, too. Not when he was so close to ending his exile.

Christina was staring at him. She didn't look impressed, exactly, but at least she appeared interested. One after another, nobles offered polite applause, though they looked uniformly confused. They were no doubt wondering whatever had possessed him to become a minstrel.

He set his mandolin aside, wishing he could abandon it forever, and he bowed dramatically. Music began from another corner, and he turned to leave. Let his presence be a mystery. He glanced toward the nobles' table, but Christina was speaking with her mother.

Only one person stood watching him. Pippa. He felt a tug of regret that he hadn't been able to impress her with a moving singing voice. He would have enjoyed that. Still in her eyes was the curiosity he'd looked for in Christina. There was curiosity and something else. A faint touch of . . . amusement?

It was not the response he wanted from any woman. He hesitated, then approached her. She didn't appear nervous as she had earlier. She waited for him, smiling. She had an interesting mouth; an upright bow that gave her a look of perpetual surprise and wonder.

Beautiful eyes. Dark and mysterious. Innocent eyes, yet capable of seeing things no one else could. She wasn't as young as he'd thought at first glance. In fact, he had no idea how old she was. She seemed young, and she seemed ancient. She seemed vulnerable, and yet she apparently relied on no one but herself.

She was the mystery he was trying to be.

He stopped in front of her, waiting for her comment. She looked at him silently for a moment, tilted her lovely head to one side, then sighed heavily as if seeing all the world's ills.

"You have, Damien of Aquitaine, the most horrifying and grating and utterly appalling singing voice I have ever heard."

Don't be kind. "So I've been told."

"It wasn't you that Eleanor cursed. It was the people of those lands that she banished you to."

"Is that so?" The muscles of his back tightened. He hated singing. Except for the songs involving battle, anyway. He had no interest in the reception of his voice. Still, that this tiny woman would point out his ineptitude, without any hint of graciousness . . .

"I wonder if she knew when she condemned you thus just how cruel a punishment it was—to England."

For reasons that eluded him entirely, Damien envisioned seizing her small body, drawing her near, and kissing her. At the very least, it would stop her from taking pleasure at his expense. "Music is a matter of taste," he said.

She laughed. "And it can be a weapon. That much, I learned tonight."

She was quick. Despite the fact that she obviously was attracted to him, she had no qualms about insulting him. Worse still, he could think of no sufficient retort.

"I noticed, good bard, that you added a few of your own verses to those ancient and hallowed lyrics celebrating brotherhood and forgiveness. Something about . . . blood spilled on a field of war, and . . . a beheading, wasn't it? Hardly Yuletide cheer." As she spoke, she gazed upward, pondering, laughter sparkling in her eyes.

"I go where inspiration carries me."

"You despise this that you are forced to do, is that not so?"

He glanced around, then back at her. "After this display, can you doubt it?"

"Yet you change the words to suit . . . what? Your own imaginings, I think."

Damien hesitated. "That is true. What of it?"

Her dark eyes softened as she watched him. Her expression turned sensual and warm. "You have a vivid—if violent—imagination."

"It whiles the hours."

"It fires the soul."

He couldn't argue with that. Imagining his redemption occupied a great deal of his time. "I am attempting, little flower, to 'become what I am.' What I was once, I will be again."

"You will be a knight with power, perhaps a noble of a castle such as . . ." She paused and waved her arm around the banquet hall. "This?"

Perceptive. She had guessed his plan. "Possibly."

"And with power, what will you do? Banish all minstrels and bards for reminding you of your exile?"

An idea he hadn't considered. But a pleasing one. Apparently, his expression gave away his thoughts, because she frowned.

"Then I will sing tonight as if tomorrow you will be king," she said.

She didn't wait for his response. She wandered toward the musicians, twirling as she moved. Damien watched, fascinated. The crowd didn't notice her. They kept talking and laughing, milling around the hall as if the tiny woman wasn't there at all.

The musicians seemed to know her, though, and they stilled their instruments. She played a note on her small harp, then another. Still, few of the revelers took any notice of the sound. Damien fought the urge to silence them on her behalf.

She didn't seem to mind. She didn't seem to notice. Christina left the table, but Lady Elisa took note of

Pippa. She drew her guests' attention to the girl, and they fell into relative quiet.

The sound of the harp increased subtly, discordant and strange, as if it had no melody, no rhyme or rhythm to it, yet growing as something not yet fully realized. Damien listened with fascination. Was it possible that Pippa was even more talentless than himself?

When she had the attention of her audience, she turned toward the nobles' table. The force of her fingers on her harp grew; the music coalesced into something far more familiar.

Just as Damien thought it might be forming into a pleasant melody, it faded. The audience was losing interest. He strained to think of a way to rescue her.

The sound of her voice came like a rumble of thunder from the halls of Olympus. A chill ran along his spine and held him motionless. From her tiny body came a sound so rich, so filled with passion that he wondered if she were human at all. Her voice was not high, but deep. Deep and low and husky, as if she aimed for every heart, and found it.

She sang in another tongue. He assumed it was Welsh, but it didn't matter. He understood. Every word brought forth images of longing and passion, and of its bitter denial. Every word summoned an ache within. An ache Damien had never encountered before.

He felt her voice as if it came from inside him.

The power of that voice grew as she sang. Her little body bent with the words. Her hair came loose from beneath her veil. It was longer and curlier than he had realized. It fell across her forehead as she twirled, but she didn't notice.

She just sang, and sang until young women wept, until the room seemed saturated with her presence. But more than that. She filled the room with all the pain and hope of every person there. His own anguish throbbed in his heart. The son of a rogue and dishonored by his father's ignoble deeds, Damien had redeemed his family, his name. He had become the most honored knight in Aquitaine, to lose it all because of a foolish woman's whim.

He ached. And Pippa kept singing. He had no idea what she said, but if it was the tale of his life, it couldn't have come nearer to his heart.

Her voice trailed off, and she resumed playing her harp. Her singing had begun as if she had been jolted from sleep. Now as she finished, her voice faded as if she were once more drifting into slumber. When the song ended, no one applauded. They just stared at each other, deeply moved.

Damien swallowed the emotions her song had released in him and looked around the room. His eyes fell on Christina, his prize. She sat looking young and defiant. She wanted something. She resisted something. He could see it in her eyes, and he understood her. She had her own life to live, and it conflicted with what her parents wanted.

The girl cast a quick glance at her mother. No, Damien realized, the girl's problem was what her mother wanted.

Lady Elisa didn't notice her daughter's sharp glance. Instead, the noblewoman looked at her husband, her face so filled with longing that Damien almost felt it himself. Her husband stared into his chalice, his expression resigned.

"Well, boy, she put *you* to shame, didn't she?"

Angus. Damien drew in an irritated breath. "She put everyone to shame."

"You, more than anyone." The Scot was persistent. Damien resolved to ignore him, then have him tossed into a dungeon when he had the opportunity.

Angus positioned himself in front of Damien, who

forced himself to gaze casually over his head. "You stay away from her," the Scot began. "You are not the one."

Damien lowered his gaze, briefly, to meet Angus's. "Your order gives me desire to do otherwise."

"You're ill-suited. Music is her sanctuary. It is your hell." Angus started away, then stopped, looking back over his shoulder. "And everyone else's, when you sing."

From the corner of his eye, Damien saw that Christina was approaching. His purpose surged forward like a dammed river, straining to be freed. But still, he found himself looking for Pippa. She was gone. He'd half-expected her to return to him, to gloat, to receive her due praise.

Cease this silliness, he told himself. He was in England by necessity, not to seduce an ethereal female minstrel. He was a practical man. He had to marry, and he would make that choice wisely, to his advantage. Not marry some landless beauty who . . . He glanced around, but saw no sign of Pippa. She put too much emotion in her songs. For her health, it seemed wise if she restrain herself more. Perhaps he should tell her so. . . .

"Come with me to the stillroom, minstrel. You are in dire need of horehound syrup."

Christina's direct, practical words startled him from his thoughts of Pippa. He turned to her, confused. "I beg your pardon, my lady?"

She eyed him with curiosity, as if taking in his good looks for the first time. Damien waited for the inevitable softening of her voice, the gentle smile.

"Your voice, minstrel, is an affront to my family and to all our guests. My mother suggested horehound syrup to cure your hoarseness. Come with me."

What a prim miss was this! he decided.

Englishwomen were in dire need of seduction and

schooling in seduction. He forced a smile and bowed. "I humbly ask your forgiveness. I will with pleasure attempt your lady mother's cure for . . . the condition of my throat."

Christina's mouth crooked to one side. "You do not sound hoarse when speaking." She didn't wait for his explanation. She sighed heavily instead. "My mother has given me the direction of the musicians." She looked proud. "It is a task I will accomplish with skill, thus proving . . ." She stopped herself, as if realizing she talked to a menial.

"Proving what, lady?"

She cast a glance toward the banquet table, and her expression changed. A tall, blond boy stood before a group of musicians, instructing them. He fingered a harp lovingly, as if teaching the harper a better tune. When he noticed Christina's attention, he turned deliberately away, but his face was red.

"Who is that?"

Christina huffed, then averted her intense gaze from the blond. "It is Wallace Davenport, the youngest son of Lord Edward, who lives not far from this castle. Wallace is both conceited and difficult."

She fancies herself in love with that boy. Damien fought an urge to groan and roll his eyes. What an inconvenience to his plans! He glanced at the youth again. Young, thin, his skin pale . . . It wouldn't take much to direct Christina's attention from that one.

Damien shook his head. "And he busies himself with musicians." He spoke disparagingly, but Christina sighed again, wistfully.

"He has admirable skill with the harp."

"A man of merit would busy himself with the sword." Damien spoke more strongly than he'd intended, and she eyed him doubtfully. "In the pursuit of honorable knighthood."

"Wallace prefers music, but he is skilled with a sword."

An implausible declaration, if ever there was one. Curse the power of infatuation! And where was Pippa? Did she also succumb to such frivolity, or was she moved by nothing but the ballads in her head? She wouldn't fall to the dubious charms of Wallace, anyway.

He spotted her across the room. No one noticed her as she mingled among the musicians. Until she drew close. Then, every man she brushed by stopped as if he'd seen an angel. Wallace Davenport stared at her wide-eyed. He smiled like a fool when she spoke to him.

How could she find such a weak man appealing? Damien's jaw clenched.

"That maiden has a lovely voice. From what little I know of the Welsh tongue, she is a woman of strong emotion." Christina didn't sound pleased. "And she's pretty." Damien tore his attention from Pippa to Christina, whose own square jaw set stubbornly.

"To the stillroom, minstrel."

Chapter Two

Pippa positioned herself outside the stillroom door and watched Damien, close enough that she could overhear his conversation with the nobleman's daughter. She had no right to spy. She wondered what had moved her to such a strange, dishonorable act.

But she already knew the answer.

He sang as if he hated every word that passed his lips. Such fury, such passion! She had listened to him in an awe she had never felt before. He turned ancient verses into vivid flashes of violent conflict. His songs' lyrics leapt from image to image, so quickly! She had listened intently, and she had seen his mind working; she had felt his anger within herself.

He fought life, struggled with it, twisted it to what he imagined in his mind. Someone had robbed him of what he'd created. Someone had taken his strength and used it against him.

So when he sang, his voice was as she'd said—a weapon.

She peeked in and saw Christina angrily shuffling through jars and pots on a shelf near the door. Damien waited in obvious confusion as she flung one iron pot aside and it clattered on the floor. "Such waste, such clutter!" She shoved several pots aside, too. Pippa smiled. A girl of strong will, young and passionate.

Damien watched her, and Pippa's amusement faded. Christina was all she herself was not. This girl's feet were grounded to the earth, yet her mind was swift and sure. Pippa lived her life surrounded in mists, in the place where images form, where songs begin. She'd found that it was the only place where life had meaning.

"Here it is." Christina seized a small jar, then took a spoon from a cluttered worktable. She filled the spoon with the syrup, then presented it to Damien.

He hesitated, suspicious, then bowed gallantly. "I will with pleasure attempt your mother's remedy, lady." *Remedy? For what?* He seemed reluctant to swallow the proffered cure. "What did you call this concoction?"

Christina puffed an impatient breath. " 'Tis horehound syrup. It will ease the hoarseness in your throat."

Pippa fought an urge to laugh. The nobles thought his grating voice due to illness. Well, it served him right.

He took the spoon from Christina's hand, then swallowed the syrup.

The expression on his face brought a burble of laughter. Pippa clamped her hand over her mouth to silence herself. Christina watched Damien closely, then filled another spoonful. He lurched backward, coughing.

"No, no . . . One is enough."

"Mother says two." Yes, this girl was strong-willed and sensible. Pippa backed away from the door. But this spitfire had met an even stronger man. He would never take that second spoonful.

"As you wish, my lady."

Surprised, Pippa peeked back in the room. He swallowed the second offering, choked back an obvious cough, then smiled. "Your attention is kind." As grating as his singing voice was, his speaking voice could melt the coldest heart. Christina apparently felt its power, for she studied him more closely and faint color tinged her cheeks.

It was the first time the girl had really looked at him. Pippa felt sure of it. She had been so tortured by his terrible singing that she hadn't noticed his good looks. Until now.

"What is your name, minstrel?" The girl's voice had softened. Pippa frowned.

"I am Damien of Aquitaine, my lady." He bowed. His long hair fell sensually over his shoulders. Pippa's fingers twitched as she imagined touching it. Perhaps placing a small braid . . .

Apparently, Christina recognized his name, because she brightened with interest. "There are rumors, Damien, that you were not always a musician."

He looked away, dramatically. "That is so. But my tale, it is long and painful in telling." He paused. "No, I cannot speak of it."

He was a master at presenting the most intriguing, mysterious face to the world. She had been right. He was suited to be an actor. She found herself leaning forward to hear his tale.

"There is no need." Christina sounded less interested in Damien's story. "I have heard it before. Your story was often told in the convent. Many girls found it romantic."

What story? Pippa clenched her fists in frustration.

"Indeed?" He sounded pleased.

"You were a knight of some prestige who disavowed

the notion of courtly love and fell into disfavor with Eleanor of Aquitaine. She condemned you to . . . this, and until you place a gold ring on the finger of a woman you love more than yourself, you have been charged to wander the hills and valleys, singing the praises of that which you scorned."

Pippa recoiled from the door, her hand clasped to her heart. *Love* was what damned him? A bitter irony. Eleanor, who praised love like a religion, had made a habit of condemning those she considered to have sinned against it. No wonder Pippa found it so easy to understand Damien of Aquitaine. She leaned against the rough wooden wall and drew a deep breath.

Christina came to the door, then turned back. Pippa darted across the hall and hid in an alcove behind a thick red curtain. Christina walked by, returning to the banquet hall. She didn't look back. Pippa remained motionless until she heard Damien leave. She held her breath, waiting for him to pass by. She couldn't let him know that she cared enough to spy on his activities.

Swish. The curtain she hid behind was pulled aside. Damien stood, assessing her as if not sure where to begin. "Well, well, well."

Her face flamed a bright, radiant pink—she knew it. Curse her light skin for showing every emotion! She longed to disappear. Instead, she cleared her throat and looked him straight in the eye.

"I was . . . lost."

"Behind a curtain?"

She smacked her lips. "Yes." She glanced around and noticed a narrow rim that might pass for a bench. She seated herself, then fiddled with a loose strand of hair beneath her veil. "Then I found it rather a comfortable spot for . . . contemplation."

"You were eavesdropping." Damien didn't seem angry. Instead he motioned for her to move to one side, which she did. Then he sat down beside her. "Why?"

She peered around, casually, as if looking for someone. No explanation for her behavior came to mind. "I don't know."

He seemed to like her answer, because he smiled. He had a beautiful smile, teasing and too knowing. And he was looking at her mouth.

Pippa's pulse quickened. She knew what he meant to do. She wanted him to kiss her, just so that she would know what he felt like that close. He studied her lips with the well-practiced eye of a master. His gaze whisked to her eyes, then back to her mouth.

He reached to brush a tendril of hair from her cheek, letting his knuckles graze her skin. She caught her breath and held it. He knew exactly what he was doing. His eyelids lowered in sensual appraisal.

She puffed a quick breath, leaned toward him, and pressed her mouth against his.

His whole body tightened in obvious surprise. For a moment, he didn't seem to know what to do in response. Pippa didn't care. She moved her mouth softly, feeling his lips beneath hers, feeling his warmth. She flicked her tongue out to taste him.

He caught her hair in his hands and pulled her closer so that she felt his chest against hers. His heart pounded as if passion raged inside him. Pippa felt as if all her dreams, all her imaginings, had come real in this moment, with this man. She wrapped her arms around his neck and lost herself in his kiss.

He kissed her mouth, then moved to her face, her temple, then her lips again. She didn't care where they were, or who might see them, but Damien stopped suddenly and stared at her, aghast.

"You kissed me!"

Her breath came swift and shallow. She felt lightheaded, but happy. A small giggle burst forth. "I did."

His mouth remained open, his eyes both stunned and ablaze with desire. She liked the image. It suited him. "I had intended to kiss *you*," he said.

"I know that. I kissed you first."

A tall knight walked down the hall, apparently preoccupied. He glanced at Pippa and Damien and smiled. His manner indicated that the antics of two peasants amused him, and offered him little surprise. Damien glared.

Pippa watched the man pass, then turned to Damien. "Were you so arrogant and sure of yourself during your knighthood?" He eyed her dubiously. "Never mind. You were."

"I earned my knighthood. I wasn't born into it."

"What makes you think *he* was?"

He glanced at the departing knight. "I can tell."

"You are right. He takes his rank for granted. To you, it means much more." Pippa paused. "What did you do that inspired Eleanor to condemn you to this fate?"

His smile faded, his eyes darkening. "She is a foolish woman."

"How much do you know of her?"

"Too much. We are related, distantly." He paused as if expecting a reaction, but Pippa waited for a more pertinent revelation. "I was born in the city of Poitiers, as was Eleanor, although my own father had no great standing in Aquitaine. I proved myself worthy despite my heritage and was granted knighthood."

Damien's eyes glowed with pride. Pippa could imagine him performing heroic deeds, all with great flair and drama. "This meant a great deal to you?" she asked.

"Of course. My skill was renowned throughout the realm."

"Matched only by your modesty."

31

He caught her teasing and frowned. "You requested my tale, did you not?"

"I did. Please continue."

"When Henry Plantagenet married Eleanor, he gained control of Aquitaine, and in theory, my fealty was sworn to England." His lips curled in distaste. "I considered transferring my allegiance to King Louis, because though an uninspired commander, he is at least French."

Something about his barely subdued arrogance provoked a desire to tease. "It is Henry who is the better warrior, despite being English," she said.

His brow furrowed into dark displeasure, but he didn't argue. "There is some truth in what you say. When Henry was crowned a year ago at Westminster Abbey and Eleanor became queen, I was asked to attend."

"A year ago . . ." At that time, Pippa had been near London giving her first performance with the troupe of actors and musicians. Until that day, she had considered her fate worse than death. But her performance had changed her life. "I understand they love each other very much." Pippa sighed, wistful, but Damien eyed her in disgust.

"They lust, which no doubt explains the swift birth of their son."

"I suppose you said as much to the queen?"

"Of course not. I am not a fool. A woman's illusions are tenderly held."

"Then what did you do to anger her?"

He shrugged, dismissing his crime, then exhaled an annoyed breath. "I had . . . been entertained by one of Eleanor's ladies-in-waiting." He paused. "Actually, several . . ."

Pippa cringed. "I would prefer not to know."

"You asked."

"I wish that I had not."

He looked even more impatient than usual. "You are not a young, foolish girl, Pippa." She wanted to interject, *"I am,"* but he was right. She had long ago left the safety of girlhood.

"No, I suppose I'm not."

"And that is for the best. I like you. You are beautiful and appealing and sincere. I would not lie to you about my true nature."

I wish you would. "Thank you." She liked him, too. She liked his impatience, the potency of the life that flowed inside him, the vibrant imagination that fueled his strength to defy a queen. "So you seduced several young, innocent women. . . ."

"They were not entirely innocent."

"Be that as it may, your behavior displeased the queen."

"It was not the seduction that displeased her, but my resistance to terming the encounters 'romantic' in nature, rather than what they were: a few hours' pleasure. I told her, truthfully, that marriage was not to be undertaken for frivolous reasons. It requires the same well-considered strategy that one prepares for battle. The conquest must be negotiated fully, and yield substantial rewards."

"I see." Pippa watched him for a moment. He was young and strong, and so beautiful that a woman could lose herself in his presence. She understood why a woman would agree to his terms—to be held in his arms, to be kissed with such passion that she would forget everything but him.

"Eleanor called me to her private chambers to discuss the issue. It may be that I lost my temper. . . ."

"Oh, no! Did you—you didn't—cast aspersions on her own marriage?"

He appeared stubborn, as if not willing to admit he had made such a grievous error. "I pointed out the foolishness of choices based on the heart, for the heart is whimsical and its passion fleeting."

Pippa sighed and her heart felt heavy in her chest. Eleanor was a strong woman. Many had said too strong. But Pippa considered her wise. "Eleven years separate Eleanor and Henry. Some say that will be their downfall. But perhaps they share secret pleasures which will make their union last a lifetime."

"Those 'secret pleasures' last but a short time, and then the passion fades to nothing. You are left with nothing but duty, and the hope of some new romance. After a time, you learn that each is as the first. A brief fire that rages, then burns out."

Pippa stared at him. "That is the most discouraging thing I have ever heard."

He moved closer to her and reached to touch her cheek. His fingers grazed over her flesh and her pulse quickened. "I tell you now so that you won't waste your passion on such illusions as Eleanor entertains. Seize its sweetness, savor it, and revel in it, for it will soon be gone."

He spoke of sensuality, but not love. Not the kind of love that would make a man give up everything for a woman. Pippa turned her face from his touch. Damien of Aquitaine was a dangerous man—he was too easy to adore. "Yet to regain your title, you must wed. Is that true?"

"I must place this ring on a woman's finger and vow that it is done in the 'sacred name of love.'" He pulled a narrow chain from around his neck, with one gold ring attached. He fingered the band, his lip curled in disgust. "This is my curse. But for duty's sake, I suppose it must be done."

"It's a pretty ring." It appeared strong and solid and enduring. Pippa watched him for a long while, as he stared at his ring as if it was his direst opponent's sword. "You are wrong, Damien of Aquitaine. You are not the one cursed, but the woman who falls in love with you."

"My story interests you. Perhaps you will put it in a ballad. Your voice would do the tale justice."

She averted her eyes and attempted to seem disinterested. Pippa restrained her pride. He liked her voice, her songs. Perhaps she had even touched his heart. "Thank you."

"Your voice is unusual and . . . stirring. Even though I do not understand the words. But you know that." He paused. "Of what do you sing?"

"Some tales from legend, Celtic and English. I sing of the world of dreams, of heroes and women who are heroes, too. Most often, I sing of love."

"You would do better to sing the praises of conquest."

Pippa laughed. "Conquest, my friend, is vastly overrated."

"Because you are a woman and have never known the thrill of battle."

"Everyone, male or female, understands the lure of power." Pippa paused and sighed. "But where one wins, another must lose. Isn't that always so?"

"Of course. Naturally." Damien studied her, then sighed. "I will never understand the way a woman reasons—or fails to reason. Unfortunately, when one is given power such as Eleanor possesses, much grief can come to those who cross her peculiar line of thinking."

"I thought so once, too. But maybe she is right."

"Power has gone to her head, and she thinks to direct the lives of all those around her. Such a woman is best kept on a short rein."

They sat close together now. Close enough so that she felt the warmth of his body, so that she detected the warm, masculine scent of him. He smelled good. "A strong will displeases you?"

"A woman who takes it upon herself to order her husband about is tiresome, yes."

"And this you call 'strong'?"

"Yes. Even 'domineering.' A woman should be . . ." He paused and studied Pippa's face thoughtfully. "Like you. Delicate and soft-spoken."

Pippa laughed. "You are right. You do not understand women at all, or at least you cannot read them."

He straightened indignantly, offended. "How so?"

"You sit with me, and you consider me frail. You are wrong." As she spoke, she leaned closer to him, pride and conviction burning in her soul. "I am stronger than Eleanor of Aquitaine, I am stronger than Christina. I am stronger than anyone I know."

Damien stared at her in astonishment. "In what way are you, the most delicate, *fragile* woman I have ever seen . . . strong?"

She smiled and looked into his beautiful eyes. "Because I'm here."

The minstrels and entertainers slept in the coldest corner of the great hall. Damien was used to such ignominious surroundings, but he would never enjoy them. Strangely, Lord Robert also slept among his guests. Obviously, marriage, too, held strife.

Pippa slept not far away from Damien, protected by Angus and several other mummers who seemed to feel her welfare was their concern. She never seemed to notice the attention paid her. She never seemed to consider the danger of being a beautiful, delicate woman alone.

When he propped himself up on one elbow, he could make out her small body as she lay on her sleeping mat. Her long hair was splayed in all directions around her head. She slept on her side, with her cheek resting in the crook of her arm. Her tiny fingers were curled, giving her an added impression of delicacy.

Strong, indeed! Never had he met a woman who seemed so vulnerable. Damien lay back and stared at the heavy, rough-hewn beams. A low firelight danced on the high ceiling. Despite their conversation, Pippa remained an enigma. She seemed self-contained, unaffected by the demands of life that plagued him.

There was a mystery about her. For one thing, he couldn't place her in the carefully ordered structure of society. At first glance, he had assumed she was a peasant wench, spirited, perhaps innocent, but no one with aspirations to the higher levels of social importance. Not a woman likely to dwell behind castle walls.

Yet nothing within those grand walls seemed to interest her. She took her lavish surroundings for granted, preferring to praise the winter garlands carried by her musician friends, or to listen quietly to their music.

Most of all, she liked to sing. When Pippa sang, she seemed to drift outside herself, or perhaps to transport herself to a place he couldn't see. Whatever world she lost herself in, it seemed more important than the one that surrounded her.

But when he was near, he sensed her desire. There was nothing vague about that. It was strong, and he surmised that it would be highly imaginative in expression. But it was the enigma of her character that had him fantasizing about her.

He wondered what she thought of him. Women all found him handsome. They found his presence powerful and stirring. He had seen evidence that Pippa felt the same. And yet, he amused her, too. There was no avoiding this fact. He made her laugh—and he didn't mean to. Still, in a way he hadn't expected he enjoyed her humor, even at his expense.

Why am I thinking about this? Why did he care what this fragile, enigmatic, and romantic woman thought of him? He should be concentrating his efforts on the daughter of the castle, Christina. Christina he understood. He could easily read what motivated her. He could guess what she would be like as a wife.

He had no burning desire for a wife, but neither did he oppose the notion, assuming she was of an even temperament. He didn't want a woman like Pippa—a beauty of endless fascination, and perhaps trouble. He wanted a woman who fit into the life he had planned, with the nobility and honor of a knight or a nobleman.

He expected a wife to be pleasing, to give him sons and daughters who would in their time forward the recognition of his household, and he expected to eventually die as an old and well-renowned man in France. If he had to marry an Englishwoman, so be it, but he would return to his homeland. He couldn't imagine life not spent in Aquitaine.

Because I'm here. The woman had been deliberately enigmatic. Had she meant "here" with him, dangerously close to a man who had every intention of seducing her? He liked that possibility—that she was toying with him, teasing his senses, daring him by recognizing what he intended.

He liked the thought, but he sensed she meant something more. Here in Menton Castle? But what had she to risk by entertaining friendly nobles behind strong castle walls? No, she meant something more than that, and he had no idea what it was.

Nor why he cared.

He had come to Menton Castle to resolve his unfortunate situation, but each time he considered his plan, his attention returned to Pippa.

He had no idea why. He had known many beautiful women. But none had been this much of a mystery.

Damien sat up. Once he understood her, she would no longer captivate him. The power of infatuation was strong. Desire had to be sated, and then it would pass. He had learned that during his youth. His solution was obvious. He would seduce this lady minstrel, thus learning of her most engaging secrets, and then proceed with his more important intentions.

December 26

A loud hubbub arose from within the great hall. A large group of young noblemen and women burst into the courtyard, led by Lord Robert's daughter. Damien rose and waited. She spotted him at once. Wallace Davenport stood behind her, but both pretended not to notice each other. The haughty knight he had seen in the hallway the night before was now accompanied by a lovely young woman. Life was so easy for some!

Christina approached Damien, her eyes glittering with youthful pleasure. "Damien! Mother has requested that we go into Menton Forest to find mistletoe." She cast a quick glance at Wallace, who frowned. "If we fail in our duty, kissing will stop entirely."

Damien stared at her, confused. The English were odd beyond compare. "Of course."

"We would like you to accompany us. So that we might have song along the way! I trust your throat is better today."

A humiliating invitation, if ever there was one, but perhaps he could turn the day to his favor. "I would . . . relish the excursion, my lady." It was almost impossible to smile, harder still to bow, but he accomplished both tasks with effort.

Wallace spotted Pippa with Angus, and tapped Christina's shoulder. She stiffened. Yes, they had obviously had some kind of quarrel. "Perhaps," the youth began, "in case Damien's throat isn't improved, we might bring the Welsh girl along as well."

Someone in Christina's group uttered a plea seconding Wallace's plan, apparently preferring the thought of Pippa's voice to Damien's. Christina looked resistant, her jaw set in a stubborn posture, but Wallace wasn't to be thwarted. "We will need a flautist as well."

Bad enough to partake in a quest for weeds, Damien thought. Having the company of a "flautist" made the prospect unbearable. Worse, it was Angus who stepped forward to answer Wallace's request.

The Scot glared at Damien and kept himself solidly in front of Pippa. Christina marshaled the group into an ordered procession, with the musicians at the rear. They waited as the guards opened the portcullis, then proceeded from the castle.

Christina led the way, followed closely by Wallace, who made a valiant attempt to seize the lead and failed. "I know the way better than you, Master Wallace," she said.

"The only place you'll lead us to is *lost*. And not for the first time, I might add. Or have you forgotten?"

Christina flushed pink with both anger and embarrassment. Yes, the two had known some sort of romantic encounter. By the look of Wallace, Damien doubted it could have involved much in the way of skilled lovemaking.

Angus rode beside Pippa, stopping Damien from joining her also, so he was left to bring up the rear. He noticed that he was the only one not garbed in some sort of festive clothing. The others had attached bright ribbons to their garments. Even Pippa had added a trailing garland of dried lavender to her white gown.

Damien wore black, with no adornment, no hat, and no mandolin.

His attire accurately reflected his mood. If he was to be treated as a serf, he could at least entertain himself by speaking with Pippa. From behind her, he could only see her long hair beneath the veil. And the sway of her hips as she rode.

That had its appeal, because he detected the swell

of a firm, feminine bottom beneath, which lent fuel to his imagination. Angus kept her engaged in conversation, but Damien suspected the memory of their kiss last night had infected her thoughts.

His own mind had rarely traveled far from the memory.

"Lady Christina!" At his call, the whole party stopped and turned around to look at him—except Pippa, who seemed to be watching a small bird hop between the branches of a chestnut tree. "You mentioned music. Perhaps the Scot could lead the party, and favor us with marching . . . riding music."

Christina seemed to like the idea. "That would be pleasing. You, Scottish person . . ."

Angus's round face reddened with displeasure. "Angus of Perth, my lady."

"Quite. Well, come up to the front of our group and commence with a suitable melody."

Angus cast a dark, threatening glare Damien's way, then eyed Pippa with obvious tenderness. "Mayhap the lady might accompany my flute with a ballad?"

Christina frowned. "A ballad would distract us from conversation. She may stay at the rear."

Damien understood Christina's resistance. She didn't want the ethereal Pippa anywhere near Wallace. Understandable. Damien didn't like the thought himself. But from what he'd seen, Wallace's interest in Pippa was displayed mainly to irritate Christina. He suspected the same reason spurred Christina's interest in himself.

They seemed so young, fighting life, yet succumbing to it utterly. For an instant, Damien imagined Christina and Wallace finding happiness in each other's company. Arguing, loving every moment together. He shook his head. It could never happen. Love was no more than a fancy. It was fleeting and ended only the bitter pain of might-have-beens.

41

Angus didn't appear willing to admit defeat. "Perhaps our noble minstrel would favor this group with a marching song."

Damien's fist clenched. Marching song, indeed! If he could drag the old Scot aside, he might easily cut his throat and leave him for dead. The entire party erupted in a rumble of displeasure at the prospect of his song.

Damien folded his arms over his chest. King Henry himself couldn't force even a note out of him now. "Sadly, I have forgotten my trusty mandolin. And my throat is still . . . recovering."

Someone breathed a muted sigh of relief. And someone else uttered a small chuckle. He knew who it was without looking. Pippa.

Angus grudgingly maneuvered his mount to the fore, positioning his flute, and the group started off again, accompanied by a tune that indeed sounded . . . martial. In contrast to the bright, cheerful Yule songs, Angus's marching music pleased Damien.

He caught up with Pippa and assumed Angus's place at her side. She didn't look at him. Her brow was furrowed as if she debated something inwardly, as if she walked on some precipice of doom and yet refused to turn away.

"You seem . . . distracted this morning, my dear."

She nodded, but didn't speak. A frustrating response.

They headed into Menton Forest, but Damien paid no attention. She was ignoring him. Perhaps she was angry. He had no idea what occupied her thoughts. "Tell me, what is the significance of mistletoe, and what has it to do with kissing?"

She still didn't look at him and seemed to resist answering. "When a girl stands beneath a sprig of mistletoe, a man is encouraged to kiss her."

How fortunate! "Does it work both ways?"

"I suppose it might." She was definitely being brusque.

"I didn't notice a sprig above my head last night, but perhaps that could explain . . ."

She stopped short. "Hush!"

Damien stopped, too, though the rest continued on ahead. "What is the matter with you?"

She turned to him, fiercely. "You know exactly!"

"I have not even the slightest idea." It was true. The woman was worse than illogical. She was unpredictable, as well.

She pointed her finger at him. She had small fingers, narrow and delicate. "You are toying with me!"

She placed her hands on her hips. Her long, curly hair fell in mingling shades of gold all around her shoulders, down to the small of her back. The hair net she wore hardly seemed to cover more than a quarter of its length.

She was even more beautiful with the sunlight glinting on her hair, reflecting in her dark, mysterious eyes. A familiar stirring tightened his loins. He wanted to know her, to understand the secrets inside her.

"I am not 'toying with you.' I simply find you beautiful and charming. I enjoy your company." *Too much.* If he could remain fixed on his task, he would easily usurp Wallace's position in Christina's young heart, and thus, regain his rank.

"You intend to marry a noblewoman, is that not so?"

Was it possible that she read his thoughts? He knew little of the Welsh, but among the French, it was rumored they had certain "gifts." He saw no reason to deny what she already knew. "It would seem a wise course."

"I am not a noblewoman."

He understood now where this line of thought was going. "Pippa . . ."

"The attention you have paid to me is for the purpose of securing me in your bed. Or whatever spot is closest, I expect. Is that not so?"

"Not at all! Yes." He almost laughed at himself, but she did not.

"I have thought of you in that capacity, also."

"Then our minds run along the same path." Damien couldn't help a surge of excitement, but something in her dark, mysterious eyes told him that this conversation wasn't heading in the direction he hoped.

"The same path, yes." Her tone indicated his guess was accurate. "But the path I see myself on with you leads into darkness and pain. I see myself abandoned. . . ." She closed her eyes and her head tipped back. For an instant, he believed she really did see images in her mind. "I see myself alone in a storm, waiting for you, hoping that you will come, and knowing you will not."

Before he could answer, her eyes popped open, and her lips tightened in intense displeasure. "You are not here for me. You are here to regain what you lost. But you can't. You will simply replace it with its likeness, but you left that part of yourself long ago."

A woman should be direct and simple in her conversation. Not mysterious and ambiguous. She shouldn't look at a man with eyes of desire, obviously contemplating him as a lover, then issue dark predictions of an uncertain fate.

His jaw felt tight from restraint. Odd that he could want her so much, yet feel such anger in her presence. Damien seized her arm, stopping her from going forward. "You are wrong, little minstrel. I will have again everything I lost, and more besides. One thing you can trust: When that day comes, the first thing I will have is you."

Chapter Three

She had called herself strong. Never had Pippa uttered a more blatant untruth. Damien rode on ahead, furious at what she had said. She couldn't restrain her feelings, but she could exercise better judgment when choosing a lover. Many men would put love first in their lives, if their hearts were deeply moved. And she deserved that.

But it seemed a dictate of Heaven's vengeance that she was falling for a man who kept his heart sealed and locked away.

Ahead, Christina and Wallace Davenport seemed to be bickering. They stopped, jarring the party into a muddled group. Christina placed her hands on her hips, her face puckered with anger. Wallace's expression, in contrast, had turned cold and impassive, distant yet superior. Pippa sighed and shook her head.

"It is this way! I know Menton Forest better than you!" Christina's voice rang with fury, but Wallace was colder still.

45

"You are confused, Christina. You have been long away. Your memory misleads you. The growth of mistletoe is found on the narrow path to your left."

Christina gestured fiercely at a small footpath off the main track. "That is nothing but a deer path! You think me incapable of the smallest decision! To you, I am a child. . . ."

"A willful one . . ."

Oh, no! Pippa cringed. Wallace had no sense with courting a young, willful woman. Christina fumed, then turned her bright, furious gaze to Damien. "We shall see. You, minstrel, accompany me on yonder path. Let the others go right or left, or wherever they think best."

Wallace glared at the invitation, then stormed back to Pippa. He seized her arm and smiled, though she knew he seethed with anger. Pippa fought an urge to groan. "Do as you will, Christina," he said. "When have you not? I will take . . ." He paused and glanced at Pippa, then lowered his voice to a whisper. "What is your name again, miss?"

She responded with equal hush. "Pippa."

"Yes. Pippa will come with me and we shall see who returns with the mistletoe."

Christina appeared livid, but she, too, forced a wide smile. "An excellent idea. We shall meet back at the castle. Several hours hence." She gripped Damien's arm and tugged him forward, but he didn't move. He glanced over to where Pippa stood with Wallace.

The rest of the group headed off down the wider path, in a hurry to leave the squabbling Christina and Wallace behind. For a moment, Pippa thought Damien might refuse Christina, and her heart skipped a beat. *Now I will know what is important to him: his ambition or his heart.*

Damien looked at Wallace, then Pippa, then glanced at Christina as if weighing the possibilities.

Please, show me I matter to you, Pippa prayed. She saw his doubt, and she saw when he made up his mind. "A contest between us—an admirable idea!"

Pippa closed her eyes and a numbness entered her chest. She had her answer. Now she knew. Damien of Aquitaine would never listen to his heart. And her own heart had never been in more danger.

"Here, I was right. Mistletoe." Wallace dismounted and yanked on the vine and began ripping mistletoe sprigs from it. "In fact, never have I seen such a growth!" He yanked another sprig and stuffed it vengefully into the sack Pippa held open. "Have you ever seen such a growth? What was your name, again?"

"Pippa." She smiled. She liked Wallace. She liked his immediately obvious emotion, his youthful petulance. He reminded her of another she had known—raised to nobility, yet so confused as to his own worth. "No, indeed. Surely you have found the greatest abundance of mistletoe in all England."

He misinterpreted her teasing words and nodded vigorously. "Lady Christina will find nothing like it on her side of the path."

Pippa touched his arm. "And you will find nothing like her on your side."

Wallace dropped a bunch of mistletoe, gaped for a moment, then bent to retrieve it. His face had turned pink. "What do you mean?"

"I think you know."

He groaned and clasped the mistletoe close to his heart. "Is it so obvious? Curse her! She is the most impossible girl! She has always been so."

"And you have always loved her."

Wallace didn't answer, but he bowed his head as if in shame. "I am such a fool."

Pippa sighed. "Why do our hearts lead us to the one most likely to make us a fool, I wonder."

Wallace stared at her for a moment. "You are not a peasant wench. Who are you?"

"I am a Welsh minstrel."

"Are you? I wonder. . . ."

Pippa caught her lip between her teeth. She was far from Cornwall. Wallace couldn't know. But he seemed to sense her surprise.

"I attended the court of King Henry in the fall. There, I met a young man my own age. Stephen, the son of Lord Philip of Cornwall and his Welsh wife."

"Oh, no!" She blurted it out before she could stop herself.

"Oh, yes. Stephen told me of his sister, Philippa, a strange and enigmatic girl, older than himself. More than passing fair, she was, and it was said her singing voice surpassed all others. Many men courted her. . . ."

"Stop!" Pippa sank to her knees and bowed her head. "He told you everything?"

"Yes." Despite what he must know about her, Wallace appeared sympathetic. "It seems you have traveled a long road since that time. You are not the same woman your brother described."

She shook her head vigorously. "I have changed. More than I ever thought possible." She paused. "Tell me of my brother. Is he well?"

Wallace smiled. "Stephen has married—his wife bears his child."

"Did he marry for love's sake?"

"He did."

"I knew he would." Pippa sighed and her gaze wandered to the snow-laden boughs of the forest. "Was he worried for my welfare?"

Wallace's brow furrowed. "Your family seemed to be abreast of your whereabouts. I guessed you sent messages to them."

"I have not. At first, I was too angry, and then later, too ashamed."

Wallace touched her shoulder, gently. "You have nothing to feel shame for, Philippa. We all follow the path laid out before us, do we not?"

She met his tender gaze. "I think we follow it too much. That is what I've learned since I left my father's home."

Wallace glanced back along the path toward where Christina must toil with Damien. "Almost . . . Almost, I understand you."

She seized his hand and held it tight. "Please, tell no one of my plight."

"I will not. But I fear for you. Your affection for that troubador . . ."

Pippa cringed. "It is fleeting, due to his good looks and eccentric manner. Nothing more."

Wallace appeared doubtful, but he nodded. "That is well. He is not the man I would choose, were I in your circumstance."

"So says Angus."

"Angus is right. You need a selfless man, Pippa. A man of the heart. The minstrel is a man of the sword. His singing voice proves *that* beyond question."

She looked into Wallace's kind eyes. *Why couldn't I love someone like you?* She realized he was thinking the same thing. They smiled at the same time.

Wallace adjusted his sheathed sword behind him and sat down beside her, then folded his arms on his knees. Her bottom felt cold on the hard snow, but the warmth in her heart returned. "In some way, I envy you the life you now lead, Pippa."

"I have found much to recommend a life of constant journeying, it's true. Not at first, but later . . . I have learned to be almost invisible. I can sing, and look out at those listening, and see when my words touch their hearts. I couldn't do that before."

"Your voice is magic. From what I am told, it always was. Perhaps like a wizard, you have only now learned to use it wisely. Gifts are power, are they not? And it is our fate to learn how to use those gifts."

"I have heard something like that before. That when you are born with a talent, you must honor it, because it is a gift from God. What you do with that gift is in turn your gift to Him."

Wallace's expression turned grave. "Yet when one is born into a situation that runs against his true strengths . . . My father wishes me to prove myself as a knight, naturally. I am the youngest son. I will not inherit his estate, nor do I desire it."

"What do you want?"

He seemed hesitant, as if shy to voice his heart's true desire. "What I favor most is the pursuit of learning. My own learning, and also, the instruction of others. It was this delight in books and letters that first bonded Christina and myself in friendship." Pride grew as he spoke. "I taught her to read, and shared my work and stories with her, though she was a girl and supposed to learn of womanly skills."

Pippa placed her hand on his arm. "Then you must follow this course. If none is laid out for you, carve it for yourself. You could ask for no one better than Christina."

Wallace gazed toward the sky. "But how can I ask her to wife with so uncertain a future? That's all that holds me back."

"You will find a way." Pippa braced herself on his shoulder and stood up. "Is this what angers her? That you haven't proposed marriage yet?"

"I believe so. She mistakenly assumes that I think her unfit to run my household."

"Then you must tell her otherwise."

Wallace looked up at her. He looked young, but certain. "Pippa, you are a wise and kind friend. Your secret is safe with me."

"Thank you . . ." Someone yelped, interrupting her, and she spun around to see three men bounding through the trees, their faces covered by cloth, each brandishing decrepit swords.

"Pippa, run!"

Wallace leapt to his feet, shouting as he struggled with his sword, but when he drew it, the ruffian leader struck it aside. Pippa scrambled for the weapon, fear coursing through her veins. Her hands shook violently as she picked it up. It was heavier than she'd expected. She gripped it with both hands, determined, but she turned to see one of their attackers strike Wallace on the head with the pommel of his weapon.

Wallace crumpled, then lay still in the snow, blood trickling from his forehead. Pippa froze. If fear overwhelmed her, if she failed to stop them, the robbers would surely kill them both.

She tried to force herself into action, to do something to save him. When she sang, she sang of bravery, but here, in reality, she seemed too terrified to move.

Wallace was a kind, good person. This couldn't happen to him.

She knew something of swordplay from watching her brother and the knights of her father's castle. The robbers wouldn't expect her to attack. But against three men, what could she do but stall them?

If that was all she could do, she would do it. Pippa positioned the weapon, and she remembered to widen her stance. No one noticed her. They were too intent on their pillage of a wealthy young nobleman.

The leader bent to rummage through Wallace's waistcoat for gold. He yanked off a ring, probably an heirloom, then started to pull off Wallace's gold-stitched tunic. Pippa stepped forward to challenge the ruffians.

"Leave him alone!"

The leader looked up in surprise, then laughed. "What say we make sport of the boy's liveliest treasure, eh, my men?"

They meant *her*. She gripped the hilt of Wallace's sword with both hands, gathered all her courage and imagined herself a Celtic queen battling Romans. Curses! Her arms ached from the weight already! Her hair came lose from its binding and fell around her face, blocking her view. She blew it fiercely aside and hoped it would stay. It did not and fell back, impeding her view, and she uttered a curse of frustration.

She mustered what she hoped was a chilling war cry, which sounded to her ears like a high, muted "whoop!" then lunged toward the thieves. Her white gown wrapped around her ankles and she stumbled, but she did not fall.

A woman screamed. Pippa hesitated and kicked her dress free. Christina stood on the narrow path, her face white, her hands clasped over her breast.

"What have we here, men? Another spoil of victory?"

Why was Christina alone? Where was Damien? Pippa didn't have long to wonder. She had to protect Christina now, too. She started forward again, but someone hissed to her from behind a tree.

"Pippa!" She started to turn. *Damien*. "Don't look at me!" As always, he sounded impatient. "Drop the sword and move aside."

She endured a painful reluctance to release her weapon, but the gown had entwined itself around her legs again, leaving her no doubt as to her capacity for battle.

She let the sword slip from her hands and she backed away. Before the robbers noticed her movements, Damien leapt from behind the tree, grabbed up the sword, and bounded toward their attackers.

He didn't fight like a nobleman, careful and practiced. He fought like a lion, with an inhuman strength. If she had ever doubted his tale of thwarted knighthood, she trusted it now. This wasn't a noble son born to careful instruction like her brother. This was a man who had fought his way up from the bottom, and whose fury and skill had lifted him above his common birth.

The robbers were overwhelmed within seconds. Bleeding and bruised, they fell over each other in their haste to depart. Damien started after them, as if he enjoyed the battle and loathed to see it end.

"Damien!" Wallace was in need of immediate care. If Damien knew this much about fighting, perhaps he knew something about healing, too. "They're gone. And Wallace is injured."

Her voice stopped him, but he turned back with acute reluctance. He tossed Wallace's sword in the air and caught it, beaming with unrestrained pride. "Well, little flower? What do you see before you now, a knight or a minstrel? *What a man is, he then becomes!*"

She fought an urge to slap him. "I see a man with too much power and skill for his own good. More importantly, I see that Wallace is in need of bandaging."

His mouth dropped and he started to sheathe his sword, then remembered it wasn't his to sheathe. "This is the gratitude I receive for coming to your rescue?"

"I had the matter well in hand." She hadn't, she knew. She had been facing certain death, but his arrogance annoyed her.

"Only if you intended to be skewered!"

She liked his indignant expression, his quick temper. She liked the way his hair fell loose to his wide shoulders and his eyes flashed in the late afternoon sun. He was everything she sang about—heroic, brave, strong, perhaps too sure of himself—but not without reason. Somehow, though, those qualities were more irritating in person.

"As it happens, my troupe has been often assailed by bands of ruffians." She felt proud. "And I have always lent a hand in our defense."

Damien groaned, and turned in a full circle uttering moans of despair. "What a pathetic troupe it must be to require the dubious skills of a tiny, fragile woman!"

"I am not tiny or fragile!" Her lips puckered as she fought an urge to take back the sword and skewer him. "The men of my troupe aren't warriors, but we defend ourselves bravely."

He mustered another groan. "And how many of your hard-earned coins have been robbed because no one had the skill to defend you *properly*?"

"Only one pouch of coins and a sack of gold!" She caught herself and bit her lip. "It was insignificant."

"Robbers, Pippa, most often choose weak groups such as your own because noblemen are defended by well-armed knights."

"Knights are too busy defending noblemen to bother protecting peasants. But once Angus joined our group, we had little to fear."

"Angus? I can't believe he has much skill with a sword."

"It surprised me also. He doesn't use a sword, though. He uses a hammer."

"A hammer? How odd."

Christina ignored Damien and Pippa as she went to Wallace's side. Tears dripped down her cheeks as she knelt beside the boy.

Wallace opened his eyes, then drew a strained breath. "*Pippa . . .*"

Christina lurched back as if she'd been slapped. Pippa bit back a groan and rolled her eyes, though Damien watched her with intense suspicion. Wallace struggled to sit up and looked around to Pippa. "Are you all right?"

"I'm fine." Why were men so insensitive and stupid, Pippa wondered. It was an ageless question.

Wallace noticed Christina and his brow arched in surprise. "Christina! What are you doing here?"

Christina braced herself and stood up. "We, Damien and I, heard shouts. Damien, being a knight of great skill and repute, crept around behind to attack and I distracted them." She went to Damien's side and slipped her arm through his. "We work well together, wouldn't you say?"

Wallace stood up, staggered, then took Pippa's hand. "We do." He held up the sack of mistletoe. "And it appears I was right. Our sack is full. . . ."

Christina glared. "I'm surprised you found time to seek it out at all."

"I don't see your sack either, mistress!"

"We left it behind when we came to rescue you. It was twice as full as that." She stopped herself, probably realizing an empty sack would have been a better weapon. Uttering a ragged growl of frustration, Christina tightened her grip on Damien's arm and aimed for the path. She refused to look at Wallace, and held her head very high. "I suppose we must return you to the castle. Mother must have some herbal concoction to tend you. Damien, you will sit at our table for dinner."

"It was nothing—nothing that a skilled knight couldn't have done, anyway." The little demon hadn't even thanked him for rescuing her. "Had the matter well in hand," indeed! And comparing his defense of her to whatever minimal deeds Angus had performed . . . Infuriating!

Damien sat at the lord of the castle's table, though Lord Robert and his wife had retired early. Still, he had Christina's full attention. For once, she didn't even glance toward Wallace Davenport. She had told the noble guests of his "tragic past," which interested everyone at the table, especially the ladies.

Everyone except Pippa.

By his deeds in the forest, he had proven himself to Christina and her father, and their acceptance set him in fine stead with the other nobles. To his annoyance, both father and daughter had decided to keep the full details of the foiled attack from the other guests lest fear of banditry disrupt the celebrations. He suspected Christina's reason had more to do with Wallace Davenport's pride than their guests' uneasiness.

Why the girl cared about Wallace's pride, Damien couldn't guess. The foolish boy clearly preferred Pippa. Even now, the youth stood beside her as they milled among the musicians. Talking intimately. Probably about the unbridled passion they'd shared in the forest.

She'd spurned him, and turned to a boy incapable of defending himself. He was also likely incapable of proper kissing, let alone true lovemaking. Damien tried to pay attention to the conversation at the dinner table, but it wasn't easy.

Things were moving too fast. Damien knew that Christina was furious with Wallace, and she had turned to him to salvage her injured pride. Since Wallace had displayed his pathetic infatuation for Pippa, Christina had seemed to look more closely at Damien. Clearly, she liked what she saw.

Better still, thanks to her raised emotion, she had already imbibed too much wine and now appeared somewhat bleary-eyed. When he spoke, she looked at his mouth and licked her lips. He should have felt desire.

Instead, he had to fight to keep from checking on

Pippa's current whereabouts and proximity to Wallace.

Even more infuriating, Pippa showed no sign of noticing him at all, nor did she seem to care that he was in the company of a young and beautiful woman. One he should most certainly bed should the opportunity arise.

She didn't care. That was obvious. Christina was jealous. Wallace was jealous. Even *he* had felt a slight flare of the emotion. But not Pippa. To all appearances, she liked Christina. She had even been willing to attack three armed bandits to protect the girl. Ridiculous, but there was no questioning her intention in the wood.

She was a brave woman. He couldn't help admiring her. She'd looked so small, struggling to hold up Wallace's broadsword, her gown wrapped around her legs. He remembered her hair falling loose from its braid at such an inconvenient moment, her annoyance when it intruded on her attack, and her muttered curses as she shoved it aside. He smiled at the image.

"Maybe we should go to the stillroom again. You could use more . . . syrup." Christina slurred slightly, but Damien winced at the mention of the dreaded medicine.

He should have complimented Pippa on her courage, at least, should have told her that she had probably saved Wallace's life by distracting her opponents long enough for Damien to reach them. But he had been too annoyed at her for not praising him. His pride had come between them. If nothing else, he liked her. He wanted her friendship.

"Damien . . . You are listening to me, aren't you?"

"Of course. My throat is much recovered, thank you."

"Take me to the stillroom."

He didn't miss her intimation this time. He glanced

toward the musicians, but instead, saw Pippa leave the hall. Wallace waited a moment, then followed. A dark heat spread through Damien's chest, settling painfully in his abdomen. Their departure looked well-planned, like that of lovers who didn't want to be found out, but couldn't wait to be alone.

Damien stood abruptly, and Christina overturned her wine goblet in surprise. "To the stillroom," he said.

He seized her hand and led her down the corridor. She tripped once and giggled. He shoved open the stillroom door and guided her inside. Only one sconce was burning, filling the room with a low, seductive glow. Christina leaned against the heavy wooden table, waiting.

"I want you to kiss me."

He needed a woman. He needed to feel her soft breasts in his hands, her warm lips pressed against his. Christina appeared willing. She looked up at him, waiting for him to kiss her. She pursed her lips, indicating an inexperience that should have thrilled him.

Instead, he just felt tired. All he had to do was kiss this beautiful, young, willing girl, and he would be on the path back to regaining his knighthood. Curse the little Welsh minstrel for distracting him from his purpose.

As he gazed down into Christina's lovely eyes, he knew he was infatuated. With Pippa. *Infatuation doesn't last. It's nothing more than a state of mind, soon past.* It had always been true. Only foolish men thought otherwise and made choices based on a whim of the heart.

Very slowly, he bent and touched his mouth to Christina's. She hesitated, uncertain, then wrapped her arms around his neck and kissed him back. She wasn't new to kissing after all. She knew what she was doing. She seemed more . . . out of practice than un-skilled.

The kiss ended. His pulse hadn't quickened. He wasn't aroused. She watched him thoughtfully for a moment, then nodded. "You are better at kissing than Wallace."

For the first time in their encounter, he smiled. He hoped Wallace would kiss Pippa so she would learn the difference.

Christina reached up and fingered his hair. "And you are much handsomer than he is, too."

He suspected she was trying to convince herself that her feelings for Wallace were unimportant, by replac-ing Wallace with Damien. She was young—it wouldn't take much effort to convince her.

But not tonight. "Should your father find you here with me, my welcome is likely to be worn thin." He touched her cheek, fondly, like a brother. "Perhaps you should retire to your chambers, my lady."

"I should." She went to the door and looked back. "Do you think he will kiss her like that?" Her inno-cence touched his heart, but he couldn't help thinking that however poor a kisser Wallace was, he'd kiss Pippa with far more passion than Damien had kissed Christina.

"I'm certain he will not." *Because I won't leave them alone for one moment longer.*

"Well, then. Good night, Damien. My father has ar-ranged a hunting party planned for tomorrow. Per-haps you will ride with me?"

"It would be my pleasure."

Christina left and Damien seated himself on the edge of the table. He drew several long breaths, then rubbed his hands over his eyes. He had no right to stop Pippa, if she wanted a night of passion with Wal-lace Davenport. He had no right to want her. But he did.

Something banged behind him and he started. A cabinet door burst open and Pippa emerged, wide-eyed with fury. Damien fought shocked laughter. Only surprise delayed its outburst.

"Were you eavesdropping again, little flower? It seems to be a habit of yours."

She didn't answer. She looked too angry for speech. She stomped across the room and placed herself in front of him. She sputtered incoherently for a moment, then slammed her fist into his chest. Apparently, it wasn't enough, because she drew back and hit him again.

Neither blow hurt. In fact, if he hadn't seen the expression on her face, he might have mistaken it for a friendly pat.

She steadied herself, stepped back from him, closed her eyes, and took a shuddering breath. But when she opened her eyes again, the same wild fury burned inside. "You! I cannot believe you kissed her!"

He felt guilty. Curse the little demon for making him doubt something he had every right to do! "She asked that I should."

"I am surprised you didn't make love to her here!"

Damien's brow rose. "You, little Pippa, have a very sordid imagination."

A faint blush deepened in her cheeks. "I do not. It is simply my understanding of your nature. Which is foul in the extreme."

"If I was going to make love with a woman, here in the stillroom . . . it would not be the daughter of the castle's lord."

Damien stepped forward and caught Pippa's veil in his fingers, toying with it. "It would be, instead, a woman with the bad manners to spy on supposed lovers." He moved a little closer. She squirmed to free herself, but he didn't release her. "It would be a woman whose every glance sparks desire in me."

He took in the sight of her round, firm breasts beneath her white dress. Then he admired her full, upturned lips. Then her long, slender neck. "It would be a woman who desires me every bit as much as I want her."

A small gasp escaped her parted lips and her dark eyes burned, not with anger, but with lust. It was strange that one so fragile could contain such powerful desire.

"Your conceit is boundless. I do not want you in any way." Her voice trembled, it quavered with need.

He took her shoulders in his firm grip and held her fast. "You are jealous of a kiss. But a kiss can be for many things, Pippa. For affection, between family, friends. For a young and vulnerable woman who needs to know that she is desirable, even though her foolish lover prefers a woman far too mysterious and wild for his simple needs."

He bent closer to her, so that he felt her soft, sweet breath on his face. "Or a kiss can be for lust, to convey a desire so strong that a man can imagine only this . . ."

She caught her breath, then dampened her lower lip as if the thought of kissing drove her as wild as it drove him.

His mouth brushed over hers and she shuddered. "Because he knows that there is no fire so strong as that which burns inside you."

They pulled each other close at the same time. Pippa entwined her fingers in his hair as if he might escape at any moment. She kissed him feverishly.

She pulled away from him, her breath coming swiftly, her eyes glazed with passion and with fear. She was afraid of what she felt, of what she wanted to do. But if she left him now, he would spend another night fighting desire, tossing and turning as he imagined her in his embrace.

He couldn't let her go. "Will you leave now, so unsatisfied?"

She gulped. "You can give me no true satisfaction." She braced herself on a chair, but Damien smiled.

"A challenge? I think I can." He caught a long tendril of loose hair in his fingers, playing with it, teasing her cheek. "Such a fever burns in you, Pippa. Do you know how to tame it?"

She shook her head. "To stay far from you, I think."

"Yes, but you can't, can you?" She didn't answer, and his smile deepened. He peered around the room. "Here, among Lady Elisa's herbs, surely we can find some way to cure your affliction."

He slid his fingers to her neck, feeling the softness, and her head tipped back. Every nerve in her delicate body had come alive, every sense his for the taking. He eased her back into his arms and kissed the corner of her mouth. She tried not to kiss him back, but the more she fought inwardly, the more he knew he would eventually have her. She was like the fox who, struggling in a trap, only succeeds in making herself more securely captured.

He kissed her cheek, then brushed back her hair to tease her small earlobe, her neck. Her pulse raced beneath his touch. His fingers found the laces of her overgown. He worked quickly, and the fabric fell loose to her feet. She gasped and pulled back, but he caught her shoulders and turned her in his arms so that she faced away from him.

Even pressed against her back, he felt her racing heart. "What are you doing to me?" she asked.

"I am satisfying you, Pippa."

She shook her head. "You're not. You're teasing me." She sounded breathless.

"Umm." He pulled the binding from her hair, letting it fall freely down her back. He buried his face in its thick mass and kissed her neck. He ran his hands up along her sides and her breath caught on a sharp gasp. Through the fabric, he touched the swells of her breasts, then their tips. He ran his thumbs back and forth over each until they hardened into firm buds, until she leaned back against him, every breath a gasp.

His own arousal burned. He felt her against his hard flesh, and she pressed closer as if to increase the sweet torment. He wanted her warm body wrapped around him, so that he could bury himself inside her, but again she moved away.

She still fought—both herself and him. She backed away from him, shaking her head. She bumped against the wooden table, and he moved in front of her. "Do you ache for me, Pippa? I ache for you."

His words affected her like music. Her eyelids drifted shut and her lips parted. He caught her waist and lifted her onto the table. She didn't resist, but she held her body frozen as if in self-defense. He slid his hand up her thigh, stroking her skin, and then he knelt before her.

It seemed right, like the worship of a goddess, though he had never approached a woman on first conquest this way. He pushed her undergown up over her knees. She squirmed, but he cupped her bottom in his hands and looked up at her.

"You do ache."

She shook her head as if in denial, but Damien didn't give her time to question his actions. He breathed against her, and he felt her violent quivering. "You will ache more."

Her undergown had fallen around her waist and she stared at him aghast, shocked by what he intended. He spread her thighs gently and brushed the tips of his fingers over her soft, damp curls. A harsh breath caught in her throat, but she didn't try to stop him. He had expected her to be ready for him, but the feel, the gentle, womanly scent of her—these things drove him past any thought of restraint.

He ran his finger along her moist cleft and she quivered. He heard a ragged whimper, then a muted groan when he found the tiny, concealed bud. He teased it and her legs stiffened. When he bent and tasted its sweetness, she bit back a cry of stunned pleasure.

He drove her past madness; and he lost all thoughts of himself. He teased her until her every breath was a raspy moan, until her legs wrapped around his shoulders and her hips writhed from his skill. He worshipped her until her fingers gripped his hair and she leaned back—attaining a woman's mystic ecstasy.

It vibrated through her body with such power that he almost shared her release. Soft cries met his ears like the sweetest music. She gripped his hair, pulling him up, and he rose in one motion. His whole body trembled as he tore off his black tunic and leggings.

He freed his erection with shaking hands, and she maneuvered herself closer to the table's edge. She seemed to know what she wanted, like a woman who had been pleasured this way many times. He didn't care. If she was his now, that alone was enough.

He gripped her waist and positioned himself at her woman's entrance. Already, hot beads of moisture formed on his blunt tip. He held himself against her, sliding along her opening until her hips bucked with desire. She clasped his shoulders tight, her head tipped back as he pressed his mouth against her throat.

He drove himself deep inside her, but an unexpected barrier slowed his advance. She tensed, as if her virginity surprised her, too. Damien hesitated, then cupped her face in his hands. Their eyes met, fire on fire, and he saw her soul in her eyes.

Here, as his lover, she was no enigma. She was a woman of such desires, of such delight, that he had never known her like. She truly was the strongest woman in the world. He kissed her, slowly, then with deepening passion as their bodies moved together. He thrust inside her and she wrapped her legs around his waist.

All his desire splintered into shattering fragments, a release that in one overpowering jolt shook him to his core. He held himself inside her, feeling their raging pulses peak and then abate like waves on a shore.

The madness cleared, leaving him still deep inside her. Her legs hung limp at his sides; her hair fell loose over her shoulders and to the table, wild around her face. His hair fell forward, too. They looked at each other, shocked yet almost too sated to speak.

After a while, when their pulses stilled, he withdrew from her body. Without speaking, he dressed her again, then himself. He replaced the binding in her hair and her sheer veil. She trembled in the aftermath of pleasure, and again she seemed vulnerable.

When both were dressed, he stood looking down into her face. She hadn't spoken. He wondered if she was sorry, but he couldn't regret their passion. Passion was fleeting, as would be the feeling that throbbed in his heart. They had seized it at its pinnacle; there was nothing left that could best this night.

"How did you know?" His question came out low, stunned, and he was surprised at the emotion in his own voice.

"Know what?"

He touched her cheek. "You were a virgin. How did you know how to respond, to please me so well?"

An enigmatic smile crossed her lips, lips that moments ago he'd thought he knew completely. "Don't you know?"

"I have no idea."

She reached up and touched his face, too. "Damien . . . The same way you knew so well how to please me. I'd imagined it."

Chapter Four

Pippa lay on her bedding amongst her fellows. Angus had positioned himself nearby for protection. It was too late, but best he not know that. He snored, but fortunately in rhythm.

She couldn't sleep, though she tried lying on her side, then her stomach, then her back again. Nothing felt right or comfortable. She should be lying beside Damien, touching him, breathing in the soft male scent of him, fingering his hair and kissing his mouth.

Instead, he had settled himself on the far side of the hall. He had been strangely quiet after they made love in the stillroom. He'd been quiet when he led her back to the great hall, and quiet when they'd all retired for the night. He hadn't argued when Angus came between them and directed Damien away.

He had wanted her. And then, when it was over, he was kind, but withdrawn. She had no idea what he was thinking. She wanted to ask, wanted to know exactly what she meant to him. She rolled over and then propped herself up on her elbow, but she couldn't see him in the darkness. She lay on her back again. Maybe he would come to her and explain.

She'd felt dazed after their interlude. Her body had gone from a sweet inner peace to a sudden quickening of her heart, then back to stillness again. Her breathing had ranged from deep to short and shallow, so swift that she'd thought she might faint.

For the first time in her life, she was truly afraid. She couldn't stop what she felt for Damien. She couldn't let go. She wanted to think of him; she wanted him to fill her thoughts and her dreams. She wished she could go on this way, taking pleasure in his company, holding on to dreams of shining love.

But time would not stand still for her to lose herself in those dreams. There would be a culmination, and a time of choice. A yes or a no. And that answer depended on Damien's ability to surrender everything he held dear for her. It seemed they were on the same road, but heading in different directions.

Pippa sat up, and her hair fell around her face. *Why did I do it?* Not for a second could she put the responsibility on him. It was she who followed him, she who desired him. He had known what she wanted, and had done what any man would do. She hadn't fully expected the immense pleasure he'd given her, her imagination hadn't quite been able to foresee the intensity of their lovemaking, but she had known he would become part of her, and that she would never forget him.

Quietly, so as not to disturb Angus, Pippa rose from her bedding, gathered her cape around her, and crept across the room. She found Damien lying on his side, with only a faint shaft of moonlight touching his face. He slept soundly, apparently untroubled by the agonies of emotion that tormented her.

She felt foolish. She couldn't wake him without seeming desperate and silly, but neither could she sleep. Pippa backed away from Damien and slipped from the room. She walked aimlessly through the corridors, along the castle walls, and to the ramparts beyond. She stood alone gazing out over Menton Forest, though a cold wind blew from the north.

Pippa drew a long, shuddering breath and closed her eyes, feeling the wind against her face. For the first time in her life, she was truly powerless. Even if she told him the secret of her past, he could do nothing to change it. Only his heart could change her fate, and he was not a man governed by the heart.

"You are restless tonight."

Pippa jumped and spun around. Christina stood behind her, a heavy woolen cloak pinned at her throat. She came to stand beside Pippa, and for a long while she didn't speak. Finally, she bowed her head and faced Pippa, her young face resolute.

"He loves you."

Pippa had no idea how to respond. She felt fairly certain that Christina cared more for Wallace than for Damien, but she had no way of being sure. "I cannot see into a man's heart, Christina."

Christina turned to gaze out over the forest. "He does. And no wonder. You are all the things I am not." It was odd that she should phrase it in such a way, considering Pippa had thought the same of her. "You are lovely and feminine and delicate. You have about you an air of romance and mystery. There is nothing mysterious about me."

Pippa smiled. "There is one thing. The man about whom you speak."

"Wallace." She said the boy's name with longing, then bowed her head again. "He confessed to me tonight that you are important to him."

"He did?" What was the boy thinking? "About what were you speaking before he 'confessed'?"

"I told him that the minstrel in black had kissed me,

68

and that my father considers him a tolerable match for me. If Damien marries me, you know, he will regain his knighthood."

"Yes, I know. But why did you tell Wallace that, if you care for him?"

"To incite his jealousy, of course. But I failed. In fact, he seemed most relieved."

"I doubt that. . . ."

Christina held up her hand and shook her head. "Say nothing. I cannot blame you, but neither can I speak more of it. I simply wanted you to know that I will not stand in your way. Wallace is yours." She paused, her jaw firming as she gazed out at the night. "I have decided tonight that I will marry the minstrel."

December 27

Fate had trapped him in a hellish quandary. Damien rode with Lord Robert's hunting party with Christina at his side, and all he thought about was Pippa. She gave love like a beneficent goddess, with her body and soul and heart given fully.

He hadn't spoken to her that morning, because he had risen early, called by Lord Robert to join the party. He should have been thrilled by the brisk morning, the thrill of the chase, but instead, he had lost track of what beast they were hunting, and now paid no attention as they rode back to the castle.

Fortunately, Christina was proving herself an undemanding companion. She rode silently beside him, lost in her own thoughts. Gloom surrounded her like a small, dark cloud. Damien felt the same.

They rode back through the gates, silent, while onlookers cheered. Damien dismounted, assisted Christina, and their eyes met. "You and I have no choice but to marry." She spoke as if announcing the inevitability of eventual death.

Damien gulped. Marrying a noblewoman was his intention after all, so her suggestion shouldn't have troubled him, but he endured a rush of panic. "The thought of marriage shouldn't be taken lightly, my lady."

She sighed, miserably, and shook her head. A page took their horses, and they walked into the castle courtyard together. "I do not take the notion of marriage lightly, Damien. I have long imagined that it is a wedding of like minds, who might profit their country and people by their joining."

"A lofty aim," he said. Christina was young, and with the serious, staid Wallace, she might have done some good. Damien wondered what *he* wanted. Regaining his title and his pride had been all that mattered to him for so long. Before that, he'd spent his youth earning the respect his father had never earned. Working to be free of his ignominious birth, to inspire awe, not pity, when he walked in a room. Yet he had gained those things, and had still been restless.

He wondered what Pippa wanted. She had her freedom. She didn't seem to care if she inspired awe. But then, whenever she sang, she inspired something much more. That was what she wanted, to enter a room, invisible, and find the ache in people's hearts with her magical voice.

But she wanted something more, too, and Damien wasn't sure what it was. He'd felt it when he'd made love to her. She wanted something for herself, to be fulfilled. To be loved, in her body and her soul. Then why had she waited for *him*, a man to whom love was a night of passion and a soft memory, nothing more?

"Marriage and love have nothing to do with each other." He caught himself, but too late. Christina stopped to stare at him, but she didn't seem offended.

"No. You're right," she said. "Marriage should be undertaken to benefit both persons involved, not because of any one heart's desire. I said the same thing to Wallace this morning. I didn't mean it at the time, but now I see you are right."

"Why did you say that to him?" While he thought any other view of marriage was foolhardy, he hadn't expected to have this young noblewoman share his view.

Christina averted her eyes as if embarrassed. "I said that he should not marry a lowborn girl because it wouldn't profit his situation." Christina's voice cracked as if emotion besieged her. "He became very angry."

"On the subject of marriage?" Damien's suspicions mounted. What "lowborn girl" interested Wallace Davenport, anyway?

"On the subject of Pippa, to be precise."

As if there had been any doubt! "Pippa?"

Christina bowed her head. "I criticized her to him. It was wrong of me, for in truth, I can find in Pippa nothing to dislike. But in my fury, I suggested to Wallace that his father would never allow him to marry a peasant wench, no matter how beautifully she sings."

"That is perhaps true." *It had better be.* Wallace was too fragile and weak a man to defy such conventions.

Christina sighed and shook her head. "It *is* true, but it appears Pippa is no lowborn wench."

Damien shifted his weight. "No?"

"She is the daughter of a Cornish nobleman. Even as a foreigner, you must have heard of him. He is known as Philip the Slayer."

Damien stared, his mouth agape. "Philip the Slayer's *daughter?* That cannot be." Philip was one of King Henry's most formidable knights, a man well skilled in warfare, whose battle strategies were legendary in their brilliance.

"It is true. She admitted her identity to Wallace yesterday in the forest. She was known as Lady Philippa, and apparently, she was much admired for both her loveliness and the beauty of her voice."

Lady Philippa. A strong, powerful name for such an ethereal woman. Pippa suited her better. Much admired? He didn't like the thought of Pippa being courted by many men. "Why? And how has such a woman, a noblewoman, come to sing in a troupe of ragged Welsh harpers?"

"I do not know the full story. I would guess that her father chose from among her suitors a husband, and she refused him." Christina paused, nodding. "I would do the same, but fortunately, my father cares more for my happiness than advancing his power through my marriage."

"It is possible. Though fragile in body, Pippa is a strong-willed woman." Too strong. No, she would never marry a man she didn't love. Was that the true explanation? "But why wouldn't Philip send men after his daughter, to bring her back by force, if necessary?" It seemed a logical solution—one he would use himself.

"That, I don't know. I expect she is in hiding."

"How did Wallace learn her identity?" If she had told Wallace, and not Damien, he would have much to say at their next meeting.

"He guessed. Apparently, he knows her brother. She swore Wallace to secrecy, but the story came out when I slighted her."

If true . . . God rewards patience after all! Damien took Christina's hand in his and pressed it firmly. "Wallace will never marry Pippa." He didn't bother to explain why. "You needn't fear for that outcome, my lady. I will see that all that has been made wrong by dark fate shall be made right again!"

He left Christina standing bewildered, and headed for the inner courtyard. Pippa wasn't there. He tried the banquet hall, though it was too soon for the evening meal. He saw her standing amidst the troupe of performers, listening as Angus played a tune on his flute. His efforts still sounded more martial than festive.

I should have known. Everything about her bespoke a privileged upbringing. Her intelligence and poise, her quiet knowledge. She was a lady in the guise of a minstrel, just as he was a knight beneath his motley garb.

He started toward her, then stopped. Why hadn't she told him? She knew of his dilemma. A vague anxiety crept into his heart. Even when she'd given him her body, she hadn't told him the truth about herself. Of course, he hadn't actually asked her, but it seemed a rather large detail to have overlooked.

Maybe she was waiting for the perfect opportunity to reveal her secret and end his misery! How perfect, how rare! He could feign innocence. He would react with great surprise when she told him—if he had the patience to wait. Time was of the essence, and he wasn't a patient man.

He would surprise her! Warmth spread through his chest. They were perfect for each other. She was the daughter of a man to whom he would be proud to serve fealty, a renowned warrior. He would restore her to her alienated father and win great respect by returning the prodigal daughter.

They would laugh about how he found her.

Perfect.

Angus's tune caught on, and the other musicians joined in. Pippa swayed to the music. Her long, curly hair was coiled down her back, as always, escaping its bindings. And as always, she didn't notice. Her eyes closed as the music surrounded her. A soft smile formed on her lips.

As Damien stepped forward, she began to sing. Her voice had altered since they'd shared that night. He recognized the change, and he understood it. Her melody contained a new dimension, more sensual and earthy, as if she sang of tangible delights rather than mystic imaginings. No dream, only reality inspired her now. Damien felt proud because he knew he was the reason.

There was no other woman like her in the world. He felt her happiness. Happiness that didn't require nobility.

His disquiet grew, but he shoved it aside, and waited for her song to end. It didn't. It went on and on, and she danced as she sang. As before, he didn't understand her words, but they had the power to enter his heart.

This time, her song didn't make him ache with longing or loss. He felt a strange, unfamiliar call: freedom. The sweet, forbidden joy of living life just as one is, bound to no convention but one's own heart.

Damien's breath grew tight in his chest, his hands felt cold. She tempted him with something worse than beauty and sweetness. It was truly the song of the damned.

"Didn't you like my song?" Pippa tapped Damien on the shoulder, but he didn't respond. He stood beneath an archway decorated with mistletoe and evergreen boughs, his head bowed, his shoulders slumped. She waited a moment, then tapped him again.

Maybe he expected her to kiss him. Oh, how she wanted to! "Damien?"

He turned slowly, looking at the floor. "Why didn't you tell me?"

"Tell you what?"

He lifted his gaze and looked at her. His green eyes had gone cold, pale with a distant light. "Tell me who you are."

She hesitated, then groaned. "Wallace." She made a

fist and punched the air. "He swore secrecy. Oh, I should never have trusted someone so young and ridiculous!"

"For what reason would you hide your identity from me?" Damien's voice grew colder still. Not with the excited passion he usually displayed, but something new and frightening. This was a man who could turn from her and never, ever look back, no matter how much he loved her. Because his pride would always be everything to him.

She tried to meet his gaze and lasted only a moment. "Because . . . because who my father is doesn't matter."

"Doesn't it? I know of your father. The name of Philip the Slayer is spoken even in Aquitaine, my dear."

"With fear and awe, I expect." Pippa saw her father in her mind—his bright face, his impenetrable dark eyes. "I spoke his name the same way when I was young."

"You must resemble your mother."

"No . . ." Pippa sighed, and an old weariness returned to surround her. "I am not much like my mother, though it was she who taught me to sing and to speak the Welsh tongue. But she was a tall woman, with black hair and green eyes, like you. I took after my father, I'm afraid."

Damien's brow angled. "That is hard to imagine."

"But it's true. He is strong-willed, small, with light hair and dark eyes."

"I pictured someone . . . larger."

"He is most imposing when mounted on his favorite steed—an immense black horse that no one else can handle."

"I have noticed that small men often choose too-large horses." Damien paused, then shook his head. "Why did you leave such a grand home, Pippa?"

She averted her gaze from his. "That, I cannot say."

"You *will* not say, more accurately." He paused, frustrated. "Were you in danger?"

"No."

"Christina suggested that you might have been forced to marry against your will, and fled for that reason."

Her lips twisted. "The subject of my potential marriage is part of the reason I am here."

"Must you always be so evasive?" He studied her in silence for a moment, frowning. "Christina says you were much desired, and courted by many."

Pippa looked at her feet. They looked small, and she pointed one toe. "That is true."

"I can understand why a woman such as yourself, who is romantic and delicate and tender, would not want to be burdened by an uncaring or cruel mate."

She winced at his words, but she didn't look up or answer.

"But Pippa, I am not those things." He stopped and shifted his weight from foot to foot uneasily. "Well, perhaps I could not be called 'romantic,' but I can be tender, should the situation call for . . . I am *not* uncaring or cruel." He paused again and cleared his throat. "Although I was considered ruthless in battle. . . ." His voice trailed and he cleared his throat again, but Pippa looked up at him and smiled.

She reached to press her palm against his face. "Damien, I understand."

He eyed her doubtfully. "Do you?"

"I do, because I am the same." He scoffed at this, but she stroked his cheek, then let her hand fall back to her side. "You are both strong and passionate, but you are strong first. You are capable of great love, but your heart is not easily reached."

His head tilted to one side as he studied her face. "Often, now, you have called yourself strong. Yet you seem the most delicate flower, unprotected from storms, vulnerable."

"No storm touches me. Except one. You."

He liked the comparison and smiled slightly. "And it is a storm you weathered well, is it not? Even delighted in. It may be that you wish to revel thus again." He moved closer to her, and she sensed the heat of his body, the controlled power inside him. "I have been given my own chambers here at Menton Castle." His bright eyes twinkled, leaving no doubt as to his intentions. "A bed, my dear, is softer by far than a table."

Her pulse quickened, her cheeks warmed. A bed would be pleasant. They could sleep in each other's arms and she would breathe his warm, masculine scent to her heart's content. She would see him sleepy-eyed and yawning in the morning. "I do not think the lord of this castle has favored you with guest chambers so that you can seduce me," she said.

Damien dismissed her comment with a wave of his hand. "He thinks I am an apt suitor for his daughter. Lord Robert would grant Christina any wish."

"He would not approve of this method of courtship."

Damien shrugged. "If Christina were truly besotted with me, I might think to feel guilt at my desire for you. But it is Wallace who occupies her thoughts. She spoke of him constantly when we were gathering mistletoe, and again today on the hunt."

"Did she?" Pippa enjoyed a warm swell of both relief and happiness. "He cares for her also."

Damien appeared skeptical. "Yet he pines obviously and loudly for you." His eyes darkened as he surveyed her body, and his attention lingered on her mouth. "Not without reason, for you do much to inspire a man's imagination."

"I don't think Wallace is possessed of a remarkable imagination. But you . . ." Her doubts faded as she found herself also staring at his lips. "You are gifted with so much. . . ." She caught herself and fiddled nervously with the tie at her throat. Damien smiled and the desire in his eyes triggered a fierce tingling in her loins.

"Let Wallace and Christina find their own path. Our lives have been made so much simpler now, Pippa. To think, I came here to find a woman who could end my curse, and found her in you, the least likely person imaginable!"

"What do you mean?" He looked too smug. "What do you want from me?"

"Isn't it obvious? You and I will marry, and I will return you to your father. I understand he's a favorite of King Henry's. Thus, the task placed upon me by Eleanor will be fulfilled, and you no longer have to wander the lonely hills and dales of England."

The longing that surged through her body almost crumpled her. If only it could be so simple! To give him everything he wanted and to have him with her always.

Pippa stared into Damien's beautiful face, loving him. Knowing him, and knowing that this moment between them had been preordained by fate.

"I cannot give you what you ask."

He grasped her shoulders, excited, unwilling to allow her inner demons to stop them. "Don't you see? All the powers of Heaven have brought us to this moment. . . ."

"I believe that is true."

"As vindication!"

"You were set to marry Christina before you learned of my heritage."

"I wasn't 'set.' It was a possibility. But this is so much better."

"Why?"

He hesitated. "Your father is more renowned in battle than Lord Robert. He is a stronger liege lord."

Pippa laughed, though she felt as though she had lost herself in a dark dream. "Not that my eyes hold you spellbound? Or that you prefer the texture of my hair to hers?"

"Of course I prefer you! We are well matched." His beautiful mouth curved into a smile. "We proved that in Lord Robert's stillroom, did we not?"

"We proved that desire is stronger than good sense." He started to speak, but she didn't let him. She touched his mouth. "Damien, do you love me? Do I matter more to you than anything?"

He looked guarded, as if he realized a wrong answer might cost him his prize. "I am smitten with you." He paused. "More smitten than I have been with any other woman." Again, his gaze raked along her body, setting fire to her nerves with memory. "You have distracted me in such a way that I find both uncomfortable and . . . impossible to ignore. I find you beautiful. I covet the touch of your body, and the smell of your skin, which is sweet and soft and feminine."

"You love me."

"I am strongly infatuated."

"And stubborn."

He bowed his head, but he was smiling. "It may be that I love you."

"More than anything?"

"A very great deal, indeed."

She had foreseen this moment when she met him. She had known it would come and could do nothing to stop it from ripping her heart asunder. "Enough to turn aside your quest, and take my love—without my father's involvement?"

His eyes snapped open, his smile disappearing. "Why should I do that?"

"Because I ask it."

He puffed an impatient breath. "And what would

you have me do? Wander dreary England at your side, singing to peasants for my dinner?"

"If it pleases me."

His sweetness turned to anger, and she saw the arrogant knight he was and always would be. "And if it pleases *me*, lady? You ask all for my love, and yet will not grant what is easily within your power to give?"

"I cannot give what you ask."

He gripped her arm. "You call me stubborn, yet no one has ever earned that title more than yourself!"

She looked up and met his flashing eyes. "You don't understand. *I cannot give you what you want.*"

Damien placed his hands on her shoulders. "Pippa, finding you . . . You are my treasure."

Tears welled in her eyes. "I am, but not in the way you think. What I can give you . . ." She paused. Was it much to offer? Would it be enough for any man, let alone a man like Damien?

She met his gaze, unwavering, sure of what she was and what she could give. "I can imagine every pleasure, such that you have never dreamed nor will ever find with another woman. I can touch you in a way no other ever has. I can tell you stories and sing to you, and make every night of your life magic." As she spoke, her voice grew in depth and in passion. "But you don't want magic. You want this . . ." She motioned to the castle around them. "You want to win. It's as if life is a game to you."

"It is a game. And I do love to win. But sometimes the object of one's quest is more important than the glory that accompanies it—"

"I know that." Pippa broke in. *"Do you?"* She touched his face again, feeling how strong he was, knowing she would never forget that. "Damien . . ."

He placed his hand over hers and held it tight.

"Pippa, if you knew all along what I wanted, and that you would refuse me, then why . . . ?"

"Don't you know?"

He shook his head, and he looked so young that she thought her heart would break. "You are my treasure, too, Damien. You touch me in a way no one ever has. When you sing, I see the stories in your head, I feel your passion. And I know, if you were not so blind, that you could make every night of my life magic."

She closed her eyes and slipped her hand from his. "And I know, because I understand you, that you never will."

She backed away from him. He stepped toward her, but she shook her head. "No, Damien. Marry Christina, for knighthood is what you truly want. I love you. I love you with all my heart and all my soul. But I can never . . . I will never give you what you need."

He pointed his finger at her, his face dark with anger. "You say you love me, mistress, but your words prove themselves false. You ask that I follow you—for what? To please your pride, I think. What I ask is fair and just. I am a man. A man, *Philippa*, who has much to do in this world. I will not be a puppet to your . . . peculiar whimsy!"

He stared at her a moment longer, as if willing her to concede, to change her mind. She stared back at him, the mist of her tears shrouding his face. Her voice came only as a tiny whisper. "I cannot."

He backed away as if she'd slapped him, stood a moment frozen, then turned to leave. She couldn't stop herself, and she stepped after him. "Where are you going?"

He looked back over his shoulder. Those eyes could turn so cold—she could imagine him in battle. She'd known that he could be ruthless, that he was armored with an icy pride, but in her heart, she had never believed that ruthlessness could be turned on her. He held her gaze for a moment, and this time, his will itself seemed a weapon.

"I am going to the guest chambers of Lord Robert." His lips curled upward at one corner as if he had issued a brutal challenge. And maybe he had. "Alone."

Chapter Five

December 31

"Lady Philippa . . . Will you do me the great honor of becoming my wife?"

On bended knee before her, Wallace reached for Pippa's hand and squeezed it tightly. She was sitting on the same bench where she'd first hidden from Damien, but now Wallace was at her feet. His luminous eyes watered with unshed tears.

What strange tide flows over us all, here during Yule! Have we all gone mad? Are we so far separated from who we truly are?

Four days had passed since her quarrel with Damien, since she'd denied him and he'd denied her. She had kept herself from going to his room, but it hadn't been easy. Each day, the need grew in her. Each night, she tossed in her bedding, dreaming of him. Always, in her dreams, he loved her more than anything else.

Always, he held her close in his arms, and she felt truly safe.

Apparently, Christina and Wallace had reached a similar impasse in their relationship. Christina had used Damien to make Wallace jealous, which had failed miserably, because he in turn doted on Pippa.

Everyone in the castle seemed sad, at odds with their hearts. Lady Elisa had requested that Pippa refrain from her more "emotive" ballads, and stick to placid Yuletide refrains. Pippa suspected that the emotion in her own songs touched too close to Lady Elisa's own heart.

Pippa stared down at the young nobleman at her feet and sighed heavily. "Get up, Wallace." Pippa waited until he obeyed, then motioned for him to sit beside her on the wooden bench. He did so, shoulders slumped, face downcast. She patted his shoulder.

"You don't love me. You love Christina."

"Hush!" He looked around to be certain they hadn't been overheard, then exhaled in relief when he saw they were alone. He resumed his serious expression and seized her hand again. "I will give up all my worldly goods for you, Pippa."

"Yes, but you wouldn't be doing it for my sake, Wallace. You would be doing it because you are grieving over Christina."

Wallace frowned and released her hand. "Christina has chosen the minstrel."

"You truly love Christina, and you both want the same life. You can be truly happy together."

"Not if her heart has turned toward the minstrel."

"It is possible that her heart has turned." Pippa chewed the inside of her lip. "If any man could change a woman's heart, it's Damien."

Wallace's shoulders slumped in defeat. "I have heard women speaking of him. Last night, two serving maids spoke of his warm heart, his gracious nature, his kindness."

Pippa's brow angled. "Strange how women conceal the truth of a man's attraction beneath favorable personality traits. What they mean is that they like the way his hair falls around his broad shoulders, the firmness of his backside, and the twinkle in his eyes which speaks of a vast knowledge of a woman's pleasure."

Wallace stared at her, aghast. Pippa shrugged. "It is true. When a woman finds a man desirable, she sees only goodness in him, and ignores that which will betray her heart."

"No one mentioned his singing voice favorably."

Pippa smiled. "And no one ever will."

Wallace shook his head. "No woman is that addled." He looked at Pippa for a moment, then touched her cheek. "Except one."

Pippa leaned back against the stone wall and drew a long breath. "Except one."

She opened seven doors, and found seven sleeping guests. The seventh, an old earl, startled, jumped up in bed shouting.

She hopped back, scrambled from his room, and darted down the hallway to the last door. She hid in an alcove just in time to avoid the irate earl, held her breath, and waited for him to close his door again. She heard a bar thump down, and repressed a smile. Perhaps her shadow was more terrifying than she'd realized.

She stood outside the eighth door, forcing her breath to come even and deep, gathering her wits. This had to be Damien's room. She placed her hand on the door and imagined him beyond, lying in bed, annoyed, frowning into the darkness. Her mind followed this path, and she imagined him not angry, but hurt. Silent tears flowing from the corners of his beautiful eyes, into his tangled hair, as he imagined that her love was untrue.

Pippa gulped and pushed open the door. She stepped inside and closed it without sound. She paused, and heard nothing. Nothing but a man's even, deep breathing. Perhaps she had, again, entered the wrong man's room.

A low fire burned in the grate, casting enough light so that she could maneuver without disrupting anything.

She crept to the side of his bed. It wasn't the grandest chamber in the castle, but the bed was high, the coverlet thick. Damien lay on his side, his black hair streaming across the bedding, looking well combed, his eyes closed, his mouth slightly parted as he *slept*.

He was asleep. She fought an urge to strike him, to wake him with a solid slap to his perfect cheek. *How dare he sleep!* How long had she lain awake, tossing and turning, unable to close her eyes, as she agonized over their thwarted love? How much pain had she endured in the pit of her stomach as she fought against going to him, as pride battled with desire and love?

A slight, soft snore emanated from his parted lips. He smacked his lips in his sleep, then rolled onto his back. His head turned to one side and his lips moved. He muttered something in another language. He seemed pleased. Sensual. He murmured softly, and she heard, unmistakably, her name.

Pippa's mood altered immediately. He was dreaming of her. Her heart's pace sped up. She discerned the powerful shape of his body beneath the coverlet. It was pushed back to reveal his broad chest, as if he'd been too warm despite the chill air.

Her fingers tingled. She wanted to touch his chest,

to feel the soft hair, to place her head against his skin and hear his heart.

Her gaze wandered lower, to a firm, distinct bulge beneath the cover. The tingle spread through her body and centered with firm insistence in the spot he had so vividly made known to her. Such a beautiful, powerful representation of maleness, of male desire and need. How sweet that a woman could simply look at this part of him and understand her own power!

Pippa felt giddy. If she woke him, he would remember their fight and they would argue more before he gave in. That is, if she woke him with words.

In the stillroom, he had seduced her with his mouth and with his tongue. He had found the most intimate spot of her and lavished it with the most tender, most erotic attention imaginable. She knew the most intimate part of him—he would be vulnerable to her touch there.

She held her breath and eased the cover from his hip, then even more painstakingly over his male length. Curious, how that part of him could seem both strong and vulnerable, how it could be both tender and demanding. Like him.

She knelt beside the bed and found herself reaching for his erect flesh. Her fingers touched his skin, and he was warm. Hard and smooth and warm. He didn't wake, his breaths still came even and deep. Her fingers closed around his shaft, without pressure, but she felt his pulse through the taut skin.

Her own pulse sped like spreading fire. She felt dizzy. What if he woke and cried out? She started to move her fingers away, but he must have sensed her touch because he moaned, a far-away sound, from deep in his dreams.

It was a moan of pleasure and encouragement. She needed little. She wrapped her fingers tighter around the thick shaft, squeezing slightly, and he tensed. Still, he didn't wake. She moved her hand up and down, mimicking the motion of lovemaking. He moaned again.

Such power! She had never known nor imagined the like of it. He was the strongest, most passionate man she knew, yet with a touch, even in sleep, she affected him. With a touch . . . or a kiss. She leaned forward and her hair slipped from its veil. So softly that she felt sure he wouldn't feel her lips, she kissed the blunt tip of him.

He moaned, and his body jerked. *He's awake.* She held herself still, her lips still touching his skin, her breath puffing softly against it. His hand clenched at his side. She heard him swallow, and his breathing turned harsh and swift.

In the silence of his chamber, her mad pulse throbbed in her ears. Her tongue swept out before she considered the act, and grazed across the hard tip. He shuddered, and she tasted him again.

His whole body tensed. Pippa rose and positioned herself higher, then took his length into her mouth. He gasped and groaned and clasped his hands in her hair. She heard her name whispered with passionate yet desperate urging.

She licked him and teased him and made love to him with an abandon that swept her beyond anything she had ever known or imagined. His muscles clenched, his hips rocked, his back arched, yet she would not relent. She loved the taste of him, the heat of his skin, the sound of his ragged breath. She loved her power, because it came from within.

His body writhed as if uncontrollable surges swept him ever closer to a place she now knew well—because he had taken her there. She increased the vigor of her attention, she felt the first pulses of him, but he curled upright, seized her shoulders, and pulled her on top of him.

She looked down into his eyes, and she saw fire there. His hands trembled as he positioned her body above his, as he parted her thighs so that she straddled him. His male length moved against her feminine core, sending shocks of pleasure through her, down her legs to her toes. She was damp, ready for him. The need for him raged within her.

"What . . . what do I do?"

He smiled and guided her hips up and over him. "Don't you know?" He reached out to touch the side of her face, his palm warm against her skin. "Use your imagination. That is what you do best, isn't it?"

"It is." Confidence swelled within her. She could do anything, because she was with him and he understood her. She braced on his chest, then lowered herself slowly, taking him inside her. The sweet pressure within, filling her, made her dizzy with need. Her fingers clenched, her toes curled, and she sank down until he filled her completely.

They looked at each other, both of them still, then each moved at the same time. His hips rose into hers, he thrust upward, and she moved to greet him. They moved together and apart. A wild tension coiled inside her, spiraling tighter and tighter.

She crumpled forward against his chest and he wrapped his arms tight around her. He rolled her onto her back—never slipping from her body—and he kissed her. His tongue played against hers, softly mimicking their bodies as he thrust into her.

He drew back to look down at her as he moved. His lips curved in an ageless smile of male power and joy as he began a deeper penetration. It was slower, but harder, sending her into an overload of pleasure. He watched her and she moaned his name as she trembled with the onslaught of ecstasy.

His eyes closed and his head tipped back, his body moving with abandon as passionate surges took control of him. She had never seen a thing so beautiful, so overwhelming. Her own body responded and the wild currents burst inside her, shattering like fragments of light in an impossible storm.

Their pulses crested and eased, and he sank down into her arms, his hair falling forward around her face. She held him close and she kissed his jaw, then his mouth as he turned to her. He kissed her with the same quiet satisfaction she felt. They were so much the same. She had known it from the beginning—they were part of each other. What he was, she had been, and all that she could ever be, she saw it all in him.

He pressed his cheek against hers, then kissed her temple. He brushed her hair from her face and kissed her cheek. "You are the sweetest lover," he said.

"And you."

He moved from her body and gathered her into his arms. She rested her cheek against his muscular arm. "We belong together, Pippa."

"I know."

He turned to look at her, but she couldn't meet his eyes. "I can't explain, Damien. Please, don't ask me. Not tonight. Tonight, I want to be with you—as close as I can get."

He hesitated. She knew he struggled with a desire to use their time of intimacy to convince and to understand her. "You give all of yourself here. You hold nothing from me. And yet . . ."

She squirmed in his arms to look down into his face. "I give you all of myself. My *self*, Damien. That is what truly matters in a person. Not the circumstances of their lives, the good fortune they've had, or the bad. I am a gift to you." She sighed, and her heart filled with both love and sorrow, because she knew this wonderful night would not be repeated. "I am a gift, but not the gift you want."

* * *

Two Turtledoves

He'd known she would sing, and he'd known that the sound of her voice would break his heart, but nothing could have prepared him for the pain. Damien sat at the banquet table beside Christina, but he couldn't tear his gaze from Pippa. She twirled and danced among the musicians, adding her deep, throaty voice to theirs. She looked so happy and so free.

Her hair hung unbound, flowing behind her when she spun. Her veil formed a gossamer train behind her, mingling with her golden locks. No, she would never go back to the life she had known, with her father. He knew that now. Almost, he understood.

For whatever the reason she had left her father's household, she had found peace and happiness here. To escape an unwanted husband, to live a life that more suited her nature—whatever the reason, she would never leave it now.

She loved him, but she would never give up this freedom she had found.

Damien watched her as her voice took command of the hall. The others lent their instruments and voices to hers.

Her little body swayed and bent as she sang. Her words touched his heart, as if the Welsh language was understood at some level deeper than his mind's capacity. As she sang, he heard pieces of himself in her music, defiant and powerful. He saw himself as he could be, stronger than he was now, unbound by the desires that relentlessly drove him, using his strength where it was needed, and not simply for his own gain.

And as she sang, he knew he was losing her, and all that might be was fading away. It had been within his grasp, and it was slipping away, vanishing to memory, to be cherished, but never touched again.

No. He would follow her. He would hold her and

stay at her side until she saw reason. But as she sang, she met his eyes across the hall, and he knew it would never be. He could follow, but he would not sway her.

She had been a gift to his life, she cast a mystical light upon him and showed him what he truly was. *What a man is, he then becomes,* she'd said. What would he be without her? What could he become that mattered now?

She had slept in his arms, then risen before dawn to leave him. She had said nothing, but she'd kissed his cheek and he'd hugged her. They'd parted without words. Surely, there were words he could say now to change her mind, to keep her.

Beside him at the table, Christina sat silently, but tears flowed down her cheeks. He knew without asking that she cried over Wallace, and what she believed to be thwarted love and dark fate. At the far end Wallace sat listening to Pippa, but it was Christina he watched. An unspoken sadness was written across his young face.

The boy was so young! Had he himself ever been that young, to believe fate controlled all matters close to his heart? Had he ever believed otherwise?

Pippa's song reached a crescendo, until everyone in the hall seemed to fade into nothing, and only she remained. Agony and ecstasy flashed from her into him, from a pain and anguish of the heart that could send a man to his knees, until he doubled over with grief, to a bliss that gave wings to a soul and kept it in flight for all time to come.

Such was love. Damien closed his eyes, and he knew he believed after all. Love was ruthless and cruel—it swept in like an army of soldiers, it slaughtered all in its path, and it left its victims forever vanquished, forever at its mercy. It was the mightiest warrior.

Her song faded, and its wake was silence, broken only by the slow thudding of his heart. She had poured all herself, all her emotion, and all her heart into this song, and he knew it was the last he would hear.

Lord Robert's guests turned quietly back to their meals. The others took up another song, lighter, as if to herald a victor's weary departure.

He knew she was leaving before she told him. He left the table and went to her, and she met him in the center of the hall. He wanted to stop her, and he didn't know how.

"I am leaving Menton Castle tonight."

He shook his head. "There is a storm brewing. Already it snows."

"I am leaving. I cannot stay."

He dampened his lips, fighting to think of something, but he knew he had already lost. "You can't leave. It is only the eighth day of Yule. There is much celebration yet, and your troupe is still needed."

"Only I will leave."

Tears welled in his eyes. He had not cried in years, not since he was a boy and his heart still held sway over his actions. "You will be missed."

"I know." She didn't cry. She just stared up at him as if committing every feature of his face to memory. In her eyes, he saw hope, though he felt only despair. "We are alike, you and I. That is why I know you, Damien. I have from the first. Don't you understand yet? I realized from the beginning this moment would come."

"You knew last night."

"Yes."

There was so much more to say between them. So much to feel and to do. "You can't leave tonight, Pippa. Not in a storm, not this way."

Christina called to him, and he exhaled an impatient breath. "You will not leave tonight. Come to me in my chambers."

"Will you give up everything you want for me?"

Stubborn woman! That she should ask him, here, when his heart ached in his chest. She wanted control of him, nothing more. The ring he bore felt cold against his chest. "You ask not for love's sake, mistress, but for something else, I think."

"Yes." She admitted it! Her response stunned him. She touched his arm and he felt that her hand was shaking. "Of course. Do you think there is anything I would deny you if I had a choice?"

"Your pride makes it so." His body ran cold with anger. She could pierce his heart, she could own him, but apparently something mattered more—something he couldn't guess, nor bear to know. "So be it."

"You think with your passions and not your heart."

"Is that so?" He couldn't restrain a sneer, or the coldness in his voice.

"Your heart must lead if you are ever to truly be happy. Isn't that what this festival tells us? The heart knows what the mind cannot."

"A fine sentiment, and one you can use in your next ballad, lady. If you followed your own heart, our fate together could be much altered this day."

"Once, that was true. . . ." She closed her eyes and her voice trailed off. "And for that, I will pay. But you—you are so perfect for me. I suppose it had to be this way." She bowed her head as if gathering strength, then looked at him again. "Will you leave it all for me?" She whispered the question as if forcing it to be spoken once more.

It came like a sword through his heart, and it turned him to ice. He met her mystical eyes; he saw her lips quiver, and her wild hair around her sweet face. She looked tiny and impenetrable, vulnerable and yet so strong that he would never break through. He stood straighter, a warrior who would never back down, no matter how powerful his foe. "No."

*   *   *

The snow fell harder than she had expected. Already, it had accumulated enough to be up and over her boots, hiding her feet in eerie white. She pulled her felt cape tighter around her body and hugged her small harp close to her heart.

She had spent a year and forty days already, facing a fate she'd never dreamed possible. A fate she had come to love. She had slipped from the castle at midnight, knowing that Damien waited for her in his chambers. No one knew that she had gone. She had waited until Angus slept, then left silently.

Pippa stopped and shivered in the cold. She was lying to herself, and it wasn't like her. Damien knew she was leaving. As soon as midnight came and she had not appeared to him, he would know. She looked back at the castle, and saw the low night firelight glowing through the windows. A deep sigh tore from inside her. Damien knew.

He knew, and he had not come for her. He had not tried to stop her. His pride would always be stronger than his love. Maybe it was what she deserved.

She didn't know where she was going. Perhaps south, but not to Cornwall. Perhaps to Wales. She felt at home there. In the last year and forty days, she had found her mother's blood inside her. The songs she'd once sung simply for pleasure now came from her heart. She had learned what it meant to be almost invisible until her voice rang out, and what it meant to know her words touched others' hearts.

She had known the blissful, yet humbling shock when a peasant would toss a small coin to her in thanks for her singing. The first time, she had cried from the joy of it. It was that day that Angus had joined their party, and had asked why she wept. She'd told him, and he had stayed by her side ever since.

She had known joy. She had learned a new kind of pride, from using the gifts she'd been granted to their fullest capacity. She had known friendship, and the sweet freedom of living among others of like minds—others who spoke of music and poetry into the night, who laughed and told stories that made her laugh, too.

Yet one thing eluded her, and with the thought of it, all joy fled. Her heart began to throb with merciless heat—because she thought of a man who was so much a part of her that she couldn't tell where she ended and he began.

Damien.

She had known his passion, and what it meant to have his body as part of hers. She knew what it meant to love.

The falling snow obscured her vision of the castle. The wind swirled the snow around her, heavier now, tossing her hair forward around her face as if directing her back to her heart's true desire. She knew what she was looking for : the sight of him following her, struggling against the storm to claim her.

Her hope, like her love, endured all. She forced herself to turn back into the wind and trudge onward. She pulled up her hood and plodded to the top of the hill, following the northern road as she remembered it from their arrival. At the top of the hill, she turned back again, knowing that when she walked onward, what was behind her would be lost to her sight forever.

Dark and beautiful in the storm, Menton Castle sat silent, unmoving, an impenetrable fortress. It was Damien's heart she saw. Nothing followed her. No footsteps besides hers divided the deep snow.

She waited for a timeless while as the snow spiraled around her. She imagined him so clearly. She could see him ordering the guards to let him out, demanding a horse so he could follow swiftly and catch up to her. She could see his black hair in the wind, in the night, sprinkled with fat snowflakes as he rode. She could imagine the sound of the horse's footfalls pounding through the snow as it galloped toward her.

She could imagine his smile as he came to her, the sweet victory of a love overcoming all obstacles.

Pippa closed her eyes and saw her life with Damien, two of a kind as they were and had always been. There was so much they could be together, so much they could do!

She opened her eyes and saw nothing but snow and a black night.

He wasn't coming. From inside, her whole being called to him, a soul to a soul, but there was no answer. Whatever they had shared was past. She sank to her knees and cried.

January 5, Twelfth Night of Yule

Her voice rang haunting and pure like a night bird's as she sang of a bird's endless flight as it called to a mate that was forever lost. A Welsh fiddler joined her song, and the villagers danced with her, filling the town's largest barn with gaiety. No one here had title or position, and many lived insufferably impoverished lives. But tonight, this night while nobles reveled in nearby castles, these peasants joyfully celebrated life beyond the reach of suffering or loss.

Tonight, her pain had become part of her, an endless ache that found expression in her song. She saw Damien's face in her mind, she felt his touch and heard his voice. She remembered the soft, manly scent of him and she knew that when she was very old, and had forgotten all else, that sweetness would linger.

Hope had died, but her love would never fade. Each memory, even the darkest, moved her heart. She sang because it was all she had left, because it was all she was. Alone, and with one gift to share: her strength.

She was strong, even when her heart ached and bled for what she had lost.

The fiddler played, echoing her song. She paused a while in her singing, letting his music carry her, her eyes closed, filled with tears. *Damien, I love you so*.

The hopeless ache filled her chest. For a while, a little while, every dream and imagining had come in from the mists and made itself real in his arms, in the light of his passionate eyes, in his wild and daring nature—there, she had lived fully.

Now, she lived in the mists again, living on dreams and memory and what might have been, but as long as she gave that lingering passion voice in a song, as long as people listened, she could find meaning in her pain.

He hadn't saved her. He couldn't, because he was so strong and she knew he must regain that for which he fought. He hadn't come to her, because she had asked too much from him.

She didn't want to stop loving him. Her love had been full, and she couldn't deny what she had found in him—a part of herself. He was all she admired, all she desired, and he was lost to her.

The fiddler eased his pace so that she could join him in song again. She opened her mouth to sing, but another voice took her place. A man's voice.

The most horrible, grating voice she'd ever heard.

No man—*no one*—had a voice that disturbing.

Except one.

She couldn't move, but a wild heat spread through her as he sang. He sang in another tongue. French. But she understood.

She stood immobile while the singer drew closer behind her.

Pippa turned around and tears flooded down her cheeks. Damien fingered his mandolin idly, his music jarring painfully against the fiddler's. He smiled and held up his mandolin.

"I never did like this much." He came closer to her, but still she couldn't move. He nodded toward the peasants, who appeared horror-stricken. "I don't think they like it much, either. But if this is what it takes, then this I will do."

She was shaking too much to go to him, too much to speak. He looked into her eyes and she saw his tears. He touched her face gently. "Pippa, my love, I am yours. I will give up everything. I will follow you wherever you go. I will sing and play this foolish instrument whenever you ask it. I will defend the coins you earn, and I will stay with you for all of my life."

She choked back a sob, and he took her in his arms, kissing her forehead, then her cheek, and her mouth. She wrapped her arms tight around his neck and kissed him back.

"God's teeth, boy, it's taken you long enough to find the lass!" Angus's voice started them from their embrace. He stomped into the barn, shoving his way passed the villagers, then dropped his flute at Pippa's feet. "He left the same night you did." Angus cast a disparaging glance at Damien, but his expression didn't reveal the same suspicion it had before. "Unbelievable. He went everywhere, *everywhere*, except the most obvious."

Pippa brushed her tears aside, but more came. She looked up at Damien, whose face contorted in a familiar, sweet frown of impatience and irritation. "If you knew where she was, you might have alerted me to her presence," he said. "And yours."

"I was following you in secret, in service to . . ." He caught himself, and his frown deepened. "I wasn't your guide, boy."

Damien glared at Angus, but Pippa rose up on tiptoes to kiss Damien's cheek. "What happened? I believed you would marry Christina."

His brow furrowed and he shook his head. "My dear, I have many wants and many desires, but I am not willing to fly in the face of true love to gain those ends. I said the same to Christina, and to Wallace. I believe she will find him a much more desirable mate."

"I am glad. Wallace is young, and somewhat misguided, but he loves her very much."

Damien eyed Angus, who watched intently as if the drama had not yet unfolded to his specifications. "There's more, boy, and I'm waiting to hear it."

"Should you refer to me as 'boy' again, I will run you through and through."

"With what, minstrel? You lost your sword to your arrogance."

Damien held up his blunt mandolin. "Then I'll bash you over the head with this."

Pippa gazed up at him with adoration. He had given her all himself, surrendered everything, but he was still Damien.

Angus ignored the threat, and turned pleasantly to Pippa. "So, my dear lass, you've won after all. As unlikely as I found it, the most arrogant, proud, and ruthless man of all has given up everything for the love of you. It seems you are free."

Pippa gave a short gasp. "I am free." She looked around at the confused villagers. "But maybe, in truth, I was free all along."

Damien's dark brow furrowed. "Free? From what?"

She looked up at him. Truly free. "From a punishment that was placed upon me, a year and forty-four days ago—by Eleanor of Aquitaine."

His mouth opened, and stayed open. "What?"

She sighed, and the blissful calm of happiness surrounded her. *This is victory. To know you have climbed the highest mountain, endured Hell and Heaven, and reached the top after all.* A contented smile curved her lips. "As it happens, Damien, my dear, I offended Eleanor, too, only a short time before she was crowned queen."

"You?" He looked as if he wanted to say more, but couldn't.

"Me. Does that surprise you?" He nodded, but didn't speak. "I told you once I was like my father. It was true. Perhaps I was like Eleanor herself. But no longer."

"That—isn't possible. Eleanor is demanding, vain, proud, and exerts her will without forethought or caution."

Pippa nodded. "That would have been an apt description of myself, yes."

"Never. You, Pippa, are sweet and kind, tender and romantic."

She laughed. "I was demanding and vain, proud and . . . not very romantic, I'm afraid, though I had many suitors. Not because of my father's power, but because they found me desirable. Does that surprise you?"

He gulped. "No."

"I could sing, I could tease, and I could promise secret pleasures with only a glance. I was a devilish monster, and I delighted in it."

Damien shifted his weight and spoke in a hushed whisper. "Pippa . . . You're arousing me."

She eyed him, then shook her head. "I knew how to inspire desire in a man, but I'd never felt it myself. I'd viewed them all, considering who best could serve me, and further my position. I'd learned to play them each against each other. . . ."

Pippa stopped and sighed heavily. "I didn't truly know what ill could come of this, only that it pleased my pride. But one young man, whom I had trifled with but cared nothing for, proved to have a more passionate heart than I imagined. He believed I returned his affections, but when he found me . . . trifling with another, he challenged the man, and they fought in a public spectacle."

"You were a demon." Pippa detected a hint of admiration in Damien's voice.

"I was. They fought, and the boy lost. At the time, I considered it a fine, dramatic display of my worth. I enjoyed it, though the boy was wounded."

Damien winced. "Tell me he didn't die."

"He did not, but his pride was savaged. I thought him foolish, and said so. In fact, I declared that I would marry the victor, who was more to my liking."

He stared at her as if he'd never known her. "I cannot imagine this."

"Eleanor of Aquitaine was likewise appalled. She and her entourage were guests of my father at the time. When I questioned my intended husband about what he could offer me, Eleanor rose and issued her proclamation. She said I had inspired love in men while waiting only for the one who would grant me all my worldly desires. Until a man was willing to give up all the same for me, Eleanor condemned me to walk England with only my songs to guide me."

"I suspect she is well practiced at such condemnations." Damien paused, searching her face as if this mystery had unfolded in unexpected directions. "You must have been furious."

"My fury knew no bounds. I wept and demanded and begged my father to make war on her. He refused, of course, although I think he was tempted."

"I was." A hooded man stepped forward from amongst the villagers, and Pippa squealed in shock.

He drew back his hood, revealing gold and silver hair and a cropped white beard. "Father!"

Philip went to her and hugged her. "Do you think I would leave my daughter to wander England alone?

Never. As soon as you left, I engaged Angus here to join you as your protector."

Pippa beamed at Angus, who offered a stoic Scot's nod and said nothing. Pippa touched her father's arm. "But you followed me, too. In disguise," she said.

Philip looked embarrassed, uneasy with his emotion. "When I could. I kept myself nearby, while Angus kept an eye on you, and reported to me." He shook his head and thumped his fist into his other hand. "That my daughter should be cursed by a foolish queen— who I am certain simply envied your beauty and charm. . . ."

Pippa hugged him, and her tears began again. "It was more than that, Father. Eleanor was right." She drew back and looked into his proud face. "I am not the girl I was a year ago. I am wiser—and I am happy."

"I see that, my dear child. And I have seen you grow and change, and I have seen all your mother's graces come alive in you. But Eleanor is still a fool."

Damien nodded, then touched her shoulder, claiming her. "With that, I must agree." Pippa pressed her lips together, then placed her hand over his heart.

"Do you, truly? You and I, we are the same. Too strong, and too proud. We didn't see the broken hearts we left in our wake. We saw only the brightness of our future, carved by our own hands. Yet there *was* no future—because our hearts were hidden—until we found each other."

The soft light of understanding gleamed in his eyes and he smiled. "There may be truth in that, but I will not credit it to Eleanor but to love instead. And for love's sake . . ." He drew forth the golden ring and took it from its chain.

While Pippa watched spellbound, he knelt before her and took her hand. "Pippa, you are my heart, and for you, I would leave all. In you, I have seen that love is sacred after all." He paused, and one tear slid down his perfect cheek. "Will you marry me?"

Her hand shook as she touched his face and wiped away his tear. "Damien . . . I will."

Damien slipped the gold ring on her finger and kissed her hand. He rose and took her in his arms, gazing down at her as if she were a legendary treasure that when discovered proved even more precious than imagined.

Philip slapped Angus on the back and beamed with pleasure. "Well! That's done, and on Twelfth Night, too. Not that I wouldn't prefer it spent in my own hall, but these villagers do indeed understand revelry." He adjusted his ragged cloak and happily looked around at Damien and Pippa. "My girl chose a manly one after all. Damien of Aquitaine! King Henry will hear of this, naturally, and he'll set them up. I'm thinking there must be a fiefdom open somewhere in Aquitaine. . . ."

Her father's words faded from Pippa's awareness. Damien had come for her. Not because of her father's power, but because he loved her. Wherever they would go, they would be together—no longer driven by pride and ambition, but by love. Whatever power they were given, they would use wisely, and it would come from their hearts.

She looked into Damien's bright eyes, and she knew he saw what she did. He cupped her face in his hands, and he smiled though there were tears of joy in his eyes. "Pippa, my dear love . . . From the moment we met, you understood me. I had no idea why, or how you could look at me and see inside me that way. To me, you were a mystery, the most challenging puzzle I had ever faced."

She smiled, too. "Do you understand why now?"

"I do." Very gently, he bent to kiss her mouth. "The mystery in you was of myself, too. Now we are one, and what we create in this world will be born of love."

The fiddler took up his tune again, and music filled the barn. The villagers laughed and drank, and her father sampled the bread and cheese. Angus relayed tales of his guardianship, and the Twelfth Night of Yule faded into morning.

All the while, Damien held Pippa in his arms, kissing her cheek and her hands, and his eyes glowed with love. When the villagers danced, he held her close and their bodies swayed together. He bent low so that his lips grazed her ear, and she shuddered.

Then very low, and deep, he began to sing just for her. And one thing she had never known came clear at last. The voice of Damien of Aquitaine was magic.

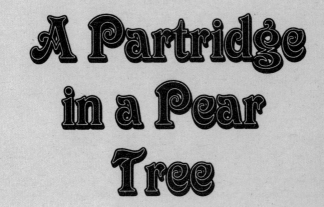

A Partridge in a Pear Tree

"The heart has its reasons, whereof reason knows nothing."
—Pascal

Chapter One

·"What did you say?" Lady Elisa stared at the man-at-arms, not quite believing what he had just told her. He could have no reason to lie, she reflected, and the message he'd brought was so typical of her husband that it must be true. Still, she repeated the most vital details in case her ears were deceiving her. "A large party of guests, including ten noblemen and nine ladies, all arriving tomorrow and staying until Twelfth Night or the day after that?"

"Aye, my lady. Lord Robert said for you to expect them at midday or in the early afternoon."

Elisa glanced quickly around the great hall. It was clean, and so was the rest of the huge castle, for she was an excellent chatelaine. In expectation of a quiet Christmas season, with the lord of the castle absent at the royal court as usual, the hall was nicely, if sparsely, decorated with pine boughs and holly. Out of consideration for the common folk who lived in the castle, the decorations also included small bunches of mistletoe dangling above the entry arch to the great hall and the passageway to the kitchen. The Yule log waited, trimmed and ready in the inner bailey, from where it would be ceremonially dragged up the steps and into one of the fireplaces in the great hall on Christmas day.

Those simple preparations would have to suffice, for there was no time to think of anything more elaborate. The band of itinerant acrobats and jugglers who had appeared at the castle gate on the previous day would have to serve for entertainment, too. If Robert, the noble baron of Menton, did not approve, let him provide his own entertainment!

Elisa dismissed all thought of decorations and entertainment in favor of a rapid consideration of clean linens, altered menus, and a mental count of the barrels of wine and casks of ale piled in the basement storerooms. Nor did she neglect her immediate duty as lady of the castle. Gritting her teeth against the resentment that filled her heart at the unanticipated demands being made upon her, steeling herself against the tumultuous emotions generated by the impending arrival of the husband, who by his very presence would shatter her lonely holiday peace, Elisa addressed the waiting man-at-arms who was her husband's messenger.

"You will be cold and weary after your long ride," she said to him. "The midday meal is not quite finished. As you can see, we are fasting before the holy day, but there is enough food. Find a place and eat your fill," she finished with a graceful wave of her hand toward the lower tables.

"Thank you, my lady." The man-at-arms bowed and

turned away, to be greeted by Sir James, the young Scottish knight who had lived at Menton for years as a hostage for his father's good behavior. Sir James and the man-at-arms were old friends from the practice yard, so when the man-at-arms was offered a pallet for sleeping, he readily accepted.

"Well, at least there is one person for whom I won't have to find a bed," Elisa muttered, watching the two.

Just then Elisa's daughter glanced up from her place at the high table. Christina possessed her father's dark hair and deep blue eyes, though where Robert's eyes were always sharp and piercing, Christina's were soft and dreamy. She was a beauty, with her father's firm jaw and straight, elegant nose. Elisa sighed, looking at her. In appearance the girl was completely unlike her golden-haired, brown-eyed, plump, and rather plain mother. In character, too, they differed, as Christina's first comment revealed.

"How lovely it will be to have Father home for a while," Christina said, smiling.

"You think so," Elisa responded, "because you pay no heed at all to domestic matters. I warned Robert about sending you to that convent school, but as usual, he refused to listen to me. You should have been kept at home or, better yet, been fostered with another noble family, so you'd have the opportunity to learn the duties of a wife and chatelaine. Instead, you spent your years away from Menton learning embroidery and reading and writing."

"There's nothing wrong with reading and writing," Christina said, rising from the high table and heading toward the edge of the dais on which the table rested.

"Certainly, there isn't," Elisa responded with some heat. She wasn't sure whether it was Christina's physical similarity to Robert or her constant, quiet rebellion bordering on surliness that rankled so deeply. Possibly, it was a bit of each. Feeling the need to defend herself, she added, "I know how to read and write."

"Barely," said Christina as she passed her mother. "And you've minimal counting skills, too."

"Stop right there." Elisa kept her voice low so none of the servants or men-at-arms would overhear the dispute, but she knew how to issue a command.

Christina obeyed, standing with shoulders hunched, head bowed, and hands folded before her as if she were a humble postulant. Which, Elisa well knew, her daughter was not. It was Elisa's fervent wish that the Church would one day declare a saint to whom the mothers of marriageable girls could pray for help when their self-control was sorely taxed. At the moment there was no such saint, so Elisa would have to help herself. And after dealing with her daughter, Elisa was going to have to deal with her husband, a much more formidable task. She thrust that unwelcome thought aside while she proceeded to settle the problem at hand.

"Since you are so expert with numbers," she said to Christina, "tell me the sum of all the guests we are to expect on less than one day's notice. Ten lords, according to your father's messenger, and each lord surely with a dozen squires and men-at-arms in his train. In addition, nine ladies, with their own servants. Your father, his squires, and all the men-at-arms from Menton who have been attending him at court these past months. What is the total number of extra mouths we will have to feed over the next fourteen days?"

"Three hundred?" Startled by the large sum her additions produced—her full attention finally captured by a domestic issue—Christina looked straight into her mother's eyes. "Where will they all sleep? How will we feed so many?"

"If you paid more attention to a noblewoman's duties instead of rashly totaling numbers without thought," Elisa told her, "you would realize that most, if not all, of the ladies will come with their lords, whether their fathers or their husbands, and thus they will not bring their own guards, but only a maid or two each. Still, it is a large number of guests and I will not have time to see to every detail myself. I am going to need your help."

"Mine?" Christina looked distinctly confused. "I don't think I—you've never asked before—" She fell silent when Elisa made an impatient gesture.

"I should have asked long ago. It is past time for you to learn what will be expected of you when you marry a nobleman," Elisa said.

"I don't want to marry," Christina said, beginning the whining protest that usually ended with her being excused from domestic chores.

"The matter of your marriage you may take up with your father," Elisa said crisply. "It is up to him to decide who—or if—you will marry. Until he reaches Menton, you will assist me and obey my every order promptly, for I have no time to quibble with you.

"Take this key," she continued, unfastening one from the cluster of keys that hung from the chain about her waist. "It unlocks the linen room. There you will count out sheets and quilts sufficient for each guest room. I will send two maidservants with clean hands to help you make up the beds. Be sure that your own hands are clean; we've no time to launder soiled linens."

"Where will you be?" Christina asked, sounding annoyed at her mother's expectation that she should do anything resembling work.

"In the kitchen," Elisa answered, "rechecking our food supplies and revising menus with the cook."

"But I have never made up a bed," Christina protested. "How is it done?"

"Learn by doing," Elisa snapped at her. "If you stop dreaming and pay attention, perhaps one of the maids will show you what you ought to know."

With that, Elisa stepped off the dais, away from the high table and the daughter she loved but could barely tolerate, and headed for the screens passage and the kitchen. Her mouth curled in a small but determined smile. She was thirty-five years old and tired of being taken for granted by her husband, scorned by her daughter, and expected by the servants always to perform her duty without complaining. In Elisa's opinion, the only person who truly understood her was her twenty-year-old, golden-haired son, William, who was squire to Robert's friend, Lord Edmund.

Surely, if Robert was bringing so large a party of guests, Edmund would be among them, and with Edmund would come his squires. William would be home for a time. Elisa would have an ally.

But whether William came to Menton or not, Elisa intended to use the Christmas season to teach her thoughtless, inconsiderate husband a lesson he would never forget.

Chapter Two

Gowned in deep green silk, wearing her best jewelry and with her hair bound into a golden net, Elisa greeted her long-absent husband in the great hall shortly after midday on Christmas Eve.

Robert came in stamping ice and mud from his boots, his blue cloak thrown back over one shoulder, his dark hair slightly tousled by the winter wind. As always his good looks, his sparkling blue eyes, and most of all, his wide, dazzling smile left his wife breathless. She reminded herself sternly that, while she had loved him since their wedding night, he did not love her at all.

"My lady." His manners faultless as always, Robert swept her a low, formal bow.

"Welcome home, my lord." As correct and formal in public as he, Elisa curtsied and extended one hand.

Privately she shivered in pleasure when Robert's warm lips brushed her fingers. At once he released her hand and straightened to look around the hall, appraising the arrangements she had made. Elisa was sure he had already forgotten her.

"Is there a shortage of green boughs in Menton Forest?" he asked, frowning.

"In case you were not aware, my lord," Elisa responded sharply, "your messenger did not appear until well into the afternoon yesterday, when it was already growing dark. There was no time before nightfall to venture into the forest to cut more greenery. All day today we have been occupied in preparing lodging and food for *your* guests," she finished with a glare that her husband blithely ignored.

"Christina!" Robert called, opening his arms to embrace his daughter. "How pretty you've grown."

While Christina smiled and dimpled at her favorite parent, Elisa regarded the crowd of folk who were entering the hall.

"I see only eight lords," she said, totaling the numbers quickly. "There are nine ladies, but only eight maidservants to attend them, unless I've miscounted. And so many knights and squires."

"More men are waiting in the bailey," Robert said. "I assume you have beds prepared for all?"

"The men-at-arms are to sleep in the barracks or the gatehouses, the squires with their masters or wherever they can find space. I leave the disposition of the men to you, my lord." Setting aside her personal feelings, Elisa responded to the call of duty, as she always did. "Christina and I will see to the ladies."

"There are several ladies in particular whose needs you should especially tend to," Robert said. He turned to a dark-haired young woman, taking her hand and leading her to Elisa. "Here is Lady Eleanor, the queen's ward and kinswoman."

Elisa would have known Lady Eleanor's high status by the richness of her blue gown, a shade that emphasized her lovely blue eyes. Elisa politely welcomed the noble guest to Menton and then, out of deference to Lady Eleanor's rank, called to escort the lady to one of the guest chambers, telling the maid to provide whatever Lady Eleanor required for her comfort.

Next Robert beckoned to a pair of guests who remained heavily cloaked and hooded by the door, still shivering from the cold. Both ladies came forward at Robert's bidding, to make their curtsies to their hostess.

"This is Edmund's daughter, Lady Joan," Robert said. "I don't expect you to recognize her; you haven't seen Joan since she was a babe in arms. She was coming to Menton with her father when Edmund was taken ill along the way. He will join us when he's feeling better, but he insisted that Joan continue her journey, believing she will be more comfortable here with us. And this other lady is Sabrina, Joan's cousin, who is serving as her companion."

There was small chance of recognizing Lady Joan, even if she had been a dear and close friend. All Elisa could see of her was a reddened nose beneath the edge of her hood. Lady Sabrina did push back her hood to reveal dark hair and eyes and a pleasant, smiling face. Elisa returned the smile but, distracted by all she still must do to make every guest feel welcome, she offered just a quick word of greeting, followed by a question directed to Lady Joan.

"I trust Lord Edmund is not seriously ill?" Elisa said, disguising her impatience to be about her duties. It was Robert and not Joan who answered her.

"It's merely a brief wintertime affliction, which is why Joan agreed to Edmund's order to leave him. Several other people who were traveling with us also have it. I'm sure all of them will recover within a few days. Meanwhile, Edmund has William to tend him, so he is in good hands and we need not concern ourselves about him, except to miss his presence while we celebrate."

"William has stayed behind?" Elisa cried out in disappointment.

"He knows his duty to his master," Robert said. "Oh, by the way, Joan's maidservant was among those taken ill. If she's well enough she will come to Menton when Edmund does. I told Joan you'd have no problem finding a suitable maid to attend her until then."

"Did you?" Elisa said. For a moment she wondered what Robert's reaction would be if she were to weep, or laugh wildly, or better yet, if she threw something at him for his thoughtless expectations of her. He always just assumed that she would respond correctly to whatever he decided to do, and he never asked about her opinions or her preferences.

"I know you have all the arrangements well in hand," Robert told her with a smile that should have warmed her heart. "You are the most competent lady I know. I leave our noble guests to your care. Don't worry about a thing, for I will see to the men-at-arms and the squires."

He headed toward the entry hall, pausing on the way to speak to a tall, slender lady whose gleaming red hair was braided and wrapped around her head and topped by a tiny, bright green hat with a long, curling feather.

Elisa's back stiffened abruptly. She knew that lady. Kasia of Salforth was a niece of the earl of Chester and, despite her colorful clothing, she was a recent widow. Kasia's presence at Menton put a prompt end to Elisa's hope of teaching Robert to pay more attention to his wife and perhaps even to show that wife some true affection. In the days when Elisa's father was trying to arrange her marriage, Kasia had been among the candidates to become Robert's wife. She was, in fact, the lady whom Robert had preferred.

Elisa stared while Robert bent over Kasia's hand and received a warm glance in return for his courtesy. The two exchanged a few words, then Robert took himself off to the bailey.

The moment he was out of sight Elisa recalled her obligations to her guests. Lady Joan was waiting, still cloaked and hooded, still shivering. Elisa had barely glanced at the girl when Robert introduced them, and she did not look closely at her now. As Lord Edmund's daughter, Joan was entitled to special treatment, and so was her companion. Elisa noticed her own daughter hovering about, doing nothing.

"Christina," Elisa said, "please show Lady Joan and Lady Sabrina where they are to sleep and see that they have something warm to drink. Then find a suitable maidservant to attend them while they are at Menton. When you are finished, return to me. I will need your help."

"You will?" Christina looked startled. "Yes, of course, Mother."

Elisa dismissed both young women from her thoughts and turned all of her attention to the remaining guests. She greeted each of them with a smile and welcoming words, including Lady Kasia. Within the hour everyone was assigned a bed and the delayed midday meal could begin.

There was no need to make excuses for the simplicity of the menu. Everyone understood the requirement to fast in anticipation of a great Holy Day, so the guests did not complain about the lack of meat, especially when they could choose among several courses of fish, along with freshly baked bread and a hearty vegetable stew. Elisa silently thanked Robert's agent in Bristol, who had sent barrels of salted herring to Menton during the autumn. The herring made delicious pies when mixed with eggs and herbs, while denizens of the castle fish pond were boiled, sauced, and presented whole on long platters. Because of the fast no sweets were served, which was a relief to the busy cook as she frantically prepared pies, cakes, and custards for the larger feasts still to come.

The simple meal was a relief to Elisa, too. Her stomach was in knots, her appetite non-existent. She sat beside Robert at the high table while he chatted easily with Lady Kasia, who was seated on his right hand out of deference to her rank as the most important lady present. The sound of Robert's laughter mingled with that of Lady Kasia was like a dagger to Elisa's heart.

She told herself she was a fool to be bitter. Nobles married for dynastic or property reasons, and seldom did they love the spouses chosen for them by their parents. Noblemen frequently took mistresses. If Robert and Kasia were involved in an affair, there was little Elisa could do about it. Even so, Elisa was surprised and deeply offended that he would bring the woman to Menton, to sit at the same table with his wife.

Looking away from her husband, Elisa assessed the well-being of the other guests. Lady Joan had sent a message by her companion, Sabrina, claiming that she was still too travel-weary and cold to attend the feast. But Sabrina appeared to be recovered from her cold journey. She was sitting near Christina, the two of them were talking together, and for once Christina was not wearing her usual sullen expression. Perhaps what Christina needed was a friend close to her own age. It was good to see her cheerful.

The nobleman sitting at Elisa's left hand asked her a question, and she returned to the duties of a hostess. Duty, always duty. Her sense of duty had seen her through twenty-one years of a polite but loveless marriage; it would see her through the next two weeks.

* * *

In the lord's chamber Robert dismissed the squire who was attending him and then lay back naked atop the huge bed. He stretched out his long legs and wiggled toes freed from his heavy boots.

"Ah," he said, "here is contentment. How I have longed for Menton."

"If you missed Menton so dearly," Elisa retorted, well aware that she sounded like a disgruntled wasp, "you could have returned sooner."

"Impossible. King Henry insisted he needed me close at hand. I was forced to beg on bended knee for permission to come home."

"Did you also beg permission for all the other lords and ladies to come with you?"

"I was pleased to invite them to my home."

"Without consulting your wife. With scarcely a day's notice of your coming."

"Is that why you're so annoyed? I knew you would manage perfectly well. You always do." He grinned at her, his blue eyes gleaming with humor. "You are far across the room, my lady. Come to bed."

Elisa regarded his well-muscled form with longing. Robert possessed the trim appearance of a man much younger than his forty years. Nor was there so much as a trace of gray in his dark hair. No sign of balding, either. Only the crinkles around his eyes and the lines at either side of his firm mouth suggested his maturity.

It was more than three months since they had lain together. Elisa ached to go into his arms, to open herself to his manly embrace. She knew she would find bodily pleasure with him. He invariably saw to it that she enjoyed their couplings. If only he loved her; if only he would think of her outside their bed.

"Come," he said again, drawing aside the quilt and sliding his powerful frame beneath it. "The night is cold and you are wearing only your shift. You will catch a chill."

"Would you care if I did?" she demanded. "Or is your concern only that any illness of mine would inconvenience you and your guests?"

"That's no way to speak to your lord." His smile did not falter and his glance was bold upon her breasts.

Elisa refused to give in to the sudden urge to fold her arms across her chest. Nor did she step nearer to the bed. She could not make her complaint if she was lying beside Robert. Once she was in bed with him the desire to touch him and draw close to him would overcome her. It always did. She could forgive him anything when he put his strong arms around her. Almost anything, she amended. This time he had gone too far.

"It's enough that you invite dozens of guests without giving me adequate notice," she said, allowing the floodgates of resentment to open wide in hope of disguising her painful love for him. "Many lords behave so, and it's true enough, their wives manage as best they can. But how could you insult me by bringing that woman here?"

"What woman?" Robert began arranging the pillows to his liking. He was no longer looking at Elisa. "Nine noble ladies came with me, and any number of female servants. Which one do you mean?"

"Kasia of Salforth," Elisa said through clenched teeth. "Your mistress."

He leaned back against the piled-up pillows and grinned at her. Elisa stood with fisted hands, fighting back both fury and fear, and trying very hard not to cry. Robert hated tears.

"Why would you imagine that Kasia is my mistress?" he asked.

"Are you saying she isn't?"

"I am wondering why you think she is."

"Your father chose me for your wife because my

dowry was larger than Kasia's. But you wanted to marry *her,* didn't you? Why shouldn't you? She was far more beautiful than I, and she is still beautiful."

"You're jealous," he said, laughing at her.

"I am wrinkled and overweight, and I've grown dull from staying always at Menton to look after your interests, while Kasia spends her days at a brilliant royal court."

"Has it never occurred to you that some men prefer a lady with a soft and comforting appearance?" he asked.

"No, it hasn't." Elisa knew she sounded like Christina in her more sullen moments, but she couldn't seem to stop herself. "I think men like women who are beautiful and slender and witty."

"You are wrong, and I am weary of this dispute. Put out the candle and come to bed." Robert rolled onto his side, turning his back on her.

Tears began to trickle down Elisa's cheeks. She bit hard on her lower lip to stop them. Keeping her own back turned in case Robert should roll over again and see her weeping, she sat on the edge of the bed and snuffed the candle.

"I apologize for my peevishness," she said. "That was no proper way to welcome you home after so long an absence. It's just that you never seem to think of me. You just tell me what to do and assume I'll do it."

"And you always do." His large hand found her smaller one beneath the quilt. Slowly he wove his fingers between hers. "You are wonderfully dependable."

"How boring that sounds." She heard his chuckle in the dark.

"My lady, if this were not a night of abstinence, I'd show you how glad I am to be home again," he said.

His words warmed her heart, until he untangled his hand from hers and turned away again, moving far to the other side of the bed. Left alone, Elisa reviewed every sentence she and Robert had spoken to each other since his return. She could discern no trace of affection for her in his speech, only acceptance of the dependable woman to whom he was bound for life by his father's choice, rather than by his own desire.

Dependable—what a dreadful word! She wanted him to yearn to return to her whenever duty took him from Menton, not because she was a dependable wife, but because he was enthralled by her charms, because he loved her too much to want to stay away. He had made an excuse of abstinence, which was reasonable enough. But if it were not Christmas Eve, would he have taken her into his arms, or would he have pleaded tiredness after a long day in the saddle?

How could she make her husband see her differently, when Lady Kasia was present to charm him and to remind him of the beauty and love he had lost years ago?

Damnation! Robert muttered under his breath. Another cursed argument. Why could he and Elisa never seem to meet in peace? No wonder he had chosen to remain three months at the royal court, which was more than twice as long as a baron's annual duty to the king required.

He grabbed the quilt and wrenched it more tightly around his bare shoulders. The lord's chamber was cold, but that was nothing unusual. All castle rooms were cold in winter. Were it not for Elisa's wild accusations, he could have wound his arms around her and held her close to warm them both and she would have welcomed him and called him Rob, and let him sleep on her soft bosom. Were it not for his pride, he'd take her in his arms anyway, and make her forget her anger with him.

It was better this way. Since he could not embrace her as tightly as he wanted or assert his husbandly rights until the next night, after the Advent fast was over, it was better to stay where he was, on his own side of the bed. Where he was cold. Where he was aching for her warmth and softness and longing to push his tongue into her mouth and his—Ah, no!

He thrashed around for a time, then settled with a pillow over his head to keep his cheeks and nose warmer. Better not think about what he wanted to do to his wife. Better to concentrate on falling asleep. Tomorrow, he'd find a way to make up their quarrel. He would explain his real reason for coming home so unexpectedly. She would understand. Elisa always understood. Well, almost always. . . .

"My lord, wake up." Elisa caught his shoulder and shook him hard. "Someone is at the main gate, requesting entrance. The sentry claims you left no orders regarding latecomers."

Robert came awake promptly and sat up in bed, shivering at the sudden jolt of cold air as the quilt fell away. Elisa, already dressed and coifed, regarded him with a cool eye. A man-at-arms, who'd apparently been sent by the guard at the gate, stood just inside the chamber door, looking around with interest.

"Do you know a man named Royce?" Elisa asked.

"Yes. Let him in at once," Robert said to the man-at-arms, who saluted his lord and left.

"Another guest?" Elisa asked, glaring at him.

"Sir Royce is Lady Joan's betrothed," Robert answered. "Edmund wanted them to have an opportunity to meet and learn to know each other. We decided between us that Christmas at Menton would be an ideal time. Royce traveled here separately from my party. He will be staying until Twelfth Night, perhaps a day or two longer."

"I see." Elisa's pretty mouth closed firmly on the comment. "Very well, my lord. I will find a bed somewhere for yet another unexpected guest. Do let me know, at your convenience of course, if there are more people still to arrive."

"It's barely daylight," Robert said, to change the subject.

"It's almost time for Mass. You ought to be up and dressed, unless you've forgotten that it's Christmas Day? I will go to the hall and greet Sir Royce and invite him to join us in the chapel."

"Damnation," Robert muttered, understanding the message conveyed by his wife's stiff spine as she departed, even while he was savoring the view of her lush and womanly figure. "This homecoming is not going at all the way I planned."

Chapter Three

The Christmas feast was almost over. This being a Holy Day, the wilder revelry would not begin until the morrow, though the guests were plainly in the mood to be entertained and someone had cajoled a traveling minstrel into singing a few carols.

Elisa frowned, irritated by the man's appearance. Minstrels usually wore bright garb and put on cheerful faces, but this one was clothed entirely in black and he appeared to be most unhappy. Furthermore, his voice was terribly hoarse. Elisa suspected he was suffering from a head cold, an affliction which boded ill for future entertainment.

With a polite word of excuse that no one acknowledged, Elisa rose from her seat and walked along the back of the dais.

"Christina," she said, bending toward the girl who was sitting a few places away, "as soon as the minstrel has finished this dreary performance, please take him to the stillroom and dose him with horehound syrup

127

to ease his throat, lest he become unable to sing at all. You'll find the jar of syrup on the second shelf to the right of the door."

"You want me to do it?" Christina responded, one hand at her bosom. "But how much shall I give him? I don't want to cause him harm."

"From the sound of his voice, nothing could make it worse," Elisa said. She winced as the minstrel hit a sour note in one of her favorite songs. "There is a large stirring spoon on my worktable. Fill it with syrup and make him swallow it. Give him a second spoonful if he'll take it. He may refuse; it is vile-tasting medicine. Here." For the second time in recent days she handed one of the household keys to her daughter.

"Why don't you do it?" Christina asked, trying to give back the key.

"I am too busy," Elisa said. "In fact, I am so busy that I'm placing you in charge of the holiday entertainment. You decide when, and how, the acrobats and jugglers are to perform. The minstrel, too. I give them all into your hands."

"Me?" Christina repeated.

"I trust you," Elisa said. "You've handled the other chores I've turned over to you very well." She touched Christina's shoulder, noting that the girl looked both surprised and pleased at being praised by her mother.

Elisa was tempted to add some pertinent advice on how to deal sternly with a minstrel who did not appear to enjoy his work, but she resisted the urge. Christina had supervised the preparation of all the guest rooms with unexpected efficiency. Perhaps she could handle the minstrel, too.

Meanwhile, since she was not needed at the high table, Elisa gave in to her restless desire to absent herself from the great hall. Robert was again ignoring his wife in favor of conversation with Lady Kasia and the gentleman who sat on Kasia's other side. The nobleman who was Elisa's partner for the meal looked half-asleep from too much wine. She would not be missed.

Elisa slipped quietly away from the dais. After a brief visit to the kitchen to be sure all was well there, she made her way to the lord's chamber. The short midwinter day was over and the sky beyond the open shutters showed only faint starlight. The room was colder than usual.

"Incompetent squire," Elisa said, hurrying to the windows. "He should have closed the shutters and fired the brazier before abandoning his chores."

As she crossed the room she stumbled and nearly fell over an unexpected obstacle. Putting down searching hands, she discovered a large basket that hadn't been there earlier.

"He just dumped it here in the middle of the floor," she exclaimed, recognizing at once from the size and shape of it what the basket probably contained. "Worthless boy! I'll speak to him myself. Robert deserves a better squire."

More cautious now in case there were other baskets left about to trip over, she made her way to the bed-side table where an oil lamp, two pieces of flint, and a small pile of lint to catch a spark were gathered. In a moment the lamp was lit and she fired the charcoal in the brazier, too. Having finally closed the shutters, she turned her attention to the basket on the floor. The leather thong that secured the lid was unfastened, and when she raised the lid she found Robert's clothing piled carelessly within.

"Not a good squire at all," she said, and set about shaking out and folding her husband's shirts, tunics, and hose, laying aside the garments that needed cleaning. "If I put Robert's belongings into his large wooden chest, then I can send this basket to the store-room and we'll have a bit more space in here."

She was almost at the bottom of the basket when

she pulled out a linen undershirt that was tightly rolled. When she straightened it to see if it needed laundering, something fell out of the crumpled linen and skipped across the floor and under the bed. By the sound there were two items, both of them solid. Elisa caught up the oil lamp and set it on the floor to help her see while she searched. What she sought was bright and thus quickly found. She knelt and reached beneath the bed, then sat back against the wooden bed frame to take a good look at the objects she held.

In the lamplight twin circles of gold gleamed softly in her hand. Each band contained a small stone as red as heart's blood. The settings were so deep that when Elisa ran a finger across one stone, she could barely feel the top of it above the smooth metal.

"As red as love, as deep as eternal devotion," she whispered. "Oh, Rob, how disgracefully easy you've made it for yourself. Two identical gold rings, one a false peace offering for your dependable, boring wife, and the other a symbol of love for your beautiful, fascinating mistress. What else can two golden rings set with rubies mean? Oh, I could kill you for this!" Her fingers closed over the rings, blocking out the soft luster of the metal and the dark red flame of the stones.

"Why did I imagine that because I am your wife, you could never break my heart? Why can't you love me just a little? And why can't I stop loving you, in spite of your indifference? Where is my noble pride?"

"Elisa, what in Heaven's name are you doing on the floor?" Robert stood in the doorway, staring at her as if she had lost her wits.

From where Elisa sat, with the oil lamp beside her on the floor, her husband appeared unnaturally tall and his face, lit from below, took on a devilish aspect, with sharp highlights and shadows.

"You are neglecting our guests," he said, frowning at her.

130

"Your guests. I never invited them. I don't even know most of them." Still clutching the rings, Elisa scrambled to her feet.

"This is my castle—" he began, but she cut him off.

"Like the dutiful wife I have always been, I was attending to practical matters, specifically to the clothing your inept squire neglected to unpack. I found these." She held out her fist and slowly opened her fingers to let him see what lay in her palm.

"Ah," he said, shaking his head, "I didn't want you to know about those yet."

"I am sure you did not. Will you still deny that Kasia is your mistress? Even with this evidence of your perfidy?"

"What evidence? Foolish woman, if you would only stop quarreling with me and listen for a while, I could explain."

"Damn you, Rob! You appreciate nothing that I do for you. Nothing! Nor do you care about me, or how you hurt me." So angry she could scarcely see, Elisa threw the rings at him, then made for the door.

"No, you don't." He caught her by one arm, swinging her around with such force that Elisa came up hard against his chest. "You will not leave until we settle this."

"There is nothing to settle," she said. "I understand perfectly. We have the usual noble marriage. You are indifferent to me, I despise you, and your mistress awaits in the great hall. *Your* great hall, my lord."

"How often must I tell you that Kasia is not my mistress? When will you believe me?"

"Never." Teeth bared in fury, she spat the single word at him.

"Then, believe this." He brought his mouth down hard on hers. His kiss was punishing, his arms like a vise around her back, crushing her so tightly against him that she could not breathe.

For a few moments she responded, rejoicing in his manly strength and in the passion he could too easily evoke in her. Then she began to struggle. He let her go at once.

"You are despicable!" she cried, and dealt him a ringing slap on the cheek.

"My lady," he said, dangerously calm, "you may not strike your lord and husband. I forbid it."

"And I forbid you to bring your mistress here."

"How many times do I have to tell you?" he roared at her. "Kasia is not my mistress!"

"You may tell me as often as you like and I still won't believe you," she said. "While Kasia is at Menton, I will not lie with you. I will sleep with Christina tonight."

"You will not!"

She did not listen to him. She walked out of the room and shut the door quietly behind her, leaving Rob to find the two golden rings. It took him a long time. After hitting his chest they had rolled far under the bed, into the shadows where the light from the oil lamp did not reach.

"Dear Lord in Heaven," Rob exclaimed when he stood holding the rings at last, "give me the wisdom to comprehend the workings of a woman's mind. And grant me the courage to face her anger until she understands."

An hour later Rob paused at the entrance to the great hall while he watched his wife. She was dazzling. She sparkled with vitality. Her green silk gown glowed in the candlelight; the gold necklace and gold hairnet she wore glittered whenever she moved close enough to the fireplace to catch the light from the burning Yule log. Elisa did not fit the tall, slender, small-breasted ideal of beauty that was current at court. Rob knew that when he cupped her breasts they would fill his large hands. Her waist remained enticingly slim in spite of two living children and several miscarriages. And hidden beneath the heavy folds of her skirt were her beautifully rounded hips and shapely legs.

Beneath her skirt. Rob smiled, relishing the surge of arousal that memory brought. It was growing late. Soon the guests would begin seeking their beds and Elisa would be able to forsake her duties as hostess to join him in the lord's chamber. The long and stringent Advent fast was over; he could take her to bed and silence all of her complaints with passion. Elisa was a passionate woman, easily aroused. He grew warm just thinking about her white arms and her lovely legs wrapped around him, and her soft cries of delight. When they were both finally sated and relaxed he would explain about Kasia, and about the rings. His smile deepened in anticipation of the night to come, and of the new freedom it would bring.

"You needn't look so smug," Elisa said, confronting him. "Everyone can see how you are eyeing your mistress."

"Actually, I was watching you," Rob responded. Unwilling to reopen the dispute about Kasia, he added, "Your gown is very becoming. Though I do confess, I have been wondering how to remove it quickly without tearing it.

"Have you noticed that we are standing beneath the mistletoe?" he asked. He reached up to pluck a berry from the small bunch hanging above the entry arch. "A berry for every kiss, isn't that right?" He lifted her wrist and dropped the waxy white berry into her hand.

Elisa stared at the berry for an instant, then glanced up at him as if wondering how to respond. While she decided between continued anger or a sweeter reaction, he wasn't going to give her the chance to say a word. He leaned forward and planted a lingering kiss on her parted lips. Then he pitched his voice to a low and seductive level.

"We have slept apart for too long. I have missed you badly."

"Don't mock me," she said, sounding as if she was on the verge of tears.

"Elisa, I wish you would listen with your heart and stop continually misunderstanding me."

"I think I understand you perfectly," she retorted, and turned her back on him.

Rob stepped closer, placing his hands on her shoulders so firmly that she could not leave him without drawing public attention to her action. He let one finger slide slowly across the bare skin that rose from the wide neckline of her dress. Gently he stroked her nape and felt her shiver in response.

He wished he could toss her over his shoulder and carry her up the stairs and throw her onto their bed. She wouldn't like that. Elisa was devoted to duty, and to propriety. She'd think he was behaving inappropriately. Besides, she was still annoyed with him. He'd have to woo her into compliance. That was a delicious thought. While he was stirring her desires, his own passion would be heightened.

It was going to be a memorable night.

He bent toward his wife and softly blew upon the nape of her neck. A few loose strands of golden hair waved in the gentle breeze he created. He'd like to grab the gold hairnet and pull it off, so her luxuriant curls could tumble down over her shoulders. He loved to weave his fingers through her hair.

Elisa whirled to face him, her eyes glittering with rage. She said nothing, just looked hard at him for a moment, then walked away and began to talk with some of the guests. Rob watched her, amused by her rejection. He knew it meant nothing.

"You will come to me in the end," he said softly, with complete confidence.

"You were stalking me," Elisa accused him the moment they were alone in the lord's chamber. "All evening long, as if you were the hunter and I your prey. Everyone noticed."

"Let them. I don't care."

"I do. Leave me my dignity," she said, striking the flints together with vicious energy in a vain attempt to light the bedside lamp. "You've left me nothing else."

"You have a great deal, if only you would forget your fevered imaginings and open your eyes to see what is real." He took the flint away from her.

With a manly efficiency that infuriated her, he struck a spark into the lint, blew on it, and used the small resulting flame to light the wick of the oil lamp.

"There," he murmured. "Now I can see you while I undress you."

"No," she said in a quiet little voice.

"Come here, Elisa." He reached for her, smiling and eager.

"No," she repeated, her voice a bit stronger this time.

"What did you say?" His smile began to fade.

"I said no. I said it twice. I have never refused you before, but I have told you, and I repeat it now, I will not lie with you while Kasia is in this castle."

"I am lord here. You will do as I command."

"If you want my body, you will have to rape me."

First he looked astonished, then he burst into laughter.

Deeply insulted by his reaction, Elisa looked around for something, anything, to throw at him. Before she could find a suitable object, he pulled her to him and kissed her in a way that left no doubt about his immediate intentions. His tongue surged into her mouth; his powerful hands forced her hips hard against him.

She clawed at his shoulders, afraid of her own rapidly rising desire. If she gave in to him now, she would never succeed in making her point. Rob would continue to believe he could disregard her feelings and do whatever he wanted.

Oh, but he was warm and strong, and she loved the sheer masculine force of his passion. Once he was thoroughly aroused, nothing deterred him. She could feel the hard evidence of his growing need. Her own need matched his. He would give her the completion she craved, and the closeness of his body—but just for a short time, and it would be only his body that would be close to her. Rob's heart lay elsewhere.

She pushed both fists hard against his chest, and when he loosened his grip on her slightly, she tore herself out of his arms.

"Either you will leave this room, or I will," she said, breathing hard, fighting to keep herself from him when all she really wanted was to lie beneath him and feel his warm skin next to hers. To feel his body inside hers. She shut her eyes to rid herself of the sight of his beloved face turning angry and cold as he realized that she meant what she was saying.

"Just as this is your castle, containing your guests, so this is your chamber," she said. "I will join Christina in her room."

"The devil you will." He was so composed, so icy-cold, that he terrified her. "There are enough warm beds in Menton where I will be welcomed. Good night, my lady."

He was gone, and Elisa collapsed onto the bed, shaking with relief. It took a few minutes before she realized what she had done. There was only one warm bed where he was likely to go. In refusing Rob his husbandly rights she had sent him from his own chamber to Kasia's bedroom.

Rob reached the great hall to find it deserted except for the few servants who routinely slept there. He tiptoed to the high table where a pitcher sat forgotten by the maids. He'd have a cup of wine while he decided how to handle his recalcitrant wife. He'd had to leave the lord's chamber. If he had stayed, he'd have done violence to the defiant wench, even though he had never struck her in the entire twenty-one years of their marriage.

He poured out the wine and gulped it down. He was damned uncomfortable, hard as a rock against his woolen hose, and it was going to be hours before that eased. He'd spent the entire afternoon and evening working up a mighty desire while he thought about the intimate pleasures of the night to come, and Elisa had refused him. Him, her lord and master! He marveled at her daring.

He ought to beat her. Another man would, without thinking twice. Ah, but if he turned Elisa over his knees and flipped up her skirts to strike the soft and rosy flesh beneath, he knew what he would do instead of administering the punishment she deserved. The realization made him harder still.

He drank another cup of wine while he considered how to make Elisa listen to what he wanted to say to her. Kasia would know exactly what to say, but Elisa would never accept Kasia's explanation. She only partly understood what lay between him and Kasia, and he wasn't sure he had the correct words in his heart with which to convince his wife. He was beginning to think Elisa would never believe what he had come home to tell her.

She would probably never let him into her bed again, either, he thought ruefully as he downed his fourth cup of wine. Recalling her declaration that he would have to rape her, he chuckled. She knew him well enough to be certain he was incapable of such an outrage.

He knew her, too—or he'd thought he did, until this day. His practical-minded, dutiful wife was growing more perplexing, and more interesting, by the moment. Still, he was not mistaken about her passionate nature. If he continued his wooing, she would soon be not only willing, but eager.

Rob poured himself another cup of wine and sat back in the lord's chair to plot the seduction of his wife.

Chapter Four

Once the holy aspects of Christmas had been properly dealt with, everyone felt free to enjoy the more earthly pleasures of food, drink, games, and other entertainments until Twelfth Night ended the long holiday.

On the day after Christmas, Elisa oversaw the huge midday feast with considerable pride. The cook at Menton was one of the finest in all England and she had outdone herself, sending to the great hall a long stream of courses: roasted fowl, manger-shaped minced-meat pies, a whole side of beef cooked to perfection, followed by steamed puddings, almond or rose-milk custards, cakes both spiced and plain, tarts made from pears, apples, and marzipan, and enough fine white bread to feed everyone at Menton, plus any beggars who waited at the castle gates.

As far as Elisa could tell, only three people were not enjoying themselves. Lady Joan sat at the high table with her head bowed, eating little, and she seldom spoke. Sir Royce was showering attention on his betrothed, so Elisa left the girl alone. Like any other noblewoman, Joan was going to have to learn to accept her father's choice of husband for her.

The second person who appeared to be unhappy was Elisa's own husband. Rob's face was so pale and he ate so little that she suspected him of having overindulged in wine after leaving her on the previous night. Perhaps he and Kasia made a habit of drinking too much when they were together, for Kasia's lovely face was also pale and drawn. With an irritated shrug Elisa dismissed the adulterous couple. Given a bit of time they would recover from their indispositions.

Meanwhile, the feast was almost over. It had begun early, so there were still a few hours of daylight left, and then the long winter evening stretched ahead. The older nobles and their ladies were content to sit in the hall watching the acrobats or listening to one of the minstrels sing, but the younger folk were growing restless. Elisa was experienced enough to know they required something vigorous to do, or else there would be serious drinking, which was sure to lead to a few fights as time wore on. She signaled to Christina to join her at the edge of the dais, then chose her words carefully, so the younger lords and ladies would not perceive what she said as an order, but only as a lighthearted suggestion.

"I must ask for your help," Elisa called out. Upon hearing her, and seeing mother and daughter standing together, the guests fell relatively quiet. Elisa waited until she could easily be heard before continuing. "Every berry has been stripped from all the branches of mistletoe that we brought in from Menton Forest three days ago. There has been entirely too much kissing!"

"In my opinion," said Rob's loud voice from the high table behind Elisa, "there has been entirely too little kissing!"

The hall erupted into laughter. Her face flaming with embarrassment, Elisa turned to glare at her husband. Unperturbed by her open disapproval, Rob grinned and lifted his wine cup as if toasting her. Then, to Elisa's surprise, Christina began to laugh and she slipped an arm around Elisa's waist.

"Whether too much kissing, or too little," Christina declared, "there will be no more kissing at all, unless we bring home enough mistletoe to last until Twelfth Night. There is daylight left, so who is with me? Who will ride into the forest in search of more kissing boughs?"

Her request brought forth cheers from every guest under the age of thirty, including Sir James the hostage knight, from a goodly number of men-at-arms, and from a few of the entertainers, too. They all began to scatter to their rooms, preparing to don warm outdoor clothing. Even Lady Joan allowed Sir Royce to take her hand and assist her down from the dais.

"Mother, what a delightful idea," Christina said, still with her arm around Elisa. "If I want to lead the expedition, I'd better hurry and change my clothes."

"I thought you hated the cold," Elisa responded in wonder at the change in her daughter. "I thought you'd far rather stay indoors and read."

"Ordinarily, I would, but you need my help. You said you do. That's true, isn't it?"

"Oh, yes," Elisa answered. "I don't want to leave the castle, not with so many guests remaining behind. It would be rude for their hostess to desert them. You will have to act as my deputy."

"I'll do it gladly. I know where the best mistletoe is. William showed me when we were children. The servants you sent out days ago never found the place, or they'd have brought in a lot more branches than they did." Christina bestowed a warm hug on her mother, then rushed off to find a suitable dress and heavy cloak. Elisa gazed after her, still astonished at the sudden change.

"Perhaps you have been doing too much for her," Rob said from directly behind Elisa. "Perhaps you are so competent and so quick at your duties that you have made Christina afraid to try, lest she fall short of your example."

"Are you criticizing me?" Elisa spun around to face him. She misjudged the distance to the edge of the dais and nearly fell backward off it. Rob caught her, holding her close and smiling down at her.

"I'd like to hold you closer still," he murmured, his lips against her cheek. "You smell of roses and cinnamon."

"You've had too much to drink," she told him.

"That was last night. I spent last night," he said, speaking so solemnly that she could not doubt his words, "sitting in the lord's chair, drinking, while I thought about you. Now I have spent more hours sitting in the lord's chair during the feast, and I grow restless."

"If you feel the need of exercise, then join the mistletoe hunt," she suggested, trying to free herself from his embrace without drawing undue notice from their guests.

"That is not the kind of exercise I want. I'd rather stay at home," he said. "I'll be far warmer, and I can enjoy watching you until the young ones return. When they do, I'll stand beneath the heaviest mistletoe bough and remove every berry, one by one. A berry for every kiss."

"You will embarrass Kasia," she snapped at him.

"Not Kasia. You. I do like to watch you blush in confusion. I'll redden your cheeks and weaken your knees before I'm done." He kissed her softly, a gentle brushing of lips over lips. "That was meant as a promise for later," he whispered.

Elisa saw the gleam of determination in his eyes and knew he was not going to be put off for a second night. He was going to lie with her that night, and it was her duty to submit. If the truth be told, and she would never tell it to him, she was not unwilling. Where Rob was concerned she had never been unwilling; she wanted him, but she wanted him to love her, not just use her. And with Kasia a guest in his castle, she feared he would never find his wife to be anything more than a convenience.

It was after dark when the mistletoe hunters returned, cheeks and noses red from the cold, eyes sparkling, their chatter filling the entry and then the great hall. One of the youths, Wallace, had been injured by a group of brigands. After Rob sent out a small party of men-at-arms to apprehend the outlaws, Elisa turned her attention to the greenery the young folk had gathered.

"Where are we to hang all of it?" Elisa asked, staring at the pile of branches wrapped in an old horse blanket that two men-at-arms carried into the hall and laid on the floor.

"You gave this project to me," Christina responded. "Please, Mother, let me handle everything."

"I'll see that she does," Rob told his daughter, before Elisa could offer any suggestions. He stooped to pluck a small branch of mistletoe from the pile on the blanket. It was heavily loaded with berries and he smiled, examining it. "This will do nicely," he said, his eyes twinkling.

"Do for what?" Christina asked, teasing him.

"Never mind, child. Just see that the rest of this stuff is hung," Rob answered her. Then, deliberately, he looked at Elisa, lifted one eyebrow in a mischievous query, and raised the mistletoe branch for her to see.

Several hours later, when Elisa had completed her evening chores and reached the lord's chamber, she discovered the branch fastened to the curtain at the head of the bed. She was trying to decide whether she possessed the courage to tear it down when Rob entered. One of his squires followed, bearing a tray with a pitcher of wine, a single silver goblet, and a small silver bowl.

"Put it on the clothing chest," Rob said to the squire, "then leave us and see that we are not disturbed unless the castle is attacked.

"Attack," he said to Elisa as the squire departed, "is most unlikely on so cold a night and during a holy season. The chances are good that we will have the entire night to ourselves." He unbuckled his belt, then pulled his tunic and linen undershirt over his head and kicked off his boots.

"I assume from the size of the wine pitcher that you intend to drink yourself into insensibility," Elisa noted rather crossly. "Go right ahead, my lord." She was trying hard not to look her fill at his manly chest, but she relished the sight of him and loved watching the way the muscles of his upper body flexed and then relaxed. He had been gone from Menton for far too long, and she had missed him entirely too much.

"I thought we could share the same goblet, as we did on our wedding night," Rob said. "Do you remember how the servants forgot to put a second goblet on the tray, and we never noticed until after everyone but the two of us was gone from our chamber? And how you wouldn't let me call anyone back, because we had already been formally put to bed?"

Elisa stared at him, unable to speak for the emotions and the memories that crowded her mind.

"You were a terrified virgin," Rob said, filling the wine goblet.

"I was never afraid of you," she declared.

"A nervous bride, then," he amended. "A virgin, certainly, and I gave you wine to stop your trembling before I took you into my arms for the first time."

"Why speak of something that happened so long ago?"

"Because I want to remember that night, how I drank and passed our single goblet to you, and you turned it until your lips pressed the very spot where mine had been. I want to remember the way you gave yourself to me in innocent trust. I believed then, and I still believe, that you were not disappointed by the way we consummated our marriage."

"You were kind and generous," she whispered, "but you did not love me."

"How could I? We had only just met that morning." His eyes on hers, Rob drank from the silver goblet, then handed it to her. "Don't believe the songs the troubadours sing, my dear. Few men fall passionately into love at first sight. Most of us have to know a woman for a while before we begin to feel anything deep and lasting for her. I will confess that most men never do fully understand any woman. I certainly don't."

"Nor do I understand you," she said, and almost bit her tongue to keep herself from asking why he wasn't with Kasia.

"Drink." Rob's fingers were warm over hers on the cool metal goblet. He lifted the goblet to her lips and she obeyed him, swallowing the honey-sweetened, spiced wine.

"You cannot recreate a night that occurred twenty-one years ago," she said. "Too much has happened since then."

"I know." Still with his hand over hers, he raised the goblet to his own mouth and drank. "There is no reason why we cannot create new memories."

"I don't want—"

"Yes, you do," he interrupted. "I see longing in your eyes. You are as starved for my embrace as I am for yours."

"I don't think you have been starving at all during your absence."

"Hush. I will permit no harsh words between us tonight." He set the goblet down on the tray, then came back to her. Before Elisa could protest or think of a way to stop him, he caught at the golden mesh of her hair net and tossed it aside. His fingers combed through her hair, loosening it till the weight of it curled across her shoulders and down her back. "I have wanted to do that ever since I came home. I do so like your hair, Elisa." He lifted a handful of the heavy locks to his face, breathing in the rose and cinnamon perfume she used to scent her hair.

A moment later his hands were on her breasts and his mouth was caressing her throat. Elisa threw back her head to give him freer access to her rapidly warming skin, knowing she was lost, as she had been lost to desire on her wedding night and on every occasion since then whenever Rob had wanted her. Loving him as she did, she was incapable of resisting his passion. He was the only man for whom she had ever yearned. She only wished that she were the one woman for him.

Spurred by injured pride, she did make a feeble effort to fight him, though she did not really want him to stop what he was doing. Her attempt lasted only a moment or two, before she gave it up and allowed him to undress her. When her gown lay in an untidy pile on top of her clothing chest, Rob sat her on the edge of the bed and knelt to pull off her shoes, to unfasten her ribbon garters and roll down her stockings.

"There," he said, kissing her ankles, "now there's only your shift between me and what I want."

He slid one arm around her back and the other beneath her knees, picking her up, holding her against his naked chest. She was keenly aware of his warmth, and of his handsome, clean-shaven face close to hers. She expected him to kiss her, but he didn't. He just grinned at her in that mischievous, infuriating way of his, as if he thought he could read her mind. Then he tossed her onto the bed. She landed with her head directly beneath the mistletoe bough.

"Oh!" she gasped in surprise. Then: "Just what do you think you are doing?"

"After all these years, you ought to know the answer to that," he said. He grabbed the silver bowl from the tray and placed it on the table beside the bed, where the flickering oil lamp set the burnished metal aglow. Then he sat and removed his hose.

"Oh, Rob." Elisa stared at the size of him, her mouth suddenly gone dry with longing.

"Aye," he said, stretching out beside her, "it's been a long time. Far too long. But I'll not rush you. We'll do this slowly. We have much to repair."

"As you wish, my lord." Elisa tried to sound demure, when in fact she was horrified to realize just how desperately she wanted him. It was not seemly for a woman to lust after her own husband. She reminded herself that she was about to perform a duty, and so was Rob.

"So solemn," he whispered, kissing the tip of her nose. "Always serious, always bound to responsibility. It's been years since I've heard you laugh."

"I take my duties seriously," she said. "My mother trained me well."

"The only complaint I have of you," he whispered, nuzzling at her neck, "is your lack of humor. I promise, I will try to cure that fault, for I think it's partly my doing."

Then, unexpectedly, he was on his knees, reaching

for the mistletoe bough, picking berries from it.

"A berry for each kiss," he said, reciting the well-known rule. "One berry, then, for each of your ankles, at least a dozen for every kiss to your throat, and one for your nose." He threw the berries into the silver bowl.

"What nonsense," she responded.

"My lady, do you dare to mock an ancient tradition?" he teased.

He was still kneeling beside her, and Elisa suspected he was deliberately flaunting his masculinity, almost in her face. She resisted the urge to touch him, to feel the hard length of him pulsing beneath her caressing fingers.

"We have a lot of kissing to do, if we are going to denude this branch before morning," Rob said. "I will require your fullest cooperation."

"You're mad," she whispered, trembling at the look in his eyes.

"Only hungry." He bent to kiss her forehead and brush the golden curls away from her face. "So hungry, for your eyes, and your ears, for your cheeks, and even for your stubborn chin." He kissed each part of her as he named it, and for every kiss he removed another mistletoe berry and tossed it into the bowl beside the bed.

"Most of all, I'm hungry for your lips." His mouth covered hers, warm and firm, enticing her into responding. His tongue teased at the corner of her lips and she opened her mouth, moaning softly as he entered and began to suck on her tongue. His large hand cupped her breast, sending heat far into her body.

"Ah," he murmured a few minutes later, "that kiss was worth at least two berries. Perhaps, even three."

"This isn't a game," she reproved him.

"Why can't it be? Why can't we play with each other?"

"That is a most improper suggestion," she exclaimed, and tried to wriggle away from him.

"Do you think I care about propriety?" he asked, laughing at her puny efforts to stop what he was doing.

He slid down to lie beside her again, thereby depriving her of the sight of his eager manhood, though she could feel it pressing against her thigh. She closed her eyes, ashamed of how much she wanted him.

"Are you truly unwilling?" he asked. "Do you really despise me so much? Shall I leave now and spend another night in the great hall?"

"No!" Elisa opened her eyes to see him grinning at her.

"That's what I thought," he said.

"You beast!" She pounded her fists against his shoulders until he rolled on top of her and took her mouth again in a deep, hot kiss that destroyed every last vestige of her resistance. Her fingers wound through his thick hair, pulling him closer.

"There's a certain pleasure in overcoming the obstacles you throw in my path," he said. "The battle only makes the victory sweeter."

His fingers were at her nipples, stroking round and round, working a slow and tormenting magic on all her senses. She cried out in protest when he finally took his hands away from her breasts. He moved on then, to caress her waist and hips, molding the soft, womanly flesh in his strong and gentle hands until Elisa felt as if her skin were on fire.

Long minutes passed. Rob took his time, as he had promised, kissing her again and again, deep, leisurely kisses, not rushing her, letting the conflagration inside her rise higher and higher. He seemed to know when she could bear no more, and chose the perfect instant to reach farther still. Gently he separated her thighs and touched her heat and moistness.

"Oh, Rob."

"Say you missed me," he whispered. "I want to hear you say it."

"I missed you." She could not tear her gaze from his vivid blue eyes.

"Say you want me," he commanded, kneeling between her thighs.

"I want you. Heaven help me, I do want you! So much."

"Heaven won't help you at this moment," he whispered. "But I will. Like this. And then, like this."

He pushed against her softness and she opened to him easily, eagerly, until he was buried in her warmth and she was complete at last.

"Oh, Rob." Her words were a long, soft sigh.

"Yes," he said, "I know. I've missed you, too."

He said something else, but Elisa was beyond hearing, and beyond reason. For those few precious moments Rob was entirely hers and she gladly returned his passion, fitting herself to his strong, smooth stroking motions, which were perfectly matched to her own needs. In this aspect of their marriage, at least, they were completely suited to each other. She would have continued their closeness indefinitely, but she felt the tension building and her release was upon her too quickly, too sweetly and irresistibly, and she cried out in mingled pleasure and sorrow.

"Elisa!"

Rob gathered her so tightly against him that she could barely breathe, but she didn't care about that. She knew that he, too, was swept away by the urgent demands of passion, that for him in that moment, she was the only other person in the world. She kept her arms around him, and kissed his cheek, and silently offered to him all the love she usually kept locked up in her heart, until he withdrew from her and rose on his elbows to look down at her.

"Why are you crying?" he asked, gently wiping away the tears she had shed.

"It's silly of me, but it was so lovely that the tears just came."

"You aren't silly at all. In fact, what we just did was worth more mistletoe berries than we have here. I shall have to ride into the forest tomorrow and search out a branch heavy enough with berries to do justice to your passion. And to mine. I'll save the new branch for tomorrow night, shall I?" he asked, his mischievous smile appearing.

"Can you never be serious?"

"I was only teasing. I do wish you could tease me back, just now and then."

"My lord, we need to have a serious talk," she said.

"Not now. Tomorrow. I have something serious to say to you, too, but I want my full wits about me when I do." With a huge yawn he settled under the quilt, resting his head upon her bosom. "Call me Rob again before I sleep," he murmured. "I much prefer it to 'my lord.'"

"Rob." She stroked his hair and kissed his brow until, when she was certain he was asleep and wouldn't hear her, she said what she had wanted to say since their first night as man and wife. "I love you, Rob. I always will."

Chapter Five

When Elisa opened her eyes the next morning the first thing she saw was the mistletoe branch, which hung bedraggled from the pin Rob had used to fasten it to the bed curtain. Only two berries were left on it. The second thing Elisa saw was the silver bowl overflowing with the berries Rob had plucked during their long night of passion. She smiled to herself and closed her eyes again, snuggling into the warmth of the quilt. She could tell without even putting out her hand that Rob was gone. His absence did not disturb her, for through the mists of sleep she could dimly recall him whispering that he would return in a little while.

The light against her closed lids told her the sun was rising. On any other morning she would have been long out of bed, dressed, and attending to her numerous duties. But not today. She wanted a few quiet moments in which to think about all the lovely things Rob had done to her—and the things he had asked her to do to him. Never in all their marriage had they been so free with each other. Rob had whispered, and groaned, and on one wild occasion toward the end of the night, he had shouted out his pleasure in a voice so loud that she feared he would waken at least some of their guests. They had kissed away almost all of the berries on the mistletoe bough.

He had not said that he loved her, had not spoken at all about his feelings for her.

Nor had he instigated the serious conversation he'd claimed they must have. A chilly draft of insecurity touched the edges of Elisa's physical contentment as she began to wonder about the subject of that deferred conversation.

The bedchamber door opened and she heard Rob's low whisper as he instructed a servant. Elisa stayed where she was, with the quilt drawn up to her ears, feigning sleep.

After another whispered conversation the door opened and closed again, and Elisa sensed that the servant was dismissed and she and Rob were alone. A moment later the mattress sank and she knew Rob was sitting on the far side of the bed.

He began to blow on the curls that covered her forehead. Elisa brushed at her hair as if a bee were buzzing around her head, and tugged the quilt higher still.

"Have you forgotten about our guests?" Rob asked, nibbling along the top of her ear. "While you've been sleeping, I've been making plans."

"What plans? What have you done?" Fully awake now, she sat up abruptly, the quilt falling back to reveal her bare shoulders and breasts.

"I knew that would wake you." Rob placed a row of kisses across her right shoulder and down to her breast, where he paused to suck and tease with his tongue.

"There are no berries left," she said a little breathlessly.

"You are mistaken, my lady. Here are two berries." He picked them with thumb and forefinger and held them before her eyes.

"You just spent those," she told him, squirming a little as the air cooled the sensitive place where his mouth had been. She wished he would kiss her breast again, but she warned herself to be sensible and pay attention to what he was saying.

"Must I pay for every kiss?" he asked.

"What is the plan you mentioned?"

"Back to duty so quickly? What a pity." He leaned across her, rubbing the woolen sleeve of his tunic against her bare breasts when he reached to dump the last mistletoe berries into the bowl. "I must find another branch to use tonight."

Elisa sat looking into his eyes, which danced with laughter and with sensual promise, and she felt the familiar heat curling low into her body.

"Do not attempt to distract me," she said, fighting her longing to put her arms around his neck and lie down on the bed, pulling him on top of her. "You spoke of a plan, my lord."

"So, it's 'my lord' now, is it?" He planted a quick kiss on her mouth and grinned, looking remarkably like a naughty boy. "I'll owe you a berry for that one, and repay it tonight. We are going hunting."

"You mean, *you* are going hunting," she corrected.

"I said 'we.' I meant 'we.' The weather is fine, though I think there may be snow tomorrow. All the more reason to hunt today. I have arranged every detail with Christina, who is proving to be remarkably capable. She has ordered the cook to prepare baskets of food for us to take along and eat in the field. All you need to do right now is break your fast with the bread and ale I have brought. I will act as your maid and help you dress. Out of bed with you, my lady!" He grabbed the edge of the quilt and pulled it to the foot of the bed, leaving Elisa naked and shivering.

"Rob, no!" She reached for the quilt, to tug it up again, but he was too quick for her. He caught her around the waist and lifted her from the bed, standing her on her feet.

"This is a novel experience for me," he said, kneeling to slide on her stockings and fasten her garters. "I'd far rather undress you than dress you, but I can't let you freeze, can I?"

There was no fighting him. He was determined that she was going to hunt with him. In just a few minutes she was bundled into a warm blue wool riding dress and soft leather boots, which Rob laced and tied for her while she tried to braid her hair neatly and eat some bread at the same time.

"What about that conversation we were going to have?" she asked, sipping a bit of ale to wash down the bread.

"My fault," he said. "I should have told you what I want to say during the night, but I was otherwise occupied. You know how busy I was."

"Plucking mistletoe berries."

"Making up for all the months I've been away." His finger traced the curve of her cheek. "You are a potent distraction from sensible thought."

"Well, the berries are all gone. Only a few leaves are left," she said, and reached to snatch the denuded branch from the bed curtain. She tossed it on top of the bowl of berries. "The distraction is ended. Tell me now what you intended to say last night."

"There's no time. I don't want to be interrupted and our guests are waiting for us. We will talk tonight."

"Will we?" she asked. "Or will you spend the night-time hours plucking more berries?"

"I'll gladly pluck whatever you are willing to give me." He tilted her chin up so he could kiss her soundly. "Come along, now. It's rude to keep our company mounted and waiting in the bailey on so cold a day. They will want to be moving."

"I need to pin up my hair." She wound the thick braid into a knot at the back of her head and secured it with a few large horn pins, conscious as she worked that Rob was holding her hooded cloak and frowning with impatience.

As soon as she finished with her hair he swung the cloak over her shoulders and grabbed her hand, pulling her down the curving stone stairway, through the entry hall, and out to the bailey.

"Where is my horse?" she asked, not seeing her usual mount.

"I've brought you a new one," he said. "Layla is a gift."

"For whom?" she demanded. "From whom?"

"For you," he answered, laughing. "From me. Come, I'll give you a hand up."

The groom holding Layla gave Elisa an apple. She fed it to the mare, then stroked Layla's neck, talking to the horse so it would become familiar with her before she mounted it. Meanwhile, she admired Layla's glossy chestnut coat and clear eyes.

"She's a beautiful animal," Elisa said to Rob.

"I think so, though at times she is a bit difficult to handle," he replied, looking at Elisa in a way that made her wonder if he was talking about Layla, or about her. She placed her foot in his cupped hands and he boosted her into the saddle. When he took the reins from the groom and gave them to Elisa, she caught his hand between both of hers.

"Thank you, Rob. Layla is a wonderful present."

"I know you well enough to think you'd rather have a fine horse than jewelry," he said.

"You were right; I would." Elisa didn't smile often,

but she smiled at Rob now. His answering smile and sparkling eyes held a warm promise.

The rest of the hunting party was already filing through the gatehouse, eager for the chance of exercise. The women all rode astride, for that was the only way to maintain control of a horse while racing across a rough countryside.

Elisa loved the feeling of freedom that riding gave her and she had no difficulty keeping up with Rob. The beat of the horses' hooves upon the frozen earth and the jingle of harness were music to her. The air was crisp and clear, with just a light coat of snow on the ground. When Rob paused to loose his falcon, Elisa drew up close to him and their breaths mingled in a frosty little cloud. She watched Rob watching the falcon take flight and knew a moment of intense, pure happiness.

Those were near-perfect hours, made all the more precious because Kasia was not among the hunters. She had chosen to remain at Menton with the older guests who preferred the fires in the great hall to the out-of-doors.

By the time the sun began to set on the short midwinter day and Rob and his guests turned homeward, they had bagged enough gamebirds to restock the larder for at least one meal, and a group of the younger knights and ladies, who had gone off on their own, returned with a small boar.

Elisa rode beside her husband in a state of contentment that was most unusual for her. Just a glance at Rob warmed her, and when he saw her looking at him and smiled at her as if he understood what she was feeling, her heart began to pound. She was looking forward to the night to come as eagerly as a young girl awaiting her lover.

* * *

As soon as she entered the castle keep Elisa consigned all of the game being brought in by the servants to Christina's care, telling her to decide what the cook was to do with it. Having relieved herself of that duty, Elisa called to her personal maidservant to follow her and hastened up the stairs to the lord's chamber.

There was no time for the full bath she wanted, but she made good use of the large pitcher of hot water the maid brought. She doused herself liberally with the rose and cinnamon perfume of her own making, then changed into a lavender silk shift and a gown of honey-colored silk. She let the maid arrange her hair. When it was piled high on her head and held in place with gold pins winking with amethysts, the maid draped over the coiffure a veil that was little more than a small scarf of sheer silk in a pale shade of lavender. The fabric drifted around Elisa's golden curls like a wisp of smoke. Over the veil, holding it in place, Elisa wore the gold circlet that was the emblem of her noble rank. Like her dangling gold earrings and the golden bracelets on each wrist, the circlet was set with amethysts.

Elisa told the maid to hold her hand mirror while she moved around, trying to catch glimpses of her reflection, so she could judge how she appeared from head to toe.

"You are beautiful, my lady," the maid said.

"I'm too old to be beautiful, but I do want to look my best. I want Rob to be proud of me." She wanted him to find her seductive, though she did not say that to the maid. Nor did she reveal that her desire for Rob's approval was the reason she was taking so much trouble with her clothing and jewels.

She pulled cautiously at the narrow line of the shift that showed above the neckline of her dress, hoping Rob would notice it and speculate about what she was wearing beneath the fine gown. She shivered in delicious anticipation to think of his reaction after he removed the heavy dress and discovered her clad in only a shift of sheer, lavender silk. Perhaps she would leave on her veil and circlet until after he undressed her, so Rob could have the pleasure of removing them, as well as her hairpins. He had said he liked her hair, so she would let him loosen it.

Suddenly, she found it difficult to breathe. Never before had she deliberately tried to entice her husband, and she found that her preparations were exciting her, too. Tonight, she would welcome Rob into their bed and repay his passion with her own mounting desire.

Her toilette completed, she dismissed the maidservant, then stood a bit uncertainly, wondering if she ought to wait for Rob to come to the lord's chamber. She decided it wasn't likely. He had told her he was going to the mews to see his favorite falcon settled, and then on to the bathhouse to wash away the sweat of hard riding. One of his squires had probably taken fresh clothing to the bathhouse for him.

Reminding herself sternly that duties awaited her below, Elisa took two deep breaths and placed a hand over her heart to calm herself before she walked out of the lord's chamber and started down the stairs on her way to the great hall. She came around the curve of the stairway and halted, shocked by the sight before her.

Rob was standing in the entry hall, at the foot of the staircase. He was wearing clean clothes, with his hair still wet from his bath—and with his arms around Kasia. Kasia's perfectly arranged red hair glowed like fire against the blue silk shoulder of Rob's tunic. Kasia murmured something that Elisa could not hear clearly, and Rob responded in a soft, reassuring tone of voice. His lips brushed across Kasia's forehead.

Elisa descended another step. Rob must have heard

the rustle of her skirt, for he looked up and their eyes met. She saw his surprise at her unexpected appearance, but she could discern no sign of guilt or remorse in him.

"My lord," Elisa said in a voice as cold as ice. "I trust you have an explanation for such a disgusting public display of illicit affection."

She could see Rob turning as cold as she was. When Kasia stirred and lifted her head from his shoulder, as if she intended to turn and face Elisa, Rob only tightened his arms around her.

"See to our guests, Elisa," Rob commanded. "Say nothing of what has happened here."

"Say nothing?" Elisa repeated. "Do you imagine I would enjoy telling *your* guests—or your daughter— what you are doing?"

"You and I will talk later," Rob said.

"Whenever it pleases you, my lord," she responded scornfully. "Whenever you can spare the time."

She descended the last few stairs, brushed past Rob and his mistress without another word, and stalked across the entry toward the arch that opened to the great hall. She kept her head up high, reminding herself that she was a noblewoman who was trained never to show her true feelings in public.

Pride and duty, she told herself. *For a woman, pride and duty are all that matter.*

Still, she could not stop herself from looking back before she stepped into the great hall.

Rob had lifted Kasia into his arms and was carrying her up the stairs. Kasia's arms were around Rob's neck. Elisa could not see her face because it was pressed tight against Rob's shoulder.

Elisa felt hollow, as if the heart and soul were ripped out of her, leaving only the shell of the person she had been just a short time ago.

You knew it all along, she reminded herself. *For

more than twenty years, you have known that he loves Kasia, and not you.

Even so, Rob's lack of shame and his willingness to let Elisa know that he was about to make love to his mistress while his wife saw to the needs of his guests were utterly bewildering to Elisa. How could he be the same man who had made tender love to her for an entire night? Was he hoping she would leave Menton and save him the trouble of dismissing her? It occurred to her that she did not really know her husband at all.

Though she would far rather have fled to the privacy of the lord's chamber, Elisa was already inside the great hall. When one of the lady guests called out a cheerful greeting to her, a lifetime of training and self-discipline took over. Scarcely aware of what she was doing, she went through the motions of being a good hostess, seeing to the comfort of the guests, supervising a lengthy late-day feast, repeatedly making the same false, trivial excuse for Rob's absence. And all the time, she was empty inside.

It was hours later before she could escape to the lord's chamber. When her maid appeared, offering to help her undress, Elisa sent the girl away, saying she wanted to be alone. From the maid's sly smile as she left, Elisa suspected her of imagining that Rob was going to arrive and take charge of the undressing himself. It was, after all, what Elisa had intended to happen, and the maid would be a fool if she had not guessed as much while assisting Elisa earlier. But it was Elisa who was the fool.

For a long time she stood in the middle of the room, unable to move. Now that no one was watching her, the noble pride that had sustained her through the interminable evening held no power to propel her any longer.

Gradually, she began to see that she was going to

have to have it out with Rob, to provoke a serious quarrel with him, if necessary. He would have to understand that she could not remain under the same roof with his mistress. Either Kasia must go from Menton at once, or Elisa would. At the moment, a quiet life in a convent held a certain attraction. Or perhaps she could go to live on one of Rob's other holdings, some distant place where he never visited.

After the day's long slide of emotion from seldom-felt happiness to complete despair, she could not think of confronting Rob that night. She was too exhausted and too close to tears, and he wasn't likely to return to his own chamber, anyway, not when he was in Kasia's warm bed.

Finally, slowly, she began to divest herself of the clothing and the ornaments she had chosen with Rob's pleasure in mind. She folded each garment carefully and put everything away in her clothing chest, then placed the gold circlet, earrings, bracelets, and hairpins neatly in her jewelry casket. She brushed out her hair and braided it for the night. She was naked and the room was cold, but Elisa felt nothing as she put out the oil lamp, climbed into the cold bed, and lay there with her eyes wide open.

Rob came to bed very late. Elisa pretended to be asleep. He undressed in the dark and stayed on his own side of the bed. Toward dawn Elisa dozed off, and when she woke, Rob was gone again.

Chapter Six

There was no escape from duty; the lady of the castle was obligated to see to the needs of castle guests, so Elisa was up and dressed as soon as the sun rose. A hasty glance into her small hand mirror revealed dark circles under her eyes and cheeks devoid of color.

"I am as pale as Kasia," she muttered to herself. She laid down the mirror, squared her shoulders, and went below to speak to the cook about the menu for the midday feast.

She was surprised to see Sir Royce and Lady Joan awake so early. They were sitting together at one end of the high table, sharing bread and talking in low voices.

"Perhaps one happy pairing can come out of this miserable Christmas season," Elisa said as she passed through the great hall on her way to the kitchen.

When she came back into the hall later, Christina and the minstrel were also there, deep in conversation. Not having the heart to think about pleasures,

Elisa decided she would continue to leave the holiday entertainment in Christina's hands.

The next person Elisa saw was Kasia.

"Good morning, my lady," Kasia said, smiling at her. "Do you know where Rob is?"

"You would know that better than I," Elisa responded coldly. Then, remembering her manners, she said more politely, "I have not seen my husband this morning. He rose before I did."

"Thank you." Kasia started to walk away, then stopped and laid a hand on Elisa's arm. "Value what you have in Rob. He's the best friend I have ever known. He has never failed me."

"I am sure he has not." Elisa spoke through stiff lips, fighting to maintain her composed demeanor.

"You must talk to him," Kasia said. "More importantly, you must *listen* to him. I think you have been sorely mistaken in your opinion of Rob."

Kasia's thin face was intent and her pale hand trembled on Elisa's sleeve. Elisa thought she knew why. No doubt Kasia expected Rob to declare to his wife that he preferred his mistress.

"Excuse me, my lady." Elisa walked away from Kasia with her fists clenched.

She retreated to the stillroom, believing she could find a few moments of peace there. But she had forgotten that Christina was holding the key. The door was unlocked, proof of great carelessness for which she was going to have to scold her daughter. Elisa's neatly arranged shelves of jars containing herbal medicines were in disarray, and a bunch of lavender that should have been hanging from the ceiling to finish drying lay on the floor, instead. There were dried leaves scattered on the worktable, some of them clinging to the stirring spoon, which contained a sticky substance.

"Horehound syrup," Elisa said, picking up the

spoon and sniffing at it. "Christina, why can't you be neater? Apparently, you brought the minstrel here to treat his sore throat and then you neglected to straighten up after yourself."

Ordinarily, she would have been greatly annoyed to find her herbal potions in such disorder, but on this particular day she was glad of an excuse to remain in the stillroom while she set things aright and, at the same time, composed her emotions. Surely, no one would disturb her.

A while later she was wiping the last of the horehound syrup off the tabletop when Rob walked into the room.

"I thought I'd find you here," he said. "Do you have any poppy syrup?"

"Good day to you, too, my lord." She glared at him, but he took no notice of her cold anger.

"Poppy syrup," he repeated. "I need as much as you have, at once."

"Is someone injured? A broken bone? Or a bad sprain?"

"No. I want it for Kasia. Her supply is almost used up."

Elisa went very still, looking directly into his eyes, silently demanding an explanation.

"I know you have some," Rob said, sounding irritated. He surveyed the shelves, frowning as he looked from jar to bottle to vial. "Where is it?"

"Why does Kasia use poppy syrup?"

"Because she's in pain, damn it!"

"Is she?" Elisa spoke almost absently, while her mind was putting together bits of information that she had noticed over the last few days, but had not thought much about. "Kasia is thin and very pale. She was trembling when I saw her earlier today. She eats little, and stays close to the fire, as if she is constantly cold. She refused to go hunting yesterday. All of which leads me to conclude that Kasia is gravely ill."

"I cannot break her confidence," Rob said when Elisa looked at him expectantly.

"You can tell me whether you carried her to her bed last evening because she suddenly felt too sick to attend the feast," Elisa said. "I deserve to know that much, Rob."

"That's what she said. But she doesn't want anyone to know. She doesn't want pity."

"How could I not have seen what was right before my eyes?" Elisa cried, genuinely puzzled.

"You are so consumed by your sense of duty, and by the practical details of everyday life, that you often fail to notice the feelings of others," Rob told her bluntly. "It is your greatest fault. You misjudged your own daughter, imagining Christina to be incapable of handling domestic problems."

"Speaking of domestic matters, Christina left this room in a sorry state, which I have just finished repairing."

"She has done a fine job of seeing that our guests are well entertained. You have misundertood me, too," Rob said. "Sometimes, I think you do it deliberately, to keep me at a distance."

"After what you've done, bringing your mistress here to Menton and spending the night with her, how dare you speak like that to me?" Elisa turned away from his accusing glance to snatch up the small bottle of poppy syrup, which she had replaced on the shelf just moments before Rob arrived.

"I'll take this," Rob said, removing the bottle from her fingers. With his free hand he caught her elbow. "You are coming with me, to administer the proper dosage to Kasia, and then to hear what she, and I, have to say." He hustled Elisa out of the stillroom and along the short corridor to the entry hall.

"Can you possibly think I am so spiteful and cruel

that I would deny medicine to a sick woman?" Elisa demanded of him. When he did not respond, she asked, "Is this to be the important conversation you were so determined to have with me? With Kasia included?"

"Definitely." They reached the stairs to the upper levels of the keep. Still with his hand gripping Elisa's elbow, Rob pushed her ahead of him up the steps. "I can think of no other way to convince you that Kasia is not my mistress, except to force you to listen to us— and I intend to make certain that, for once, you do not misunderstand my meaning."

Rob's brusque manner changed as soon as they reached Kasia's room. The maidservant who was attending Kasia left at his quiet order. He released Elisa's elbow and went to the bed where Kasia lay, still dressed, atop the covers.

"I've brought help," Rob told her softly.

"Elisa, I am sorry to trouble you when you are so busy," Kasia said.

"I apologize for not recognizing earlier that you are ill," Elisa responded, thoroughly ashamed of the jealousy that had prevented her from seeing what was so obvious now. She moved closer to the bed, looking hard at Kasia's drawn face and her wraithlike form. Elisa noted an unpleasantly sweet odor that overcame the rather heavy perfume that Kasia doubtless wore to cover up the smell. It was the same odor that had surrounded Elisa's mother for weeks before she died of a cancer in her breast. Understanding and sympathy banished the last traces of jealousy.

"You are in pain," Elisa said, "and probably nauseated, too. I'll mix the syrup with some wine, to make it easier to swallow." She took a cup from the bedside table and set to work.

"Please, don't tell anyone else about this," Kasia begged.

"I won't," Elisa promised.

"I wouldn't have let Rob ask you for medicine, but I've used all of my own syrup. I seem to need more and more of it."

"So did my mother," Elisa said, handing the cup of wine and syrup to Kasia. "I have a good supply of poppy juice in the stillroom, so I can easily make more of the syrup, or if you need help quickly, we can simply put some drops of the juice into sweetened wine. If you are queasy, it will need disguising. In its raw state the stuff has a dreadful taste."

"Thank you." Kasia drank some of the wine. "Let me repay your kindness, Elisa. Rob has told me that you believe I am his lover. I am not. I never have been."

"Kasia," Rob protested, "after the pain you endured last night, you are worn out. You ought to rest. Let me do the talking."

"I don't have time to rest," Kasia told him with a wistful smile. "But I am weary, so I will allow you to tell Elisa the truth, while I listen and correct you when necessary. Please, Elisa, sit here." Kasia patted the bed and Elisa, too startled and curious to refuse, sat beside her rival and prepared to listen.

"Elisa, you have always been right about one thing," Rob began. "I did prefer Kasia to you all those years ago, in large part because she and I were often together as children. Kasia was the one girl I knew well—or thought I knew. I was not particularly overjoyed by my father's choice of you as my wife. I vowed to be honorable in my marriage to you but, being a romantic young fool, I considered Kasia my secret love, and all the more so after she was married off to a man old enough to be her grandfather. Later, as I grew to know you better, I began to realize how misplaced my youthful infatuation was. As for Kasia, all her life she has loved another."

"Let me tell this part, Rob," Kasia said, taking his hand. "The syrup is working and the pain is receding. Before I fall asleep, let me say what Elisa deserves to hear.

"I never wanted to marry any man. From the time I was a little girl, my hope was to enter a convent. When I told my father, he said he could not allow it, that he needed to use me to make an alliance with another noble family. But he wasn't a heartless man, so he chose an elderly spouse for me, a baron who already had three sons for heirs and thus did not require more children, a kindly husband who only wanted a wife to be a nurse to him in his declining years. I did take care of him, and he always treated me well. Many noblewomen lead harsher lives. When he died last summer, I honestly grieved for him. But now I am free at last to follow my first and only love. When I leave Menton I will enter a convent, and there I will marry my Holy Bridegroom."

"Until late yesterday," Elisa said when Kasia paused to drink a little more wine, "you seemed to me to be a happy woman—radiantly happy."

"What you see in Kasia is the shining light of conviction," Rob said, "the joyous knowledge that she is following her own true path toward a world that she believes will be far better than this one. The two of us talked a great deal on our way to Menton from court," he ended with a smile for the sick woman.

"That's true," Kasia said, returning his smile. "I came to Menton to spend a last Christmas with the friend who has been like a brother to me for most of my life.

"A brother," Kasia repeated, her voice growing slurred from the syrup that was easing her into sleep. "A constant friend. Never a lover. You must believe that, Elisa."

"I do believe it." Elisa took the empty cup from Kasia's hand. "Thank you for telling me the truth."

She set the cup down. Finding an extra quilt atop the clothes chest, she covered Kasia, who appeared to have fallen into a deep and peaceful sleep. Rob was still holding Kasia's hand when Elisa slipped out of the room.

Elisa had to get out of the castle, away from the demands made on her and away from Rob. She ran up the stairs to the lord's chamber to snatch her heaviest cloak from the clothes chest, then down the steps again and out into the bailey, where she stopped the first stableboy she met.

"Saddle my horse," she ordered, not pausing on her way to the stables, sweeping the lad along with her in her haste.

"You'll want a groom to ride with you," the stable boy said. "Or I could go," he added hopefully.

"I intend to ride alone. No, not that horse," she said, seeing him heading for the stall where her usual mount was kept. "I want to ride Layla."

"Layla has been giving us some trouble this morning," the boy said.

"All the more reason to ride her. I'll tire her out so she'll be less difficult to handle."

"Yes, my lady." The stable boy knew better than to insist that a noblewoman should follow his suggestion.

Layla refused to take the bit until Elisa went into the stall to gentle her, and the horse tossed her head and balked when the stable boy led her into the bailey. Elisa was waiting at the mounting block. She swung a leg over Layla's back and settled into the saddle.

"My lady, are you sure you don't want someone to go with you?" the boy asked, looking worried as Layla sidled and danced across the bailey.

"I said no," Elisa told him. "I can handle this horse."

She proved it by keeping Layla under tight control until they were out of the gatehouse and across the moat. Then she bent to speak into Layla's ear.

"All right, girl. You need to run till your demons are banished, and I need to ride away mine, too. Go!" She touched her heels to Layla's flanks and the horse bolted forward, hooves pounding on the frozen ground. The air was bitterly cold, the wind sharp and damp with the threat of impending snow. Dark gray clouds hung heavy above.

Elisa cared nothing for the weather. Too many conflicting emotions were surging through her heart and her mind. She knew for certain that Rob and Kasia had never been lovers, for the words spoken by a dying woman were unquestionably true. All Elisa's former dislike of Kasia was gone, replaced by understanding and compassion, and by a wish that she knew of a way to cure Kasia's illness. Lacking a cure, Elisa would willingly prepare as much poppy syrup as was necessary to ease Kasia's pain.

But how, Elisa wondered, was she to deal with her heartache at hearing Rob admit that Kasia was his youthful love? He loved her still, she knew. The knowledge was bitter.

Layla slowed her headlong pace a little, and Elisa began to think of the overheated horse, and to realize that they were a surprising distance from the castle.

"I don't want to return," she said to Layla, "but you need your stall and a groom to care for you, and I have responsibilities I cannot shirk. Both of us are tethered to Menton."

She turned the horse to begin the ride back. When she looked across the intervening fields she noticed a lone rider approaching at a gallop.

"It's Rob. I'd know that bright blue cloak anywhere," she said with a sigh. "We cannot avoid him, Layla, so let us boldly go to meet him."

"What in the name of all the saints do you think you're doing?" Rob shouted at her, grabbing Layla's reins to make her stop. "Have a care for your horse, if you don't care about your own life. You know perfectly well that frozen fields and rutted roads can be dangerous. Layla could break a leg and if you are thrown when she goes down, you could freeze to death before anyone finds you."

"Which would trouble you more, my lord, the loss of a valuable horse or the loss of a dutiful chatelaine?" she demanded. She tried to pull the reins out of Rob's hands, but he refused to let them go.

"Be careful!" he scolded. "You are upsetting the horses."

"*You* are upsetting *me!*"

"Elisa, sometimes I think you are mad." He dropped Layla's reins and caught Elisa's uncovered hair, instead, almost pulling her from her saddle in his impatience. "There's no doubt that you are close to driving me mad." Leaning out of his saddle he forced her nearer, his fingers tight in her braided hair. His sudden kiss was savage, bruising her lips.

"Stop it!" She pushed him away, and came near to falling off Layla in the process. Both horses shied and turned, protesting the loud voices and sudden movements of their riders. "Now it's you who are upsetting the horses."

"You are unlike any other woman," Rob declared, watching in open admiration as Elisa regained her seat and calmed Layla. "You learn that your husband does not have a mistress, and what is the first thing you do in response to that knowledge? You go flying off across the fields like a madwoman. If it weren't for a responsible stable boy who reported to me as soon as you left, I'd not have known where to look for you. What am I to do with you?"

Say you love me, and mean it. She couldn't speak the

words. She just sat there on Layla, looking at him through tear-misted eyes, while snow began sifting down between them like a thin veil separating them.

"Elisa." He sounded calmer, and he put out his hand as if he wanted to take hers.

"You are quite right, my lord," she said, choosing to ignore his conciliatory gesture. "I believe my wits must be at least slightly deranged. However, I do have sense enough to know how wrong it is to keep an over-heated horse standing about in the cold air and snow." She nudged Layla gently and set off in the direction of the castle, leaving Rob to follow, or not, as he chose.

Chapter Seven

There was little time over the next three days for Elisa and Rob to talk—or to quarrel again. In order to keep Kasia's illness a secret as she wished, they took turns caring for her, with Kasia's maid also helping. Elisa quickly developed a deep respect for the uncomplaining way in which Kasia accepted her inevitable fate. Though it hurt to think of it, Elisa could understand why Rob was so devoted to Kasia.

"Thanks to your good herbal remedies, I've been able to sleep hours longer, and even to eat more," Kasia said to Elisa as the last day of the old year lengthened into evening. "Perhaps by tomorrow or the next day I'll be strong enough to travel and I can leave for the convent."

But when the morning came it was snowing, and when Rob joined them in Kasia's chamber, he decreed that Kasia must stay at Menton until the weather cleared.

"In that case," Kasia said, "I will test my newfound

strength by going to the great hall to sit by the fire, so you and Elisa won't have to neglect your guests any longer for my sake."

"I doubt if we'd be missed," Elisa responded. "Everyone seems remarkably content. Christina is managing very well in my place." Elisa thought with a pang of guilt that she should have been paying more attention to what Christina was doing, and she should have been watching over Lady Joan, too. She owed it to Lord Edmund to see that his daughter was enjoying herself. But then, whenever she saw Joan, the girl was with Sir Royce, and they didn't look as if they cared to be interrupted.

During those days of caring for Kasia, Elisa learned to know a Rob she had never seen before. The quiet and efficient way he cared for Kasia's needs, and his gentleness with her, revealed new aspects of Rob's character. When Elisa mentioned her surprise at his patience and at his ability to cheer Kasia, Rob responded as if there was nothing special in his kindness.

"You forget," he said, "that I have seen battle, and I've been responsible for the care my men received when they were wounded. The sick, the injured, the dying are not unfamiliar to me."

"I should have considered that," Elisa said, meeting his smile with a warm glance. "I know Kasia is grateful for your presence."

She also knew that Kasia's illness was taking its toll on Rob. There was a night when he came to the lord's chamber very late and, instead of tumbling into bed and into a deep sleep, which was his recent habit, he put his arms around Elisa and began to kiss her. She was aching for his touch, longing for another night like the one after Christmas, so she gladly accepted his caresses. His possession of her was slow and tender, and Elisa soon realized that what he was seeking in her was not passion, but comfort. Loving him, sorrowing for his grief, she opened herself to him without reservation, giving him what he needed. Afterward she held him close until he fell asleep.

Elisa told herself sadly that this was the way it would always be between them in the future, for within a few days Kasia would be gone, leaving Rob with only a bittersweet memory, one he was going to cherish for the rest of his life—and how could a mere wife compete with the memory of a man's lost first love?

On the tenth day of Christmas the sun reappeared and the snow began to melt. On the next day, the roads having cleared enough for travel, Lord Edmund finally arrived at Menton, restored to health and bringing with him his squires, including William, a few men-at-arms, and Lady Joan's maidservant, who was also recovered from her illness.

Elisa had been longing to see her handsome, golden-haired son again, yet William was clearly more engaged by the concerns of his fellow squires than by his mother's affection. He clasped his father's hand in manly greeting and bestowed a casual hug on his sister, before submitting with ill-concealed impatience to Elisa's effusive welcome.

"Mother, please!" William disentangled himself from Elisa's embrace. "Could you be a little more restrained when my friends are present?"

"I have missed you," Elisa cried, wounded by his apparent lack of caring. "I love you."

"So do I love you," William responded in a voice too low to be overheard by his companions. "But you must understand that I am no longer a little boy. I am a man, with a man's work to do. My lady, I must ask you to excuse me now." With a graceful formal bow William left his mother and hurried across the great hall to where the other squires were gathered.

"I've lost my son," Elisa whispered, half to herself.

"What did you expect?" Rob asked, seeing her crest-fallen expression. "William is right, you know; he's not a child anymore. Our boy has grown into a fine young man, who will be knighted when spring comes. We will have to think about finding a wife for him."

"I wish he could love his wife," Elisa said wistfully.

"Perhaps we'll find someone he likes and can grow to love." Rob put a hand on Elisa's shoulder as if to offer comfort for the loss she was feeling. "I do think that's the best way."

To welcome Lord Edmund as that nobleman deserved, the midday feast was especially exuberant, with the main course featuring six fine roasted geese. The men stayed up late, drinking and talking into the night long after the ladies had retired. Elisa was given no hint as to the subject of their discussion until almost noon of the day of Twelfth Night, when she was already deeply involved in preparations for the festivities of that afternoon and evening.

"Here is wonderful news," Rob said to her. "It will delight you, I know, for it's just the sort of thing women like. There is to be a wedding."

"Whose wedding?" she asked. Then, recalling their conversation of the previous day, she added, "Not William, surely. Not without telling me before you make the decision."

"No, of course not." Rob flung an arm across her shoulders as if he intended the gesture to banish her concerns over William. "It's Joan and Sir Royce. Edmund has decided they ought to marry tomorrow."

"What?" She stared at him in disbelief.

"Well, they have been formally betrothed for months," Rob said. "Edmund only delayed the official marriage ceremony until they'd had a chance to know each other. Which they certainly have done since they've been here with us. From what I've seen, they've been together almost constantly. Edmund says everyone he would want to invite to the wedding is already present at Menton, so he spoke to the priest and it's all arranged. Joan and Royce will be wed immediately after Mass tomorrow morning."

"Indeed?" Elisa put all of her displeasure into her voice. "How kind of you to inform me, my lord. I suppose I am expected to see to a special marriage feast, and to have a bridal chamber made ready for the newlyweds?"

"You were preparing a great feast for tomorrow, anyway. It's the last great feast of Christmastide, after all," Rob said, unabashed by the sharpness of her tone or by her frown. "As for the bridal chamber, I know you will manage everything splendidly."

"Thank you for your confidence in me," she responded dryly. "Really, Rob, sometimes you ask too much. This is Twelfth Night, for heaven's sake! How can we have a noble wedding complete with a grand feast on the very next morning? The great hall will be a shambles before tonight's celebration is over. You know how uproarious the servants can be, and how much they drink on this night."

"I do know it," he said, grinning at her. "I also know I can depend on you. It will be a night for high revelry. Put on your best gown, my lady. I have something important to tell you, and something to give you, too."

By the look he bestowed on her when he seized her hands and kissed her fingers, Elisa thought she knew exactly what it was that he intended to give her.

Lady Joan appeared to be an unusually shy bride-to-be, scarcely saying a word when Elisa spoke to her about the arrangements for the wedding and the feast that was to follow the ceremony. It did occur to Elisa that she had seen remarkably little of the girl while

Joan was at Menton, and she wondered if she ought to say something about what would be expected of Joan on her wedding night. After a moment's consideration she decided to keep quiet. There would be time enough in the morning to approach so delicate a subject, but at present Elisa was too busy to deal with the issue. Instead, she went looking for Christina.

"You've heard the news, I'm sure," Elisa said to her daughter. "We will require special entertainment in honor of the wedding tomorrow."

"I will see to it," Christina responded.

Elisa was about to ask what sort of entertainment Christina could arrange with several of the minstrels gone, when one of the kitchen maids approached her with an urgent request from the cook. Elisa excused herself and hastened to the kitchen. There, faced with a temperamental cook and two hysterical maid-servants, she quickly forgot all about the entertainment.

The revels on that Twelfth Night were as cheerfully noisy as the servants could possibly devise. They began by choosing as their Lord of Misrule a rather dim-witted lad whose usual job was to turn the spit in the kitchen. While the boy howled with delight, they sat him in the lord's chair and crowned him with an old cooking pot. Once that act was completed, the social order of the castle was officially turned upside down.

Immediately thereafter, Rob and Elisa, assisted by their younger guests, proceeded to serve the feast to the servants, while the servants sat at the long tables enjoying the change in their state and taking advantage of the situation by calling out ridiculous commands to their masters.

Two of the noblemen guests assumed the roles of minstrels. Garbed in particolored costumes, they strolled about the great hall, one carrying a lute, the other with a rebec and bow. They played off-key tunes on those instruments while singing loudly in voices even more dreadfully unmusical than the real minstrel's husky tones.

"They are a marvel," Elisa observed, chuckling when one of the make-believe minstrels forgot the words to his song.

"Most likely, no one has noticed how badly they sing," Rob said. "Everyone is having too much fun to care. Now that the meal is over, we can safely leave guests and servants alike to their own pleasures. Come away with me, my lady."

"Come where?" she asked, resisting his tug on her hand.

"To the lord's chamber." His attempt at a wicked leer dissolved into a warm and inviting smile. "I want to be private with my wife, and I have a gift for you."

"Tomorrow is the proper day for giving gifts," she reminded him sternly.

"Tomorrow, you will be distracted by wedding details and I will be busy consoling Edmund upon the loss of his daughter."

Elisa could think of no argument against that statement of obvious fact, so she allowed him to lead her across the hall toward the entry and the stairs. Kasia smiled and waved at them as they passed. She looked perfectly comfortable sitting close to the fire with two of the quieter guests, all of them observing with considerable amusement the antics of both servants and nobles.

Rob paused to pick up a candle to light the way, though he never let go of Elisa's hand until they were in the lord's chamber with the door closed and bolted. Then he released her just long enough to set down the candle before he grasped her shoulders and pulled her close.

"I've been waiting all day for this," he said, and kissed her.

"Rob, please." She attempted to push him away. "We ought to go downstairs again. We have responsibilities to our guests."

"Your first responsibility is to me. I want you here, alone with me, not below in the great hall."

"Well, my lord, that's plain speaking." Still locked in his embrace, she leaned back a little to look up into his eyes. What she saw there made her heart beat faster, and frightened her a little, too. She took refuge in an accusation. "How can you rudely neglect the guests *you* invited? I don't understand you."

"You never have," he said. "For a woman so intelligent, you can be remarkably blind. Tonight I plan to open your eyes. Shall I tell you the real reason why I came home for Christmas?"

"I assume it was to torment me." Her voice was a whisper because suddenly it was difficult to speak with his gaze so intent upon her face.

"I will admit that I do delight in challenging you, so I can watch the way you overcome the domestic obstacles I set before you," he said, laughing. Then, more seriously: "Have you ever wondered why I depend on you so completely? It's because I trust you. I learned early in our marriage that you would never play me false." He stopped, took a deep breath, and continued.

"Just two weeks ago, when Kasia told me about her illness, my first reaction was that she is too young to be so sick. Then I realized that she and I are the same age, both of us forty, and fortunate to have lived as long as we have. Since that hour I have thought constantly of how few years there are in anyone's life, and how much time you and I have wasted in foolish quarreling. Elisa, I know you do not love me, but can we be friends?"

181

"Friends?" she repeated, thinking what a poor substitute friendship was for what she really desired from him.

"The truth is," Rob said, "I want no other woman. While I was young and my duty to King Henry took me away from home for long months, I did from time to time consider straying. I am only a weak man, after all, and subject to temptations of the flesh, of which there many at the royal court. But I never gave in to any of those temptations. I have never been unfaithful to our marriage vows because always—*always*, Elisa!—it was you I really wanted. No one else could possibly be a substitute for you."

"What are you saying?" she cried, stunned by his words. "Rob, I beg of you, don't mock me. I know you love Kasia. I understand that you always will."

"There you are wrong," he told her with great firmness. "Completely, utterly wrong. Kasia was a boy's romantic dream, a naive young man's image of love. Out of my overwrought emotions and Kasia's good sense and honesty, she and I have built a friendship that will endure until life's end. I grew up and grew out of my youthful passion for her with surprising speed. As for you, Elisa—" He hesitated, looking down at her.

"Yes?" She was almost afraid to speak, not daring to credit the sudden hope that was sprouting in her heart like the first fragile blossoms of springtime.

"What is between you and me began on our wedding night," Rob said, "when you gave yourself to me in complete trust. My admiration and respect for you took root during that first night and has grown over the years."

"Admiration?" she repeated. "Respect?" When first she had learned he was coming to Menton for the holiday, that was what she was determined to win from him. Now he was telling her she'd had both all along. She was glad to hear him say so, but unfortunately for her, she wanted far more.

She pulled out of his grasp and turned away, trying to blink the tears out of her eyes before he could see them. She was so busy hiding her feelings from him that at first she did not see what he was doing until, through a teary mist, she realized that the chamber was steadily growing brighter.

"What's this?" She stared as Rob finished lighting the dozens of ivory-colored candles that, in her intense concentration on him and what he was saying, she had not previously noticed. The candles were set all around the room, on the clothing chests and the bedside table, and on a pair of tall, branching candelabra. The thick tapers of pure beeswax ranged in height from short stubs to middle-size to two-foot-long candles that surely had never before been lit.

"You stole them from the chapel supplies," she accused him. "I know because I supervised the making of these candles."

"I borrowed them," he said, "though I suppose I could claim that since the chapel is part of my castle, the candles in it belong to me, to use as I wish. However, I am not minded to argue with you just now."

"This is a wasteful extravagance." She was confused and more than a little disturbed by his unusual behavior. Sensing a need to defend herself, she reacted with anger, which seemed to her a far safer emotion than the trembling desire that threatened her self-control. "No one should burn so many costly candles at one time."

"There have been moments during our marriage, and this is one of them," he told her, "when I have been sorely tempted to strangle you for your willful and stubborn misreading of my character, and of my intentions. Listen well, Elisa, for I may never have the courage to say again what I am about to tell you.

"On the first night of our marriage, I began to love you. I tried to deny it to myself, for a nobleman ought not to love his wife. Love makes a man soft and overly indulgent, when a noble's first duty is always to be strong and ready to ride into battle for his liege lord. Yet despite my struggle against it, my love for you has only grown deeper over the years."

"You love me?" She met his glance and saw the terrifying truth shining there so clearly that even she—stubborn, willful, convinced he would never love her as she loved him—even she could not mistake his meaning. "You have never said it before."

"Because I have been as foolish and as filled with misplaced pride as you," he said. "But cold pride seemed pointless after I learned Kasia is dying. That was the hour when I finally realized how wrong it is to deny what is in my heart. Let me say it straight out.

"Elisa, you are the love of my life. The longer I know you, the more I love you and the more I value your honesty and your devotion to duty. What I said to you on the night after Christmas is true. The instantaneous love that minstrels sing about is best left to the very young; it has its joys. But I have learned to prefer a mature love that has grown through the years, through separations and disappointments and passionate homecomings. That is the love I offer you, if you want it. I swear my love is true, and it will endure to the end of my life. If such love as mine is allowed in Heaven, then I will love you there, too."

"You married me because your father ordered it," she said, beginning the old, bitter litany. He stopped her with his hand over her mouth.

"Foolish woman, set aside the past! Let it go. It is over, finished. This is a new day, in a new year. Our children are grown and about to begin their own lives, independent of us. You and I are all we have. Let us seize whatever time is left to us. Can you return my love?"

"You must know that I do," she cried, "unless you have misunderstood me as completely as I have misunderstood you for all these years."

"Then say it. You needed to hear the words; so do I."

"I love you, Rob. I always have." Tears streamed down her face. He gently wiped them away. "But Rob, those rings I found—"

"Ah, yes," he said. "You misunderstood that gesture, too."

"Well, if you would just explain what you intend," she began irritably.

"Well, if you would only control your anger and stop scolding until I have a chance to explain," he said.

They stared at each other in silence for a long, thoughtful moment.

"My lord, if we are to begin anew, then we both have much to learn," Elisa said.

"Agreed. In the future, I will explain my intentions to you, unless I am sworn by oath to King Henry to keep a particular secret. And I will inform you in advance when I want to invite guests to Menton." He raised his eyebrows and waited expectantly.

"I will cease my scolding," she said, "and I will try not to leap to hasty conclusions."

"I'm glad to hear it." His smile was slow and full of a wonderful, boyish mischief that made him appear years younger than his actual age. He tucked a hand into the folds of his tunic and drew forth the two golden rings that had caused Elisa so much anguish. "You were so angry that you did not look closely at them. Look now and tell me what you see." He opened his hand. The gold circles laying side by side on his palm shone in the candlelight.

"Set with rubies," Elisa murmured, "rubies red as heart's blood."

"Red as true love," Rob said. "Note their sizes."

"I don't understand." She transferred her gaze from the rings to his blue eyes.

"One is a lady's ring," he said. "About that you were correct. The other is a large size, made to fit a man's finger. One for you. One for me."

"Oh."

Her lips formed a perfect, enchanting circle. Rob longed to kiss her, but he wasn't finished yet. He wanted to be absolutely certain that on this particular subject, she would never misunderstand or doubt him again.

"I had them specially made," he told her. "They are new, never worn before this day. Elisa, I want to renew our marriage vows, with a truer meaning to what we promise each other, for this time I will speak the words out of love, and out of my own free choice. Can you do the same?"

"Will we be friends, and lovers, too?" she asked softly, as if considering the possibility.

"It is my dearest wish," he whispered, feeling the tears rise to his eyes, yet not at all afraid of appearing unmanly before her. "That is why I came home this Christmas—to tell you that I love you."

"It's all I've ever really wanted," she said, "for you to love me, and to speak the words aloud."

"I will say the words every day, for the rest of our lives," he promised.

"What shall we do now?" she asked with a nervous little laugh. "I don't think the Church has a form for what you want."

"Then, we will invent our own form." He took her hands in his, and in the candlelight his eyes were blue as the sea, deep as the love he professed.

"Elisa," he said, sliding the smaller of the golden

rings onto the finger of her left hand from which, as everyone knew, the blood returned directly to the heart, "I do swear, upon my honor and my life, to love you, and only you, forever, to be faithful and true, and to keep you always by my side, wherever I may go."

"Even to court?" she asked, surprised out of her solemn mood by his last words.

"Even there," he promised. "Even to France, or to Spain. Wherever King Henry may send me, you will go, too. I will never leave you alone again. Now you, Elisa." He laid the larger ring in her hand.

"I do swear, upon my honor and my life," she said in a voice far clearer and more certain than the weak, girlish tones in which she had spoken her original vows so long ago, "to love you forever—for I do love you, with all my heart—to be faithful and true—as I have always been—and to stay by your side and follow you willingly, wherever you may go." She pushed his ring onto his finger. The ruby gleamed when his hand encircled hers.

"I love you," he said, tightening his clasp on her fingers. Then the mischief he could never repress for long overcame him. He grinned at her and lifted her into his arms. "Since we've already feasted, I'd say it's time for bed. Time to consummate our vows, my lady."

"Rob, stop it this instant!" Then she was laughing with him, her feeble protest merely a teasing way to prolong the delights to come.

Rob sat down on the bed, holding Elisa in his lap, and began to rain kisses down her throat to the neckline of her gown.

"You are an overeager bridegroom," she told him, wriggling against his growing hardness. She sighed when he groaned in acknowledgment of her provocative action.

"My dearest lady, you have no idea how eager I am," he murmured.

"Have I not?" She unbuckled his belt, pulled it off, and tossed it across the room, then tugged his tunic over his head. Meanwhile, he worked at her clothing so eagerly that Elisa heard a faint tearing sound as stitches gave way. "My lord, you are shameless."

"We are both shameless," he declared when they were undressed. He slid into bed beside her. "Now, if I recall the rules correctly, a marriage contract is not legal until the man's naked thigh touches the lady's naked thigh." He proceeded to make the marriage legal, relishing the smoothness of her skin against his rougher flesh.

"Indeed, my lord, I believe you are correct," Elisa responded, her eyelids lowered, suddenly shy and demure as any virgin on her wedding night. "Though I hope you don't intend to stop there, as I have been told many aged bridegrooms must do."

"Aged?" Laughing, Rob flung himself upon his wife's lovely and willing body, to kiss and caress her until she trembled with helpless desire. "Is this the act of an aged man? Or this?" He subjected her to a most determined thrust.

"No, my lord. I do believe you grow younger by the moment." Elisa looked into Rob's eyes as they became one and knew, finally and indisputably, in her heart and her very soul, that he loved her as much as she loved him. Secure in that happy knowledge she released all of her old resentments, all irritations and jealousies and hopeless pain, letting those unworthy emotions burn to ashes in the passionate fire of a true and everlasting love.

Epilogue

"It's difficult to comprehend what has happened," Elisa said to Kasia. "Who would have thought that Lord Edmund would keep such a secret for so long?"

"We all have secrets," Kasia responded, catching Elisa's hand to admire the gold and ruby ring. "Especially romantic secrets, which are hidden the deepest in anyone's heart. How can you be surprised that Edmund has kept silent about his youthful romance? You and Rob have been hiding your love from each other for years. I'm glad to know your secret is finally told. You look happier now. So does Rob."

"I am happy. It's partly your doing, you know. Kasia, I wish you would stay longer. I would like to know you better. We have wasted valuable years when we could have been friends. Can you believe I'm saying those words to you?" she added with a laugh.

"Thank you," Kasia said. "Don't ever grieve for me, Elisa. I am as happy as you are for, like you, I am going to spend the rest of my life with my one true love. I leave Menton knowing I have two good friends to remember me and, perhaps, to visit me occasionally. I do intend to live for a while longer, thanks to your medicines. You and I will have time enough to learn to know each other."

Elisa and the woman who was no longer her rival embraced each other with genuine affection. Then Rob helped Kasia down the steps to the inner bailey, where a gentle palfrey awaited her. Rob lifted her into the saddle. With a wave of one gloved hand, Kasia rode out of the gate, escorted by a band of Rob's men-at-arms. She would reach the convent that was her destination before full darkness descended.

Most of the other guests were leaving, too, having delayed their departures just long enough to witness the wedding that morning and to attend the feast that followed it. Only a few guests would stay until the morrow. Lord Edmund was planning to remain for another day or two, which meant William would be at Menton for a while longer.

The servants, most of them looking a bit green after their night of revelry and the excitement of the morning, were beginning to clean up the great hall. The long Christmas season was finally over.

"I, for one, am glad of it," Elisa said to Rob as they made their way up the stairs to the lord's chamber. "I would like to be alone with my husband for a while."

"Look at them," said William from the archway into the great hall, his youthful voice carrying clearly to his parents' ears. "What's happened to them, Christina? They've always been polite and formal with each other, but now they're like two turtledoves."

"It's about time," his sister answered him.

"Past time, if you ask me," Rob called down the

191

stairwell. He emphasized the words with a wink and a wicked grin for Elisa. Below them William and Christina burst into laughter.

"My lord, once again I must tell you that you are a man without shame," Elisa declared as she watched him latch and bolt the door of the lord's chamber.

"There. At last we are alone, just as you desired. Unless, of course," Rob teased, ever mischievous, "those lowering clouds I noticed produce a great snowstorm, which will keep our remaining guests at Menton, eating and drinking and wanting entertainment as they continue the celebration for another week or so. If that should happen, you may be certain that one of the servants will soon come knocking at the door to remind you that you will be responsible for concocting new menus from our depleted larder."

"Guests staying longer? More menus to plan? Don't even think of it!" In mock anger Elisa grabbed a pillow from the bed and began to pummel her lord and master about the head with it.

"In the last day and night, my lady, you have shown a remarkable lack of respect for my august person," Rob observed, just before he tossed her onto the bed and fell on top of her.

"It was bound to happen once you admitted you love me," she said, allowing her hands to roam over him in a most disrespectful fashion.

"I would like more of the same treatment," Rob told her, and buried his face in her bosom. Elisa put her arms around him and, except for a few sighs, they both fell silent for a long, sweet while.

"Speaking of entertainment for the guests, what was that you were saying earlier today, about Christina, Wallace and the minstrels?" Elisa asked suddenly. She sat up to look down at Rob.

"Never mind. I promise, you'll hear all about it

later." Rob slung an arm around her to pull her down beside him again.

Having gotten her where he wanted her, he kissed her so thoroughly that Elisa forgot all about her daughter, and about her son, too. As Rob's kiss deepened, she even forgot her duties as chatelaine. In fact, Elisa forgot everything except the beloved husband who was holding her in his arms and demonstrating with a fierce and unstoppable passion just how much he loved her.

Eleven Pipers Piping

Constance O'Banyon

Here's to Ken, James, and the whole gang at Anderson News in Fayetteville, North Carolina. What fun eating pizza in the warehouse and getting to know such great people! I don't know when I spent a more enjoyable afternoon. Thanks.

Prologue

Lady Eleanor walked behind the servant, clutching her fur cloak tightly about her neck as protection against the drafts in the dark hallway. A chill penetrated the tapestried walls and invaded her whole body.

Was she shivering from the cold? she wondered. Or from fear?

She took a deep breath and let it out slowly to gain courage.

Although the queen was a distant kinswoman, it was seldom that Lady Eleanor was summoned to a private audience. Lady Eleanor's mother had named her after her illustrious cousin, but there had never been any warmth between them. Sometimes she wondered if the queen even remembered her existence.

She paused before the door while she waited to be announced. She heard the queen bid her enter, and she took her courage in hand. Queen Eleanor had been most displeased with her of late, and Lady

Eleanor wondered if she had been summoned to be reprimanded . . . or worse.

It was not her fault that King Henry had lavished much attention on her, and she had certainly not welcomed his interest, or encouraged him in any way. In fact, she was frightened of him and wanted only to turn away from his unwelcome attentions.

But the queen, enduring her second pregnancy of the year, was jealous of any attention her much younger husband paid to other women.

Lady Eleanor stepped into the room, her eyes going at once to the woman she'd been named for.

The queen was seated before her dressing table, her lady-in-waiting brushing her long golden tresses until they crackled. Queen Eleanor was remarkably beautiful, even though she was already thirty-three years of age and had borne four children.

She was the ruler of the Aquitaine in her own right, and the wealthiest woman in the world. She had ended her fifteen-year marriage with the king of France and abandoned two young daughters, all for love of Henry of England.

She was a formidable woman, devious and conniving, and Lady Eleanor knew she would not hesitate to eliminate any rival for the king's affections, even her own kinswoman.

"Your Majesty," Eleanor said, nervously dipping into a respectful curtsy. "You summoned me?"

Queen Eleanor swiveled, met her cousin's frightened gaze, and waved her attendant to leave the room.

"Of course I summoned you, else you would not be here, would you?"

"No, Your Majesty."

"You know why I wanted to see you?"

Lady Eleanor held her head at a proud tilt, refusing to be intimidated. After all, she had done nothing wrong.

"I believe so, Your Majesty."

The queen's brow knitted in a frown. "If you know that, then you must also know that you can no longer remain here at court."

Lady Eleanor wondered if she would finally be sent home to Aquitaine. She had yearned for her homeland, but she did not want to return to her father in disgrace and out of favor with the queen.

"I have done nothing wrong, Your Majesty," she said with gentle dignity.

"Have you not?" Then the queen's voice softened, although there was still an edge to her tone. "I think you speak true. But all the same, you have caught my husband's attention, and for that reason, I am forced to send you away."

Lady Eleanor lowered her eyes. "Will I be returning to Aquitaine, Your Majesty?"

"Never! You know that cannot be, else everyone will speculate as to why the queen has suddenly sent her beautiful young kinswoman away from court when the king had shown marked pleasure in her company." Queen Eleanor's hands clenched and unclenched in agitation. "You, my girl, are going to spend the Yule season at Menton Castle, getting to know your betrothed! Immediately thereafter, I will expect the two of you to journey to London, where you will be married. As soon as Sir James has sworn fealty to Henry, you will journey with your husband to his home in Scotland, and there you will remain."

Lady Eleanor blinked her eyes in astonishment. Though she had been betrothed to Sir James of Glencairn since shortly after Henry had ascended to the throne of England, she had thought that their marriage would be years away. After all, her betrothed was yet a hostage at Menton.

Eleanor tried not to show her joy. Even though their betrothal was a political alliance, her maiden's heart

199

had fantasized about her James, and she even fancied herself in love with him—if one could love someone one had never seen.

Sir James had been taken as a lad of nine from his home in Scotland and placed under the tutelage of Lord and Lady Menton, to keep his father, the powerful Duke of Calkannon, from waging war against England. Lady Eleanor had pictured him as a lonely boy in a strange land, just as she was far from her beloved Aquitaine, and also lonely.

Through the years she had been in England, she had heard scattered reports about Sir James. She'd been overjoyed the day she had learned that he'd won his spurs and had been knighted. Then there had been the reports that he continued to be rebellious and detested anything English. They had something in common there, for she was not so fond of England herself.

With a young girl's yearning, she hoped to be the one to heal Sir James's wounded heart and bring love and contentment into his lonely existence.

Did he ever think of her? she wondered. Did he ever wonder about the wife King Henry had chosen for him?

"When do I leave, Your Majesty?"

"On the morrow. Charge your maids to make ready your trunks, and be prepared to leave in early morn with Lord Menton and his party."

"What if Sir James does not like me?" Lady Eleanor asked, voicing her worst fear.

The queen looked at her speculatively. "You are a comely wench, rich and well-connected, so you should have no difficulty making him like you. But no matter how Sir James feels about you, he will treat you with the respect that your station demands. A woman can expect no more than that."

"But I want more," Eleanor said earnestly. "I want him to love me."

The queen shook her head, and compassion shone in her eyes. "You are so young to be thrust into such a situation. Perhaps I should have prepared you better." She smiled slightly when she saw the worried expression on her young cousin's face. "Put your fears aside. Many men prefer youth and innocence. It seems my husband is fascinated by those two qualities." She waved her hand in dismissal. "Leave me now. You have much to do before your journey."

Lady Eleanor bowed and backed toward the door. She was filled with excitement and trepidation at the same time.

What *if* Sir James did not like her?

How would she bear it?

Chapter One

December 23

Seamus Glencairn, the future Duke of Calkannon, bravely faced his enemy.

As he balanced the heavy hilt of his broadsword in both hands, he drew in a ragged breath. In his vision-like state, he could almost smell the scent of sun-drenched heather, and it filled his nostrils and seeped into his soul. He had to stand fast to protect his people and keep the invaders away from his home.

Gripping the sword, he moved forward, and with a powerful swing, made contact with his hated foe.

A burst of laughter from behind him made him turn. All of a sudden, he felt the cold of the bleak English winter, and his adversary became naught but a wooden pole. He scowled at the man who sauntered up to him.

"Well met, James," the man said, using the English translation of Seamus's Scottish name, as did everyone at the castle, as ordered by Lord Robert. The man observed the deep gash the young knight had made in the sturdy wooden target post. "You may be the best of us all. Pity you are a Scot and not English. But a man cannot change his nationality merely by taking on English trappings."

James looked at Miles impassively, knowing that his words were meant to provoke. He and the Englishman had grown into manhood together, and Miles resented the fact that the Scot had won his spurs and he had not. His pettiness oft manifested itself in the form of ridicule.

"It is *Sir* James to you, Miles."

The young Englishman laughed. "Ah, yes, you fancy yourself a true English knight now. I hear that you are soon to be married and returned to Scotland with the queen's kinswoman as trophy. Though why anyone would want to leave civilized life for your barbaric homeland is a mystery to me. I wonder what your bride will think of her new homeland."

James narrowed his gaze, and his words were edged with fury. "It has not escaped my notice that many things are a mystery to you, Miles. Mayhaps if you spent more time at your studies and less in the hay with some wench, life would hold fewer riddles for you and more answers."

"Scottish pig!" Miles cried, wielding his own broadsword, only to have it parried by Sir James's mighty thrust.

For several moments, the two men were locked in a furious battle, the sound of their swords echoing through the practice grounds, bouncing off the castle's high stone walls, and reaching the far recesses of the keep.

Suddenly James's forward thrust yanked the sword from Miles's hand and sent it clattering to the ground. Just as James placed the point of his blade to the frightened man's throat, another sword crossed his, forcing it to the ground.

"What is this!" Yates, the master-at-arms, raged. "I will not have my students turning on each other. And you, Sir James, already a knight, and fighting with one who has not yet won his spurs. Have you no honor?"

James held his tongue, partly out of respect for the man who had taught him, and partly because he'd learned to keep his own counsel in the dozen years he'd been a prisoner in this household. Lord Robert and his lady treated him well, but a hostage he was nonetheless, something he could never forget.

"It will not happen again," James said, sheathing his sword.

"What was this all about?" Yates demanded.

Miles's gaze met James's, and the Scot spoke first. "It was naught but a minor disagreement."

"It looked more like a large disagreement to me," Yates said, eyeing James. He liked and respected the young knight who met with challenges daily. Over the years he'd watched James struggle with homesickness and ridicule from many of the English students, and Yates had pitied him at first. But James had approached his training with the same enthusiasm as he studied Latin with Father Hides. Everything James did was better than, faster than, or greater than anything done by his fellows. This did not make the young lad popular with his peers; it only made his life more lonesome.

"Sir James, walk with me," Yates said. "I have something of import to relate to you."

James eyed Miles for a moment and then fell into step beside his former instructor. "I do not suppose you are going to tell me that I am being sent home?" The question was spoken as a jest, but there was also hope in the young knight's piercing brown eyes.

"Not as yet. But the time may be sooner than you

think." Yates stopped and glanced at the young knight. "I am instructed to inform you that your betrothed, Lady Eleanor, is among the guests expected for the Yuletide season."

James glared at his old mentor as if faulting him for this untimely news. "I have never accepted the queen's kinswoman as my chosen wife, nor will I give her my name."

"I hear that the lady is endowed with a large fortune. And I know your family's castle has fallen into disrepair since the last war. Take the woman as your wife, for if you do not, the king will see that you never leave England. He will take it as a personal affront if you reject his wife's kinswoman, and King Henry is not a man to gainsay."

James struggled with his troubled thoughts. Yates was right. He would never leave England if he rejected the king's choice of wife for him. "Suppose the lady rejects me?" he asked worriedly.

The old man shook his head, knowing that the young knight had much to learn apart from training in weaponry and knowledge found in the written word. The boy had to find himself; he had become lost in his love for his homeland and his hatred for England and all things English.

"Then, Sir James," the instructor said at last, "you would be free of the commitment. But I do not think that will happen. The lady is cousin to the queen. She will know where her duty lies."

James's thoughts turned inward. When she appeared at Menton, he would make certain that the lady despised him and would ultimately reject him as her husband. He said none of this to Yates, however. "When will Lady Eleanor arrive?"

"I am told she will arrive on the morrow. I was instructed by her ladyship that you must make yourself presentable to your betrothed when she arrives."

James nodded. "I will be ready for her."

Lady Eleanor had worn her finest blue gown so that she would look her best when she met her betrothed. She was so nervous she could hardly concentrate on what her hostess was saying. Her gaze swept the great room, searching the face of each man present, wondering which one would be Sir James. She dismissed them all as too old, too young, or a mere servant. It soon became apparent to her that the man she was supposed to spend the rest of her life with was not there to welcome her. Her heart plummeted.

She turned her attention back to her hostess. "Lady Elisa, thank you for receiving me as a guest in your home. It is most kind of you to share your holiday with strangers."

The lady of the castle made the correct reply, but it seemed to Eleanor that the woman's mind was on other matters. She was grateful when Lady Elisa instructed her personal maid to escort her upstairs to her room.

It was a pleasant room, with velvet and lace bed hangings, but Eleanor paid little attention to her surroundings. She stared out the window, to the keep below, while her maid, Marie, unpacked her trunks. Where was Sir James? Why had he not been present when she arrived?

It had never occurred to her that he might not want to meet her. She had always imagined that they were connected in some way. Because she felt so strongly about him, she assumed that he'd at least be curious about her.

She watched snowflakes drift lazily past the window. Was it possible to love a man she had never met and could not even put a face to? Perhaps she only loved what she had imagined him to be.

She reached for her blue veil and left the room. She was frightened and felt very alone. She would seek comfort in the chapel.

The morning had passed quietly for James. He'd studied Latin with Father Hides for two hours. At last he looked up from the book he'd been reading aloud and closed the cover.

The priest nodded in approval. "I can teach you nothing further, James. It seems the student has outgrown the teacher."

"There is still much I do not understand, Father, answers that I cannot find in books."

"And what would that be?" Father Hides asked kindly. "What is troubling you, my son?"

"It has nothing to do with my studies, Father, but is rather a question of right and wrong."

In a symbolic gesture, Father Hides made a steeple with his hands and spoke softly. "In what respect, James?"

"Is it right in the eyes of God to take a lad from his home, teach him his enemies' ways, and choose a wife from among those enemies? And what about Lady Eleanor? If I take her to Scotland with me, the poor woman will be no less a hostage than I have been here. Where is the sense in such an arrangement? Would I not be within my rights to ensure her rejection so she will be free to marry one of her own?"

"Ask yourself if your motives are pure—are you concerned for the well-being of Lady Eleanor, or are you only thinking of a solution to your own troubles?"

James met the priest's questioning gaze, and he knew that he must speak with honesty. "In truth, Father, I have given the lady no more than a passing thought since the day when Lord Robert told me of the betrothal. At the time, a marriage between us was in the distant future and was unreal to me. Now the day is at hand, I must meet the lady, and I have no interest in her at all."

"Meaning that what you reject as fact, you put out of your mind. That kind of thinking can be dangerous. Let me impress upon you, Sir James, the seriousness of rejecting such an illustrious personage as Lady Eleanor Gilbert. Her wealth and lands in Aquitaine have been coveted by many."

"Not by me."

Father Hides held up a hand to silence the young knight. "That the lady has been offered to you is testimony to your importance to England as the future Duke of Calkannon. The truce between your people and ours is a tenuous one at best, so pray, do nothing foolish that will land you in the Tower. King Henry is not a man to cross. His punishments can be fast and deadly, especially where his pride is concerned."

"I have considered this, and I am willing to take a chance. In truth, I have little to risk that is not already risked, have I, Father?"

The priest laid a comforting hand on James's shoulder. "It is nearing the time for the guests to arrive—truth to tell, they are most likely here as we speak. You should pay the lady the courtesy of greeting her on arrival."

"I will not do that. I have no wish to see her, and I will delay it as long as I am able."

Eleanor knelt on the stone floor of the chapel, feeling more alone than she had ever felt in her life. She remembered other Christmases, when she had been a girl in Aquitaine, when she had laughed and felt happy, basking in the love of her family.

Hearing a raised voice, she turned her head to the half-open door that must lead to the priest's chamber. For a moment she considered making her presence known, but then she decided to attend to her prayer.

But the voice reached her deepest meditating.

"Then, Father, I shall make certain that the lady looks elsewhere for affection, for I will never give her mine."

"Think what you are saying, my son."

"I may be the lady's choice, but she is not mine. I will make certain that she quickly becomes disenchanted with me."

"But, my son—"

"Do not lecture me, Father."

"Think of the woman."

"I will be rid of her—I promise you that, Father."

Eleanor squeezed her eyes tightly together, trying to block out the intruder's words. Her lips moved quickly as she stared at the holy icon of Mary, and at last the voices fell silent or the two men had moved away from the door, for she heard nothing further.

She tried to imagine what woman would want a man who so fiercely rejected her. Whoever the woman was, Eleanor pitied her. Her mind went back to her prayer, and she asked for God's blessing on her impending marriage and the man who would be her husband.

Chapter Two

James left Father Hides's study, his mind racing with thoughts of what he could do to induce Lady Eleanor to reject him as a would-be-husband. His footsteps were noiseless as he passed into the chapel, the short-cut to the courtyard.

He heard the slight whisper of silk and turned to the altar, where a woman dressed in blue knelt with her head bowed. From his vantage point, James could see her face illuminated in the soft candlelight, and he stood transfixed, certain that he'd never before seen anyone so lovely.

Her face was angelic, and it reflected goodness and purity of heart. Each feature complemented the others, and the result was that she was a stunning beauty. Her skin was creamy-white and her mouth full and rosy, as if formed for a man's kiss. A long curl had escaped her veil, and it was as black as ebony.

James was not aware that he'd been holding his breath, and when he exhaled, she must have heard him because she turned in his direction. The lady scampered to her feet, and in her haste, the blue veil fluttered downward to land at her feet on the stone floor.

"Forgive me, lady, for disturbing you at your prayer." He retrieved her veil, raised it to his lips, and was overcome by a sweet, intoxicating scent. Bowing, he extended the cloth to her, and when their fingers brushed, he felt something twist inside of him.

Had she felt it too? he wondered.

Eleanor stared at the young knight for a moment and then dropped her eyes, as if concentrating on her trailing sleeve, when actually her heart was throbbing and her pulse quickening. Oh, this was a fair lord, who stood tall and proud, his black hair curling at the nape of his leather jerkin, his dark eyes fathomless and wonderful to behold. "Pray do not disturb yourself, *monsieur*," she managed to say. "I had finished my prayer."

There was a long silence, and Eleanor's cheeks burned because she could tell he was staring at her. Raising her gaze to his, she was stunned by the intensity of his dark eyes. His face was handsome to behold, and she had to look away. "I must leave, sir. If you will excuse me?"

He stepped forward. "I have deduced that you are French, but I do not know your name. Can you not tell me at least that much?"

She backed away. "We have not been properly introduced, sir. Therefore, I am not permitted to speak to you or know your name." Who was he? Was this William—the son of the lord of Menton Castle? She turned and hurried away, wishing that she had never met the young knight in the chapel. She was to be married soon; she should not feel such strange emotions for another man.

She had just experienced her first glimpse into what

it felt like to be in the company of a man who made her maiden's heart soar. Oh, but she must not be disloyal to Sir James. After all, had she not loved her betrothed in her heart?

Even as she told herself this, she knew that as long as she lived, she would remember the soft dark eyes and the deep voice of that stranger.

James watched the French lady in blue walk away, fearing he'd just found something very precious and lost it at the same time.

Who *was* she?

She must have arrived with Lord Robert's party. She could even be married, for all he knew. He had to know who she was. "What harm is there in telling me your name?" he called out.

She paused and glanced back at him. "I belong to another," she said, before rushing out the door of the chapel.

He stood there in the shadow of the altar, her face imprinted on his memory. Surely she had been as affected by him as he had been by her. It tore at his heart to know that she was out of his reach and belonged to another man.

Mechanically, he moved out of the chapel, climbed the steps, and made his way to the bailey, where he knew he'd find Yates. He had to get away from the castle. Hawking would give him time to clear his head.

Shaking inside, Eleanor sought her room. Sitting on the edge of the bed, she raised her veil to her lips, remembering that the knight's lips had also touched it. What was the matter with her—she'd never reacted to a man in this way before. She felt ashamed of her wayward thoughts—after all, she was here to meet the man to whom she was to be wed.

The door opened and Marie entered, puffing as if

she had raced up the stone steps. "My poor lady, 'tis such a shame." Her maid shook her head. "I do not know where to begin."

Eleanor sighed in resignation. Marie was often given to woeful lamentations, and would oft depict the worst possible face of any situation. The maid's gray eyes were sorrowful at the moment.

"What is a shame?" Eleanor asked patiently.

The flaxen-haired Marie, who was but two years older than Eleanor, rolled her eyes. "I shouldn't tell you, my lady. 'Tis just too dreadful!"

"Very well, then you had better keep it to yourself." Eleanor stood and stepped out of her soft leather shoes. "Help me dress for dinner."

Marie bit her lips. "You must know, and who's to tell you if I don't?"

"Very well. What is it that troubles you so?"

"It's about him."

"Him?"

"Your intended—Sir James."

Now, Marie had piqued her interest. "What about Sir James?"

Marie's eyes took on an eager light. "Well, you know how the servants talk, and I can tell you that they have plenty to say about his lordship. It seems the ladies like him very well, and he is far from discouraging them."

"Is that all?" Eleanor tugged at a stray curl that had escaped Marie's cap. "I had heard much the same before I left London. We are not yet married, and a man rarely lives the life of a cloistered monk."

Marie shook her head. "If it was only that, my lady, I would not think anything was amiss. But there is more."

Eleanor was growing impatient. "Then say it, and have done with it. I weary of all this chatter."

"He doesn't want to marry you," Marie blurted out.

"He is willing to face the king's displeasure to be rid of you," she said, looking sorrowful. "Oh, my poor lady, he will not have you. One of the kitchen lads heard him talking just today to the priest. Sir James intends to make you reject him, so that you can take the king's displeasure on *your* shoulders. What a beastly man. Oh, my poor, poor, lady."

Eleanor was stunned for a moment. Dear merciful God—it was Sir James that she had overheard in the chapel. That meant that *she* was the poor, unwanted woman that she had pitied. She felt her anger rising, but with an effort, she turned a calm face to the servant. "Hush. I will not have you talk so of Sir James. It is unwise to chatter with the servants of Menton Castle."

But Marie would not be deterred. She knew her mistress was kind and gentle, and she feared for Lady Eleanor's future. The king and queen would surely punish her severely if she returned to London without her Scottish bridegroom. "Have a care, my lady. He is up to tricks and stratagems. I beg you, trust nothing Sir James says or does."

Eleanor nodded. The servants knew everything that went on behind the castle walls, and she had no doubt that Marie had been told the truth about Sir James. But it did not matter so much as it should. The man she had fancied herself in love with was still faceless, and the man she had lost her heart to was very much alive. Oh, how could she be rid of a man who did not want her? He didn't want to be the one to reject her, and she must not be the one to reject him.

She pressed her fingers against her temples and sighed. What a tangle it was, but she would not be bound to a man who did not want her. Remembering the man in the chapel, she longed for her freedom. Then, perhaps . . . just maybe . . . the knight who had touched her heart so deeply . . .

But, no, those were forbidden thoughts. But still, she could dream—she always had that. Only this time the man had a face, he had a voice, and she would remember him always.

Chapter Three

Lady Eleanor was seated at the high table in an honored position, as befitted her rank and consequence. The place to her left was vacant, and they were awaiting the arrival of her betrothed.

It was hard, after one's dreams had turned to dust, to smile and be gracious and act as if there was naught amiss. Sitting there among the merrymakers, Eleanor realized how childish all her dreams of her faceless betrothed had been, how foolish she had been to imagine a future of love and happiness for them.

Each step into maturity had caused her to scrutinize herself, to wonder if her fiancé would be pleased with the woman she was becoming. For so long, thoughts of him had never been far from the front of her mind. She had been prepared to love him with her whole being, but to him she was an unwanted encumbrance, a nuisance—a . . . nothing.

Unbidden, her mind turned to the knight she had encountered earlier in the day. She wondered who he was and why she hadn't also seen him someplace other than the chapel. He had seemed gentle and handsome and noble, and oh, so kind to her, a true example of how a chivalrous knight should be. And he had been as attracted to her as she was to him, she knew it.

Angry with herself, Eleanor removed every thought of him from her mind. It was her dreams that had left her open for pain and disillusionment. She would have to live in the here and now, a prisoner to her fate.

Noticing her frown and mistaking its reason, Lord Robert leaned in her direction and said quietly, so no one else could hear, "Fear not, my lady, at Sir James's absence. He is a conscientious man, and if he is not here, there is a reason. He has been well taught and would do nothing to show his future wife dishonor."

Eleanor blushed slightly because her thoughts had not been on Sir James, but on another man. "I know we shall meet soon enough, Lord Robert. Please do not concern yourself."

The banquet began with a toast to the health of the king and the queen, and then an acknowledgment of the honored guests. And still Sir James did not arrive.

Now it was Lord Robert who was frowning as the vassals began serving the food. He had known that his hostage oft spoke against being forced to marry a woman at the English king's bidding. Through the years, Lord Robert had often received complaints of James's supposed misdeeds, and most of them had been based upon the jealousy and spite of those who were not as strong a fighter, or as apt in their studies as the Scottish lad. Even so, Lord Robert was concerned in this instance. Yates, the knights' instructor, had emphatically dismissed the notion that Sir James would ever behave dishonorably. Even the castle priest had told him that James would not refuse to accept the Lady Eleanor as his wife. He supposed he should have talked to James himself, but it had been a long, problem-filled day, and he hadn't wanted to seek out more trouble than he already had.

Lady Eleanor found herself searching each face at the lower tables for the man she had conversed with earlier. She wished she'd told him her name and found out his as well, but she'd been so bemused by him that all other thoughts had fled her mind.

Just then she felt a movement behind her, and looked up to see her gallant knight standing behind Sir James's empty place, a stunned look on his face as he stared at her.

Oh, no, that could not be Sir James! Her eyes flashed with sudden anger as she realized it *was* her betrothed. Had he tricked her by pretending an ignorance of her identity—or by pretending to be attracted to her? Or had he been as surprised as she was to find out that she was his bride-to-be?

Not that it really mattered. He would not know that she'd overheard him reject her to the priest, for she would never tell him.

Mostly, she would never forgive him for destroying her dreams.

"Ah, Sir James, at last," Lord Robert called out with obvious relief. "We had begun to suspect that there was something amiss when you did not show yourself at table."

James made a slight bow in Lord Robert's direction and murmured an apology, but his eyes remained on the beautiful lady who, remarkably, one day soon, would be his wife. He was hardly able to suppress his delight as he bowed to her in response to Lord Robert's introduction, but she just barely acknowledged him with a nod of her head.

There was an awkward moment as James, who had never been at a loss for something to say to a woman—no matter her age or station—could think of nothing to say to this woman that he suddenly wanted to impress.

He took his place at the table and they sat side by side for long, silent moments.

At last James tried to catch her attention, but she stared straight ahead, refusing to acknowledge him. For all the attention she was lavishing on the minstrel who was entertaining the company, he might have been one of the finest singers of his time, instead of one of the worst.

He started to feel uneasy, wondering back to what he had said to her earlier in the day that would make her so angry with him.

Eleanor was struggling to maintain her composure, willing away the tears that threatened to spill from her eyes. So this was Sir James, the man she had dreamed of for years, the man she must swear to honor above all others, the man she must give her body to and obey without fail—the man who didn't want her.

"It would seem that fate has played a cruel trick upon us, my lady," James said softly.

Curious, despite herself, Eleanor turned to him. "What mean you by that, Sir James?"

"To make us both believe this afternoon in the chapel that we had no hope."

Still not understanding his meaning, she looked at him questioningly.

"That we had met each other too late, that we were obligated to other people and could never be together."

After what she had heard him say to the priest, she did not trust him. She forced herself to shrug with feigned indifference. "It matters not to me whom I wed. One man is much the same as another."

Eleanor turned away from James and concentrated on eating her meal, which was well-prepared, yet so seasoned with her misery, it might as well have been as tasteless as a bone.

After a while, she stood and excused herself, rushing to her room so she could be alone with her wretchedness and confusion.

Early the next morning, Sir James was once again at the practice grounds, punishing the wooden target post with fierce blows from his broadsword. This time, instead of facing an English foe in the heather-scented Highlands of his homeland, he was facing another invader, a dark-haired lass with a faint French accent who had curled herself around his heart.

He was bewildered. She did not seem English at all. He should have remembered that as a native of Aquitaine, she would be French. How could he go from trying to rid himself of the encumbrance of a wife he did not want, to trying to find a way to win her reluctant heart? She had comported herself so well, he'd felt like a lowly peasant beside her. Although both their fathers were dukes, she was a lady of the grandest scale and she appeared high above him.

He became aware of the squires and knights-in-training who were waiting on the edge of the practice field, shivering in the cold, waiting for him, a knight, to leave before they could begin their daily training.

Drawing in a disgruntled breath, he sheathed his sword. It was time for him to face the Lady Eleanor and mend any trouble that stood between them.

Eleanor had been reluctant to return to the chapel in case she encountered Sir James there. She certainly did not want him to think she was seeking him out. But he had confided to the priest that he did not want to marry her, so to the priest she must go for the answers to her questions.

To her relief, Father Hides was alone.

He turned to her and smiled. "Lady Eleanor," he said, bowing his head in deference, obviously remembering her from the banquet the night before. "What brings you to the chapel so early this morning?"

She hesitated, but he held out his hand and beckoned her to him.

"I have come to seek your counsel, Father."

"Then, my lady, come back into a room off the confessional so that we may be undisturbed."

Eleanor followed him to a sparse room, furnished only with a rough table and two sturdy chairs. She sat in the chair he indicated and waited to speak until he was also seated.

"Father, I hardly know how to begin," she whispered.

"How about at the beginning, my child? The more I know, the better advice I can give you."

She nodded. "The beginning was when I was told that I had been chosen to be the wife of a young Scottish hostage and would one day live with him in the cold, bleak northern lands, among an uncivilized, barbaric people. That wasn't, perhaps, the best way for a young, impressionable girl to be told about her predetermined fate, but my cousin, Queen Eleanor, is a practical woman, and she wanted me to be practical too."

At this point in her story, Eleanor became choked with tears, and Father Hides waited patiently until she was ready to continue.

"I suppose I couldn't reconcile myself to such a bleak future, so I began thinking about my future husband and building an image of him in my mind, an image of a chivalrous, honorable knight-in-training who worshiped me and worked every day to make himself worthy of me and my love."

Eleanor hung her head. "I was foolish, I know that now, but I imagined that we had a lot in common. He was a hostage here, forced to grow up in a foreign land, outside the shelter of his family's love. I, also, had to leave my beloved family and my homeland, and although I wasn't a hostage here in England, I might as well have been by how confined my life has been."

She looked at Father Hides.

"I often thought of him and dreamed of him, and I believed that he thought of me as well. I imagined a bond between us that wasn't there."

She stopped, looking at Father Hides with a wistful expression, waiting for him to advise her.

"In what way can I help you, Lady Eleanor?" he asked.

"Tell me how I can release Sir James from his betrothal. It's what we both want. He because he does not want me, and I because I do not want to be wife to a man who will not treasure all I have to give him."

Father Hides's face was etched with concern, and he took her hand comfortingly. "You and Lord James are as bound to each other as surely as if the wedding vows had already been spoken. You both made a sacred oath."

"Not I. The queen initiated the prenuptial agreement. And unless I am mistaken, I would venture that Lord James made no such promise either."

"That is true. But Lord Robert accepted the terms for him. 'Tis just as binding."

"Have I no say over how I will live the rest of my life, Father?"

"Such is the way of the nobility, my child. But I know Sir James, and he is a man of pride and honor. I have just met you, but I have looked into your heart and found you worthy. I believe that this will be a good match."

She lowered her head. "There must be a way to end this torment, Father. I no longer want to be his wife."

"Put your faith in God, my child, and all will be well."

Tears of helplessness stung her eyes. "I have faith, Father, and I will put it in God's hands. But who will say the same to Sir James?" It was a question that needed no answer. She stood, and walked to the door. "Thank you, Father. I know what I must do. I just do not know how it will be accomplished."

Chapter Four

Cloistered in her room, Eleanor reflected on the events as they had happened since her arrival at Menton Castle. Father Hides had been little help, so she would just have to come up with a solution on her own. She was prepared to turn Sir James's strategy against him and force him to reject her.

What she really wanted to do was ride to the closest seaport and take ship for Aquitaine as soon as possible. What she *would* do, however, was her duty. She was a guest in Menton Castle and would do nothing to reflect unfavorably on her hosts and bring the wrath of the king and queen down upon them.

A heavy rapping sounded on her door, and she waited for Marie to answer it, until she remembered that her maid had gone to the kitchen for hot milk. Eleanor's head was throbbing, and she needed the hot milk to ease the chills that wracked her body.

Opening the door, she found a page standing there. With a slight smile, he bowed and asked, "My Lady, if it please you, Lady Elisa has asked if you would like to join the party that will be riding out to hunt for mistletoe."

Eleanor sighed inwardly. She could hardly refuse, else it might seem that she was discourteous. "Tell her ladyship that I would be pleased to go."

"Very well, my lady. I believe they will be gathering in one hour."

Eleanor gripped the door and watched the young page move further down the hallway and knock on another door. The last thing she wanted to do was be among merrymakers.

She closed the door and moved to her trunk. If there was the slightest chance that she would run into Sir James, she wanted to prove to him that she was as indifferent to him as he was to her. She lifted out her all-white velvet riding habit that was trimmed with fur. At the time her mother had charged the seamstress to make the garment for her, she'd thought it frivolous; after all, no one wore a white riding habit—it just wasn't practical.

With a quick glance out the window she noted that it had begun to snow. The garment would be just fine. The other ladies would probably wear their brightest creations, and she would fade into nothingness against the backdrop of snow.

James watched the stairs for Eleanor to descend. He had decided that the best way to win her was by courtly manners and flattery. After all, they had always worked for him with other women, why not his betrothed? True, the two of them had gotten off to a bad start, but he was sure he could rectify their troubles before the day was over.

When he saw movement at the top of the stairs, he could only stare at the lovely vision in white that floated gracefully downward. To have such a wife would be all he could ask for. James didn't believe that love came so quickly, but if not love, what was the strong emotion he felt for her? Eleanor possessed a peacefulness and calmness of spirit that seemed to heal his tormented soul. He'd witnessed it when he first saw her at prayer in the chapel. He found himself worrying about whether she was dressed warmly enough and fearing she might catch a chill. He'd never felt such concern for any other woman.

She was exactly the right woman for him.

Eleanor caught a brief glimpse of James before she turned her head away. *Why did her heart beat so fast when he was near?* she wondered. Surely he could guess how she felt just by looking at her flushed face. She would have to be careful to hide her feelings from him.

When her foot touched the bottom step, he was there to greet her. He was dressed in a rust-colored surcoat and brown trousers with a long brown cape thrown carelessly across his broad shoulders. Why did he have to be so handsome?

"My lady, I am pleased to see that you are going on the mistletoe hunt. In spite of the cold, it should be good sport."

Even though she was still standing on the step, he was taller and she had to look up at him. "I cannot imagine you attending such frivolous entertainment, Sir James. Will you not find it a bit tedious?"

He held his arm out to her, and she had no choice but to place her hand upon his sleeve. "I can assure you, Eleanor, I shall not be bored for a moment."

Her eyes widened when he said her name without using her title. "As you say, Sir James."

He threw back his head and laughed heartily, as if he knew that she was trying to make a point. "Do you not think with the bond we share, that we might dispense with titles?"

"We did not heretofore share a bond, *Sir* James," she answered stubbornly. "There has yet to be a betrothal that could not be broken if one or the other partner is not satisfied with the arrangement."

He paused, turning her to face him. "And do you find me unsatisfactory, my lady?"

She had to drop her glance because she could not look into his stunning dark eyes. "I hardly know you, my lord. I have had to rely on others' accounts of you to form my judgment."

He smiled and raised her gloved hand to his lips, looking far too handsome for her inexperienced heart to contend with.

"Then you have not my true likeness at all if you pay heed to others' words. Let me show you who I really am, and in so doing, find out who you are."

She had the strongest urge to run back upstairs and bolt the door behind her. Oh, what could he be planning that he had made himself so pleasant to her? If she was not watchful, he would break her poor, foolish heart.

Stiffening her spine, she allowed James to escort her into the outer courtyard, where most of the others were already mounted and ready to ride. James gave her a hand up to her mount, and she arranged her gown before grasping the reins.

As they rode away from the keep and James fell in beside her, she glanced around at the others, wishing she was acquainted with just one of them. But even on the journey to Menton Castle, the others had kept their distance. She imagined they were aware that she was the queen's ward, and therefore hesitated to approach her. If only they knew how badly she needed a friend at the moment. Even Father Hides had brought her no comfort.

"Are you warm enough, my lady?" James inquired.

"I am comfortable enough," she said, urging her mount to a faster pace and forcing him to do the same to keep up with her.

After they had ridden for twenty minutes over snow-packed fields, they came to the woods. It was at this point that she turned back and saw that the rest of their party were not following. She halted her horse and glanced at James.

"Where are the others?"

"They went the long way. Since I grew up here and have hunted the woods many times, I know where the best mistletoe is to be found."

"Oh." She tugged at her gloves and glanced at the rise, hoping to see the others appear. "Should we not ride back to find them?"

His voice deepened as he gazed into her eyes. "Are you afraid to be alone with me, Eleanor? I can assure you that you will come to no harm."

"I was thinking more of my reputation," she answered bitingly. "I cannot imagine what the others will think about our unconventional actions."

He looked toward the nearby woods, and she studied his profile, immediately struck by some deep sense of sadness about him. But surely she was mistaken? She must not forget that he wanted nothing but to be rid of her.

"They will merely surmise that I want to be alone with my betrothed," he said lightly. "And they would be right." He glanced back at her, as if he'd revealed too much of his inner thought. "Tell me, Eleanor, do you miss your home?"

"Most of the time. I oft yearn for warmth on my cheeks and the heady breezes of Aquitaine," she said plaintively.

He watched the sadness that clouded her features. "I know so little about you, Eleanor."

She turned to him. "Sir James, you do not know me at all, and I doubt you ever shall."

"You could tell me about yourself."

Her vexation was increased by his temerity. Why should he pretend an interest he did not feel? Had she not heard him with her own ears telling Father Hides that he wanted only to be rid of her? Now, he was trying to lull her into passiveness by pretending to care about her.

"Tell me something about yourself," James prodded. "I confess I know nothing past the fact that you are a ward of the English court. Knowing so little of your country, I always imagined you to be more like the English."

She ached at his words, since from the first mention of a possibility of their marriage, she had gleaned any scrap of information she could about him. He had not even cared to learn about her circumstances. "You did not trouble to inquire into the background of your future bride?"

He looked regretful. "I beg you to understand my position in this country. I am a hostage, unable to use my own name and forced to learn the English customs and deny my Scottish heritage. If we are to be honest with each other, I confess that I thought of you only as another English punishment that I would be forced to endure before I could be returned to my home."

Tears stung the back of Eleanor's eyelids, but she would rather die than let James see how deeply his words affected her. "You thought of me as a punishment, and I thought of you as . . . as a kindred spirit— a stranger in a stranger land, forced to leave your home, as I was. Neither of us was asked if we sanctioned the marriage. I was given no more choice in the matter than you were, Sir James."

He glanced at her, puzzled. He'd never thought of her as a hostage, not when she was a member of the queen's family. "You say you did not like living at court, but surely there were many noblemen to attend you and offer you solace in your plight?"

"I may be kinswoman to Queen Eleanor, but she seldom acknowledged my existence. So few would risk her displeasure by even speaking to me." She averted her gaze. "I was kept in virtual seclusion."

James frowned. "Is this true?"

"I can assure you it is." Her eyes reflected defiance. "I know you have been away from Scotland longer than I have my beloved Aquitaine, but I missed my father and my brother as much as you missed your home." Her voice softened. "I long to return to my family and the land of my birth as surely as you do."

Her sadness seemed to cut through his heart. "I never imagined you were . . . that you missed your home as I miss mine."

Her gaze fastened on his. "Did you not? Did you think that I was anxious to wed a man I had never met? Did you imagine I wanted to live the rest of my life in your cold, dreary Scotland when I was accustomed to walking in the sunshine of my native country?"

Her description of Scotland as cold and dreary rankled, and his response was therefore harsh. "As I said, I did not think of you at all."

She gazed upward, willing herself to push the stinging retort from her mind and not give it voice. "I see mistletoe on your branch. It is high up, but you are, after all, a well-trained knight and must have knowledge enough to bring it down.

James glanced upward and saw that the branch she referred to was almost at the top of the tree and extended on a branch too thin for a man to climb. He smiled to himself and unsheathed his sword. After hacking several small branches out of the way so that he had a better vision of the object, he glanced at her.

"Move aside, my lady. I would not want you to be in harm's way."

Eleanor looked from him to the branch. "Surely you do not think you can cast your sword so accurately that it will cut the mistletoe?"

He merely glanced at her with tolerance. "As you pointed out, my lady—I am a knight well trained."

With fluid grace, he swung onto a wide branch and smiled down at her. "This may well be the most formidable challenge I have yet faced," he said with bravado he did not feel.

Eleanor held her breath as his broadsword flew through the air, sliced through the mistletoe, and sent it plummeting to her feet. He reached out his hand and recaptured the falling sword.

He leaped to the ground, sheathed his sword, retrieved the mistletoe, and bowed, handing it to Eleanor.

"Your slightest wish is as a command to me, my lady."

Her eyes were wide with amazement as she gazed at him in awe. "I have never seen such a feat. You are truly a master with the sword."

James thanked Providence and his steady hand, for in truth, he was as astounded as Eleanor that he had accomplished the deed. It was nothing he would ever attempt again because next time he would not be so fortunate. It had been mere happenstance that had guided his sword.

He would not tempt fate again.

Chapter Five

Eleanor stared at James in bewilderment. If he wanted to make her reject him, as she had overheard him say in the chapel, he was going about it in the wrong way. He was gallant and attentive, and when he looked at her with those dark eyes, it made her heart beat faster.

He was actually becoming the man she'd always imagined him to be.

What trickery was he about? Did he want to win her heart and then humiliate her in some way?

Suddenly, she shivered.

"My lord, it grows cold. Should we not find the others and make our way back to the castle?" She gazed up at the overcast sky. "It looks like it will soon snow again."

James could almost see the distrust in her clear blue eyes. Since she was Queen Eleanor's ward and kinswoman, he had expected her to be frivolous and promiscuous. He had heard stories about the queen's immoral behavior, and he'd assumed that she had schooled her kinswoman after her own likeness. But one look at Lady Eleanor's face told of her goodness and purity of heart. The softness of the white fur on her hood encircled her face, brushing against her cheek, and she seemed like an angel come to earth.

A snowflake had settled on her brow, and he moved closer to her, like a man caught in a trance. Before he knew what he was going to do, he cupped both sides of her head and brushed her brow with his lips.

James knew he'd made a mistake when his body came to life with yearning and desire curled in his gut so strong that he wanted to crush her to him and never let her go.

Eleanor had never been kissed by a man before, but instinctively she parted her lips and offered them to James. She heard him suck in his breath; then his arms tightened about her and his mouth settled on hers so softly it was like butterfly wings.

She melted against him, wanting to be absorbed by the heat he generated within her. Feelings so new and stunning took possession of her, and she pressed her body to his, feeling, rather than hearing, him groan.

His lips became harder, more demanding, and wildly wonderful as he deepened the kiss. His mouth moved to the corner of hers, upward to brush against her closed eyes, then back to partake of her lips once more.

Oh, what was happening to her? she wondered, as her arms went around his shoulders. She wanted him to never stop kissing her. A thrill went through her, and she knew for the first time in her life why man and woman had been created.

"My sweet, sweet lady," he murmured against her lips. This was meant to be, I know that now."

Sudden sanity returned to Eleanor and she tore herself out of his arms. "You had no right to do that." Her voice sounded shaky and breathless because she really wanted to go back into his arms and feel his kiss on her lips. "You take liberties with me, Sir Seamus," she said, unwittingly using his Scottish name as she had so often done in her daydreams.

James gripped her hand, and his gaze fell to her neck where her pulse was throbbing, and he smiled because he could feel the blood pounding through his body as well. "You wanted me to kiss you as much as I wanted to kiss you. Do you deny it?"

"I . . . was taken unaware."

"You kissed me back."

She jerked her hand free of his. "I had never kissed a man before, and I did not know what to expect."

His eyes softened. "So mine were the first lips that touched the sweetness of your mouth?"

She turned away from him. "As I told you, I have been like a prisoner at court. This was the first time I have ventured forth without the queen's ladies at my heels."

She felt his hand on her shoulder, but she dared not turn around or he might see the love for him carved on her expression.

"Eleanor, why did you call me by my Scottish name? No one ever does, and I was not aware that you knew my true name."

She decided to be truthful, but she would never reveal all to him. She would not tell him how as a young girl she had loved him wholeheartedly, and how disillusioned she had been when she met him. She turned slowly to look into his dark eyes. "The name just slipped out because I have always thought of you as Seamus. I pitied you because you were forced to abandon your country and your true name. Even now, when I think of you, it is as Seamus."

His voice deepened. "And do you think of me often, Eleanor?"

She stiffened her spine. "Lately, I have been thinking of you in the most unflattering way. Pity you could not be the man I dreamed you were."

He smiled slightly. "So you dreamed of me?"

"As will any foolish young girl when she is told she is to marry. I imagined what you would be like. I also imagined you would be wondering about me. I found out that you had not given me a thought, other than to wish me gone." She stared directly into his eyes. "The man fell far short of the dream."

James felt shame sweep over him. He suspected she must have heard some of the castle gossip about how he'd rejected her as his bride-to-be. But that was before he'd met her. Now it was different. This was no angel facing him now, but a woman who knew her own mind and who would not allow him or any man to best her. Her hood had fallen away and her black hair was caught by the breeze. If she looked like an angel now, it was an avenging one.

"If I have erred in some way, I beg your forgiveness, my lady." He bowed to her. "I am truly contrite and humbled, but I do not apologize for tasting the sweetness of your mouth."

Her voice was cold. "I forgive you. Now, can we join the others?"

He drew in his breath. So far, he had made a muddle of things. "As you wish."

He fell in beside her as she walked to her horse. She waited for him to lift her onto the saddle, and when his hands encircled her waist, he found he could span it with his two hands. He wished in his heart that he could turn back two days. He would be waiting for her to arrive, and he would be the chivalrous knight she'd imagined him to be.

Eleanor brought out the best in him, and he wanted to slay dragons and make her his lady love. He wanted to spend the rest of his life with her. He wanted her in his bed, to make love to her, to plant his seed in her stomach, and to clasp her hand in his for the rest of their lives.

As they rode back toward the castle, they were both silent, lost in their own thoughts. James glanced at Eleanor, but she stared straight ahead and did not once look in his direction.

Had he lost her?

James heard the sound of a rider coming toward them, and a man emerged from the woods. As he drew closer, James did not recognize him, but apparently Eleanor did.

When the man drew even with them, Eleanor slid off her horse and straight into the arms of the man, who had dismounted and enclosed her in an embrace.

"Oh, Gregory," she cried, laying her head on the tall stranger's shoulder. "You are here!"

Anger and jealousy twisted inside James when the man named Gregory kissed Eleanor on the cheek and continued to hold her to him. Perhaps she had indeed been corrupted by the queen's court.

Beside the man, Eleanor pulled back and smiled. "I have so many questions to ask you, but first let me present you to Sir James."

Gregory stalled her, lowering his voice so only she could hear. "Not just yet. I am not supposed to be in England. If King Henry finds out I am here, he will not be pleased."

Eleanor looked surprised. "Why are you here?"

"Send your escort away. What I have to say is for your ears alone." Gregory glanced up at the mounted knight, who glared back at him. "Make any excuse necessary, but send him away so we may converse alone. And no one, not even your betrothed, must know my identity."

Gregory was acting very secretive, and she knew

that he had come to England for some reason she did not fully understand, but which must be important.

She walked to James and spoke softly. "I beg you to forgive me and return to the castle without me. My . . . an old friend from home has something to say to me alone."

James's hand went to the hilt of his sword. "Just how close to you is this old friend?"

Eleanor saw her chance to release James from their marriage pledge, although it would be built on half-truths and near-lies. James wanted her out of his life, and she would give him the chance to release her with honor, at least on his part. Of course, her reputation would be ruined for all time, and the queen and king would be furious with her, but she found she cared more for his happiness than her own.

"I have known and loved this man all my life," she said at last.

James's expression was stormy, and she watched his hand grip his sword. Then with relief, she watched him release his sword and look down at her.

James stared at the man, who stood as tall as himself, and was princely in appearance. He supposed that women would think the man handsome. He was richly dressed and appeared to be someone of consequence, although some years older than Eleanor.

"Go to your lover," he said angrily. "We will speak of this later. I will also want to speak to that man, but we will do our talking with swords."

James whirled his mount around her and rode away in a cloud of spraying snow.

Eleanor stared at him until he disappeared over the rise. She felt as if her heart would break, but she had given James his excuse to rid himself of what he could call an unworthy wife-to-be.

She turned back to Gregory and he came to her. "If you ask, I will explain all to that man later. But when

I tell you my dilemma, you will see why no one must know that I have set foot in England."

"Tell me everything, Gregory."

He gripped her hands in his. "I am sorry to tell you like this, but there is great need for haste." His hand tightened on hers and his voice broke. "Our father is dead."

She gasped, and her head fell against her brother's shoulder as anguished sobs shook her body. Her brother held her and spoke soothingly, until at last she had spent all her tears.

"How did it happen?" she asked, wiping her eyes on the handkerchief he handed her.

"It was not a natural death, Eleanor. He was murdered by Sir Rochester. When the plot was uncovered it was too late. You know Rochester has always hated our father and coveted his death."

"Yes, but—"

"We found out that Rochester has fled here to England. I have traced him as far as London, and my men keep an eye on him even now."

"What are you to do?"

"End his miserable life. That's why no one must know I am here, so blame for his death will not be laid at my feet. You do understand that mine must be the hand that strikes him down since he slew our father?"

Eleanor nodded. "If you did not do it, then mine would be the hand to end his life."

She went back into her brother's embrace, and they were silent, sharing their anguish. Their father had been loved by them both.

At last he lifted her onto her saddle. "I must be in London before nightfall tomorrow. I will send you word, or come myself when the deed is done."

"Gregory, be careful. Rochester is a coward, and that kind of man can be the most dangerous."

"Think of him as dead," he said, swinging into the

saddle. "Now, you go after your bridegroom and try to soothe him. I will soon give you leave to tell him all—if you can trust him to keep my secret."

Gregory was on a dangerous mission, and he didn't need to worry about her situation with James. "Do not think of anything but your safety. I will be praying for you."

"Yes, little sister, do that." He gave her a salute and rode off toward London.

Eleanor said a quick prayer that God would keep her brother safe. Then she rode toward the castle with sadness heavy on her shoulders.

Chapter Six

Eleanor was glad that she encountered no one when she rode to the stable. The steward informed her that many of the others had not yet returned to the castle and were still hunting mistletoe.

She hurried toward the castle, thankful at finding the great hall empty but for a servant who was laying a fire in the massive fireplace. When she finally reached her room, she found Marie waiting for her. After Marie had helped her disrobe, Eleanor sent her away, saying she wouldn't need her until she dressed for the evening meal.

When she was alone, Eleanor dropped down on the bed and buried her face in the pillow to muffle her sobs. Her beloved father was dead and Gregory might be in danger at this very moment. She would not rest easy until she heard that her brother was safely out of England.

Her thoughts turned to James. He would probably demand to know about her relationship with Gregory, and she couldn't tell him, even if she wanted to. Oh, what a tangle her life had become. Right now, all she wanted to do was return to Aquitaine with her brother and never set foot in England again.

There was a soft knock on the door, and Eleanor moved to open it. She was surprised to find the Lady Elisa there. "Will you not come in," she invited her hostess.

"Thank you, my dear. I have not seen much of you and wanted to inquire if you have all you need."

"Indeed I do. You are a wonderful hostess, madame, and I am grateful for your hospitality."

Elisa ventured further into the room. "I do not know how to say this, Lady Eleanor, but I would like to tell you something about Sir James. He came to us as a young boy and received the best of instruction. He excelled as a warrior, as well as in scholarly pursuits."

Eleanor nodded, not sure what Lady Elisa was trying to tell her. "It must have been satisfying to both you and your husband to witness Lord James's excellent progress."

"Indeed it was. But I have just come to realize that there is a part of James's life that we neglected. We did not pull him into our family life, and this is my fault."

"How so, lady?"

"I am not . . . have never been outgoing with my feelings. I have ofttimes felt uncomfortable with my own children's demands."

Eleanor felt pity for the pretty woman who seemed so capable as a housekeeper and hostess, but she had noticed how she often rebuffed her own husband for all to witness. "I am not sure what you are trying to tell me."

"I just want you to know that if Sir James seems distant and distrustful, there are reasons for his behavior. I beg that you will be forbearing with him. He is close to Yates, his trainer, and Father Hides, but I think he trusts few others here at Menton."

"I am glad you told me about Sir James, Lady Elisa."

Elisa nodded. "I hope you will deal well together. Arranged marriages are not always—" The lady broke off. "I have taken up too much of your time. I just hope you will remember what I said about James."

Eleanor was puzzled by her feelings about arranged marriages. Hadn't the woman's own marriage been arranged? "Thank you for your advice. I shall certainly consider it."

When Elisa left and closed the door behind her, Eleanor was more puzzled than ever.

James was seated at the high table, his eyes on the doorway, ever watchful for Eleanor to appear. His pose was still, his anger barely in check. Her behavior that afternoon had been unforgivable. He intended to discover the identity of the man who had known her so well and find out why he'd come to Menton.

James had not seen the servant girl who'd come up behind him. "Excuse me, my lord," Marie whispered near his ear so no one else would hear. "I have a message from my mistress, Lady Eleanor. She begs to be excused from this evening's entertainment."

He swung his head around and pinned the girl with a heated glare. "Did your lady give a reason?"

"Just that she is not feeling well."

James rose, his anger unleashed. "Take me to her."

"Sir James, I cannot do that." Marie's eyes rounded. "It is not proper."

He grasped the girl's arm. "I said, take me to her at once! I am sure your lady would not want me to make a scene in front of all the others."

"Follow me, my lord," Marie said reluctantly. "Although I know not what my lady will say to all this."

*   *   *

Eleanor fixed the last hook on her high-necked night-gown and arranged her dark hair, which fell to her waist. She was glad she didn't have to face anyone tonight, especially James. She needed time to think about her father and remember the wonderful childhood he'd made for her after her mother died. She had never understood why her father had sent her to England, but she had always known her marriage would be political—marriages of her class always were.

She climbed into bed and lay back against the pillow, staring at the lone candle that cast the room in shadow. "Oh, Father, I do miss you so."

The door was unceremoniously thrust open, and Eleanor stared into the angry eyes of her betrothed.

Eleanor came to her knees. "What mean you by entering my room, sir? Where is my maid?"

"I have sent her away. I will have a word with you, lady, and you will tell me what I want to know."

"You must leave at once. If it is discovered that you are in my bedchamber, I will be ruined, as will you."

James looked at her grimly. "Madam, if that outrageous exhibition this afternoon, where you allowed that man many liberties, did not bring about your downfall, I doubt that my presence here will. My question to you is, just how well did you learn from your cyprian kinswoman who calls herself queen of England?"

She glared at him. "How dare you insult me and the queen."

He waved her objections aside. "Answer me."

Eleanor slipped out of bed, and too late became aware that James could probably see much of her nakedness through her thin nightgown. "I have no intention of answering any of your questions. Not when you come into my bedchamber uninvited and unwelcome."

"And the man today, has he ever been in your bed-chamber, invited and welcomed?"

Her anger made her want to strike out at him. "Many times."

Before Eleanor knew what was happening, James was at her side, gripping her arms and bringing her against his hard chest. "Then I feel no compunction for inviting myself here." His hands were rough as he pulled her tightly against him, while his hands clasped her head and forced her to look at him.

"Am I being sold damaged goods?"

She felt the heat of his body through the thinness of her gown, and could only shake her head to deny his insulting words.

He dipped his head, his mouth sliding up her arched neck to hover above her parted lips. "I will taste the sweetness of your body, since it seems to be available to all who thirst."

Eleanor felt him swell against her, and she experienced a new sensation—passion, sweeping through her virginal body. "I never—"

His mouth cut off what she was about to say, and she thought she might faint in his arms. When his hand went to the neck of her gown and he unhooked it, his hand slid inside and cupped her breast, making her tremble with powerful emotions that shook her to her toes. The only sound that issued from her mouth was a breathless whisper of his name.

James pushed the neck of her gown aside so he had better access to her creamy white breasts. Eleanor bit her lip to keep from screaming out when his tongue circled, enticing the nipple to harden against his lips.

What had started out with James as a way to vent his anger had turned into a passion such as he'd never known. He wanted her more than he'd ever wanted any woman. She was soft and willing in his arms, and he cared little that she had known another man. She was going to be his wife. After this night there would be no doubt of that.

He lifted her in his arms, staring into luminous blue eyes. If he hadn't known better, he would think that this was her first time because there was an innocence about her and uncertainty, but it could be just the play of the candlelight against her face. She said nothing—she merely seemed ready to submit to him—and that suited him just fine.

When he came down on the bed beside her, she reached out and extinguished the candle, throwing the room in darkness.

"If that is your wish, my lady. Although I would rather see your beautiful body." With a smooth motion, he lifted her and swept her nightgown over her shoulders, tossing it aside.

Eleanor trembled when James pressed his body against hers. She had never known that a man could do this to a woman, make her quake with longing and ache for the touch of his hand.

But this was wrong, and she knew it deep in her heart. Even though she wanted him to show her what it meant to be a woman, she should tell him the truth, that Gregory was her brother. If she did, James would stop—she knew he would.

His hands moved across her hips, and he turned her so their bodies fit as if they were made for each other.

"I want you," he whispered next to her ear. "No matter what you have done before, I need you."

When his hand slid slowly between her legs, Eleanor stiffened, trying to fight against a new and more powerful emotion. She wanted all that James could give her, everything!

"Just relax," he said in a deep voice. "You know what comes next."

She shook her head, and tears crept from her eyes

and fell across her cheek. She did not know what came next, but he thought she did.

James turned his head to find her mouth, and tasted the saltiness of her tears. She felt him tense. He drew his hand away and was quiet for a long moment.

"I have made you cry, the last thing I would ever want to do." She felt him leave the bed, and soon she felt something soft hit her face. He'd retrieved her gown and tossed it to her.

"You will forgive me, Eleanor. It seems I lost my head. No matter what you are, or what you have done with another man, I have no right to do this to you."

She clutched her gown in front of her, half-sorry that he'd stopped, but the gesture redeemed him in her eyes. He, believing she had been with another man, had pulled back at the last moment when he felt her tears. That proved there was goodness in him.

"I am sorry, James. I have much to tell you, but I cannot just yet."

"Save your secrets, Eleanor. If you still want the marriage, I will go through with it. If you do not, then I will find a way to set you free."

"I do not—"

"Say nothing more for now. Think on what almost happened tonight, and then judge if you want me for a husband."

Eleanor cried softly, glad that the darkness hid her sorrow. She wanted more than anything to be his wife, but he did not really want her. He simply felt honor-bound to marry her.

"James, I heard you speaking to Father Hides the day I arrived. I know you do not want me as your wife."

She heard his sharp intake of breath, followed by a long silence. When he spoke, it was with feeling. "So that is what happened—why you have been so reluctant with me." Again there was a long pause. When he spoke, there was sorrow in his tone. "You were not intended to hear what I said. I am sorry, but understand, that was before I had met you, Eleanor."

She heard him open the door, and dim light from the sconces in the hallway revealed him as only a shadow. He closed the door, and she was alone in the darkness.

"What shall I do?" she said aloud. "I want to be his wife, now more than ever."

She pulled her gown over her head and climbed into bed. It was a long time before she fell asleep.

Chapter Seven

It was a dreary day, overcast and looking as if it might snow. Eleanor wore her warm gray woolen gown, caring little about dressing to please anyone. She missed the morning meal, not wanting to face James after the incident of the night before. On the washstand, she found a crumpled bit of mistletoe and held it to her heart.

Eleanor was in love—really in love—not the yearnings of a young girl waiting for the perfect knight, but a woman with desires and forgiveness in her heart. Even if she never saw James again, she would always love him.

If only she had told him about the death of her father, and that the man he thought was her lover was really her brother. Last night he had only reacted to the lies she had let him believe. She had hurt him, she knew that—but he had hurt her, too. How could he have believed that she had been with another man, even if she had allowed him to draw that conclusion?

She came downstairs for the noon repast, and a servant led her to a small dining room where the family usually took their meals, rather than the grand dining room, which would have been far less hospitable.

Eleanor found only two other ladies at the table. She had met them briefly on the journey to Menton; the younger one was Jane Simpson, and the elder, Lady Graves. She greeted them cordially and they acknowledged her in kind. Then they put their heads together, and Eleanor had a feeling they were talking about her.

"My lady," Jane Simpson asked between sips of cider, "may I inquire when you and Sir James are to be married?"

Eleanor blinked at the unexpected question. "We met for the first time here at Menton Castle. The final plans have not yet been discussed."

Lady Graves, a woman in her fifties and recently widowed, sniffed. "I find these things are best done quickly, and apparently the queen agrees. I had heard that Lord Robert has received a letter from Her Majesty, asking that the wedding take precedence over the Yule season."

Eleanor could hardly speak for the lump forming in her throat. "We all know that any kind of celebrated event, such as a wedding, is forbidden during the holy season. I am sure there is some mistake."

"Perhaps," Lady Graves said doubtfully. "But I overheard Lord Robert telling Sir James himself."

Eleanor concentrated on the cheese that had been set in front of her, blinking her eyes and wishing she could flee to her room. Oh, what could it mean? Surely, there must be some way to delay the wedding until she could speak to her brother. Gregory was the new Duke of Lancingworth now that their father had died, and she knew that if she asked it of him, he would take her back to Aquitaine with him—even if it angered the king and queen. But did she want to cast her brother at odds with King Henry?

What was she to do?

"Lady Eleanor," Jane said eagerly, "I think you are the most fortunate of women, and I know many ladies who feel the same."

Her older companion gasped at the girl's lack of manners.

Eleanor spoke softly to the young, dewy-eyed girl who, if she were older, would have known that she was breaching the lines of etiquette. "In what way?"

"He . . . Sir James is quite the most handsome of knights. If I—" She must have been kicked under the table, because she cried out and fell silent.

Eleanor rose and excused herself, wanting to get away from the two ladies as fast as possible. She paused in the great hall not wanting to return to her room, where she would only worry about Gregory or brood because Queen Eleanor wanted her married as quickly as possible.

She chose instead to go into the chapel and pray for her brother's safety.

James had joined the hunt, not because he wanted to, but because he wanted to avoid Eleanor. He was angry with himself for what he'd done to her the night before. She would probably never forgive him, and who could blame her?

Then there was the message from the queen, instructing him and Eleanor to marry as soon as it was possible. That was strange, and he wondered why the queen would want the ceremony to take place so quickly.

He halted his horse and watched the high spirits and antics of those in pursuit of a wild boar—he was not in the mood to join in the merriment. As he watched the others disappear into the thickets, he was struck by an idea—he knew why the queen wanted the marriage so soon. She had found out about the other man—the one who had so brazenly sought Eleanor out here at Menton. Could it be that the lady was with child and needed a husband as soon as possible?

Brooding, he stared straight ahead, wondering where his life would go from here. Eleanor loved the stranger, she'd admitted that. He should have struck the man down when he'd had the chance—but that would not have won the lady's heart, now would it?

Since meeting Eleanor he knew that she was the perfect wife for him, but he did not want her if her heart was tied to another man. Or if she carried that man's child.

Silently, he turned his horse back toward the castle, deciding he'd go directly to the tournament field. A round of practice with Yates and their broadswords would go a long way toward clearing his mind.

Eleanor entered the feast hall to find that James had already arrived. Their eyes met, and she glanced away, blushing. She knew that he was remembering the night before—how would she ever face him?

Reluctantly, she made her way to her place beside him, and when she drew near, Lord Robert approached and bowed before her. "My lady, I would have word with you and James before the meal begins. Will you both accompany me at once?"

Curious stares followed them as they left and walked with Lord Robert into a small room off the great hall. When Eleanor was seated, and James stood stiffly nearby, Lord Robert spoke.

"Lady Eleanor, James has already been informed about the message I received from Her Majesty this morning, and I wanted to tell you what it contained."

Eleanor waited for Lord Robert to continue. There

251

was no reason for her to tell him that she already knew what the letter said.

Lord Robert cleared his throat and looked somewhat uncomfortable. "It should come as no great surprise to you since you are betrothed to Sir James."

She decided not to make it easy on her host. She merely watched him silently, while he continued.

"Her Majesty has insisted . . . er . . . requested that you and Sir James be married at once, and that the wedding be conducted with the utmost secrecy. I have no instructions after that, and do not know if you will be traveling to Scotland right away or joining Their Majesties at court. I have sent a messenger to ask the queen for further instructions." He waited for her to reply, and when she said nothing, he pressed her. "Is this to your satisfaction?"

"I am at the queen's command. I am sure the orders to leave England will come swiftly," she said with bitterness, realizing that her kinswoman would not be satisfied until she was out of the country. Did the queen trust King Henry so little that she still saw Eleanor as a threat?

Again, Lord Robert cleared his throat. "Well, I will leave you two young people alone. I am sure you have much to say to each other."

Eleanor stood. "When will the wedding take place, my lord?"

Robert looked uncomfortable. "Tonight."

Eleanor glanced up at James, who did not look pleased. She turned beseeching eyes on her host. "Surely, it is too soon."

"As I stated, the ceremony will be held in private," Lord Robert said, "in the anteroom off the chapel, and not announced until we have received word from the queen. After you have supped, my lady, you will have time to make whatever preparations you wish." He bowed and moved out of the room, softly closing the door behind him.

There was a long silence in the room. At last, when she could stand it no longer, Eleanor glanced at James, to find him staring at her.

"I can prevent this, you know," he said with feeling.

"Is that what you want, James?"

"What I want is of little consequence. If I wed you, I can return to Scotland. That is my one desire."

His words stung, but she raised her head proudly. Her eyes never flinched, nor did her pain show. "Do I understand that you want the marriage?"

"To the end I just stated, aye. But perhaps you would rather refuse and marry the man you say you love."

She shook her head, wishing she could bare her soul to James. But she couldn't tell anyone, not even him, that her brother was in England. "I cannot marry Gregory."

"He has a wife then?"

Eleanor thought of her dear sister-in-law, who was even now close to delivering Gregory's second child. Poor Katherine must be out of her mind, worrying about her husband in London. "Yes. He is married."

"Then shall we strike a bargain, my lady? Since you cannot have the man of your choice, will you settle for me?"

Oh, she could see the anger in his eyes, and it cut into her heart. He did not want to marry her, but doing so was his only way to go home.

"Yes, James, I will strike a bargain with you, but I will say more. Do not judge me too harshly. There is much I cannot tell you at this time. I know it is hard to ask you to trust me when you know so little of me, but I ask it all the same."

"Trust you, my lady? Nay. But marry you I shall."

She moved to the door and he fell in beside her.

"I will await your pleasure in the chapel, my lady."

Chapter Eight

Eleanor watched James walk away from her, realizing what a tangled web she'd made of her life. If she'd come here with the intention of ruining any chance they had for happiness, she could not have done so more effectively.

If only they'd met under different circumstances— if they'd developed a friendship first, then perhaps she could have won his love.

Now it was too late.

Her footsteps were slow as she approached the chapel. There was no one she could go to for advice except Father Hides. If she spoke to him in confidence before the wedding, he would have to keep her secret, wouldn't he?

She found the priest at his prayers, but he heard her soft footsteps and crossed himself, then rose to his feet.

"I understand that there is to be a wedding this very night," he said, smiling.

"A secret wedding, Father. The queen told me we would travel to London and be married there, but she changed her mind, it seems."

"So it appears." Father Hides had some knowledge of the queen's jealousy when it came to her husband and any lovely young girl he showed an interest in. He could imagine why she had sent Lady Eleanor to Menton Castle and why she wanted to rush the wedding. "Do not fret about that, Lady Eleanor."

His eyes were kind, and feeling his sympathy, she blurted out, "Oh, Father, that is not the worst of it."

"Why are you so troubled, my child? Did you want to talk to me about something?"

"If I do, you will tell no one what is said here tonight?"

"You can trust me, my child. I am bound by God's law to keep all confidences."

She let out a sigh of relief. "Then I will trust you." She ducked her head to hide the tears gathering in her eyes. "My father was killed, and I cannot show my grief, or many will question my reason."

"My lady, I am so sorry. While I did not know His Grace, I had heard much of his goodness."

She quickly told him about her father's death and of her brother pursuing the killer to England. She expressed her concerns for her brother's safety, while Father Hides listened attentively, sometimes nodding, at other times shaking his head. She omitted the part about James going to her room the night before, and when she had finished, she looked into his clear eyes.

"Under the law of the Holy Church, is it permitted for me to marry James with this lie between us?"

"Untruthfulness is never a good start for marriage, my lady, but I can see your need for concealment. We will just both pray that your brother finds a satisfactory and worthy conclusion to his trouble so that you can tell Sir James everything."

James and Lord Robert chose that moment to enter the chapel, and Eleanor whispered quickly to the priest, "Say nothing, Father."

"Your secret is sealed inside me, my child." He turned to greet the others. "Ah, we are all gathered and the ceremony can began. Sir James, you stand before the altar, and Lady Eleanor should stand at his left."

Eleanor was trembling so badly that her voice shook when she spoke the vows. She was hardly aware of what was happening, and it was over so quickly that she was dazed when she heard Father Hides blessing the union.

She glanced down at the plain gold band on her finger and then met James's gaze.

"Well, madame," he said, "it seems that you have tied your life to mine." He reached forward and brushed his lips against her cheek in a stiff movement. "Pray that neither of us live to regret it," he whispered so only she could hear.

Sir Robert smiled at each of them, clapping James on the back. "What a jewel you have won, James." He bowed to Eleanor. "Please excuse my hasty departure, but I have a friend that is ailing." He looked regretful. "Pity there could not be a more public ceremony for the wedding." He smiled again. "But you are no less married than if it had been in London before Their Majesties and all the court."

Eleanor realized that James still held her hand, but she did not feel married to him. And from the look on his face, he did not enjoy the prospect any more than she did. Not knowing what to say, she murmured, "Now you can return to Scotland."

"When the king wills it so."

She sighed. "I believe we can expect the queen to will it so. We will see you on the road home very soon or I do not know my kinswoman."

Before he could reply, Father Hides motioned them forward. "You are man and wife; go and begin your life together."

James dropped her hand and stalked to the door. "We will go to your room, my lady, since we are both familiar with it."

Eleanor had no choice but to hurry after him. She was confused and heartsick. She was a bitter bride, and he was a reluctant husband. She saw no happiness ahead for the two of them.

Marie's eyes rounded when she saw Sir James in her lady's bedchamber. She hovered near the door, not knowing whether to back out or come forward.

"Marie," Eleanor said patiently, "come in and close the door. I have something to to say to you."

The girl did as she was told, stealing a look every so often at Sir James, who stood with his back to them, staring out on the inner bailey as if he was unaware of what was going on between mistress and servant.

"Marie," Eleanor began to explain, "Sir James and I were married tonight. You must tell no one until Lord Robert announces it to the other guests."

Marie's mouth rounded. "Married, your ladyship?"

"That's right, Marie. Eventually we will be going to Scotland. I am telling you this because I will be giving you the choice to either go with me, or return to Aquitaine."

"I'll be going with you, my lady. I serve you."

Eleanor smiled. "Thank you, Marie. You may seek your own bed now. I will not be needing you tonight."

The servant bobbed in a quick curtsy. "My lady, *monsieur*." She left, closing the door firmly behind her.

James swung around to Eleanor. "Will she talk, do you think?"

"No. She will not."

"Most servants do."

"Not Marie. I trust her with my life."

He was cold and still, and she was aware that he would rather be anywhere but in her chamber. "My lord, I asked you to trust me. Can you not do that?"

His dark gaze bore into hers. "I do not know you as well as you know your Marie, do I?"

"No, my lord. You do not know me at all."

She looked at the bed and her nightgown, which was spread across the foot. "What sleeping arrangements will we make, my lord?"

He drew in an exasperated breath. "Eleanor, call me James. We are, after all, man and wife."

She nodded. "As you wish, James."

He moved to a chair and sat down, his gaze on her. "Tell me about yourself. Perhaps I can better understand you if I know something about your past."

She climbed on the high bed and sat facing him. "Very well. You know I grew up in Aquitaine and you know my father was the Duke of—"

A frown creased his forehead and he interrupted her. "*Was* the Duke? Do you not mean *is* the Duke?"

She dropped her gaze and rushed on with what she was saying, hoping he would forget her slip. "I have one brother, and he is married, with a family and a new baby on the way."

"When did you come to England?"

"Not long after Henry became king. I always knew that I would have to make a political marriage. My father was a powerful man, as is yours. I knew when the queen sent for me that she had found a husband for me. I learned when I reached London that you were that choice." She looked at him, noticing that he was gripping the arms of the chair so tightly that his knuckles were white. "I suppose you found out when I did."

"I have just one question for you, Eleanor, and I

258

want you to tell me the truth. I promise you that I will know if you speak false. A man can always tell if a lady is not pure."

She swallowed hard. "You want to know if I have ever been with a man?"

"Have you?"

"No, James. I have never even kissed a man besides you."

He shot to his feet, his face etched in fury. "That is not quite true, madame. I saw you kiss another man, the one you call Gregory. And if you kissed him—"

She slid off the bed, angry now herself. "Do not say it! I have told you the truth. Whether or not you believe me is up to you. I do not care."

"Who is that man, and what is he to you?"

She wanted to tell James; it was on the tip of her tongue to tell him everything, but she dared not. Not until Gregory was safely out of England.

He stood over her like a menacing force. "Then, I will bid you good night and seek my own bed."

She nodded. "If that is your wish."

She watched him leave, knowing the confusion he must be feeling. She wanted to call him back, but she dared not. She had asked him to trust her, and he hadn't. His pride was more important to him then his feelings for her.

She unhooked her gown and let it slide to the floor. After she was prepared for bed, she climbed under the covers, shivering with cold.

She would sleep alone on her wedding night.

Chapter Nine

The next two days Eleanor did not see James at all, nor did she care to. She loved him, but she'd asked him to trust her, and he chose to believe the worst of her.

But a young girl's dreams die hard, and she still believed that her new husband was an honorable and chivalrous knight, and he would one day prove it to her.

Each day she went to the chapel and prayed for hours for her brother's safety and for the soul of her dead father.

As of yet, she had received no word from Gregory, and she began to fear the worst.

Eleanor had spent another sleepless night. It was just after sunup that she donned her hooded cape and ventured out in the fresh air, with Marie at her side. The snow was beginning to melt, and the wind was not so cold.

"My lady," Marie said almost shyly. "Sir James inquires about you every day."

Eleanor stared at the blackbirds circling the keep. "He would have done better to find out for himself," she said frostily.

"I am told by the other servants that he stalks around brooding and is more difficult to get along with than ever. They wonder what change has come over him."

Eleanor was in no mood to listen to the servants' gossip. "If you would spend your time more fruitfully, Marie, you would have no time to listen to gossip."

The girl looked stricken. "Yes, my lady. It's just that I worry about you."

Eleanor's voice was softer now, and she regretted speaking so harshly to Marie. "These are troublesome times, but they will soon pass. All will be well in the end." But her hope was not as strong as her words indicated.

A shadow fell across her face, and a man-at-arms approached her. "Lady Eleanor, His Lordship has asked that you come at once. If you will follow me, I will take you to him."

Eleanor dismissed her maid with a nod and fell in step with the man-at-arms. He led her through the great hall to the same room they had occupied the night she found out she was to marry James.

The guard bowed to her at the door and departed to take up his other duties.

Eleanor stepped into the room expecting to find Lord Robert, but instead she found her brother.

With joy in her heart, she flew across the room and into Gregory's embrace. "God be blessed, you are safe! I was so fearful for you."

"I am sorry you were worried." His arms tightened about her. "All has ended in the best possible way."

Eleanor drew back and looked into his eyes. "Tell me what has happened?"

"Come forward by the fire and warm yourself," Gregory said, "and tell me about this wedding that took place while I was in London."

Lord Robert had bidden James to go to the anteroom to join his wife there. James now stood in the doorway, witnessing the tender scene between his wife and the man he had come to despise. His hand went to his sword and he tensed. Eleanor would tell him just what this man was to her before he drove his sword into him.

"I will tell you everything later, Gregory," she said, squeezing his hand. "First, tell me what happened in London."

"I will tell you as soon as your husband arrives. He has every right to know what has occurred." Gregory glanced up and smiled. "Ah, I believe he is here now."

James advanced into the room, his dark gaze on his rival. He didn't know why Lord Robert had sent him here, but he was about to find out. His gaze dropped to his wife, who had just moved out of the man's embrace.

"I do not believe we have been introduced," Gregory said smiling. "I am—"

"Take your hands off my wife!" James said in a menacing voice that came out as a harsh whisper.

Gregory looked from the man to his sister. "You have not told him about us?"

She shook her head, stepping between the two of them. "You asked me to keep your presence in England a secret."

"There are far too many secrets going on now," James said, unsheathing his sword. "Move out of the way, Eleanor!"

"No, I will not. Are you crazed, James?"

Gregory stepped around her and smiled at the hot-headed youth. "I believe you should know the name and circumstance of the man you want to kill—do you not think so?"

James lowered his sword, not really wanting to kill anyone, but jealousy twisted in his heart, and he would not stay his hand for long. "State your name," he said impatiently, hardly able to bear the thought of this man touching his wife.

"I am Gregory Gilbert, Duke of Lancingworth."

James stared at his rival through half-closed eyelids. He raised his sword and placed it at the duke's throat. "Now that I know who you are, prepare to die."

Gregory casually moved the point of the sword with his finger, knowing a knight would never cut down an unarmed man. "You do not understand. I am—"

"Although you are married, you lavish your affections on my wife," James interrupted him. "And for that you shall die."

Some deviltry in Gregory made him goad the young bridegroom further. "I adore your wife. She is dearer to me than my own life."

James looked at Eleanor, who had her hand at her throat and had turned quite pale. "Gregory, please tell him," she pleaded.

"Very well. Sir James, I have the dubious honor of being your brother-in-law. Of course I love Eleanor. She is my sister!"

Feeling like an utter fool, James stared from brother and sister, seeing the resemblance for the first time. They had the same color hair, the same blue eyes, and some facial likenesses. "Please accept my most sincere apologies, Your Grace."

"Call me, Gregory," the duke told him. "After all, you are married to my sister."

"Gregory, had I known, I—" James looked at Eleanor, suddenly feeling unworthy of her, but irritated, too, because she had let him believe the worst. "Why did you not tell me he was your brother?"

"I could not," she said, moving closer to James, wishing she could erase the misery from his heart. "I had to keep my silence for a good reason."

"I will explain it to you," Gregory said, drawing Eleanor into the circle of his arms. "You see, our father was murdered. I followed the murderer, Sir Rochester, to England with the intention of ending his life, thus avenging my father. I did not want anyone to know I was in England."

"I see," James said, looking at his wife. "Did you learn for the first time about your father's death the day of the mistletoe hunt?"

"Yes," she said, leaning her head against her brother's shoulder and feeling his arms tighten about her. "I could not even grieve openly, for fear people would question the cause."

James glanced up at the ceiling for a moment so he could gather his thoughts. "How can you ever forgive me? I should have been a comfort to you, and that night I—"

"Let us speak no more of that," Eleanor said quickly, not wanting her brother to know about the night James had come to her room. "What about Sir Rochester?" she asked Gregory.

"You may well ask. The villain is locked in the Tower and is awaiting sentence. King Henry assures me that Rochester will lose his head, and I will have to be satisfied with that, although I wish I could have been the one to avenge our father."

Eleanor clasped her hands and moved to the fire to warm herself. "I am glad you had no hand in it, Gregory. 'Tis better if the law takes its true course." Her glance went to her husband, whose face was etched with torment. "Do not trouble yourself about what passed between us, James. Had I been able to tell you the truth, you would have reacted differently, I know that."

Gregory had been watching the stiff exchange between his sister and her husband. "I have something that must be asked before I give you King Henry's message. Eleanor, do you want to remain married to this man? Do you want to make your home in Scotland with him? If you so desire, I am prepared to take you back to Aquitaine with me, where I will contact the Holy Father to have this marriage set aside."

She was quiet for a moment while she searched James's eyes. She saw something like fear reflected there. But, fear of what—that she wanted to stay with him, or that she would leave? "It is my wish that my husband make that decision," she said at last.

James took a step toward her. "I would be honored if you would be my wife. If I cannot have you, I will have no other."

She moved out of her brother's arms and flew into the arms of her husband.

James held her close to him, absorbing her sweetness. "I do love you, my lady wife. You may as well know it, because everyone else here at Menton Castle knows."

She pulled back and touched his face. "I loved you before I met you, and that has never changed, but only grown stronger."

James was smiling broadly as he looked at Gregory. "You see how it is—the lady prefers Scotland to Aquitaine."

Gregory smiled. "I see how it is." He drew in a deep breath, glad to see his sister so happy. "I have heard much about your . . . shall we say, reluctance to embrace anything English. I have a message for you from King Henry."

"And that is?"

"That if you will swear fidelity to him in the company of myself and Lord Robert, you and my sister can leave thereafter for Scotland."

Eleanor's face was radiant with happiness. "Oh, please, James, swear the oath. I want to go home with you so we can start our life together."

Only for a fleeting moment was there a look of the old rebelliousness on James's face. Then he looked into the loving eyes of his wife and nodded.

"I will so swear."

Gregory laughed. "I could not have let her go if you were not ready to sacrifice for her. And after all I have heard about your years of being a hostage here, I was not sure you would agree."

James smiled at his wife, wanting badly to take her upstairs and make love to her. "Your sister is very persuasive."

Gregory moved across the room to a door that connected with the great hall. "I was not here for your wedding, but I have arranged for a celebration to do you honor."

James and Eleanor looked puzzled as her brother motioned to someone beyond the door. Suddenly the air was filled with the haunting sound of many Scottish bagpipes, and eleven clansmen from Clan Glencairn marched into the room. They circled the married couple, who were now beaming.

James looked down at his wife, his eyes misty—it had been a long time since he had heard the music of home.

Her hand went into his, and there were tears in her eyes.

He pulled her to him as the sweet music from his past wove its way through his mind. "My love for you is endless," he whispered against her ear. "Let us go home," he said, dipping his head and kissing her lips, unmindful of those who watched.

Eleanor's heart was singing with the bagpipes. Her reality was more precious than any girlhood dream she had conjured up in the past.

Her gallant knight loved her—and she him.

Three French Hens

Lynsay Sands

Chapter One

December 24

"Ye'd best set that aside and wipe yer hands, girl. Cook'll be wantin' ye in a minute."

"Hmm?" Brinna glanced up from the pot she had been scrubbing and frowned slightly at the old woman now setting to work beside her. "Why?"

"I was talkin' to Mabel ere I came back to the kitchen and she says one o' them guests His Lordship brought with him don't have no maid. Fell ill or something and they left her at court."

"So?"

"*So*, Lady Menton sent Christina in here to fetch a woman to replace her," she said dryly, and nodded toward the opposite end of the kitchen.

Following the gesture, Brinna saw that Aggie was right. Lady Christina was indeed in the kitchen speaking with Cook. A rare sight, that. You were more likely to find the daughter of the house with her nose buried

in one of those musty old books she was forever dragging about than sniffing near anything domestic. It
had been a bone of contention between her and her
mother since the girl's return from the convent school.

"I still don't see what that's to do with me," Brinna
muttered, turning to frown at the older woman again,
and Aggie tut-tutted impatiently.

"I didn't raise ye to be a fool, girl. Just look about.
Do you see any likely lady's maids 'sides yerself?"

Letting the pot she had been scrubbing slide down
to rest on the table before her, Brinna glanced around
the kitchen. Two boys ground herbs with a mortar and
pestle in a corner, while another boy worked at the
monotonous task of turning a pig on its spit over the
fire. But other than Lady Christina and Cook, she and
Aggie were the only women present at the moment.
The others were all rushing about trying to finish
preparations for the sudden influx of guests that Lord
Menton had brought home with him. Aggie herself
was just returning from one such task.

"From what I heard as I entered, they've settled on
ye as the most likely lady's maid," Aggie murmured.

"Mayhap they'll send you now that yer back,"
Brinna murmured. "That would make a nice change
fer ye."

"Oh, aye," Aggie said dryly. "Me runnin' up an' down
those stairs, chasin' after some spoilt little girl. A nice
change, that. Here it comes," Aggie added with satisfaction as Lady Christina left and Cook turned toward
them.

"Brinna!"

"See. Now, off with ye and make me proud."

Releasing her breath in a sigh, Brinna wiped her
hands dry on her skirts and hurried to Cook's side as
she returned to the table that she had been working
at before Lady Christina's arrival. "Ma'am?"

"Lady Christina was just here," the older woman announced as she bent to open a bag squirming beneath the table.

"Aye, ma'am. I saw her."

"Hmm." She straightened from the bag, holding a frantically squawking and flapping chicken by its legs. "Well, it seems one of the lady's maids fell ill and remained behind at court. A replacement is needed while the girl is here. You're that replacement."

"Oh. But, well, yer awful short-staffed at the moment and—"

"Aye. I said as much to Lady Christina," Cook interrupted dryly as she picked up a small hatchet with her free hand. "And she suggested I go down to the village in search of extra help . . . just as soon as I dispatch you to assist the lady in question."

"But—oh, nay, ma'am, I never could. Why I can't. I . . ."

"You could, you can, and you will," Cook declared, slamming the bird she held on the table with enough force to stun it, stilling it for the moment necessary for her to sever its head from its body with one smooth stroke of her ax. Pushing the twitching body aside, she wiped her hands on her apron, then removed it and set it aside before catching Brinna's elbow in her strong hand and directing her toward the door.

"Ye've been a scullery maid under me now for ten of yer twenty years, Brinna, and I've watched ye turn away one chance after another to advance up the ranks. And yet God has seen fit to send ye another, and if you think to turn this away for yer dear Aggie's sake—"

She paused and rolled her eyes skyward at Brinna's gasp of surprise. "Did ye think I was so dense that I'd believe ye actually enjoy washing pans all day every day? Or did ye think I was too blind to notice that ye start afore the others have risen and stay at it until well after they've quit for the night—all in an effort to cover the fact that Aggie has slowed down in her old age?" Sighing, the cook shook her head and continued forward, propelling Brinna along with her. "I know you are reluctant to leave Aggie. She raised ye from a babe, mothered ye through chills, colds, and child-hood injuries. And I know too that ye've been the best daughter a woman could hope for, mothering and caring for her in return these last many years. Covering for her as age crept over her, making the job too hard for her old body. But ye needn't have bothered. I am not so cruel that I would throw an old woman out on her duff after years of faithful service because she can not work as she used to. She does her best, as do you, and that leaves me well satisfied.

"So . . ." Pausing, she eyed Brinna grimly. "If you don't accept this opportunity to prove yourself and maybe move up the ranks through it, I'll swat ye up the side o' the head with me favorite ladle. And don't think I won't. Now." Cook turned her abruptly, showing Brinna that while she had been distracted by the woman's words, Cook had marched her out to the great hall and to the foot of the stairs leading to the bedchambers. "Get upstairs and be the best lady's maid ye can be. It's Lady Joan Laythem, third room on the right. Get to it."

She gave her a little push, and Brinna stumbled up several steps before turning to glance down at the woman uncertainly. "Ye'll really keep Aggie on, despite her being a bit slower than she used to be?"

"I told you so, didn't I?"

Brinna nodded, then cocked her head. "Why're ye only telling me now and not sooner?"

Surprise crossed the other woman's face. "What? And lose the best scullion I've ever had? Why it will take two women to replace you. Speaking of which, I'd best get down to the village and find half a dozen or so girls to help out while the guests are here. You get on up there now and do your best."

Nodding, Brinna turned away and hurried up stairs, not slowing until she reached the door Cook had directed her to. Pausing then, she glanced down at her stained and threadbare skirt, brushed it a couple of times in the vain hope that some of the stains might be crumbs she could easily brush away, then gave up the task with a sigh and knocked at the door. Hearing a muffled murmur to enter, she pasted a bright smile on her lips, opened the door, and stepped inside the room.

"Oh, fustian!" The snarled words preceded the crash of a water basin hitting the floor as Lady Joan bumped it while peeling off her glove. Stomping her foot, the girl gave a moan of frustration. "Now look what I have done. My hands are so frozen they will not do what I want and—"

"I'll tend it, m'lady." Pushing the door closed, Brinna rushed around the bed toward the mess. "Why don't you cozy yerself by the fire for a bit and warm up."

Heaving a sigh, Lady Laythem moved away to stand by the fire as Brinna knelt to tend to the mess. She had set the basin back on the chest and gathered the worst of the soaked rushes up to take them below to discard, when the bedroom door burst open and a pretty brunette bustled into the room.

"What a relief to be spending the night within the walls of a castle again. I swear! One more night camping by the roadside and—" Spying Brinna's head poking up curiously over the side of the bed, the woman came to a halt, eyes round with amazement. "Joan! What on earth are you doing on the floor?"

"Whatever are you talking about, Sabrina? I am over here."

Whirling toward the fireplace, the newcomer

gasped. "Joan! I thought—" She turned abruptly back toward Brinna as if suddenly doubting that she had seen what she thought she had. She shook her head in amazement as Brinna straightened slowly, the damp rushes in her hands "Good Lord," Sabrina breathed. "Who are you?"

"I-I was sent to replace Lady Laythem's maid," Brinna murmured uncertainly.

This news was accepted with silence; then the brunette glanced toward Lady Laythem, who was now staring at Brinna with a rather stunned expression as well. "It is not just me," the cousin said with relief. "You see it, too."

"Aye," Lady Joan murmured, moving slowly forward. "I did not really look at her when she entered, but there is a resemblance."

"A resemblance?" the brunette cried in amazement, her gaze sliding back to Brinna again. "She is almost a mirror image of you, Joan. Except for that hair, of course. Yours has never been so limp and dirty."

Brinna raised a hand self-consciously to her head, glancing around in dismay as she realized that the ratty old strip of cloth that usually covered her head was gone. Seeing it lying on the floor, she bent quickly to pick it up, dropping the rushes so that she could quickly replace it. The cloth kept the hair out of her face while she scrubbed pots in the steaming kitchen, and half-hid the length of time between baths during the winter when the cold made daily dips in the river impossible. She, like the rest of the servants, had to make do with pots of water and a quick scrub for most of the winter. The opportunity to actually wash her hair was rare during this season.

"She does look like me, does she not?" Lady Laythem murmured slowly now, and hearing her, Brinna shook her head. She herself didn't see a resemblance. Lady Joan's hair was as fine as flax and fell in waves around her fair face. Her eyes were green, while Brinna had always been told that her own were gray. She supposed their noses and lips were similar, but she wasn't really sure. She had only ever seen her reflection in the surface of water, and didn't believe she was anywhere near as lovely as Lady Laythem.

"Aye." The cousin circled Brinna, inspecting every inch of her. "She could almost be your twin. In fact, had she been wearing one of your dresses and not those pitiful rags, you could have fooled me into thinking she was you."

Lady Laythem seemed to suck in a shaky gasp at that, her body stilling briefly before a sudden smile split her face. "That is a brilliant idea, Sabrina."

"It is?" The brunette glanced at her with the beginnings of excitement, then frowned slightly. "What is?"

"That we dress her up as me and let her take my place during this horrid holiday."

"What?" Brinna and Sabrina gasped as one; then Sabrina rushed to her cousin's side anxiously. "Oh, Joan, what are you thinking of?"

"Just what I said." Smiling brightly, she moved to stand in front of Brinna. "It will be grand. You can wear my gowns, eat at the high table with the other nobles. Why, 'twill be a wonderful experience for you! Aye. I think it might actually even work. Of course, your speech needs a little work, and your hands—"

When the lady reached for her callused and chapped hands, Brinna put them quickly behind her back and out of reach as she began to shake her head frantically. "Oh, nay. 'Tis sorry I am, m'lady, but I couldn't be takin' yer place. Why, it's a punishable offense fer a free woman to pass herself off as a noble. Why they'd—well, I'm not sure what they'd do, but 'tis sure I am 'twould be horrible."

"Do you think so?" Lady Laythem glanced toward her cousin questioningly, but found no help there. Her cousin was gaping at them both as if they had sprouted a third head between them. Sighing, Joan turned back to beam at Brinna reassuringly. "Well, it does not matter. 'Twill not be a worry. If you are discovered, I shall simply say 'twas all my idea. That 'twas a jest."

"Aye, well . . ." Eyes wide and wary, Brinna began backing away. "I don't think—"

"I will pay you."

Pausing, she blinked at that. "Pay me?"

"Handsomely," Joan assured her, then mentioned a sum that made Brinna press a hand to her chest and drop onto the end of the bed to sit as her head spun. With that sum, Aggie could retire. She could while away the rest of her days in relative comfort and peace. Aggie deserved such a boon.

"Joan!" Dismay covering her face, Sabrina hurried forward now. "Whatever do you think you are doing? You can't have this—this *maid* impersonate you!"

"Of course I can. Don't you see? If she is me, I won't have to suffer the clumsy wooing of that backwoods oaf to whom my father is determined to marry me off. I may even find a way out of this mess."

"There is no way out of this mess—I mean, marriage. It was contracted when you were but a babe. It is—"

"There is always a way out of things," Joan insisted grimly. "And I will find it if I just have time to think. Having her pretend to be me will give me that time. I would already have figured a way out of it if Father had deigned to mention this betrothal ere he did. Why, when he sent for me from court, I thought, I thought—well, I certainly did not think it was simply to ship me here so that some country bumpkin could look me over for a marriage I did not even know about."

"I understand you are upset," Sabrina murmured

gently. "But you have yet to even meet Royce of Thurleah. He may be a very nice man. He may be—"

"He is a lesser baron of Lord Menton's. He was the son of a wealthy land baron some fifteen years ago when my father made the betrothal, but his father ran the estate into the ground and left his son with a burdensome debt and a passel of trouble. He made a name for himself in battle while in service to the king, then retired to his estates where he is said to work as hard as his few vassals. He does not attend court, and does not travel much. In fact, he spends most of his time out there on his estate trying to wring some profit from his land."

Sabrina bit her lip guiltily. It was she herself who had gained all this information for Joan during the trip here from court. It had been easy enough to attain, a question here, a question there. Everyone seemed to know and respect the man. She pointed that out now, adding, "And he is succeeding at the task he has set for himself. He is slowly rebuilding the estate to its original glory."

"Oh, aye, with my dower, Thurleah shall no doubt be returned to its original wealth and grandeur . . . in about five, maybe ten years. But by the time that happens, I shall have died at childbirth or be too old to enjoy the benefits. Nay. I'll not marry him, cousin. This is the first time in my nineteen and a half years that I have even set foot outside of Laythem. I have dreamed my whole life that someday things would be different. That I would marry, leave Laythem, and visit court whenever I wish. I will not trade one prison for another and marry a man who stays on his estate all the time, a man who will expect me to work myself to death beside him."

"But—" Sabrina glanced between her cousin and Brinna with a frown. "Well, can you not simply go along with meeting and getting to know him until you come up with a plan to avoid the wedding? Why must you make the girl take your place?"

"Because 'twill give me more time to think. Besides, why should I suffer the wooing of a country bumpkin who probably does not even know what courtly love is? Let him woo the maid. His coarse words and ignorant manners will no doubt seem charming to her after the rough attentions she probably suffers daily as a serf."

"I am a free woman," Brinna said with quiet dignity. But neither woman seemed to hear, much less care about what she had to say, as Sabrina frowned, her eyes narrowing on Joan.

"I have never said anyone called Thurleah a country bumpkin or said that his manners were poor," Sabrina declared.

"Did you not?" Joan was suddenly avoiding her cousin's gaze. "Well, it does not matter. Someone did, and this maid can save me from all that by taking my place."

"Nay. She cannot," Sabrina said firmly. "It would not work. While you are similar in looks, you are not identical. She is even an inch or two taller than you."

"You are right, of course. If Father were here I would never dare try it, but it's almost providential that he fell ill and had to remain behind at court. But no one here has seen me before except for Lord Menton on the journey here, and then I was bundled up in my mantle and hood, with furs wrapped around me to keep warm. The only thing he saw was my nose poking out into the cold, and she has the same nose. The same is true of Lady Menton when we arrived. She greeted us on arrival, but 'twas only for a mere moment or two and I was still all bundled up."

"Mayhap, but what of the difference in height?"

Joan shrugged. "I was on my horse most of the journey and no doubt my mantle adds some height to me

They will not notice. It will work."

"But she is a *peasant*, Joan. She does not know how to behave as a lady."

"We will teach her what she needs to know," Joan announced blithely.

"You expect to instill nineteen years' worth of training into her in a matter of hours?" Sabrina gasped in disbelief.

"Well . . ." The first signs of doubt played on Joan's face. "Perhaps not in hours. We can claim that I am weary from the journey and wish to rest in my room rather than join the others below for dinner tonight And I shall tutor her all evening." At Sabrina's doubtful look, she gestured impatiently. "It is not as if I must teach her to run a household or play the harp. She need only walk and talk like a lady, remember to say as little as possible, and not disgrace me. Besides she need only fool Lord Thurleah, and he could not possibly spend much time around proper ladies. He does not even go to court," she muttered with disgust. She turned to the maid.

"Girl?" Joan began, then frowned. "What is your name?"

"Brinna, m'lady."

"Well, Brinna, will you agree to be me?" When Brinna hesitated briefly, Joan moved quickly to a chest at the foot of the bed and tossed it open. Rifling through the contents, she found a small purse, opened it, and poured out several coins. "This is half of what I promised you. Agree and I will give them to you now. I shall give you the other half when 'tis over."

Brinna stared at those coins and swallowed as visions of Aggie resting in a chair by the fire in a cozy cottage filled her mind. The old woman had worked hard to feed and clothe Brinna and deserved to enjoy her last days so. With the coins from this chore, she could see that she did. And it wasn't as if it was dangerous. Lady Joan would explain that it was her idea if they got caught, she assured herself, then quickly nodded her head before she could lose her courage.

"Marvelous!" Grabbing her hand, Joan dropped the coins into her open palm, then folded her fingers closed over them and squeezed firmly. "Now, the first thing we must do is—"

The three of them froze, gazes shooting guiltily to the door, as a knock sounded. At Joan's muttered "Enter," the door opened and Lady Christina peered in.

"Mother sent me to see that all is well with your maid."

"Aye. She will do fine," Joan said quickly, a panicked look about her face. Brinna realized at once that the girl feared that seeing them together, Lady Christina might notice the similarity in their looks and somehow put paid to her plans. There was no way to reassure her that the other girl wasn't likely to notice such things. It was well known at Menton that Lady Christina paid little attention to the world around her unless it had something to do with her beloved books. Which was the reason Brinna was so startled when the girl suddenly tilted her head to the side, her deep blue eyes actually focusing for a moment as she gave a light laugh and murmured, "Look at the three of you. All huddled together with your heads cocked up. You look like three French hens at the arrival of the butcher. Except, of course, only two of you are from Normandy and therefore French. Still . . . "

Brinna felt Joan stiffen beside her as an odd expression crossed over Christina's face. But then it faded and her gaze slid around the room. "They have not brought your bath up yet? I shall see about that for you." Turning, she slid out of the room as quickly as she had entered, leaving the women sighing after her.

* * *

"Why ye've made me as beautiful as yerself," Brinna breathed in wonder as she was finally allowed to peer in the looking glass at herself.

It was dawn of the morning after Brinna had stepped through the door of Lady Joan's room as her temporary maid. The hours since then had been incredibly busy ones. While Sabrina had carried Joan's message that she was too tired to dine with the others to the dinner table, Brinna had reported to the kitchens, informing Cook that the lady required her to sleep on the floor in front of her door in her room as her own maid usually did. She had then grabbed a quick bite to eat from the kitchen and spared a moment to assure herself that all was well with Aggie before preparing a trencher and delivering it to the lady, only to find her in the bath Lady Christina had had sent up. After tending her in the bath, then helping her out, Brinna had found herself ordered into the now-chill water.

Ignoring her meal, Joan had seen to it that Brinna scrubbed herself from head to toe, then again, and yet again, until Brinna was sure that half of her skin had been taken off with the dirt. She had even insisted on scrubbing Brinna's long tresses and rinsing them three times before allowing her to get out of the water. Once out, however, she had not been allowed to redon her "filthy peasant's clothes," but had been given one of Joan's old shifts instead. They had dried their hair before the fire, brushing each other's tresses by turn.

The situation had become extremely odd for Brinna at that point as the boundary between lady and servant became blurred by Joan's asking her about her childhood and life in service, then volunteering information about her own life. To Brinnā, the other girl's life had sounded poor indeed. For while she had had everything wealth and privilege could buy, it did seem that Joan had been terribly lonely. Her mother had died while she was still a child and her father seemed always away on court business. This had left the girl in the care and company of the servants. Brinna may not have had the lovely clothes and jewels the other girl had, but she'd had Aggie, had always known she was loved, had always had the woman to run to with scraped knees or for a hug. From Joan's descriptions of her childhood, she'd never had that. It seemed sad to Brinna. She actually felt sorry for the girl. . . . Until their hair was dry and the actual "lessons" began. Brinna quickly lost all sympathy for the little tyrant as the girl barked out orders, slapped her, smacked her, and prodded and poked her in an effort to get her to walk, talk, and hold her head "properly." It was obvious that she was determined that this should work. It was also equally obvious to Brinna that it would not. Lady Sabrina had not helped with her snide comments and dark predictions once she had returned to the room. By the time dawn had rolled around, Brinna was positive that this was the most foolish thing she had ever agreed to. . . .

Until she saw herself in that looking glass. She had thought, on first looking into the glass that Lady Joan held between them, that 'twas just an empty gilt frame and that 'twas Lady Joan herself she peered at. But then she realized that the eyes looking back at her were a soft blue gray, not the sharp green of the other girl's. Other than that, she did look almost exactly like Lady Joan. It was enough to boost her confidence.

"You see?" Joan laughed, lowering the mirror and moving away to set it on her chest before turning back to survey Brinna in the dark blue gown she had made her don. "Aye. You will do," she decided with satisfaction. "Now, one more time. When you meet Lord Thurleah you . . . ?" She raised a brow questioningly and Brinna, still a little dazed by what she had seen in that glass, bobbed quickly and murmured, "Greetings, m'lord. I—"

"Nay, nay, nay." Joan snapped impatiently. "Why can you not remember? When you first greet him you must curtsy low, lower your eyes to the floor, then sweep them back up and say—"

"Greetings, my lord. I am honored to finally meet you," Brinna interrupted impatiently. "Aye. I remember now. I only forgot it for a moment because—"

"It doesn't matter why you forgot. You *must* remember, else you will shame me with your ignorance."

Brinna sighed, feeling all of the confidence that the glimpse of herself in the looking glass had briefly given her seep away like water out of a leaky pail. "Mayhap we'd best be fergettin' all about this tomfoolery."

"Mayhap we had best forget all about this foolishness," Joan corrected her automatically, then frowned. "You must remember to try to speak with—"

"Enough," Brinna interrupted impatiently. "Ye know ye can't be makin' a lady of me. 'Tis hopeless."

"Nay," Joan assured her quickly "You were doing wonderfully well. You are a quick study. 'Tis just that you are tired now."

"We are all tired now," Sabrina muttered wearily from where she sat slumped on the bed. "Why do you not give it up while you can?"

"She is right," Brinna admitted on a sigh. " 'Tisn't workin'. We should give it all up for the foolishness it is and—" A knock at the door made her pause. She moved automatically to open it, then stood blinking in amazement at the man before her.

He was a glorious vision. His hair was a nimbus of gold in the torchlight that lit the halls in the early morning gloom. His tall, strong body was encased in a fine amber-colored outfit. His skin glowed with the health and vitality of a man used to the outdoors, and his eyes shone down on her as true a blue as the northern English sky on a cloudless summer day. He was the most beautiful human Brinna had ever laid eyes on.

"Lady Joan? I am Lord Royce of Thurleah."

"Gor," Brinna breathed, her eyes wide. This was the backwoods oaf? The country bumpkin whose clumsy attentions they wanted her to suffer? She could die smiling while suffering such attentions. When his eyebrows flew up in surprise, and a pinch of her behind came from Joan, who was hiding out of sight behind the door, she realized what had slipped from her lips, and alarm entered her face briefly before she remembered to curtsy, performing the move flawlessly and glancing briefly at the floor before sweeping her eyes up to his face and smiling.

"My lord," she breathed, her smile widening as he took her hand to help her up, but that smile slipped when she saw his expression.

He was frowning, not looking the least pleased, and Brinna bit her lips uncertainly, wracking her brain for the reason behind it. Had she muffed the curtsy? Said the words wrong? What, she wondered with dismay, until he shifted impatiently.

"I arrived but a moment ago," he said.

Brinna's eyes dilated somewhat as she tried to think of what she should say to that.

"I hope your journey was pleasant." She glanced around at those hissed words, her wide eyes blank as they took in Joan's impatient face peeking at her from behind the door. *"Say it. I hope your journey—"*

"Who are you talking to?"

Brinna turned back to him abruptly, stepping forward to block his entrance as he would have tried to peek around the door. The move stopped his advance, but also put them extremely close to each other, and Brinna felt a quiver go through her as she caught the musky outdoors scent of him. "Just a servant," she lied huskily, ignoring the indignant gasp from behind the door.

"Oh." Royce stared at the girl, his mind gone blank as he took in her features. She was not what he had expected. His cousin, Phillip of Radfurn, had spent several months in France in late fall, had traveled through Normandy on his way home, and had stopped a while at Laythem on his travels. He had then hied his way to Thurleah to regale Royce with his impressions of his betrothed. He had spoken a lot about her unpleasant nature, her snobbery, the airs she put on, the fact that she ran her father's home as similarly to court as she could manage. . . .

He had never once mentioned the impish, turned-up nose she had, the sweet bow-shaped lips, the large dewy eyes, or that her hair was like spun sunshine. Damn. He could have prepared a body and mentioned such things. Realizing that he had stood there for several moments merely gaping at the girl, Royce cleared his throat. "I came to escort you to Mass."

"Oh." She cast one uncertain glance back into the room, then seemed to make a decision and stepped into the hall. Pulling the door closed behind her, she rested her hand on the muscled arm he extended and smiled a bit uncertainly as he led her down the hallway.

"Well?"

Sabrina turned away from the door she had cracked open to spy on the departing couple and glanced questioningly at Joan. "Well, what?"

"You are going with her, are you not? She will need help to carry this off."

Sabrina's eyes widened in surprise. "But I am your companion. I am not to leave you alone."

"Aye. And she is me just now. It will look odd if you leave her alone with him."

Sabrina opened her mouth to argue the point, then closed it with a sigh as she realized Joan was right. Sighing again, she hurried out the door after Royce and Brinna.

Chapter Two

"The things I do for Joan."

Brinna sighed inwardly as Sabrina continued her tirade. The woman seemed to have a lot to say on the subject. Brinna just wished she wasn't the one to have to listen to it. Unfortunately, she was rather a captive audience, unable to escape the other girl. Sabrina attached herself to Brinna every time she left Lady Joan's room, and did not unattach herself until they returned.

It was the day after Christmas, the day after Lord Thurleah had arrived at Menton and come to Lady Joan's room to escort her to Holy Mass. And that was the last moment of peace Brinna had had. Mass had been longer than usual, it being Christmas Day, and Brinna had spent the entire time allowing the priest's words to flow over her as she had stared rather bemusedly at Lord Thurleah from beneath her lashes. He truly was a beautiful man, and Brinna could have continued to stare at him all day long, but of course,

Mass had eventually come to an end and Lord Thurleah had turned to smile at her and ask if she would not like to take a walk to stretch their legs after the long ceremony.

Brinna had smiled back and opened her mouth to speak, only to snap it closed again as Sabrina had suddenly appeared beside her, declining the offer. Using the risk of getting a chill as an excuse, she had then grabbed Brinna's arm and dragged her from the chapel and back to the great hall, hissing at her to remember to keep her head down to hide her gray eyes, and to try to slouch a bit to hide the difference in height.

Brinna had spent the rest of that first day as Lady Joan, staring at her feet and keeping her shoulders hunched as Sabrina had led her in a game of what appeared to be musical chairs. She would insist they sit one place, spend several moments hissing about "the things I do for Joan," then suddenly leap up and drag her off to another spot should anyone dare to come near them or approach to speak to her. Eventually, of course, there had been nowhere left to hide in plain view, and Sabrina had stopped moving about, switching her tactics to simply blocking any communication with Brinna/Joan by answering every single question addressed to Brinna as if she were a deaf mute. Most of those questions she answered had been addressed by Lord Thurleah, who had followed them around the great hall determinedly, then had seated himself beside Sabrina at dinner. He had tried to sit beside Brinna—who he thought was his betrothed Joan—but Sabrina had promptly stood and made Brinna switch seats on some lame pretext or other that Brinna hadn't even really caught. She had been too distracted by the frustration and anger that had flashed briefly on Lord Thurleah's face at Sabrina's antics to notice. It had been a great relief to her when the meal had been over and Sabrina had suggested, meaningfully and quite loudly, that she looked tired and might wish to retire early for the night.

Leaving Sabrina behind to beam obliviously at an obviously irate Lord Thurleah, Brinna had returned to Joan's room to find it empty of the lady who was supposed to occupy it. After a moment of uncertainty, Brinna had shrugged inwardly and set to work putting the room to rights, finding that she actually enjoyed the task. Working in the kitchen, and usually sleeping there as well on a bed of straw with the other kitchen help, made solitude a rare and valued commodity to Brinna. She had reveled in the silence and peace as she had puttered about the room, putting things away, then removing Lady Joan's fine gown and lying down to sleep on the pallet by the door in her shift. She had dozed off, only to awaken hours later when the door had cracked open to allow Joan to slip inside.

Brinna's eyes had widened in amazement as the dying embers from the fireplace had revealed her own worn clothes on the girl and that the strip of cloth she usually wore on her head was now hiding Joan's golden curls. But she had not said anything to let Joan know that she had seen her return dressed so when Joan had removed the tired old rags. It wasn't her place to question the lady as to her goings on. Besides, the stealthy way she had crept about and crawled into bed warned Brinna that her questions wouldn't be welcome. Pretending she hadn't seen her, Brinna had merely closed her eyes and drifted back to sleep.

Joan had still been sleeping when Lord Thurleah had arrived at the room that morning, but Brinna had been up and dressed and ready to continue the charade. Once again he had escorted her to Mass, and once again as they had prepared to leave the chapel, Sabrina had whisked her away into her game of musical chairs. Until the nooning meal, when Lady Menton had announced a need for more mistletoe. Christina had quickly arranged a party of the younger set to go out in search of the "kissing boughs." Most of the guests, Lord Royce included, were on horseback, but a wagon had been brought along to put the mistletoe in and Sabrina had managed to make some excuse to Lady Christina as to why she and "Joan" would rather ride in the wagon. So here Brinna sat, trapped in the back of a wagon with Sabrina, stuck listening to her rant about her cousin.

Who would have thought that being a lady could be so *boring*, she thought idly, her gaze slipping over the rest of the group traveling ahead of the wagon. Well, at least she was just bored and not miserable like that poor Lady Gibert, she thought wryly as her gaze settled on the other woman.

Eleanor was the girl's name. She had tried to introduce herself to Brinna/Joan the day before, and Sabrina had blocked her as she had everyone else. It was one of the few times that Brinna had been really angry at Joan's cousin and not just irritated. Eleanor was obviously terribly unhappy and in need of a friend, and Brinna felt Sabrina could have been a bit kinder about it.

Her gaze slid to the man who rode beside Lady Eleanor, and Brinna grimaced. James Glencairn. He was the girl's betrothed and also the one to blame for Eleanor's misery. The man had come to Menton as a boy, and had had a chip on his shoulders as wide as Menton's moat since arriving. Not surprising perhaps since, despite being treated well, he had been and still was a virtual hostage, kept and trained at Menton to ensure his father's good behavior in Scotland. Sadly, it appeared he was making the unfortunate Lady Eleanor just as miserable.

"You are not even listening to me," Sabrina hissed

suddenly, elbowing Brinna in an effort to get her attention.

Taken by surprise by that blow to her stomach, Brinna swung back in her seat on the edge of the wagon, lost her balance, and tumbled backward out of the cart to Sabrina's distressed squeak. She landed on her back in the hard-packed snow of the lane and was left gasping for the breath that had been knocked out of her as Sabrina's assurances caroled in her ears. "Nay, nay, all is fine. Lady Joan and I have merely decided to walk. You keep on going."

"But—" the anxious driver's voice sounded before Sabrina cut him off.

"Go on now. Off with you."

Sighing as she was finally able to suck some small amount of air into her lungs, Brinna lifted her head slightly to see that the riders on horseback had not noticed her mishap and only the wagon driver was peering anxiously over his shoulder at her as he reluctantly urged his horses back into a walk. Sabrina was trudging back toward her through the snow, glaring daggers.

"What on earth are you trying to do? Kill me with embarrassment? Ruin Joan?"

"Me?" Brinna squealed in amazement.

"Aye, you. Ladies do not muck about in the snow, you know."

"I—"

"I do not want to hear your excuses," Sabrina interrupted sharply, perching her hands on her hips to mutter with disgust, "Peasants! Honestly! Get up off your—"

"Is everything all right, ladies?"

Sabrina's mouth snapped closed on whatever she had been about to say, her eyes widening in horror as Lord Thurleah's voice sounded behind her. They had both been too distracted to realize that he and his man had taken note of their predicament and ridden back to assist. Forcing a wide, obviously strained smile to her lips, Sabrina whirled to face both men as they dismounted. "Oh, my, yes. Everything is fine. Why ever would you think otherwise?"

Brinna rolled her eyes at the panicky sound to the other girl's voice and the way her hands slid down to clutch at her skirts, tugging them to the side as if she thought she might hide Brinna's undignified position in the snow. By craning her neck, Brinna could just see Lord Thurleah's face as he arched one eyebrow, his lips appearing to struggle to hold back an amused smile. "Mayhap because Lady Joan has fallen in the snow?"

"Fallen?" Lady Sabrina's genuine horror seemed to suggest ladies simply did not *do* anything as embarrassing as fall off the back of the wagon into the snow. . . . And if they did, gentlemen shouldn't deign to notice or mention it. Sabrina's fingers twitched briefly where they held her skirts, then suddenly tugged them out wider as she gasped, "Oh, nay. You must be mistaken, my lord. Why, Lady Joan would never have fallen. She is the epitome of grace and beauty. She is as nimble as a fawn, as graceful as a swan. She is—"

"Presently lying in the snow," Lord Thurleah pointed out dryly.

Sabrina whirled around at that, feigning surprise as she peered at Brinna. "Oh, dear! However did that happen? It must have been the driver's fault. Oh, do get up, dear." Leaning forward, she clasped Brinna's arm and began a useless tugging even as Lord Thurleah bent to catch Brinna under the arms and lift her to her feet, then quickly helped Sabrina brush down her skirts before straightening to smile at Brinna gently. "Better?"

"Oh, yes, that is much better," Sabrina assured him,

cutting off any reply Brinna might have given. "Thank you for your aid, my lord. Lady Joan is usually—"

"The epitome of grace," Royce murmured wryly.

"Aye. Exactly." She beamed at him as if he were a student who had just figured out a difficult sum. "Why, she has been trained in dance."

"Has she?" he asked politely, turning to smile down at Brinna.

"Aye. And that is not all," Sabrina assured him, stepping between him and Brinna to block his view of the girl. Apparently eager to convince him that this little mishap was an aberration, she began to rattle off Lady Joan's abilities. "She speaks French, Latin, and German. Knows her herbs and medicinals like the back of her hand. Is meticulous in the running of the household. Is trained in the harp and lute—"

"The harp?" Lord Thurleah interrupted, leaning sideways to peer around the brunette at Brinna.

"Oh, aye. She plays it like a dream," Sabrina assured him, shifting to block his vision again.

"Really?" Straightening, he smiled at Brinna. "Then mayhap you could be persuaded to play for us tonight after our meal? 'Twould make a nice break from that minstrel who attempted to sing for us last night."

"Aye, it would, would it not?" Sabrina laughed gaily.

Brinna's mouth dropped open in horror as the brunette continued. "Why, he was absolutely horrid. Joan would be much more pleasant to listen to." She glanced to the side then, as if to look proudly at Brinna, then frowned as she caught the girl's expression. "What are you—" she began anxiously, turning toward her fully. Then her own eyes rounded as she suddenly grasped the reason for Brinna's abject horror. Her own face suddenly mirroring it, she whirled back toward Lord Thurleah, shaking her head frantically. "Oh, nay. Nay! She couldn't possibly play. Why she . . . er . . . she . . ."

When Sabrina peered at her wild-eyed, Brinna sighed and moved forward, murmuring, "I am afraid I injured my hand quite recently. I would be no good at the harp just now. Mayhap later on during the holidays."

"Aye," Sabrina gasped with relief, and turned to beam at Royce. "She hurt her hand." Realizing that she looked far too pleased as she said that, Sabrina managed a frown. "Terrible, really. Awful accident. Sad. Horribly painful. She almost lost full use of her hand."

Brinna rolled her eyes as the girl raved on, not terribly surprised when her comments made Lord Thurleah lean forward to glance down at the hands she was presently hiding within Lady Joan's cloak "It sounds awful. Whatever happened?" he asked.

"Happened?" Sabrina blinked at the question, her face going blank briefly, then filling with desperation. "She . . . er . . . she . . . er . . . pricked her finger doing embroidery!" she finished triumphantly, and Brinna nearly groaned aloud as what sounded suspiciously like a snort of laughter burst from Lord Thurleah, before he could cover his mouth with his hand. Turning away, he made a great show of coughing violently, then cleared his throat several times before turning a solemn face back to them.

"Aye. Well, that *is* tragic." His voice broke on the last word, and he had to turn away again for a few more chortling coughs. By the time he turned back, Brinna was biting her upper lip to keep from laughing herself at the ridiculous story. Unaware that her eyes were sparkling with merriment as she met his gaze, that her cheeks were pink with health, and that she seemed almost to glow with vitality, she blinked in confusion when he suddenly gasped and stilled.

Frowning now, Sabrina glanced at the man, her mouth working briefly before she assured him, "Aye, well, it may not sound like much, but 'twas an awful prick."

Royce blinked at that, seeming startled out of his reverie. For a moment, Brinna thought he might have to turn away for another coughing fit, but he managed to restrain himself and murmur, "Aye, well, then we must not let her play the harp. Mayhap something less strenuous on her *pricked* finger. Chess perhaps?"

"I am sorry, my lord," Sabrina answered. "I fear chess is out of the question as well. Joan has . . . a . . . er . . . tendency to suffer the . . . er . . . aching head." At his startled glance, she nodded solemnly. "They come on any time she thinks too hard."

Brinna closed her eyes and groaned at that one. She couldn't help it. Really! It was hard to imagine that the girl was supposed to be on Lady Joan's side.

"So, thinking is out of the question?" she heard Lord Thurleah murmur with unmistakable amusement.

"I am afraid so."

"Aye. Well, it must be a family trait."

Brinna's eyes popped open at that. She was hardly able to believe that he had said that. To her it sounded as if he had just insulted Sabrina. Surely he hadn't meant it that way, she thought, but when she glanced at his face, he gave her a wink that assured her that she was brighter than Lady Sabrina would have him believe. He had just insulted the girl. Fortunately, Sabrina obviously hadn't caught on to the insult. Making a sad grimace with her lips, she nodded solemnly and murmured, "Aye, I believe the aching head does run in the family."

"Ah," Lord Thurleah murmured, then gestured up the path to where the others were now disappearing around a curve in the lane. "Mayhap we should catch up to the others?"

"Oh, dear." Sabrina frowned. "They *have* left us quite far behind, have they not?"

"Aye, but my man and I can take the two of you on our horses and catch up rather quickly, I am sure," he said gently, taking Sabrina's arm and leading her the few steps to where his man waited by the horses. Brinna followed more slowly, her gaze dropping of its own accord over his wide strong back, his firm buttocks, and muscled legs as he assisted Lady Sabrina onto his mount.

At least she had assumed it was his mount. Sabrina apparently had, too, Brinna realized as he suddenly stepped out of the way to allow his man to mount behind the girl and the brunette gasped anxiously. "Oh, but—"

"Lady Joan and I will be right behind you," Lord Thurleah said gaily over her protests, nodding to his man, then slapping the horse on the derriere so that it took off with a burst of speed, carrying away the suddenly struggling and protesting Lady Sabrina. She was squawking and flapping her arms not unlike the chicken Cook had held by the legs while talking to her the other day, and Brinna bit her lip to keep from laughing aloud at the wicked comparison. Lord Thurleah turned to face her.

"Now," he began, then paused, his thoughts arrested as he took in her amused expression.

"My lord?" she questioned gently after an uncomfortable moment had passed.

"I have heard people speak of eyes that twinkle merrily, but never really knew what it meant until today," he said quietly "Your eyes sparkle with life and laughter when you are amused. Did you know that?"

Brinna swallowed and shook her head. This must be the rough wooing Joan had spoken of, she realized, but for the life of her could find no fault with it. His voice and even his words seemed as smooth as the softest down to her.

"They do," he assured her solemnly, reaching out to brush a feather-light tress away from her cheek. "And your hair . . . It's as soft as a duckling's down, and seems to reflect the sun's light with a thousand different shades of gold. It's, quite simply, beautiful."

"Gor—" Brinna murmured faintly enough that he could not have caught the word, then paused uncertainly and swallowed as his eyes turned their focus on her mouth.

"And your lips. All I can think of when I peer at them is what it would feel like to kiss you."

"Oh," she breathed shakily, a blush suffusing her face even as her chest seemed to constrict somewhat and make it harder to breathe.

"Aye, you might very well blush did you know my thoughts. How I imagine covering your mouth with my own, nibbling at the edges, sucking your lower lip into my mouth, then slipping my tongue—"

"Oh, Mother," Brinna gasped, beginning to fan her suddenly heated face as if it were a hot summer day instead of a frigid winter one. His voice and what he was saying were having an amazing affect on her body, making it tingle in spots, and sending bursts of warm gushy feelings to others. Maybe she was coming down with something, she thought with a bit of distress as his face began to lower toward hers.

"Joan! Oh, Joan!"

Royce and Brinna both straightened abruptly and turned to see Lady Sabrina walking determinedly toward them, Lord Thurleah's mounted man following behind, an apologetic expression on his face as he met his lord's glance.

"Your cousin appears to be most persistent," Royce muttered dryly, and Brinna sighed.

"Aye. She's rather like a dog with a bone, isn't she?"

"The group has stopped just beyond that bend," Sabrina announced triumphantly as she neared. "It seems the spot is just crawling with mistletoe. Even as I speak, servants are climbing and shimmying up trees to bring down some of the vines."

Reaching them, Sabrina hooked her arm firmly through Brinna's and turned to lead her determinedly in the direction from which she had come, trilling, "It is fortunate, is it not? Else you may have gotten separated from the group and not caught up at all. Then you would have missed all the fun. Imagine that."

"Aye, just imagine." Royce sighed as he watched the brunette march his betrothed off around the bend.

"He is—"

"Aye, I know," Joan interrupted Brinna dryly. "He is a very nice man. You have said so at least ten times since returning to this room."

"Well, he is," Brinna insisted determinedly. They had arrived back at Menton nearly an hour ago. Sabrina had rushed her upstairs, then insisted Brinna wait in the hall while she went in and spoke to Joan alone. Brinna had stood there, alternately worrying over what was being said inside the room and fretting over how she would explain why she was loitering about in the hall should anyone happen upon her. Fortunately, no one had come along before Sabrina had reappeared. Stepping into the hall, she had gestured for Brinna to enter the room, then walked off, leaving her staring after.

A moment later, Brinna had straightened her shoulders and slid into the room to find Joan seated in the chair by the fire awaiting her. Brinna had not hesitated then, but had walked determinedly toward her. After rejoining the group, she had spent the better part of that afternoon considering everything she had learned to date. And it had seemed to her that, while

Lady Joan was reluctant to marry Royce, it was due to some obvious misconceptions. Someone had misled her. Lord Thurleah was neither a backward oaf nor a country bumpkin given to rough wooing. He was just as polite and polished as any of the other lords. And it seemed to Brinna that she was in a position to correct this situation. All she had to do was tell Lady Joan the truth about Lord Thurleah's nature and the girl would resign herself to being his bride. Lady Joan, however, did not appear to wish to hear what she was trying to tell her. Still, she'd decided she had to try. "He isn't what you said. He doesn't woo roughly. He—"

"Brinna, please." Joan laughed, digging through her chest for Lord knows what as she went on gently. "My dear girl, you are hardly in a position to judge that. It is not as if you have spent a great deal of time around nobility."

"Aye, but, he-he spoke real pretty. He—"

"You mean he was very complimentary?" Joan asked, pausing to frown at her as Brinna nodded quickly. "Well, then, say that. Ladies do not say things like 'he spoke real pretty.' And do try to slow your speech somewhat. That is when you make the most mistakes."

Brinna sighed in frustration, then took a moment to calm herself before continuing in the modulated tones Joan had spent that first night trying to hammer into her head. "You are correct, of course," she enunciated grimly. "I apologize. But he truly is not the way you think he is. He was very *complimentary*. He said your eyes twinkled, your hair was as soft as down, and your lips—"

"It doesn't matter. I am not marrying him," Joan declared firmly, then closed the lid of the chest with a sigh and turned to face her. "Now, Sabrina told me

301

about the little incident of your falling out of the wagon."

Brinna felt herself flush and sighed unhappily. "Aye. She nudged me and—"

"It doesn't matter. All I wanted to say was to be more careful in future. And try to remember that you are a lady while pretending to be me and should comport yourself accordingly."

"Aye, my lady," she murmured.

"So, you'd best change quickly and make your way down to the meal."

Brinna's eyes widened at that. "Should I not go below and fetch you something to eat first?"

Joan arched an eyebrow at that "That would look odd, do you not think? A lady fetching a meal for her servant?"

"Nay, I meant that I could change into my own dress and—"

"That will not be necessary. I have already eaten."

Brinna stilled at that news, confusion on her face as she considered how that could have come about. One look at Lady Joan's closed expression told her that she was not to dare ask. Sighing, she shook her head. "Still, I should at least go down to the kitchens for a minute. They will wonder if they don't see me every once in a while."

"They saw you today." When Brinna blinked at that news, the other girl smiled wryly and admitted, "I donned your dress and the cloth you wore over your hair in case anyone came looking for you while you were out on the mistletoe hunt as me. Someone did. I think it was your Aggie. At least she seemed a lot like the old woman you described to me."

"What happened?" Brinna gasped.

Joan shrugged. "Nothing. She said Cook had said 'twas all right for her to bring you something to eat and check on you. I told her that 'Lady Joan' had left a whole list of chores to do while she was gone and thanked her for the food. They won't expect to see you again today. That is why I told you to inform them that I wanted you to sleep in my room. So they wouldn't expect to see much of you."

"And she didn't suspect that you were not me?" Brinna asked with disbelief.

"Who else would she have thought I was?" Joan laughed dryly. "No one would suspect that a lady of nobility would willingly don the clothes of the servant class."

"Nay, I suppose not," Brinna agreed slowly, but felt an odd pinch somewhere in the vicinity of her chest. Aggie had raised her. Watched her grow into womanhood. Surely the woman could tell the difference between her own daughter and an impostor?

"Come now." Joan clapped her hands together. "Change and get downstairs, else you will be late for the meal."

"Aye, my lady."

Chapter Three

"Riding? On that great beast?"

Brinna stared at the mount before her with nothing short of terror. This was the fourth day of her escapade, but it was the first day that she did not have Sabrina dragging her about, lecturing her as she avoided the rest of the guests while a frustrated Lord Thurleah trailed them, doing his best to be charming and friendly to the back of Brinna's head. Brinna had actually begun to feel sorry for the poor man as he'd tried to shower attendance on her while Sabrina blocked his every advance. His Lordship was not finding this courting easy. Or at least he hadn't been until this morning, for this morning Sabrina was bundled up in bed, attempting to fight off the same chills and nausea that had kept Lady Joan's maid and father from accompanying the others to Menton for Christmas.

Sabrina had started coming down ill the day before, and it had shown. She had lacked her usual bulldog-like promptness in blocking any speech between Brinna and the others, to the point that Brinna had actually had the opportunity to murmur, "Aye, my lord," twice. Brinna had also made their excuses when, after sitting down to sup with the others, Sabrina had stared at the food before them, her face turning several shades of an interesting green before she had suddenly clawed at Brinna's arm, gasping that they had to leave the table . . . at once!

Recognizing the urgency to her tone, Brinna had risen quickly and escorted Joan's cousin upstairs, where thee girl had made brief friends with the chamber pot before collapsing onto the bed clutching the stomach she had just emptied, proclaiming that she was surely dying. And if she wasn't, she wished she were.

She hadn't looked much better this morning. If anything she had seemed weaker, which was hardly surprising since she had spent the better part of the night with her head hanging over the chamber pot until there had simply been nothing left for her stomach to toss into it. Perhaps it was due to that weakness that she had not fought too hard to convince Joan to keep Brinna from impersonating her that day and to send a message that they were both ill. Whatever the case, she had not argued too vigorously, and Joan had decided that Brinna should go ahead, saying that Brinna had had several days in the company of the other nobles and would most likely be fine. Joan had merely reminded Brinna to try to say as little as possible, keep her head bowed, and not allow herself to be alone with Lord Thurleah.

Trying to tamp down the excitement whirling inside her, Brinna had nodded solemnly, then gone to the door to greet Lord Thurleah as he had arrived to escort her to Mass. If she had felt a secret pleasure at the idea of spending the day alone with Lord Thurleah, well, as alone as one could be in the company of the rest of the Menton guests, he had looked decidedly pleased by the news that Sabrina was too ill to accompany them that day.

Smiling charmingly, he had clasped her hand on his arm and escorted her to Mass as usual, but afterward, rather than steer her toward the great hall as he had every other morning, he instead had led her here to the stables, explaining that he had planned a surprise for her and Sabrina that morning. He had thought that a ride might be a nice change and had sent word to the stables to prepare their horses. Which was how she found herself standing before the three great beasts now eyeing her suspiciously, her heart stuck somewhere in the vicinity of her throat as she contemplated dying trampled beneath their hooves. For surely that was what would happen should she attempt to ride one of the saddled animals before her. Lord Thurleah might think that a ride would be a nice change, but Brinna could not help but disagree with him. Scullery maids did not have reason to be around the beasts much, and certainly didn't get the chance to ride them.

"Did I make a mistake, m'lady? This is your mount, isn't it?" the stable boy asked anxiously. Brinna cleared her throat and forced a smile.

"Aye. 'Tis my horse. I. . . . I just thought. . . . Well, 'twas a long journey here. Mayhap 'twould be better if she was allowed to rest," she finished lamely, and wasn't surprised when the stable lad and Royce exchanged slightly amused smiles before Royce murmured, "I was told you arrived at noon the day before I did. If so, then your mount has had four days to rest, my lady. No doubt she would enjoy a bit of exercise about now."

"Oh, aye," she murmured reluctantly, and wondered what to do. Lady Joan had not prepared her for a situation like this. Though she probably would have had she had a horse handy in her room at the time, Brinna thought wryly. She blinked suddenly as a thought came to her. Mayhap the girl had prepared her. Managing a grimace of disappointment, she turned to face Royce and the stable boy.

"What a lovely surprise, and it would have made a nice change too," she said, careful to enunciate clearly as Joan had taught her. "But as Sabrina is too ill to accompany us, and it isn't proper for a lady to be alone with a man who isn't her husband, well . . . " She paused to add a dramatic little sigh before finishing with, "I fear the ride shall have to be put off until Sabrina can accompany us."

"Aye, you are right, of course." Frowning thoughtfully, Royce turned to pace several steps away, and Brinna was just beginning to relax when he suddenly snapped his fingers and whirled back. "My man can accompany us."

"What?" she cried in alarm.

"My man Cedric can accompany us. He will make a fine chaperon. Unsaddle Lady Sabrina's mount, lad, and prepare Cedric's instead," he instructed as Brinna's eyes widened in horror.

"Oh, but—" she began, panic stealing any sensible argument she might have come up with. She was left gaping after him as he strode out of the stables determinedly.

"Bloody hell," she breathed as he disappeared, then turned back to eye the mount that would be hers as the stable boy led Sabrina's horse off. Joan's mare didn't look any happier at this turn of events than she felt. The beast was eyeing her rather suspiciously, and Brinna couldn't help thinking the horse knew that she wasn't Joan and was wondering what had become of the girl. Brinna was so sure of what the look in the beast's eyes meant that she shifted uncomfortably and murmured, "I haven't harmed 'er. Yer lady's alive and well." Noting that the horse didn't look particularly convinced, Brinna frowned. "It's true. 'Sides, this is all her doin'. She—"

"Who are you talking to?"

Brinna gave a start at that question, and glanced over her shoulder to find that Royce had returned and now towered over her shoulder. He was big. Very big. Why, she imagined if they stood in the sun side by side, he would cast a fine patch of shade for her to stand in. "My mare," she murmured absently, trying to judge how much wider he was. Probably twice as wide as she, she decided a bit breathlessly, not noticing the way he shook his head before sharing an amused glance with the older man who now accompanied him.

"This is my man Cedric. You may remember him from the mistletoe hunt?"

"Oh, aye. Greetings, my lord," Brinna murmured, and recalling her lessons on greeting people, started to sweep into a graceful curtsy that Lord Thurleah halted by catching her elbow. "He is a knight, not a lord," Thurleah explained gently, and Brinna felt herself flush.

"Oh, well." She hesitated, unsure how to greet the man now, then merely nodded and offered a smile, which was gently returned.

"Here you are, m'lord. I returned the lady's horse to its stall and prepared Sir Cedric's." The stable lad led the new horse forward to join the other two.

"Ah. Very good. Fast work, boy," Giving him an approving nod, Royce turned Brinna toward the door and led her out of the stables, offering her a smile as he went. Swallowing, Brinna managed a weak smile in return, but her attention was on the three horses Sir Cedric was now leading out behind them.

"I . . ." Brinna began faintly as he brought the

horses to a halt beside them, but whatever she would have said died in her throat and she nearly bit her tongue off as Royce suddenly turned, caught her at the waist, and lifted her up onto the animal that was Lady Joan's. Once he had set her down on the side-saddle, he paused to eye her solemnly, his eyebrows rising slightly.

"Are you all right, Lady Joan? You have gone white as a clean linen."

"Fine," Brinna squeaked.

"You are not afraid of horses, are you?"

"Nay, nay," she gasped.

"Nay, of course not," he murmured to himself "You rode here on this beast."

"Ahhhaye." The lie came out as a moan.

Royce nodded almost to himself, then cleared his throat and murmured, "Then, if you are not afraid, my lady, why is it you are clutching me so tightly?"

Brinna blinked at the question, then shot her eyes to her hands. They had tangled themselves in the material of his golden tunic and now clawed into it with all the determination of someone who was positive that should he release her, she would surely fall to her death. Lady Joan would not do that, of course, she told herself firmly. Forcing a smile that felt as stiff as wood, she forced her hands to release their death grip and smoothed the material down. " 'Tis fair soft material, my lord. Quite good quality."

"Ah." Looking unsure as to what to make of her behavior, he released his hold on her waist and started to move away, only to step quickly back and catch her once more as she immediately started to slip off the sidesaddle. "I am sorry, I thought you had already braced your feet," he muttered, easing her back onto the saddle again.

Swallowing, Brinna dug about the animal's side with her feet under her skirts in search of whatever it was he thought would be there to brace her feet. She found it after a moment, an inch or so higher than her feet fell. Of course, Lady Joan was a couple of inches shorter than her, and of course that would have been the perfect height for *her*. For Brinna it meant bending her legs more than she should have had to and resting at a most awkward position. This time when he released her, she managed to keep her seat, and even summoned a wobbly smile as she accepted the reins he handed her.

As he turned to mount his own horse, Brinna wrapped the reins desperately around her hands to be sure she did not lose them. Only then did she risk a glance toward the ground. As she had feared, it appeared to be a mile or more away. Aye, the ground was a long, long way down, and she could actually almost see it rushing toward her as if she were already falling off the beast. Shutting her eyes, she sat perfectly still, afraid to even breathe as she frantically wondered what the order was to make the animal move when the time came to do so. She needn't have worried. The moment Royce urged his own mount forward, and his man Cedric followed, the mare fell into line behind them.

They started at a sedate pace, but even that was enough to make Brinna wobble precariously in her seat and tighten her grasp on the reins desperately as they moved through the bailey. She was positive she would not make it out of the gates, but much to her amazement she did, and even began to relax a bit. But then they crossed the bridge and reached the land surrounding the castle and Royce suddenly urged his mount into a canter.

Brinna's horse followed suit at once, and she began to bounce around on the animal's back like a sack of turnips in the back of a cart on a rutted path. Every bone in her body was soon aching from the jarring they were taking. Still, she held on, her teeth gritting together, as she told herself that it would soon be over. It seemed to her that they had been riding for hours when Royce and his man suddenly turned to glance back at her. Forcing her lips into a tight smile, she freed a hand to wave at them in what she hoped was a careless manner. They had barely turned forward again when her foot slipped off the bar brace and she slid off the horse. All would have been well had she not wrapped the reins around her hands as she had. She would have tumbled from the horse into a nice pile of snow and that would have been that. Unfortunately, the reins were wrapped around her hand and she didn't at first have the presence of mind to unwrap them. She hung down the side of the mount, shrieking in terror as her feet and lower legs were dragged through the snow. Her shrieks, of course, just managed to terrify her mount and urge it into a faster run, which made her scream all the louder.

Royce glanced over his shoulder toward Lady Laythem, saw her wave, and glanced back the way he was heading. He had decided on this ride in an effort to get her alone. He had heard a great deal about her being spoiled and snobbish from his cousin, but so far the woman had not quite fit that description. While it was true she was silent most of the time, which could be mistaken for snobbery, he was beginning to think it merely shyness. Truly, the girl seemed to shrink within herself when in the company of others. Of course, that cousin of hers didn't help any. Sabrina answered every question he addressed to the girl in an effort to draw her out, and usually positioned herself between the two of them. It was most annoying. He was hoping that once alone Lady Laythem would shed some of that shyness and show her true nature.

"She's not much of a rider," Cedric commented,

drawing Royce from his thoughts and making him nod in silent agreement. "When do you want me to drop back and give you some privacy?" Cedric asked, having been apprised of his lord's wishes when he had fetched him.

Before Royce could respond, a sudden shrieking made them both turn back again. They were just in time to see the lady's mount come flying up and pass them, dragging the lady herself behind, kicking and screaming like a madwoman.

"My God." They both gaped after the fleeing horse briefly, until Brinna finally managed to regain her scattered wits and untangle her hand from the reins. She slid free of the mount, disappearing into the deep snow alongside the trail as the mare raced wildly off into the woods.

"I shall fetch the mare," Cedric choked out around what sounded suspiciously like laughter before urging his horse into a gallop and chasing off into the woods after the beast.

Shaking his head, Royce bit his lip in his own amusement and urged his mount forward along the trail until he reached the spot where Lady Joan had disappeared. It was easy enough to find; she had left a trail as she had been dragged along through the snow. Where the trail ended was where she must have slid off the horse. But as he stopped his mount, Royce couldn't see any evidence of her presence. His amusement replaced by concern, Royce slid off of his horse and waded into the snow calling her name, shocked to find himself waist-deep in snow as fluffy as a newborn lamb's wool. Stumbling forward, he nearly tripped over her body, then bent quickly, shoveling some of the top snow away with his bare hands before reaching into the icy fluff to find her and drag her upward, turning her at the same time until he had her head resting against his bent knee.

"Joan?" he murmured worriedly, taking in her closed eyes and the icy pallor of her cheeks. Brinna opened one eye to peer at him, then closed it again on a groan. "Are you all right? Is anything broken?"

"Only me pride," she muttered, then opened both eyes to admit wryly. "I was rather hoping ye'd just leave me here to die in shame alone."

Royce blinked at that, then felt his mouth stretch into a slow smile before he asked again, "Were you hurt? Is anything broken?"

"Nay." She sighed wryly. "But the snow went up me skirts so far me arse is a block of ice." When his eyes widened incredulously at that and a choked sound slid from his throat, Brinna stiffened anxiously She supposed ladies wouldn't refer to their behinds as arses. Or mayhap they wouldn't mention them at all. Arses or what they were called had not come up during Lady Joan's lessons. Still, from Lord Thurleah's reaction, she was pretty sure that she hadn't chosen the right word to use. The poor man looked as if he were choking on a stone.

Sitting up in his arms, she reached around to pat his back solicitously. The next moment, she clutched at his shirt with both hands under his mantle as he suddenly lunged to his feet, dragging her with him until they both stood in the small clearing he had made in the snow while digging her out. Once she was standing, he immediately began brushing down her skirts, but Brinna couldn't help noticing the way he avoided looking at her and the fact that his face was terribly red. She was trying to decide if this was from anger or embarrassment when he straightened and cleared his throat.

"Better?"

Brinna hesitated, gave her skirts a shake, then wiggled her bottom about a bit beneath them to allow the snow underneath to fall back out before allowing her skirts to drop back around her legs. Then she gave a wry shrug. " 'Tis as good as 'tis likely to get 'til I can change, my lord."

"Aye." He sighed as he saw his plans to get her alone being dashed. "We had best head right back to see to that."

Taking her arm, he led her to his horse, mounted, then bent to the side and down, grasped her beneath her arms, and lifted her onto the horse before him. Settling her there with one arm around her waist to anchor her, he reached with the other for the reins.

Clutching his arm nervously, Brinna tried to relax and get her mind off the fact that she was actually on a horse again. It was as he started to turn his mount back the way that they had come when she realized that one of the sounds that she was hearing didn't quite belong. "What is that?"

Royce paused and glanced at her, then glanced around as he too became aware of the muffled sounds she had noticed just moments earlier. It sounded like someone cursing up a blue streak. After a brief hesitation, Royce turned his horse away from the castle again and urged his mount forward until they turned the bend and came upon a loaded-down wagon stopped at the side of the path. At first it looked abandoned, but then a man straightened up from the rear, shaking his head and muttering under his breath with disgust.

"A problem?" Royce asked, drawing the man's startled gaze to them and bringing him around the wagon.

"I'm sorry, m'lord. Is my wagon in yer way?"

"Nay. There's more than enough room to get by you should I wish to," Royce assured him. "Are you stuck?"

"Aye." He glanced back to his wagon with a sigh. "I was trying to stay to the side of the path to be sure there was room fer others to pass, but it seems I strayed too far. The wagon slid off to the side and now she won't budge."

Royce shifted behind her, and she glanced up just as a decision entered his eyes. "Wait here, my lady. I won't be a moment," he murmured, then slid from the mount.

Brinna hesitated, clutched the pommel of his mount as the animal shifted restlessly beneath her, then slid from the saddle and followed to where the two men examined the situation. "Can I help?"

Both men glanced up with surprise at her question, but it was Royce who answered with a surprised smile. "Nay, Lady Joan, just stand you over there out of the way. We shall have this fellow out and on his way in a moment."

Biting her lip, Brinna nodded and moved aside, aware that ladies wouldn't trouble themselves with such problems. She stayed there as the men decided on a course of action, and even managed to restrain herself when Royce put his shoulder to the cart while the wagon driver moved to the horse's head to urge the animal forward. The wagon moved forward a bare inch or so, but then Royce's foot slid on the icy path and the wagon promptly slid back into its rut. When they paused long enough for Royce to reposition himself, Brinna couldn't restrain herself further. She wasn't used to standing on the sidelines twiddling her thumbs when there was work to be done. Giving up her ladylike pose, she hurried forward, positioning herself beside Royce to add her weight and strength to the task at hand. Royce straightened at once, alarm on his face.

"Oh, nay, Joan. Wait you over there. This is no job for a lady."

"He's right, m'lady. 'Tis kind of ye to wish to assist, but yer more like to be a hindrance than a help. You might get hurt."

Brinna rolled her eyes at that. A decade working in the kitchens carting heavy pots and vats around had made her quite strong. Of course they could hardly know that, and she could hardly tell them as much, so she merely lifted her chin stubbornly and murmured, "I am stronger than I look, sirs. And while I may not be of much help, it would seem to me you could use any little help you can get at the moment." On that note, she put her shoulder to the cart once more and arched a brow at first one man, then the other. "Are we ready? On the count of three, then."

After exchanging a glance, the two men shrugged and gave up trying to dissuade her from helping. Instead, they waited as she counted off, then applied their energies to shifting the wagon when she reached three. Brinna dug her heels into the icy ground and put all of her slight weight behind the cart, straining muscles that had been lax these last several days, grunting along with the men under the effort as the cart finally shifted, at first just an inch, then another, and another, until it suddenly began to roll smoothly forward and right back onto the path. She nearly tumbled to the ground then as the cart pulled away, but Royce reached out, catching her arm to steady her as he straightened.

"Whew." Brinna laughed, grinning at him widely before turning to the wagon driver as he hurried back to them.

"Thank ye, m'lord, and you too, m'lady," he gushed gratefully. "Thank ye so much. I didn't know how I was going to get out of that one."

"You are welcome." Royce assured him. "Just stick to the center of the path the rest of the way to the castle."

"Aye, m'lord. Aye." Tugging off his hat, the fellow made a quick bow to them both, then hurried back around the wagon to mount the driver's bench again and set off.

"Well—" Brinna straightened as the cart disappeared around the bend in the path, the clip-clop of the horse's hooves fading to silence. "That was fun."

"Fun?" Royce peered at her doubtfully.

"Well, perhaps not fun," she admitted uncertainly. "But there's a certain feeling of satisfaction when you get a job done well."

He nodded solemn agreement, then frowned as his gaze slid over her. "Your dress is ruined."

Brinna glanced down with disinterest, noting that aside from being soaked, it was now mud-splattered. " 'Tis but mud. 'Twill wash out," she said lightly, then glanced back up, her eyebrows rising at his expression.

"You are a surprise, Lady Laythem," he murmured, then explained. "When you fell off the horse and were soaked, you did not cry that your gown was ruined, coif destroyed, or curse all four-legged beasts. You picked yourself up, dried yourself off, and said 'twas the best to be done until you could change."

"Actually, you picked me up," Brinna pointed out teasingly and he smiled, but continued.

"Then, when we came across the farmer with his wagon stuck in the snow, you did not whine that I would stop to help him before seeing you safely back to the castle, changed, and ensconced before the fire. Nay. You put your own shoulder to the man's wagon in an effort to help free it."

"Ah," Brinna murmured on a sigh as she considered just how out of character her actions must seem for a lady of nobility. "I suppose most ladies wouldn't have behaved so . . . um . . . hoydenishly." She murmured the last word uncertainly, for while Aggie had often called her a hoyden as a child, Brinna wasn't sure if "hoydenishly" was a word.

"Hoydenishly?" Royce murmured with a laugh that had Brinna convinced that it wasn't a word until he added, " 'Twas not hoydenish behavior. 'Twas unselfish and thoughtful, and completely opposed to the behavior I expected from a woman who was described as a snobbish little brat to me."

"Who called me that?" Brinna demanded before she could recall that it wasn't herself that had been described that way, but Joan.

"My cousin. Phillip of Radfurn." When she peered at him blankly, he added, "He visited Laythem some weeks ago."

"Oh. Of course."

"Aye, well, I fear he took your shyness and reticence as signs of snobbery and a . . . er, slightly spoilt nature. He had me quite convinced you were a terror."

"Really?" she asked curiously. "Then why did you come to Menton?" Her eyes widened. "Did you come here to cancel the betrothal?" That would be a fine thing, wouldn't it? If he had come to cancel it and she had put paid to his intentions with her actions.

"Oh, nay I could never cancel it. My people are counting on your dower." The last word was followed by silence as his eyes widened in alarm. "I mean—"

" 'Tis all right," Brinna assured him gently when he began to look rather guilty. "I already knew that you needed the dower."

He sighed unhappily, looking not the least reassured. "Aye, well, without it I fear my people will not fare well through this spring."

"And you will do your best to provide them with what they need? Whether you want to or not?"

"Well . . ." Taking her arm, he turned to lead her back toward his horse. "It is the responsibility we have as members of the nobility, is it not? Tending to our people, fulfilling their needs to the best of our ability."

"Some of the nobility do not see it that way," she pointed out gently, and he grimaced.

"Aye. Well, some of them have no more honor than a gnat."

"But you are different."

When he gave a start at the certainty in her tone, she shrugged. "Most *lords* would not have troubled themselves to offer aid to a poor farmer either."

He smiled wryly. "I suppose not."

"But then from what I have heard, you are not like other lords. I was told that you are trying to correct neglect and damage done by those who came before you."

He remained silent, but grimaced, and she went on. "I was also told that you work very hard, even side by side with your vassals, in an effort to better things?"

His gaze turned wary, but he nodded. "I do what must be done and am not ashamed to work hard." He hesitated. "I realize that some ladies would be upset to have their husbands work side by side with the servants, but—"

"I think it is admirable," Brinna interrupted quickly, wishing to remove the worry from his face. It wasn't until she saw his tension ease that she recalled that Lady Joan had not seemed to be at all impressed by it. Before she could worry overly much about that, Royce turned to face her, taking her hands in his own.

"I need the dower. My people need it desperately. And to be honest, I would have married you for it whether you were hag, brat, whore, or simpleton— just to see my people fed and safe." He grimaced as her eyes widened incredulously at his words, then went on. "But you are none of those. You have proven to be giving and to be willing to do whatever is necessary when the need arises to help those less fortunate around you. And I want you to know that, the dower aside, I am beginning to see that I and my people will be fortunate to have you as their lady, Joan. I think we shall deal well together."

Joan. Brinna felt the name prick at her like the sharp end of a sword. She too was beginning to think that they would have dealt well together. Unfortunately, she wasn't the one he was going to marry. It was Joan. Her thoughts died abruptly as his face suddenly lowered, blocking the winter sun as his lips covered her own.

Heat. That was the first thing Brinna noticed. While her lips were chill and even seemed a bit stiff with cold, his were warm and soft as they slid across hers. They were also incredibly skilled, she realized with a sigh as he urged her own lips open and his tongue slid in to invade and conquer.

The kiss could have lasted mere moments or hours for all Brinna knew. Time seemed to have no meaning as she was overwhelmed with purely tactile sensations. She was lost in the musky scent of him, the taste and feel of him. She wanted the kiss to go on forever, and released an unabashed sigh of disappointment when it ended. When she finally opened her eyes, it was to find him eyeing her with a bit of bemusement as he caressed her cheek with his chill fingers.

"You are not at all what I expected, Joan Laythem. You are as lovely as a newly bloomed rose. Sweet. Unselfish . . . I never thought to meet a woman like you, let alone be lucky enough to marry her." With that he drew her into his arms again, kissing her with a passion that fairly stole her breath, made her dizzy, and left her clutching weakly at his tunic when he lifted his head and smiled at her. "We had best return. Else they will wonder what became of us."

"Aye." Brinna murmured, following docilely when he led her by the hand back to his mount. She would have followed him to the ends of the earth at that moment.

Three French Hens

"Good Lord!"

Brinna turned from closing the bedroom door to spy Joan pushing herself from the seat by the fireplace and rushing toward her. She was wearing Brinna's own dress. The fact that Joan was there took Brinna a bit by surprise. The other girl had usually been absent until late at night, when she'd crept in like a thief and slid silently into bed to awake the next morning and act as if nothing were amiss. But then, Sabrina wasn't usually around this room either, and that was the cause. Brinna supposed it was possible Joan had stuck around to keep an eye on the ailing girl. On the other hand, it was equally possible that she had stuck around to avoid having the fact discovered that she usually slipped out as soon as they were gone. The lady was up to something.

"Look at you!" Joan cried now, clasping her hands and taking in her sodden clothes with a frown. "You are soaked through. What did he do to you?"

"He didn't do anything," Brinna assured her quickly. "I fell off your horse and—"

"Fell off my horse!" Joan screeched, interrupting her. "You don't ride. Do you?" she asked uncertainly.

"Nay. That is why I fell off," Brinna said dryly, and pulled away to move to the chest at the end of the bed.

Joan took a moment to digest that, then her eyes narrowed. "You didn't go out with him alone, did you?"

"Nay. Of course not. His man accompanied us," Brinna assured her as she sifted through the gowns in the chest. Picking one, she straightened and turned to face Joan unhappily. "Mayhap you should play you from now on."

Joan blinked at that. "Whatever for?"

"Well . . ." Brinna turned away and began to remove the gown she wore. "You are to be married. You really should get to know him."

Joan grimaced at that. "Not bloody likely. I'll not marry him. I shall join a convent before consenting to marry an oaf like that."

"He's not an oaf," Brinna got out from between gritted teeth as she flung the dress on the bed. She turned to face Joan grimly. "He's a very nice man. You could do worse than marry him."

Joan's eyes widened at her ferocious expression and attitude, then rounded in amazement. "Why, you are sweet on him."

"I am not," Brinna snapped stiffly.

"Aye, you are," she insisted with amusement, then tilted her head to the side and eyed Brinna consideringly. "Your color seems a bit high and you had a dreamy expression on your face when you came into the room. Are you falling in love with him?"

Brinna turned away, her mind running rife with memories of his body pressed close to hers, his lips soft on her own. Aye, she had most likely looked dreamy-eyed when she had entered. She had certainly felt dreamy-eyed until Joan had started screeching. And she would even admit to herself that she might very well be falling in love with him. It was hard not to. He was as handsome as sin, with a voice like Scottish whisky, and kisses just as intoxicating. But even worse, he was a good man. She had been told as much of course, or if not exactly told, she had heard Lady Joan and her cousin discussing what they considered to be his flaws. Which to her were recommendations of his character. The fact that he worked so hard to help his people, that he was determined to better things for them . . . He put their needs before his own, even in matters of marriage. How could one not admire that?

Aside from that, he had been nothing but gentleness

itself in all his dealings with her. He was no backward oaf or country idiot. Or at least, if he was, Brinna couldn't tell. Nay, he had treated her sweetly and well, staying near her side during Mass and throughout every day since Christmas morning. Despite Sabrina's interference, she had felt protected. And he had not taken advantage of her reaction to those kisses in the woods, though the Good Lord knows he could have. Brinna suspected that had he wished it, she would have let the man throw her skirts up and have her right there at the side of the path, and all it would have taken was a couple more kisses. She suspected he had known as much too, but he hadn't taken advantage of that fact. Nay, he was a good man. A man she could easily love with her whole heart. But if she gave her heart to him, it would be lost forever, for he was engaged to Joan, and he had to marry her, else he would lose the dower that his people needed so desperately.

He couldn't do that. She knew it. He wouldn't do it. She had not known him long, but she knew already that he was a man who took his responsibilities seriously. His people needed that dower, so he would marry to attain it and Brinna had no hope of having him. She couldn't go on with this charade. Couldn't risk her heart so. Not even for Aggie and the possibility of seeing her comfortable. She would not do this anymore. She had to convince Joan to resign herself to this marriage, but to do that, she had to convince her that he wasn't the backwards oaf someone had led her to believe he was.

"Who is it that told you that Lord Thurleah was a country bumpkin and oaf?" Brinna asked determinedly, and Joan got a wary look about her suddenly.

"Who?" she echoed faintly, then shrugged. "It must have been Sabrina. She questioned people on the journey here to find out more about him for me."

Brinna's gaze narrowed suspiciously. "But didn't

she say the day I became your maid that she hadn't said that he was an oaf—just that he worked hard to improve his lot in life?"

Joan shrugged, avoiding her eyes. "Then someone else must have mentioned it."

"Could it have been Phillip of Radfurn?" Brinna asked carefully, feeling triumph steal up within her as the other girl gave a guilty start, her eyes wide with shock. "It *was* him, wasn't it? He is deliberately making trouble between the two of you. He visited you at Laythem, told you that Royce was a backward oaf, with no social graces, then went on to his cousin's to tell him that you were a—"

When she cut herself off abruptly, Joan's gaze narrowed. "To tell him that I was what?"

"Oh, well . . ." Now it was Brinna's turn to avoid eye contact. "I don't really recall exactly."

"You are lying," Joan accused grimly. "What did he say?"

Brinna hesitated, then decided to follow one of Aggie's maxims. The one that went, *If yer in a spot and don't know what to do or say, honesty is yer best option.* "He told Lord Thurleah that you were a selfish, spoilt brat."

"What?" The blood rushed out of Joan's face, leaving her looking slightly gray for a moment, then poured back in to color her red with rage. "Why, that—" Her eyes, cold and flinty, jerked to Brinna. "Change and return below," she ordered coldly, moving to the door. "And no more riding or anything else alone with Lord Thurleah. His man is not a suitable chaperon." Then she slid out of the room, pulling the door closed with a snap.

Chapter Four

"I think you are improving."

"Oh, aye." Brinna laughed dryly as she clutched at the hands Royce held at her waist to steady her as they skimmed along on the lake's frozen surface on the narrow-edged bones he had insisted she try. Royce called them skates, and claimed that what they were doing was skating. It was something he had picked up while on his travels in the Nordic countries. Brinna called it foolish, for a body was sure to fall and break something trying to balance on the sharp edge of the bones that he had strapped to her soft leather boots and his own.

He had been trying for days to convince her to try skating. Ever since the afternoon they had gone for the ride. The day Sabrina had felt under the weather. But it wasn't until today that she had given in and agreed, and that was only because she had wanted to please him. She caught herself doing that more and more often these days; doing things to try to please him. It was worrisome when she thought about it, so she tried not to.

"Nay, he is right, you are improving," Sabina called. Having overheard his comment and Brinna's answer as they had skated past where she stood on the edge of the frozen lake, Sabrina had called out the words cheerfully. "At least you have stopped screaming."

Brinna laughed good-naturedly at the taunt. Sabrina had relaxed somewhat during the past several days. She had recovered quickly from her illness and returned to her chore as chaperone the morning after the ride. But she had taken a different approach on her return. She still accompanied Brinna everywhere, but no longer bothered to try to keep her from talking to everyone, Royce included. She had also stopped forcing herself between the two of them when they walked about or sat for a bit. Brinna supposed she had decided it wasn't worth the trouble when they had already spent a day together without her interference.

"You are starting to shiver," Royce murmured by her ear. "We have been out here quite a while. Mayhap we should head back to the castle to warm up."

"Aye," Brinna agreed as he steered them both back toward Sabrina. "Mayhap we should. 'Tis almost time to sup anyway."

Sabrina seemed to greet the decision to return with relief. She herself had refused to be persuaded to try the "sharp bones" as she called them, so she had stood on the side, watching Brinna's antics instead. While it had been amusing, her lack of activity meant that she was a bit chill and so was eager to return to the warmth of the castle. She waited a bit impatiently as they removed the bones from their feet, then accompanied them back to the castle, teasing "Lady Joan" gently about her ineptitude on the ice.

As it turned out, it was later than any of them had

realized, and the others were already seated at table when Brinna, Royce, and Sabrina entered. They were laughing over Brinna's less-than-stellar performance on skates that afternoon, but fell silent as they realized that they were late. Not that most people noticed their entrance—the great hall was abuzz with excited chatter and laughter—but Lady Menton spotted them arriving.

Casting apologetic glances toward their hostess, the three of them hurried to the nearest spot with an opening and managed to squeeze themselves in. It meant they ended up seated among the knights and villeins at the low tables, but such things couldn't be helped—besides, the high table seemed quite full even without them.

"It looks like a celebratory feast," Brinna murmured as the kitchen doors opened and six women filed out, each bearing a tray holding a succulent roast goose on it.

"Aye," Sabrina agreed with surprise. "I don't recall Lady Menton saying anything this morning about—"

Brinna glanced at the brunette sharply when her unfinished sentence was interrupted by a gasp. Spotting the alarm on Sabrina's face and the way she had blanched, Brinna frowned and touched her hand gently. "What is it? Are you not feeling well again?"

Sabrina's turned to her, mouth working but nothing coming out.

"Joan? My lady?"

Brinna glanced distractedly at Royce when he touched her arm. "Aye?"

"Is that not your father?"

"My father?" she asked blankly, but followed his gesture to the head table. Her gaze slid over the people seated there, and she suddenly understood why the table was full even without them. William of Menton and an older man now helped fill it. Her gaze fixed on the older man. He was handsome with blond hair graying at the temples, strong features, and a nice smile. Brinna would have recognized him anywhere. He was Lord Edmund Laythem, a good friend of Lord Menton's and a frequent visitor at Menton. He was also Joan's father.

Brinna's gaze was drawn to Lady Menton as the woman leaned toward her husband to murmur something. Whatever it was made the two men glance across the room toward Brinna. For a moment she felt frozen, pinned to her seat like a bug stuck in sticky syrup as her heart began to hammer in panic and her breathing became fast and shallow. What if he stood and came to greet her? He would know. They would all know. But he didn't rise. Edmund Laythem merely smiled slightly and nodded a greeting.

It took an elbow in her side from Sabrina to make Brinna nod back and force what she hoped was a smile to her own lips.

"Mayhap we should go greet him," Royce murmured beside her and started to rise, but Brinna clawed at his arm at once.

"Oh, nay! Nay. I—there is no sense disrupting Lady Menton's feast. Time enough to greet him afterward."

Royce hesitated, then settled in his seat reluctantly. "As you say, my lady," he murmured, then smiled wryly. "Well, now we know the reason behind the feast. Lady Menton must have put it on to welcome your father and her son."

"Aye," Brinna murmured faintly, then tore her eyes away from the high table and swiveled abruptly toward Sabrina.

"What are we going to do?" Sabrina asked in a panic before she could say a word, and Brinna's heart sank as she realized the brunette would be of little help.

"Are you not going to eat?"

Forcing a smile, Brinna turned to face forward at

Royce's question. "Of course. Aye. We shall eat," she murmured, casting Sabrina a meaningful sideways glance.

Nodding, Sabrina set to her meal, but there was a frown between her eyes as she did, and she was still as tense as the strings on a harp as she cast nervous glances toward the head table. Brinna was aware of of her actions, but avoided looking at the head table at all costs herself. She kept her head bowed, eyes fastened on her meal as she ate, and slowly began to shrink in her seat.

It was the most excruciating meal Brinna had ever sat through. Worse even than her first night as Joan's fill-in. She wasn't even sure what she ate. It all tasted like dust in her mouth as her mind raced about in circles like a dog chasing its tail, desperately searching for a way out of this mess. An excuse to hurry up stairs right after the meal and avoid Lord Laythem was needed, but her mind seemed consumed with the fact that this was the end of the road for her. She had thought she had a couple more days at least to bask in the warmth of Lord Thurleah's attention, but this was it. The end. These were her last moments with him. If only—

She cut the wish off abruptly. It was no good. She could not have Royce. He was a lord and she just a scullery maid. He needed a large dower such as Joan could provide. She had nothing but the ragged clothes presently on Lady Joan's back. Still, he had come to her on Christmas Day like a gift from God that had brightened her life and made her experience things she had never thought to feel. It broke her heart that he was a gift meant for someone else and that she could not keep him.

"Are you done?" Royce asked after finishing off the last of his ale. The meal was coming to a close. Several people at the lower tables around them had already risen to return to their chores, or to find a place to relax and listen to the minstrel, who was even now preparing to torture them some more with his version of music. Even Brinna had finished off what Royce had served her with, though she couldn't recall actually eating a thing. "Shall we go greet your father now?"

"Oh, I-I should . . . er . . ."

"Aye, we should," Royce agreed, misunderstanding her stammering and taking her arm as he rose to his feet.

Brinna remained silent, following reluctantly as he led her toward the head table where most of the guests still sat chatting over their ales, her mind still squirming about in search of escape. Luck lent a hand as the others began to rise in groups now to leave the tables, slowing them down and making Royce and Brinna proceed in single file as they weaved through the crowd. Royce let go of her hand then, and Brinna walked behind him for a couple of steps, then simply turned on her heel and made a beeline for the steps that led upstairs.

She had to get to Joan's room. She had to find Joan, and the only place she could think to look was the room. Not that she would normally be there at this hour. Joan didn't even sleep in her own room anymore. She had fallen into the pattern of leaving as soon as Brinna departed with Royce for Mass, then not returning until just ere dawn on the next morning. She had been doing so since the day Brinna had told her what Royce's cousin, Phillip of Radfurn, had said. The girl had stormed out in a fury, been absent through the night, then returned just moments before Royce had arrived to escort the woman he thought was Lady Joan to Mass. The fact that Lady Joan had been out all night had been worrisome enough to

Brinna, but the fact that she had returned in a fabulous mood, and had actually glowed with satisfaction and happiness as she had insisted that they continue with the charade, had made Brinna fear that whatever was going on did not bode well for Royce.

Now, Brinna just hoped that the girl, wherever she normally spent her time, had heard about her father's arrival and had returned to the room, prepared to take over her role as a member of nobility.

Royce stepped onto the dais directly behind Lord Laythem and tapped the man on the shoulder, offering a polite smile when he turned on his seat to glance at him.

"Royce. Greetings, son." The older man stood at once, as did Lord Menton and his son William. "I hope you are having a good Christmas here with Robert and his family? I am sorry I haven't been here from the beginning, but I fear the ague and chills felled me where many men have failed."

Royce smiled at his wry words and nodded reassuringly. "I was told that you were ill. I hope you are recovered now?"

"Aye, aye. I'm still regaining my strength and I've a stone or two to put back on, but I feel much better."

"I'm glad to hear it. Your daughter and I—" He turned slightly to gesture Joan forward as he spoke, then paused, blinking in surprise as he saw that she was no longer with him. "Where did she—" he began in bewilderment, and Lord Laythem clapped a hand on his shoulder and smiled wryly.

"I think she slipped away when you moved through that one group halfway up the room," Edmund Laythem told him dryly, revealing that he had watched their approach.

Royce's eyes widened at this news. "Why would she—"

"She was none too pleased with me when last we met," the older man confessed, then shrugged. "I fear I handled things badly. I never really bothered to mention the betrothal agreement until she arrived at court on her way here. It was all a great surprise to her and she was understandably upset by my neglect."

"I see," Royce murmured thoughtfully.

"Aye, well, I am sorry if she has caused you any trouble because of it?" It was a question as well as an apology, and Royce reassured him quickly.

"Oh, nay. She has been delightful. Of course, Lady Sabrina was another matter at first. She would not even let me talk to Joan for the first few days."

Lord Laythem's eyebrows rose at that, but he shrugged. "Sabrina can be a bit overeager when a task is set to her. No doubt that is all that was." He smiled wryly, his gaze moving to the brunette, who still sat in her seat at the table, watching them anxiously. "Actually, I must have a word with her. Her father was at court over the holidays and arranged a marriage for her. He sent some men with me to retrieve her back to prepare for it. If you will excuse me?"

"Of course." Royce stepped aside to allow the man past him, then took a moment to greet William of Menton and compliment Lord and Lady Menton on the feast he had just enjoyed before turning to survey the room in search of Joan. Catching a glimpse of her disappearing up the stairs, he excused himself and hurried after her.

Brinna opened the door to enter Joan's room, and found herself pushed back out by a hand on her chest.

"I just have to check on something," Joan trilled gaily before allowing her body to follow her arm out of the room.

"What—" Brinna began in confusion as the girl pulled the door closed, but Joan waved her to silence, then glanced quickly up and down the hall before dragging her to the shadows near the top of the stairs to keep an eye on the people below.

"My father arrived today," Joan said.

"Aye, I know. 'Tis why I came up here. To avoid him."

Joan nodded at that, but frowned as she rubbed her forehead. "This complicates things."

"Complicates things?" Brinna goggled at her, but Joan didn't notice.

"Aye. My maid came with him. That is who I was talking to in our room."

"Your room," Brinna said firmly. "And to my mind this doesn't complicate things. It ends them. You shall have to go back to being you. 'Tis for the best anyway."

Joan did not appear to see the sense behind the suggestion as she shook her head grimly. "Nay. I cannot I need to—" Her expression closed as she caught herself, then said more calmly, "There is no need to end it now. I shall insist my maid rest for the remainder of my stay to recover from her recent illness and the journey here. That way you will not be expected to return to the kitchens, she will not get in the way, and we can continue with our agreement."

"What of your father?"

"Oh, damn, here comes Lord Thurleah."

Brinna glanced down the stairs at Joan's anxious tones, her heart skipping a beat as she saw him start up the stairs toward them. Her gaze returned to the other girl in a panic. They were both dressed as Lady Joan at the moment. It would not do to be seen together. "What—"

Joan cut her off by giving her a shove toward the stairs. "Get him out of here. He must not see us together."

"But your father!" Brinna cried in dismay, resisting her push.

"Just avoid him," Joan snapped impatiently. "Now, get going."

The shove she gave her this time nearly sent Brinna tumbling down the stairs. Catching herself at the last moment, she cast a glare back toward the shadows that hid Joan, then hurried down the stairs to meet Royce.

"Where did you go?" were his first words. "One moment you were behind me and the next you were gone."

"Oh . . . I . . . I went to my room to greet my maid," she lied lamely, not surprised when Royce arched one eyebrow doubtfully.

"Before greeting your father?"

"Well, she was very ill when I left her at court."

"As was your father," he pointed out dryly, and Brinna grimaced.

"Aye, but—"

"Your father told me that you were angered with him for keeping the news of our betrothal to himself and not giving you warning," he interrupted before she could say something else stupid.

"Aye, well . . . "

"And while he should have perhaps given you more warning, he seems to regret the rift between you."

"Yes, well—"

"Besides, you do not mind so much, do you? About marrying me, I mean?"

"Nay, of course not," she assured him quickly.

"There you are then. 'Tis only polite to greet him. Now, where has he got to?" Pausing halfway up the stairs, he peered about until he spotted Lord Laythem below talking to Sabrina. "Oh. He is still with your cousin. He is passing on a message from her father, your uncle." Hesitating, he glanced back at Brinna, smiling wryly. "Mayhap we should leave them in peace until they finish. Would you care for a beverage while we wait?"

"Aye," she murmured, then continued down the stairs with him until they reached the bottom and she spied a knight and one of the kitchen girls slipping outside. An idea springing to mind, Brinna stopped abruptly, tugging on his hand. "Nay."

He turned to her in surprise. "Nay?"

"Nay." She paled slightly as her gaze slid past him to see that Lord Laythem had finished speaking to Sabrina and was now rising, his gaze on where she and Royce stood. "I-I need . . . air."

Frowning with concern, Royce clasped her lightly by the arms. "Are you all right? You've gone quite pale."

Brinna dragged her gaze away from the approaching Lord Laythem and focused on Royce. "Nay," she said firmly. "I am not all right. 'Tis the heat. Do I not get out into the fresh air this minute, I'm sure to faint."

It was all she had to say. She barely had time for one more glance over his shoulder at Lord Laythem as he weaved his way toward them; then Royce had whirled her toward the great hall's doors and propelled her to and through them.

"Better?" he asked solicitously as the doors closed behind them.

Her arms moving automatically to hug herself against the cold winter night, Brinna glanced uncertainly about the courtyard. Lord Laythem had been close enough to see where they had gone to, and she very much feared his following them. Standing on the steps, handy for him to find on exiting the hall, hardly seemed the wisest thing to do.

"Perhaps the stables," she murmured thoughtfully. Surely Lord Laythem would never look for them there? Certainly it was the last place Brinna would have chosen to go were she not desperate to hide.

"The stables?"

"What a wonderful idea." Brinna beamed at him as if it had been his idea. "No doubt the stables shall make me feel better." Taking his arm, she attempted to move him down the steps. It was like trying to shift a centuries-old tree. The man was immovable. Certainly too damn big for her slight weight. "My lord? Will you not come with me to the stables? Tis warmer there," she coaxed, tugging at his arm.

Heaving a sigh, he started forward down the stairs. "I thought you said that the castle was too hot and you needed to be outside else you might faint. Now you wish to go to the stables because 'tis warmer?"

"Aye, well, the castle is too warm, and the night too cold. The stables shall be just right, I am sure," she muttered, dragging at his arm in an effort to speed him up. "Do you not think we might walk faster?"

"You were faint a moment ago," he protested.

"Aye, but the exercise will do me good."

Muttering under his breath, he picked up his pace a bit, hurrying across the courtyard behind her as she began a jog toward the stables.

"I am not sure this is a good idea," Royce complained as they reached the stables.

Ignoring him, Brinna tugged the stable doors open and slid inside. Turning to glance back the way they had come as he slid in behind her, she spied a dark shape that could have been Lord Laythem standing on the stairs staring after them, and felt her heart skip a beat. Whirling away as he closed the door, she eyed the stables almost desperately, searching for somewhere to hide lest Joan's father follow them. Then she started down the row of stalls determinedly.

"What are you doing?" Royce asked curiously, following her the length of the building until they reached the last stall.

"I thought to check on my mare," she lied grimly.

"She was back near the door," he pointed out dryly, and Brinna rolled her eyes at that bit of news, then for want of any other thought of what to do, whirled, caught him by the tunic, and reached up onto her tiptoes to plaster her lips on his. It was the only thing she could think to do. His kisses made her thought processes fuzzy and scattered and made her willing to follow him anywhere unquestioningly. She could only hope they had the same effect on him and would stop his questions. Unfortunately, it did seem to her that he was better at this. While their earlier kisses had been fiery and passionate, now, without his participation, it did seem to be a wasted exercise. Brinna was about to pull away when he suddenly relaxed and kissed her back.

Sighing in relief, Brinna leaned into him and let her arms creep up about his neck. She had the curious urge to arch and stretch against him like a cat, but he pulled away before she could, a question in his eyes.

"How do you feel now?"

"Wonderful," Brinna purred, leaning her head on his chest with a small sigh, only to stiffen at his next words.

"Then mayhap we should head back."

"Oh, nay," she gasped anxiously.

"We shouldn't be here alone. It isn't proper, Joan."

Joan. She stared at him silently. He was Joan's. But for just this moment in time, she wanted to pretend he was hers. Joan wouldn't care. She didn't want him. But Brinna did. She wanted to hold him close for one night. Then hold those memories close for all the days of her future as she worked in her little cottage.

"Joan?"

"Mayhap I don't feel proper," she whispered huskily, and Royce's eyes widened incredulously. For a moment they stood frozen in silence. Then he suddenly groaned and pulled her back into his arms, his mouth lowering to cover hers in a kiss that made her legs weak. This time there was no restraint. Nothing held back. He gave her all his passion, overwhelming her with it as his hands closed over her breasts through her gown.

Pressing her back against the stall, he broke the kiss and turned his attention briefly to undo the lacings of her dress. Brinna gasped as the neckline slid apart and he tugged the collar of her shift down, revealing her naked breasts. Cold winter air chilled them briefly before Royce covered them with his hands. Growling deep in his throat, he cupped them, his thumbs running over her erect nipples as he pressed another hard, fast kiss to her lips. Then he made a trail down her throat, across her collarbone, and down to the erect tip of one breast, which he sucked into his mouth hungrily.

Brinna shuddered. Her hands clenched in his hair, then dragged his face back up for a kiss, and she thrust her own tongue into his mouth as he had done to her. Releasing his head, she dropped her hands down to slide her fingers beneath his tunic, fanning them over his hard flat stomach, then running them up over his ribs to his chest.

She felt the cool breeze creep its way up her left leg with some peripheral part of her mind, but really didn't realize what it meant until his hand brushed against her hip. Before she could register surprise, his hand had slid around between her legs and up the inside of her thigh, a warm caress. Brinna gasped into his mouth, jerking in his arms as his hand covered her womanhood, cupping it briefly before he slid a finger between her folds to investigate her warmth and heat as he urged her legs further apart with a knee between her own.

She heard the keening whimpers for quite a while before she realized that they were coming from her own throat. Suddenly embarrassed, she tugged her mouth away and turned her head until she found his shoulder. Pressing her mouth against it, she retrieved her hands from beneath his shirt, then wasn't sure what to do with them. When Royce caught one of her hands and drew it down to the front of his braies, pressing it against the solid hardness that had grown there, she froze, raising fear-filled eyes to him. He met her gaze, read her fear, and paused, his hand stilling between her legs. She saw uncertainty burst to life in his eyes, and would have kicked herself had she been able to.

"You are afraid. Mayhap we should stop and—" he began, his voice dying, eyes widening in shock as she suddenly moved the hand that clasped him through his braies, and slid it down the front of his braies to touch his bare flesh.

"Move to the straw," she suggested huskily, giving him a gentle squeeze.

Uncertainty fleeing under passion, Royce caught her by the backs of her thighs and lifted her up. Brinna wrapped her legs around his hips, and caught them at the ankles to help hold them up as he turned to walk to the back corner of the stables where several bales of hay rested. He set her on one that would keep her at the same height, then reached up to tug her gown and shift off her shoulders as she released her legs and flattened them against the front of the bale she sat on. Once the cloth lay in a pool around her waist, Brinna leaned back, tilting her head back as she arched her breasts upward for his attention.

He did not disappoint her. His hands and mouth paid homage, touching, caressing, licking, nibbling, and sucking at her goose-bumped flesh until she moaned aloud with her desire for him. It wasn't until then that he caught at the hem of her skirt again. Sliding his hands beneath it, he clasped her ankles, then ran his hands up the flesh of her calves to her thighs, pushing the material before him, urging her legs apart as he did. His mouth moved to cover her gasps as she shuddered beneath his touch, and she drank of him deeply, then bit his lower lip as his hands met at her center. He caressed her, then slid one finger smoothly into her, and Brinna arched into the invasion, her hands shifting to his shoulders and clutching him desperately as she wriggled into the caress.

Tearing her mouth away then, she shook her head desperately and gasped as he slid his finger out, then back in. Reaching down into his braies again, she grasped him almost roughly, trying to tell him what she wanted as she bit into his shoulder to prevent crying out. She felt the cloth loosen around her hand, then felt it no longer as he sprang free in her hand. Brinna ran her hand the length of his shaft, then pressed her feet against the bale, sliding her behind to the edge of it in search of him.

Chuckling roughly at her eagerness, Royce gave in to her request and edged closer, brushing her hand away to grasp his manhood himself and steer it on the course it needed to follow. She felt him rub against her, caressing her as his hand had done a moment ago, and wiggled impatiently, but still he did not enter her, but teased and caressed and rubbed until Brinna thought she would go mad. It was at that point that the tension that had been building inside of her suddenly broke. Taken by surprise, Brinna cried out, her legs snapping closed on either side of his hips as she arched backward.

Covering her mouth with his own, Royce chose that moment to thrust into her. A sudden sharp pain flared briefly where they joined, and Brinna stiffened against it, then gasped and relaxed somewhat as it passed. When he began to draw himself out then, Brinna's eyes popped open, dismay covering her face as she clutched at his buttocks to keep him inside her.

"Nay," she gasped in protest, then blinked in surprise as he drove into her again. "Oh," she breathed, arching automatically and returning his smile a bit distractedly as she felt the tension begin to build again. "Oh."

"Aye," Royce murmured, slipping his hands beneath her buttocks and lifting her into his thrusts.

"Joan?"

Brinna blinked her eyes open with a sigh, sorry to see her stolen moment pass so swiftly. They had just finished the ride she had started. Royce had spilled his seed with a triumphant cry that had made the horses shift and whinny nervously in their stalls in response. Brinna had followed him quickly, biting into the cloth of his tunic as her body spasmed and twitched around him. Then he had slumped against her slightly, holding her even as she held him. Now it was over, it seemed, and he had brought reality back with that one name. *Joan*.

"Joan?" Straightening, he smiled down at her with a combination of uncertainty and gentleness. "Are you all right? I did not hurt—"

"Joan?"

They both stiffened at that shout from out of the darkness.

Brinna peered anxiously over Royce's shoulder even as he cast a glance that way himself. They both saw that the stable door was open and someone was walking up the shadowed aisle toward them. Cursing, Royce pulled out of her and quickly tugged her skirt down into place. Replacing himself inside his braies, he turned away, hiding her with his back as he faced the approaching man.

"Who goes there?" he asked tensely, reaching for his sword.

"Lord Laythem."

Brinna heard the breath whoosh out of Royce at that announcement, and bit her lip as she clasped Joan's gown to her breasts and ducked fully behind him. There was a moment of tense silence as the man approached, then the crunch of straw under his feet ended and there was a weary sigh.

"Well, it would seem I waited too long to see if you would return to the hall," he murmured, then added wryly, "Or perhaps not long enough."

"I am sorry, my lord," Royce began grimly. "I—"

"Do not be sorry, lad. I was young once myself. Besides, this makes me feel better. At least now I won't have to feel that I forced Joan into something."

Brinna saw Royce's hands unclench as he relaxed. Then Lord Laythem cleared his throat and murmured, "Though it may be a good idea to move the wedding date forward a bit."

"Aye. Of course," Royce agreed promptly. "Tomorrow?"

"Eager, are you?" Lord Laythem laughed. "I shall talk to Robert, but I do not think tomorrow is likely. We crown the Lord of Misrule tomorrow," he reminded him. "I'll see what I can arrange and let you know."

"As you wish, my lord." Brinna could hear the grin in Royce's voice and knew he was pleased. Her own heart seemed suddenly leaden. But then, she wasn't the one he would be marrying.

"Aye. Well, you had best collect yourselves and return to the hall. I would not want anyone else to catch the two of you so."

"Aye, my lord."

"Good." There was a rustle as he turned to leave, then he paused. "Joan, I want to talk to you ere Mass on the morrow . . . Joan?"

"Aye," Brinna whispered, afraid to speak lest he notice that her voice differed from his daughter's. Not apparently noticing anything amiss, he wished them good night and left.

Royce whirled to face her as soon as Lord Laythem was gone. He was jubilant as he helped her redon Joan's gown, talking excitedly about how this was a wonderful thing. How the arrival of the dower early would aid his people. They would leave the day after the wedding. They would travel to Thurleah, purchase this, repair that, and spend every spare moment in bed. Brinna listened to all this, forcing herself to smile and nod, and doing her best to hide the fact that her heart was breaking.

Chapter Five

"Here, put this on."

Brinna turned from straightening the bed linens as Lady Joan slammed into the room. "My lady?"

"Put this on," Joan repeated grimly, stripping her gown even as she spoke. "And give me your dress."

"But—"

"Now, Brinna. There is no time."

Brinna started to undress, responding automatically to the authority in Joan's voice, then halted. "Nay We can not do this. *I* cannot. Your father is here now. He will—"

"Today they appoint the Lord of Misrule. All will be chaos all day. 'Sides, he will not bother with me—*you*. He will be drinking and carousing with Lord Menton. You can easily avoid him."

Brinna shook her head grimly. "I cannot."

"You must," Joan hissed, grabbing her hand desperately and giving it a squeeze. "Just this one last time."

"But—"

"You got me into this," Joan said accusingly, her patience snapping, and Brinna's eyes widened in amazement.

"Me?"

"Aye, you. If you hadn't let Royce drag you off to the stables for a quick tumble like some cheap—" She snapped her mouth closed on the rest of what she was going to say and sighed.

"How did you find out?" Brinna asked, her voice heavy with guilt.

"What do you think Father wished to speak to me about?" she asked grimacing, then bit her lip miserably. "The wedding is tomorrow. I have to warn—" She snapped her mouth closed again and frowned, then turned away, took two steps, then turned back. "Please? Just this one last time. You will not be discovered. I promise. Truly, you know as well as I that 'twill be chaotic today."

"Not at Mass it won't be."

Sensing that she was weakening, Joan pounced. "You shall leave late for Mass. That way, Father will be seated at the front with Lord and Lady Menton, and you and Lord Thurleah will be at the back of the chapel. Just don't let Thurleah dawdle once Mass is over and it should be all right."

Brinna blew her breath out on a sigh, then nodded and continued to undress, wondering as she did why she had even hesitated. She wanted to do this. She was eager to spend any little moment of time with Royce that she could while she could.

"Oh, good," Joan said.

Brinna whirled from closing the bedroom door to stare at Joan in amazement as she rushed toward her. Truly, she had not expected the other girl to be there yet. She had thought Joan would spend every last moment of freedom she had as far from this room as possible. Actually, she had rather hoped that Joan would. After the day she had had, Brinna could have used a few moments of peace and quiet.

As per Joan's instructions, Brinna had kept Royce waiting that morning, leaving him cooling his heels in the hall as she and Joan had paced nervously inside the room until Joan had determined that enough time had passed so that Brinna and Royce would be late for Mass and end up seated far from Lord Laythem and the possibility of his noticing something amiss. And the girl had been right. Mass was already started when they reached the chapel. Royce ushered her to the nearest seat, as far from her "father" as Brinna could have wished, and they had sat silently through the Mass.

Royce would have waited then to return to the great hall with the other Menton guests, but Brinna had exited the moment it was over, forcing him to follow or leave her without an escort. She had apologized prettily once they were out of the chapel, claiming a need for air with a suggestive smile that had made his eyes glow with the memory of the last time she had proclaimed a desire for air. Moments later Brinna had found herself locked in his arms in a handy alcove, being kissed silly. And so the day had gone, with Brinna spending half her time dodging Joan's father and the other half locked in Royce's arms in some handy secluded spot. The only chance she had had to relax was during the feast itself. She, along with everyone else, had cheered the crowning of the kitchen lad who usually manned the spit as the Lord of Misrule, then had helped Lord and Lady Menton and most of their younger guests in serving the servants while Joan's father and another guest had taken on the role of minstrels and attempted to provide music for the celebrants.

Once it was over, however, Brinna had again found herself dodging Lord Laythem and spending more and more time in dim corners and dark alcoves, her head growing increasingly fuzzy with a combination of drink and lust. Royce had not gone unaffected by the revelry and their passion himself. The last time she had dragged him off to avoid Lord Laythem, he had nearly taken her in the shadows at the head of the stairs before recalling himself and putting an end to their embrace. Then he had suggested a little breathlessly that mayhap they should end that evening early so that their wedding day would come that much quicker. Which was why Brinna was now back in Joan's room before the usual time.

"I am glad you are here," Joan went on, clasping her hands with a smile. "I was afraid I would not have the opportunity to thank you and say good-bye ere I left."

"Left?" Brinna echoed faintly.

"Aye. I am leaving. Phillip and I are running away to be married."

"Phillip?" Brinna stared at her blankly, sure the drink had affected her more than she had realized.

"Phillip of Radfurn. Lord Thurleah's cousin?" Joan prompted with amusement. "When he visited Laythem we—" She shrugged. "We fell in love. He followed me to court, then on here, and has been staying in the village so that we could see each other."

"But he told Royce that you were a spoiled brat," Brinna reminded her in confusion.

"Aye. He was hoping to convince him to break the contract. He wanted me for himself, you see."

"I see," Brinna murmured, but shook her head. She didn't really see at all. "Did you say you were running away?"

"Aye. To be married. Phillip is fetching the horses now."

"But you can't. You are supposed to marry Royce tomorrow morning."

"Well, obviously I will not be there."

"But you cannot do this. He's—"

"I know, I know," Joan rolled her eyes as she moved to the window to peer down into the darkness of the courtyard below. "He is a nice man. Well, if you like him so much, why do you not marry him? He will be looking for a wife now that I am out of the picture anyway. As for me, Phillip is more my sort. We understand each other. And we will not spend our days moldering out on some old estate. He adores court as much as I do."

"What of your father?"

Joan grimaced. "He will be furious. He may even withhold my dower. But Phillip does not care. He loves me and will take me with or without—" She paused suddenly, then smiled. "There he is. He has the horses. Well, I'm off."

Whirling away from the window, she pulled the hood of her mantle over her head and hurried to the door. Pausing there, she glanced back. "I left the rest of the coins I promised you in the chest. Thank you for everything, Brinna."

She was gone before Brinna could think of a thing to say to stop her. Sighing as the door snapped closed, Brinna sank down on the edge of the bed in dismay.

What a mess. It was all a mess. Joan was rushing off with Lord Radfurn. Royce's plans would be ruined. His hopes for his people crushed. And she was at fault, she realized with horror. She had ruined everything for him. If she had not masqueraded as Joan, Joan would have been forced to remain here and spend time with him and—

Oh, dear Lord, how could she have done this to him?

"Joan!" Sabrina rushed into the room, slamming

the door behind her with a sigh. "It is madness out there. Everyone is drunk and I thought I saw Brinna slipping out of the keep—" She paused as she drew close enough to see the color of Brinna's eyes and the miserable expression on her face. "Brinna?"

She nodded solemnly.

"Then that was Joan I saw slipping out of the keep?"

"Aye," Brinna sighed "She is running off with Phillip of Radfurn."

"What?" Sabrina shrieked. "Oh, I knew that man was trouble."

Brinna's eyes widened in surprise. "Phillip of Radfurn?"

"Aye. He was all over her at Laythem. Trailing after her like a puppy dog. Going on and on about how grand Henry's court is. As if Joan's head wasn't already stuffed with the thought herself." She shook her head in disgust and dropped to sit on the bed beside Brinna. "He must have followed us here."

"Aye, he did."

"Then she has probably been slipping out to see him every day. No wonder she wanted me to accompany you. That way she could flit about unchaperoned. Lord knows what they have been getting up to. They— oh, my God!" Sabrina turned on her in horror as if just understanding the significance of Joan's running away. "What are we going to do? Lord Laythem will be furious when he finds out."

"No doubt," Brinna agreed, thinking that the man would also be mightily confused after coming across someone he thought was Joan messing about with Royce in the stables just last night. He would be furious to think that after that, she had then run off with Radfurn. Royce would be just as confused and angry.

"Oh, dear Lord." Sabrina stood abruptly and moved toward the door. "I am getting out of here."

349

"Out of here?" Brinna stood up anxiously. "What do you mean out of here?"

"My father sent men with Uncle Edmund to escort me home to be married. I had insisted that we wait until after the wedding to go, but now . . ." Pausing at the door, she turned back to shake her head. "I will insist we leave first thing on the morrow. I do not want to be here when Uncle Edmund discovers this. He will skin me alive for my involvement. And I would rather be far and away from here before he finds out."

"But should we not tell them? They will worry and—"

"Worry? Girl, what are you thinking of? Forget their worry and think of yourself."

Brinna blinked in surprise. "I have nothing to worry about. I am just a servant."

"Who has been parading as a noble for the past nearly two weeks," Sabrina pointed out, then bit her lip. "Oh, dear Lord, I knew I should have told you this sooner."

"What?" Brinna asked warily.

Sabrina shook her head "I was talking to Christina that first night at table. The night Joan stayed up here to train you to be a lady," she explained. "She happened to mention that a neighbor's smithy got caught impersonating Lord Menton this last summer. It seems the lord had commissioned a new suit of mail. The smithy finished it earlier than expected, but rather than take it at once to his lord, he donned it and paraded about, masquerading as him. He was caught, and they buried him alive with the mail saying that since he coveted it so much he could spend eternity with it."

Brinna paled and winced at the story, then shook her head. "Aye, but that was different. Lady Joan insisted I masquerade as her. She said she would say 'twas all a jest and all would be well. She—"

"She is not here to tell anyone that, is she? And as it turns out, 'tis not much of a jest. At least I don't think Lord Laythem or Lord Thurleah will see it as one." Sabrina nodded as Brinna's eyes widened in dawning horror. "Mark my words. Dirty your face and hair with soot, redon your kerchief and clothes, then get you on that pallet by the door and feign sleep until the morrow. When they come looking for Joan, claim she did not return last night and you know not where she is, then just get out of the way. As for me, I am going to speak to my father's man and see if 'tis too late to leave tonight."

Brinna leapt into action the moment the door was closed, rushing to the chest to begin digging through it for her ratty old gown and the strip of cloth to cover her hair. She had just sunk to her knees by the chest in horror as she recalled that Joan had been wearing her clothes when she left, when the door to the room opened again.

"Ah, yer here already," the old crone who entered murmured with disappointment as she spotted Brinna by the chest. "I was hoping to beat ye here and see yer bed turned down ere ye arrived."

Brinna made a choking sound and the old woman smiled benignly. "Now, now. I know ye insisted I rest a bit longer to be sure I'm recovered, but really, I am well now and ready to take on my duties again. 'Sides, I wouldn't leave ye in the hands of some inexperienced little kitchen maid on the eve of yer wedding."

Brinna held her breath in horror as the woman, who could only be Joan's maid, approached. At any moment the woman would cry out in horror once she saw Brinna up close and realized that her eye color was all wrong and her features just a touch off—but it never happened. Instead, Brinna's eyes were the ones to widen in realization as she saw the clouds that obscured the woman's eyes leaving her nearly blind.

Brinna was safe for now, so long as she kept her mouth shut. But she had to figure a way out of this mess by morning, else she might find herself spending the day watching them dig a grave to bury her alive in.

Brinna stood silently between Royce and Lord Laythem, her head bowed to hide the color of her eyes and her shaking knees. She couldn't be sure whether they shook from her fear of discovery, or the fact that she had been standing with her knees slightly bent all throughout the priest's short morning Mass in an effort to appear an inch or so shorter so as not to give herself away to Joan's father.

It was fate that had brought her here. Fickle fate, blocking her at every turn, making escape impossible. First her clothes had left the room on Joan's back; then Joan's maid had arrived to usher her to bed before settling herself on the pallet before the door, ensuring that no one entered . . . and that Brinna couldn't leave. She had spent the night wide awake, tossing and turning, as she tried to find a way out of this cauldron of trouble. The only thing she had been able to come up with was to simply slip away at her first opportunity, find Aggie, get her to find her something more appropriate for a servant to wear, then do as Sabrina had suggested.

Fate had stepped in to remove that opportunity as well. She simply had not been given the chance. Joan's maid had barely risen in the morning and begun to fuss around Brinna before the door had burst open to allow Lady Menton and a bevy of servants to enter. Aggie had been among them, and Brinna had waited stiffly for her to say something, but the woman who had raised her from birth seemed not to recognize her as Brinna was bathed, dressed, and primped. It wasn't until just before Royce arrived that Brinna had realized that the woman had known who she was all along. The bath had been removed and Lady Menton and the rest of the servants had left with it when Aggie had suddenly stepped up to her and placed a silver chain about her neck.

"Yer necklace, m'lady. Ye can't be getting married without this," she had murmured. " 'Twas yer mother's."

Brinna had lifted the amulet that hung from the chain in her hand and peered down at it, her eyes widening as she recognized it as the one that Aggie had worn for as long as she had known her.

"All will be well," the old woman had whispered gently, and Brinna had gasped.

"You know!"

Giving her a sharp look of warning, Aggie had gestured to Joan's maid, who was busy digging through the chest, then chided Brinna gently. "I've known from the beginning. Did ye think I wouldn't when I met that other girl in here?"

"But what do I do?"

"You love him, don't you?"

Brinna's answer had been in her eyes, and Aggie had smiled. "Then marry him."

"But—"

"Here we are." Joan's maid had approached then with a veil for her to wear, and Aggie had merely offered Brinna a reassuring smile and slipped from the room. Then Joan's maid had veiled her, Royce had arrived, and she had found herself making the walk she had made every day since taking on this foolish masquerade. Only this morning she had known she was walking to her death.

Mass this morning had been delayed and shortened due to the wedding, but now the priest had finished it and moved on to the ceremony while Brinna struggled with what to do. She knew what she *should* do. Throw off the veil that half-hid her features and proclaim who she really was before this went any further. Unfortunately, fear was riding her just now. While Brinna loved Royce, she certainly did not think that she could not live without him. She was quite attached to living actually. In fact, the more she considered how some poor smithy had been killed for daring to misrepresent himself as his lord, the more she loved life.

"Do you, Joan Jean Laythem, take Royce to be your . . ."

A rushing in her ears drowned out the priest's voice briefly, and Brinna felt the sweat break out on her forehead as she swallowed some of the bile rising up in her throat.

"Love, honor, and obey . . ."

Love, she thought faintly. Aye, she loved him. And she thought he might actually love her, too. But how long would that last once he realized how she had tricked him? Good Lord, he would loathe her. How could he not when she was taking the choice away from him. Tricking him into marriage with a scullery maid.

"My lady?"

Blinking, she peered at the priest, suddenly aware of the silence that surrounded her. They were waiting for her answer. Her gaze slid to Royce, taking in the expression on his face. It was two parts loving admiration, and one part concern as he awaited her response. Swallowing, she tried to get the words out. I do, she thought. I do. I do. "I don't."

"What?"

Brinna hardly heard Lord Laythem's indignant roar as she watched the shock and alarm fill Royce's face. Shaking her head, she gave up her slouching and stood up straight and tall, wondering even as she did what madness had overcome her. "I cannot do it."

"Joan?" The confusion and pain on Royce's face tore at her.

"You need the dower for your people. If that were not so . . . But it is, and I cannot do this to you. You would never forgive me. And you shouldn't forgive a woman who could do that to you."

Royce shook his head in confusion. "What are you saying?"

"I am not Joan."

There was silence for a moment, then Royce gave an incredulous laugh. "You jest!"

"Nay. I am not Joan Laythem!" Brinna insisted, and her heart thundering in her chest, she ripped the veil from her head. As those there to witness the occasion leaned forward in confusion, wondering what they were suppose to be seeing, she whirled to face Lord Laythem. "I am naught but a scullery maid. I—your daughter—I was sent to tend to Lady Laythem when she arrived because her lady's maid was ill. When she realized how similar we were in looks, she insisted I take her place for Lord Royce to woo," she ended lamely, despair and resignation on her face.

"Joan." Lord Laythem turned her to face him, then paused in surprise as he noted the extra inches she suddenly sported. Frowning, he shook his head and looked her grimly in the eye. "Joan, I—green," he declared with dismay.

Royce frowned, his stomach clenching in concern at the expression on the man's face. "My lord?" he asked warily.

"Her eyes are green," Lord Laythem said faintly.

"Nay, my lord." Royce frowned at him, his own eyes moving to the lovely gray orbs now filling with tears of fear and loss. "Her eyes are as gray as your own."

"Aye, but my daughter's are green."

Royce blinked at that, then shook his head with horror. "Are you saying this is not your daughter?"

"Aye," he murmured, his gaze now moving slowly over her features, taking in the tiniest differences, the smallest variations with amazement, before he recalled the problem before them and asked. "Girl— what is your name?"

"Brinna," she breathed miserably.

"Well, Brinna, are you saying that since my daughter has arrived here, you have been Joan?"

"Aye," she confessed, shamefaced.

"Even in the stables?"

Her face suffusing with color, Brinna nodded, wincing as Royce cursed harshly.

"And where is my daughter now?" Lord Laythem asked, ignoring the younger man.

"She ran off to marry Phillip of Radfurn last night," Brinna murmured, turning to peer at Royce as she said the words and wincing at the way he blanched. Knowing that all his hopes for his people were now ashes at his feet, she turned away in shame, flinching when he grasped her arm and jerked her back around.

"You knew her plan all along? You helped her?" he said accusingly with bewildered hurt, and Brinna bit her lip as she shook her head.

"I helped her, aye, but I didn't know of her plan. Well, I mean, I knew she did not want to marry you and that she was looking for a way to avoid it, but I did not know how she planned to do so. And . . . and had I—I didn't know you when I agreed to help her, I just—she offered me more coins than I had ever hoped to see and I thought I could use them to make Aggie comfortable and—" Recognizing the contempt on his face and the fact that nothing she was saying was helping any, Brinna unconsciously clutched her mother's amulet and whispered, "I'm sorry."

"Look, girl," Lord Laythem began impatiently, only to pause as his gaze landed on the amulet she was clutching so desperately. Stilling, he reached a trembling hand to snatch at the charm. "Where did you get this?" he asked shakily, and Brinna swallowed nervously, afraid of next being accused of being a thief.

"It is my mother's," she murmured, recalling what Aggie had said as she placed it around her neck. Brinna had always known that Aggie was not the woman who had birthed her, but since Aggie had always avoided speaking of it, Brinna had never questioned her on the subject.

"Your mother's?" Paling, Lord Laythem stared at her blankly for a moment. Then, "What is her name?"

"I don't know."

"Of course you know, you must know." He gave her an impatient little shake. "What is her name?"

"She doesn't know."

They all turned at those words to see Aggie framed in the chapel door. Mouth tight with anger, she moved her wretched old body slowly through the parting crowd toward them. "She's telling the truth. She doesn't know. I never told her. What good would it have done?"

"Aggie?" Brinna stepped to the old woman's side, uncertainty on her face.

"I am sorry, child. There was no sense in yer knowing until now. I feared ye would grow bitter and angry. But now ye must know." Turning, she glared at Lord Laythem grimly. "Her mother was a fine lady. A real and true lady in every sense of the word. She arrived in the village twenty-one years ago, young and as beautiful as Brinna herself. The only difference between the two was that her eyes were green."

Her gaze moved from Brinna's gray eyes to Lord Laythem's own eyes of the same gray-blue shade before she continued. "I was the first person she met when she arrived. She told me she was looking to buy a cottage and perhaps set up shop. My husband had just passed on and we had no children. We used to run an alehouse from our cottage, but it was too much for a woman alone to handle, so I sold her our cottage. When she asked me to stay on and work with her, I agreed.

"As time passed, we became friends and she told me a tale, of a pretty young girl, the older of two daughters born to a fine lord and lady in the south. The girl was sent to foster with another fine lord and lady in the north, where she stayed until her eighteenth year, when the son of this lord and lady got married. The son returned from earning his knight's spurs three months before the wedding."

She glanced at Lord Menton meaningfully, nodding when his eyes widened at the realization that she spoke of him. Then her gaze slid to Lord Laythem again. "He brought with him a friend—and it was this friend who changed our girl's life. She fell in love with him. And he claimed to love her, and to want to marry her. Young as she was, she believed him," Aggie spat bitterly, making Lord Laythem wince despite his confusion.

"They became lovers, and then just before his friend's marriage, her lover was called home. His father had died and he had to take up his role as lord of the manor. He left, but not before once again vowing his undying love and giving our girl *that*." She pointed to the amulet that hung around Brinna's neck and grimaced. "He swore to return for her. Two weeks later a messenger arrived to collect our girl and take her home. She returned reluctantly only to learn that her parents had arranged a marriage for her. She refused, of course, for she loved another. But her parents would hear none of it. Marriage was about position, not love. Then she found out she was pregnant. She thought surely her parents would cancel the marriage and send for her lover then, but they merely pushed up the date of the marriage, hoping that the intended groom would think the babe his own. Our girl collected all the jewels she had and took part of the coins meant for her dower and fled for here, where she knew her 'love' would eventually return for her as he had promised.

"She came to the village because she knew that if she approached Lady Menton . . . your mother, my lord"—she explained, with a glance at Robert—"she would have sent her home. She thought that if she hid in the village, she would hear news of when her lover returned, yet not be noticed by the people in the castle. So, she waited and worked, and grew daily with child.

"Time passed, and I began to doubt her lover, but she never did. 'Oh, Aggie,' she'd laugh lightly. 'Do not be silly. He loves me. He will come.' " She was glaring so fiercely at Lord Laythem as she said that, that Brinna was getting the uncomfortable feeling that she knew how this was going to end.

"He didn't, of course, but she kept her faith right up until the day she died. The day Brinna was born. She had walked to the village market as she did every day for news, and she returned pale and sobbing, desperately clutching her stomach. She was in labor. A month early and angry at the upset that had brought about her birth, the babe came hard and fast. She was barely a handful when she was out. So wee I didn't think she'd survive the night."

Aggie smiled affectionately at the tall strong girl beside her as she spoke. "But you did. It was your mother who didn't. She was bleeding inside and nothing I did could stop it. She held you in her arms and named you Brinna, telling you and me both that it meant of nobility. Then as her life bled out of her, she told me what had upset her and brought about her early labor. She had heard in the village that her lover had returned. He was here visiting the young Lord Menton. He had arrived early that morning. . . . With his new bride, our girl's own younger sister." Aggie's hard eyes fixed on Edmund Laythem. "Brinna's mother was Sarah Margaret Atherton, whose sister was Louise May Atherton Laythem."

Brinna gasped and turned accusing eyes on the older man standing beside Royce. She was blind at first to the tears coursing down his face.

"They told me she was dead," he whispered brokenly, then met Brinna's gaze beseechingly. "Robert knew of my love for your mother and sent word to me that she had been called home. I moved as quickly as I could, but winter struck before I got affairs in order and could leave. As soon as the spring thaw set in I hied my way south to Atherton, but when I arrived, it was only to be told that she was dead. Her parents offered me her younger sister, Louise, in her place. I was the lord now and expected to produce heirs as quickly as possible to ensure the line, and she looked so like Sarah I thought I could pretend . . ." His voice trailed away in misery. "It didn't work, of course. In the end I simply made her miserable. She wasn't my Sarah. Sarah was full of laughter and joy, she had a love for life. Louise was more sullen in nature and shy, and all her presence managed to do was remind me of what I had lost. In the end I couldn't bear to be around her, to even see her. I avoided Laythem to avoid the pain of that reminder."

Taking Brinna's hands, he met her pained gaze firmly. "I loved your mother with all of my heart. She was the one bright light in my life. I would give anything to be able to change the way things worked out in the past, but I can only work with the now. I am pleased to claim you as my daughter." Pausing, he glanced at Royce, then squeezed her hands and asked. "You love him?"

"Aye," Brinna whispered, lowering her eyes unhappily.

Nodding, he then turned to Royce. "Am I right in assuming that you love my daughter?"

Royce hesitated, then said grimly, "I don't know who your daughter is. I thought she"—he gestured toward Brinna unhappily—"I thought this was your daughter, Joan. Now, it seems she is a scullery maid who is your illegitimate daughter and that she was pretending to be Joan so that the real Joan could run off with my own cousin. I won't be married, I won't get the dowry my people need, I—" He paused in his angry tirade as Brinna gave a despairing sob and turned to hurry out of the church.

Lord Laythem watched his daughter flee, then turning determinedly on Royce, he straightened his shoulders. "Leave your anger at her deception aside and search your heart. Do you love Brinna?"

Royce didn't have to think long at all before saying, "Aye, I love the girl, whether she is Joan or Brinna, lady or scullery maid. I love her. But it matters not one whit. My people depend upon me. I have a duty to them. I have to marry a woman with a large dower." He heaved a sigh, then straightened grimly. "Now if you will excuse me, I shall leave and see if I cannot accomplish that duty and at least—"

"You have the dower." At Royce's startled look, Laythem nodded. "We had a contract. Joan has broken it. Her dower is forfeit. Now you need not marry for a dower. You may marry as you wish. If you love Brinna, I would still be proud to have you for a son-in-law."

Royce blinked once as that knowledge sank in, then whirled to the priest and grabbed him by the lower arms. "Wait here, Father. We'll be right back," he assured him, then whirled to chase after Brinna.

Lord Laythem watched him go with a sigh, then smiled at his friend Lord Menton as he and his wife stepped forward to join him.

"I didn't know," Robert murmured, and Lady Menton stepped forward to squeeze Edmund's hand. "Had I realized that Sarah was in the village, I would have sent a messenger to you at once. And had I known she had a daughter here—"

"I know," Edmund interrupted quietly, then arched an eyebrow at his friend's daughter, Christina, as she stared after the absent Royce, shaking her head with slight bemusement. "What is it?" he asked her.

"Oh nothing really," she murmured, giving a small laugh. "I was just thinking that if Brinna is your daughter, she too is half-Norman and they really were three French hens after all." When he and her parents stared at her blankly, she opened her mouth to explain about the day she had found Sabrina, Brinna, and Joan in a huddle, and the comment she had made about "three French hens," then shook her head and murmured, "Never mind. 'Twas nothing."

Royce rushed out of the chapel just in time to see Brinna disappear into the stables. Following, he found her kneeling in the straw where they had made love, sobbing miserably. Swallowing, he moved silently up behind her and knelt at her side. "J-Brinna?"

Her sobs dying an abrupt death, she straightened and turned, her eyes growing wide as she peered at him. Then she scrambled to her feet, turning away to face the wall as she wiped the tears from her face. "Is there something you wished, my lord? A pot you need scrubbed or a—" Her voice died in her throat as he turned her to face him.

"I need you," he told her gently. "If you will have me."

Her face crumpled like an empty gown, and she shook her head miserably as tears welled in her eyes. " 'Tis cruel of you to jest so, my lord."

"I am not jesting."

"Aye, you are. You must marry someone with a dower. Your people need that to survive the winter and I—" Pausing suddenly, she bent to dig under her skirt until she found the small sack she had fastened at her waist. The sack jingled with the coins Joan had given her as she held them out to him. "I have this. It is not much, and I know it won't make up for what you lost with Joan, but mayhap it will help until you find a bride with a dower large enough—"

"I have the dower." He pushed the hand holding the sack away and drew her closer. "Now I need the bride."

"I-I don't understand," Brinna stuttered as his arms closed around her.

"Joan broke the contract. The dower is mine even though we won't marry. My responsibility to my people is fulfilled. Now I can marry whom I wish," he whispered into her ear before dropping a kiss on the lobe of that shell-like appendage.

"You can?" she asked huskily.

"Aye, and I wish to marry you."

"Oh, Royce," she half-sobbed, pressing her face into his neck. "You don't know. . . . I hoped, I dreamed, I prayed that if God would just let me have this one gift, I would never ask for anything ever again."

"This gift?" Royce asked uncertainly, leaning back to peer down at her.

"You," Brinna explained. "You came to me on Christmas Day, my lord. And you were the most wonderful Christmas gift I could ever have hoped for." She laughed suddenly, happiness glowing in her face. "And I even get to keep you."

"That you do, my love. That you do."

The CAT'S MEOW

Victoria Alexander, Nina Coombs, Coral Smith Saxe & Colleen Shannon

*"To persons of good character,
free feline to stable home"*

The ad seems perfect for what Gisella Lowell, an eccentric Bostonian gypsy, intends. While the newspaper ad offers only the possible adoption of four adorable cats, Gisella's plans are a whisker more complex: four individual tales of magic and romance. As the October nights grow chill and the winds begin to howl, four couples will cuddle before their hearths, protected from the things that go bump in the night. And by Halloween, each will realize that they have been rewarded with the most fulfilling gift of all: a warm, affectionate feline. And, of course, true love.

___52279-9 $5.99 US/$6.99 CAN

Dorchester Publishing Co., Inc.
P.O. Box 6640
Wayne, PA 19087-8640

Please add $1.75 for shipping and handling for the first book and $.50 for each book thereafter. NY, NYC, and PA residents, please add appropriate sales tax. No cash, stamps, or C.O.D.s. All orders shipped within 6 weeks via postal service book rate. Canadian orders require $2.00 extra postage and must be paid in U.S. dollars through a U.S. banking facility.

Name_____
Address_____
City_____State_____Zip_____
I have enclosed $_____ in payment for the checked book(s).
Payment <u>must</u> accompany all orders. ❑ Please send a free catalog.
       CHECK OUT OUR WEBSITE! www.dorchesterpub.com

Swept Away

Marilyn Campbell,
Thea Devine,
Connie Mason

Whether you're on a secluded Caribbean island or right in your own backyard, these sensual stories will transport you to the greatest vacation spot of all, where passion burns hotter than the summer sun. Let today's bestselling writers bring this fantasy to life as they prove that romance can blossom anywhere—often where you least expect it.

___4415-3 $5.50 US/$6.50 CAN

Dorchester Publishing Co., Inc.
P.O. Box 6640
Wayne, PA 19087-8640

Please add $1.75 for shipping and handling for the first book and $.50 for each book thereafter. NY, NYC, and PA residents, please add appropriate sales tax. No cash, stamps, or C.O.D.s. All orders shipped within 6 weeks via postal service book rate. Canadian orders require $2.00 extra postage and must be paid in U.S. dollars through a U.S. banking facility.

Name_____
Address_____
City_____State_____Zip_____
I have enclosed $_____ in payment for the checked book(s).
Payment <u>must</u> accompany all orders. ☐ Please send a free catalog.
CHECK OUT OUR WEBSITE! www.dorchesterpub.com

BLUE CHRISTMAS

Sandra Hill,
Linda Jones,
Sharon Pisacreta,
Amy Elizabeth Saunders

The ghost of Elvis returns in all of his rhinestone splendor to make sure that this Christmas is anything but blue for four Memphis couples. Put on your blue suede shoes for these holiday stories by four of romance's hottest writers.

___4447-1 $5.50 US/$6.50 CAN

Dorchester Publishing Co., Inc.
P.O. Box 6640
Wayne, PA 19087-8640

Please add $1.75 for shipping and handling for the first book and $.50 for each book thereafter. NY, NYC, and PA residents, please add appropriate sales tax. No cash, stamps, or C.O.D.s. All orders shipped within 6 weeks via postal service book rate. Canadian orders require $2.00 extra postage and must be paid in U.S. dollars through a U.S. banking facility.

Name_____

Address_____

City_____ State_____ Zip_____

I have enclosed $_____ in payment for the checked book(s).

Payment <u>must</u> accompany all orders. ❏ Please send a free catalog.